THE TURNCOAT KING

The Rising Wave

MICHELLE DIENER

This is a work of fiction and all names, people, places and incidents are either used fictitiously or are a product of the author's imagination.

Created with Vellum

ALSO BY MICHELLE DIENER

FANTASY NOVELS BY MICHELLE DIENER

The Rising Wave series:

The Rising Wave (Prequel novella to THE TURNCOAT KING, found in Warlords, Witches & Wolves: A Fantasy Romance Anthology)

The Turncoat King

The Threadbare Queen (Coming late 2021)

Mistress of the Wind

The Dark Forest series:

The Golden Apple

The Silver Pear

SCIENCE FICTION NOVELS

Sky Raiders series:

Intended (Short Story Prequel)

Sky Raiders

Calling the Change

Shadow Warrior

Class 5 series:

Dark Horse

Dark Deeds

Dark Minds

Dark Matters

Verdant String series:

Interference & Insurgency Box Set

Breakaway

Breakeven

Trailblazer

High Flyer

HISTORICAL FICTION NOVELS

Susanna Horenbout and John Parker series:

In a Treacherous Court

Keeper of the King's Secrets

In Defense of the Queen

Regency London series:

The Emperor's Conspiracy

Banquet of Lies

A Dangerous Madness

Other historical novels:

Daughter of the Sky

SHORT PARANORMAL FICTION

Breaking Out: Part I (Short story)

Breaking Out: Part II (Novella)

To receive notification when a new book is released, sign up on michellediener.com.

CHAPTER 1

She was being hunted.

Ava stood still, at the very edge of the forest, and looked back among the trees as she'd done over and over since the attack the night before.

Last evening, as she'd slid off her horse to make camp, an arrow had just missed her, embedding itself in the bark above her head with a hard thud. She had leaped back onto her mount and ridden away as fast as she could.

Now she would have to move out of the protection the trees had given her and onto the steppes—into the open.

It would be a lot easier to aim an arrow at her out on the plain.

That's what worried her.

And yet, she had to move forward. There was certainly no going back.

It worked both ways, though.

The people chasing her had so far not been willing to reveal themselves, only attacking from a distance—if she counted last night as being the first attack.

There had been another—much more personal—attack on her at her grandmother's estate. And she had wondered since last night if the two men responsible for that attempted kidnapping were the same men chasing her now.

No way to know until she caught sight of them.

She peered around the tree she was hiding behind again and saw no movement through the trees.

They were out there, though. She could sense them.

Perhaps they would wait until she was out of the woods to get a good shot.

She could make sure they never did.

She pulled a sewing kit from her pocket, removed her cloak, and began to embroider along the back of it, high up where it fell across her shoulder blades.

The horse moved restlessly beneath her, and her heart beat in rapid, bird-like hops. She was the most vulnerable she had been since the attack last night.

She had removed the only thing protecting her.

The thick wool was already decorated, but now she stitched in bows and flying arrows, grateful they were not difficult to create. Like everything else she'd woven into the cloak, she kept the color the same as the cloak itself, dark brown, making it difficult to see what she had done.

No sense proclaiming her protections if she didn't need to. Most people, she knew, wouldn't understand what they were looking at, even if she'd done it all in gold silk.

A twig snapped underfoot a little way away, and her hand trembled as she tied off the thread.

She fumbled as she pulled the cloak on again, her breath speeding up as she secured it around her throat.

"Just be calm," she told herself, and patted her horse's neck before urging her forward.

The mare leaped from the trees into the open as if she had been waiting for the chance. After the slow stop-start of the steep hills and the thick forest, the speed felt glorious.

Ava bent over her horse's neck and an arrow flew past her, the feathered fletching brushing her cheek, almost in a caress.

She laughed—she couldn't help herself—and urged the horse on, turning to see if she could catch sight of her hunter.

He stayed hidden in the gloom of the trees, and all she saw was the line of the forest edge behind her and the mountain rising above it.

She was out of Grimwalt at last, and into Venyatu, and she whooped as the mare plunged down the first hill and got her out of arrow range.

She had only escaped from the prison where her cousin had held her four weeks ago, and years of confinement meant she did not take the open space, the blue sky above, and the cut of the wind on her face, for granted.

The wide-open vista lifted her spirits, and she realized the dark gloom of the forest and the feeling of being prey had weighed her down these last few days.

The hill leveled out and then dropped away again, and the sight below forced a gasp from her.

An army was moving, horses and foot soldiers, wagons pulled by the ungainly but ground-eating yakkuna so beloved and entwined in Venyatux culture. Trailing behind them were the camp supporters, from cooks to engineers.

She let the mare have her head, not slowing or trying to hide as she headed for the column.

This was a good thing.

A place to hide. A place where she wouldn't have to worry about her dwindling food supply, and a place where she could sleep at night, instead of being in a permanent state of watchfulness.

Her hunters could hide here, too, she conceded, and it would be harder, amongst so many people, to see them coming if they snuck up on her. But avoiding the army was impossible. She would rather be with them than try to skirt around them.

Anyway, the column of soldiers was surely headed for the same place she was. The thought made her heart leap in her chest and her eyes tear up.

She blinked the tears away.

She had a lot going for her here.

She could pretend to be a convincing Venyatux. She sorely doubted whoever followed her could do the same. They would be outsiders.

She would not.

“Halt.”

The shout was snatched away by the wind, so it took Ava a moment to hear it, even though the soldier who'd called out seemed to rise up in front of her like an apparition. By the time she had reined her horse in, the guard had his arrow notched and pointed at her.

He was massive, wearing his hair high in a ponytail on the crown of his head. It fell in a thick, twisted rope down his back.

“Sorry.” She smiled at him winningly while her mare danced beneath her, and wondered if the working she had embroidered into her cloak would protect her from an arrow shot at this close distance. “The wind made it hard to hear you.”

She had been taught official court Venyatux by Carila, her weapons and defense master, but she used the thick, regional accent from his home town which he had spoken in casual moments.

Her fluent use of his language had the guard lowering his arrow. “What are you doing away from the column?”

“I am joining it.” Ava kept her smile bright. “I missed the call to arms. My aunt didn't want me to leave and I think she kept it from me, but I heard about it in the end, and here I am.” She hit her chest with a closed fist in the Venyatux salute and bowed her head. “I am ready to serve in the name of the Whispering Grasses.”

The guard groaned, as if in pain. “Where are you from?”

“The border.” She nudged her horse closer to his, and with a sigh he slid his arrow back into its sheath and slung his bow over his shoulder.

“The border with Skäddar?”

“Yes.” She tilted her head. “Near Grai.” Carila had been from Grai. She knew more about it than anywhere else in Venyatu.

“So why are you coming from the direction of Grimwalt?” He eyed her suspiciously as he turned his horse back toward the column.

“It's the quickest route,” she said with a shrug. “Although I did keep out of sight when I cut through there. Didn't know if I needed some kind of permission.”

The guard snorted. “I don't either, but I'm guessing you do.”

She laughed. "Good thing I wasn't caught then."

He grinned back at her.

They were close enough to the column now that Ava could smell the dust being kicked up by thousands of hooves. She gave a happy sigh, and it truly was heartfelt. People, excitement, movement. Everything she hadn't had for two years. "I can't wait to fight."

The guard chuckled. "Don't get too excited. I'm not sure what position they'll give you. We need competent fighters."

"I'm more than competent." Ava realized she'd have to play this just right. "I am happy to fight someone to show you."

"It's not me you'll have to convince," he said. "But I'll put in a good word for you."

"I'm Avasu." Ava touched her forehead and bowed, and when she looked up she saw the guard was looking at her strangely.

"I am Deni. I never knew people at the border were so formal."

"Maybe it's because we are representing the nation with the Skäddar?" she said lightly, and shrugged.

Deni gave a slow nod. "Maybe." He raised his arm and hailed another guard heading toward them, a woman with a similar style of high ponytail and long plait, like Deni.

Ava wondered if it was a regional style.

"What do we have here? A little stray?" The woman looked Ava over with quick, suspicious eyes.

"A straggler. Heard about the call to arms and wanted to join. She's come from the border with Skäddar." There was a slight warning in Deni's voice, as if admonishing the woman to be nice, and Ava felt a flare of warmth for the big man.

"A goat herd?" The woman tilted her head so she looked down her nose as Ava.

"What's wrong with goat herding?" Ava asked. "I bet there are plenty here eating border mountain goat and are happy to be doing so."

Deni laughed. "She's got you there, Sybyl."

"Anyway, while I may herd the occasional flock of goats, I also protect them from the mountain lions and the thieving Skäddar that come across the border. So I can fight as well as anyone."

The woman looked at her again, a little less dismissively. "All right, we'll take you to the lieutenant, and she can decide what to do with you."

"That's all I ask." Ava smiled. She didn't really mind what task she ended up with, but she preferred to fight. She wanted the practice for when they joined the Rising Wave.

She wanted to ask how far they were from Luc's army, but she kept her mouth shut.

She would hopefully find out soon enough anyway.

This was surely the fastest, safest way to meet up with her lover, so she would do what she had to do to fit in and be accepted.

She followed behind Deni and Sybyl as they trotted forward, toward the front of the column, and allowed herself a last look back.

There was no one on the hills behind her, but that meant nothing.

She was sure the man who'd called himself a messenger from the Speaker of Grimwalt's court was still out there, along with his companion.

They'd tried unsuccessfully to kidnap her seven days ago from her grandmother's house, and she was sure it was them who had followed her when she'd packed up and run. It was also possible his accomplice had gone back to report their failure to the Grimwalt court at some point, while the messenger tried to run her to ground. Or they could still be working together.

In the last two days they'd tried to attack her twice.

She would need to watch her back.

She was sure they weren't going to let a little thing like an army on the move get in their way.

CHAPTER 2

Luc walked through the camp, nodding to the soldiers who hailed him, stopping here and there for a short exchange, but heading inexorably to the open plain beyond the tents.

He'd left his horse behind, even though he'd have preferred to ride out a little way, leave the whole army behind him for a bit.

If he'd taken it, though, someone would have insisted on coming with him, and he wanted to be alone.

His friends thought being alone was a dangerous thing for him right now, but no more dangerous, in his mind, than being in a group.

He'd been attacked by assassins three times since he'd returned to the Rising Wave after his escape. Once while sitting with his three top lieutenants, not two hours after he'd found his way back from the Kassian fortress he'd been held in. No one had been fast enough to save him then.

He'd saved himself.

He gripped the fabric over his chest at the thought, and looking down at his fist, forced himself to release it.

"You do that a lot."

He managed not to show his surprise at the voice to his left, and simply turned to look at Massi as she fell into step beside him.

He sighed.

Even sneaking off on foot hadn't been enough to fool her.

"Do I?"

"You know you do. It worries you." Massi looked over at him. "Why?"

"I took an arrow there, when Ava and I were escaping the Kassian. It's natural for me to rub it." Except, if anyone asked to see the scar, he couldn't oblige.

It was gone.

"What's going on, Luc? I'd ask what they did to you while they had you prisoner, but you and I both know nothing could have been as bad as the Chosen camps."

"No, they beat me a little, that's all." He shrugged. "It was nothing." Not even the knife they'd stabbed into his side to see if he was truly unconscious had worried him.

The scar from that wound was gone, too, he reminded himself. As was the one on his forearm. The one he'd gotten fighting the Kassian soldiers when they'd ambushed him before his capture.

Everything that Ava had touched with her needle and thread had healed completely.

"Then what?" Massi's exasperation came out on a puff of white because of the chill in the air.

"Ava . . ." He hesitated. He didn't understand what Ava had done to him, and was reluctant to share anything about her with anyone else. Even Massi, who had been by his side since he was fifteen. They were family in every way that mattered.

"Ava." Massi said her name neutrally, but Luc detected a hint of censor in her voice.

"Ava," he agreed. He shielded his eyes against the bright midday sun and looked out in the direction of Grimwalt.

"She has some hold on your mind. Your happiness." Massi kicked out at a small pebble in her path and it skittered off into the long grass.

"She does," he agreed.

She made a sound of surprise. "You admit it?"

"It's true. I'm worried about her, worried something has happened to keep her away so long, and given what she was planning to do . . ."

He shrugged. "Not a day goes by I don't struggle not to get on my horse and ride off to find her."

Massi was silent, so he turned to look at her, and found her staring at him in horror.

"You would leave the Rising Wave?"

"I'm still here, aren't I?" He lifted his hand to shield his eyes again. "But it's not without regrets and doubts."

"You knew her for all of three days." Massi's words were soft, as if she was unable to speak properly.

"And yet, I miss her." This time, he put a fist over his heart, and Massi's silence was beyond shocked.

She knew what that meant. Everyone from the Chosen camps knew.

"Does she feel the same?" Massi whispered.

Luc didn't know the answer to that. Ava had asked him if her coming to join him would be acceptable to him, after she was done trying to wreak her revenge on the Queen's Herald. That sounded like she at least cared.

"I hope so."

"You hope—" Massi swore. "I'm worried about you, Luc. We finally have the fruits of our labor all around us. The Funabi are finally here, and settled in. Most of our own people from the plains have come, and those who aren't here yet will join us soon. The Venyatux are on their way. And while Grimwalt won't stand with us, it at least has chosen to close its borders and give Kassia no aide or even trade. We're in a position of strength, headed for Fernwell with no army ranged against us yet, and instead of making plans, you are sneaking out of camp to search the horizon for a woman who you met for a few days nearly two months ago."

"When you put it like that . . ." Luc shrugged. "Perhaps I should step down as the commander."

"What?" She took a step back. "That's not what I meant."

"Then what you meant," he said, turning to look her straight in the eye for the first time, "is that I should shake my feelings for Ava off and pretend I never met her."

Massi was quiet. "That *is* what I meant, and it was wrong of me, and I'm sorry." She sighed. "I don't know your Ava, but she must be quite something for you to . . . think so highly of her." She put out a hand and rubbed Luc's arm. "I'm inclined to think highly of her myself for her part in saving you, but I also don't like that we don't know a lot about her. The way the thought of her distracts you makes me worry we'll be less prepared against the Kassian, and that is ungenerous of me. You've given everything to the Rising Wave. If anyone deserves something good, it's you."

Luc pulled her close, slinging an arm over her shoulder. "You deserve it, too, Massi. We all do."

They had been rounded up as teenagers, impressed into Kassia's service, and had had to make their own families, their own joy. He thought they'd been successful.

But Ava had lit something in him that he hadn't experienced before.

"Are you spelled?"

Luc stilled at the question, dropped his arm as he stepped back with a neutral face. "Now why would you ask me a question like that?"

Massi shook her head. "It's one of the rumors going around the camp. That you move faster than a man has any right to. That when you train you never miss what you aim for, never allow a blow to land." She tipped her head back to look at him. "You were stronger than anyone I've ever known before you were captured, but since you've been back, you're . . . more. Better at everything. You've managed to fend off three assassination attempts single-handedly. And that first one, when that Funabi assassin tried to kill you the night of your return?" She shrugged. "I didn't even clearly see you move you were so fast."

If Massi had been a bit more generous in her thoughts of Ava, maybe he'd have shared his worries that perhaps he had been spelled, but he refused to make Ava more vulnerable when she arrived.

He wanted Ava to be accepted and befriended when she reached the Rising Wave. Not treated with the awe and fear that known spell casters usually encountered as their welcome.

She was his lover. She would be living with him, if he could persuade her to agree.

He would not have her viewed with suspicion, even if he suspected her himself.

"I'd been on alert for days before that attack, expecting the Kassian to track me down and kill me. You were sitting in your own tent, feeling safe, wine cup in hand." His voice was mild.

Massi laughed in relief. "That's true. But to be honest, that sword you brought back from the Kassian stronghold . . ." She shrugged. "It's much admired. There are stories now that it's enchanted. Giving you special powers. Strength and accuracy. If I were you, I'd be careful someone didn't try to steal it."

With a grunt of surprise, Luc pulled the sword from the sheath at his back and held it out in front of him. He had come to appreciate it more and more, the longer he had it. The intricate gold work on the hilt, the weight and balance and reach of it.

It had been in a box in a long-forgotten storeroom in the Kassian fortress where he and Ava had been held, and they wouldn't have escaped if he hadn't found it.

"I don't think I'm any different in training to how I was before. Maybe a bit more focused." Was he better? He didn't feel like he was.

"You know soldiers." Massi turned back to the camp, and reluctantly, Luc turned with her. "They'll make a story out of anything. When it comes to you, they embellish even more."

"Is this spelled sword nonsense making them have doubts about me? About the Wave?"

Massi shrugged. "The opposite. The story is only a righteous leader could hold such a sword. That only makes your legend bigger than before." She hesitated. "The other story—the one I mentioned before—is that you were spelled by a fey witch who was imprisoned with you, but that's a lot less popular than the sword one."

A chill ran down his spine, and he struggled to pull up a lighthearted smile. "I'd like to find who's spreading that story. No one should know I escaped with anyone. I've only told you, Revek and Dak the full truth."

She glanced at him. "You have told the camp you're expecting a friend to join you, though. And that friend is a woman."

"There's a long jump from letting them know to be on the lookout for a friend of mine, to my escaping the Kassian with a fey witch."

Massi studied his face and shook her head. "I've seen that look before. We need to keep things friendly, Luc. Not go around intimidating our allies."

"I just want to know who's spreading rumors. Find out for me. I won't approach them."

Massi rolled her eyes. "Fine. But don't engage. We've got enough on our plate without you beating up the troops."

"I won't beat anyone up." But he did want to find out who was telling that particular story. Because it was unsettlingly close to the truth.

CHAPTER 3

They had made it off the steppes and onto the flat plains that formed the far north of Kassia three days ago.

No army had stopped them.

Ava heard there were a few scouts who rode away as soon as they saw the column, so someone would know they had crossed into enemy territory.

But it would be days at least before the news reached Fernwell.

Herron's war on the border of Jatan, to the west, had diverted all of Kassia's resources away from the far north border with Grimwalt and Venyatu.

That's what she'd heard before she left Grimwalt, anyway.

It looked to be true.

Ava kept to the front of the column and looked out over the sweeping grasslands. They were golden, the grasses dry after the long summer.

This was Cervantes.

Kassia had ambushed the people who lived here, decimated them, and rounded their children up into camps and called them the Chosen.

This was Luc's former homeland she was traveling through.

He had the light eyes and dark hair of his people, the broad shoulders and the height.

She lifted a hand from the reins and hugged herself as she thought of how he looked, staring daggers at her as he crouched, naked, in the river, and demanded she tell him what she had done to him.

She had not answered. And she had gone on to do even more.

Had that been wrong?

She had so little guidance in this but her own conscience, and it had felt right. Felt good to lay a working of health, speed and accuracy over him.

To give him something that would protect him.

She couldn't regret it, but he may well feel differently.

And soon she would be able to find out for herself.

Was that why she was suddenly nervous as they approached the Rising Wave?

Right now, she could imagine him as he had been at their final farewell, pulling her close for a desperate kiss.

What if she arrived and he had another woman? Had given up waiting for her?

Or perhaps worse, was angry at the workings she had woven into his very skin.

And then, of course, there was the matter of her lies to Deni and the other Venyatux she had befriended since she'd joined the column.

She did not want to hurt them, or lose their friendship, but she knew when the truth came out, she would.

"Avasu!" Deni's shout came from her right, and she turned in her saddle to look. She was using the name Carila had given her, and it made her think of him every time someone in the Venyatux column called her.

She missed the old man, and his raucous laugh.

Deni waved his arm, and she urged her horse into a canter to reach him, trying to shake off the melancholy of what was to come when the truth was revealed.

Deni was a friend, and she had so few of those.

"You speak Skäddar, don't you?" He smiled at her as the wind played with his long plait.

"Yes." Very fortunately for the lie she was living here, she did.

Carila had spoken it, and he had taught her everything he knew.

"There's a missive for the general from the Skäddar, but it's in their language, and the general doesn't read or write Skäddar."

That was interesting.

Ava followed Deni to the very head of the column.

She hadn't come into contact with the general yet, and only interacted briefly with her lieutenants when she was assigned her duties for the day.

She was in no hurry to attract their attention, but it might be worth it to find out what the Skäddar had to say about the Rising Wave and the war Luc was taking to Kassia's capital.

Sybyl was waiting for them, off to the side, and they joined her.

The general and two of her lieutenants were bent over a missive, and a Skäddar warrior sat on a short, sturdy pony near them, the blue and green whorls of decoration on his face absolutely fascinating to Ava.

She nudged her mare toward him, until she was right beside him. "Greetings."

He looked away from the general slowly, eyes narrowed.

"Do you mind if I look at the beautiful patterns on your face?"

The Skäddar's eyes narrowed a little more. "Why?"

"The design is complex and beautiful and I'm interested in patterns."

"Your Skäddar is rough." The warrior went back to watching the general.

"I know. I'm sorry. I think I'm the best you're going to get."

"I can understand you, so that is all that is necessary."

Ava couldn't help moving a little closer, her gaze still fixed on his face. The design looked very complex from afar, but she had the sense that if she got a little closer, she would discover it was actually simple but clever.

"No closer."

With a sigh, Ava backed away. "Whatever they mean and whoever painted them, my compliments."

The Skäddar flashed her a look of surprise, but before he could say anything, Deni rode up.

"The general wants you now."

With a nod to the warrior, she turned her horse and trotted up to the general with her gaze lowered.

"You spoke to him?" The general's voice made her look up and catch her gaze.

She nodded.

"What did he say?"

Ava's mouth quirked. "That my Skäddar is rough but he can understand me well enough."

The general looked at her with what seemed to be expressionless eyes.

Ava held still in her saddle, her gaze steady.

"What does this say?" The general had not plaited her hair, unlike most of the soldiers around her, although she had gathered it at the top of her head, and the wind blew it in long, silky strands of black and silver behind her, like a banner.

Ava took the proffered roll of parchment and opened it.

She took her time reading it, wanting to make sure she understood.

She had always spoken Skäddar better than she had read it.

"Well?" The general's impatience was communicated only by her horse, which danced beneath her.

"It says you are rude." She lifted her gaze from the missive and shrugged.

The general made a sound at the back of her throat. "That is not all it says."

Ava shook her head. "It says you asked them to spy on the Jatan and to let you know what the Jatan decided to do after the Kassian attack on their border. Then you left to join the Rising Wave without waiting for their leaders to discuss your request and the offer that accompanied it. This has forced them to send one of their best warriors down through Venyatux territory with a message on their decision."

The general slid a look at the Skäddar warrior and then turned back to her, her face neutral.

"It says they will do as you ask if you agree to not only grant Skäddar special trade status, but create a trade treaty that includes

Grimwalt, so all three northern lands have preferential trade agreements." Ava couldn't help the lift of her eyebrows.

Her parents had been trade emissaries for Grimwalt. Since their murder at Kassia's hands, she had no idea who had taken their place, but she knew for sure the general did not have the authority to speak on Grimwalt's behalf.

Grimwalt had never bowed to any country—although they did have a special relationship with Venyatu. They may even agree to a request from Venyatu for a three-way trade treaty with Skäddar. But that wasn't something the general could promise.

"That's all?" the general asked.

She nodded.

"How do they end the missive? Who signed it?"

She looked down again. "We await your response. The Skäddar Collective."

The general made the sound at the back of her throat again. Then she lifted a hand and beckoned the warrior over.

The wiry, muscular man moved his mountain pony over slowly, in no rush to obey.

Ava kept her gaze on his face and he shot her an exasperated look.

"Ask him if he can stay one more day and travel with us."

Ava didn't realize the general was speaking to her for a moment, then remembered why she was here.

She repeated the request in Skäddar and the warrior's lips thinned.

"Why?"

Before she could translate, the general moved in even closer, and lowered her voice. "Tell him we will join with the Rising Wave tomorrow. Two of our scouts have already encountered the rear units and they are going to stop moving and wait for us to join them. Tell him it would be good for the Commander of the Rising Wave to have an opportunity to send a letter to his leaders as well."

Ava hadn't known they were so close.

Her heart leaped in her chest and she forced her gaze to her hands to hide her reaction. She repeated the request, and the warrior looked at her suspiciously.

"Is this true?"

"It is the first time I've heard we are so close, but I am but a lowly soldier, I hold no rank, so I wouldn't have been told." She narrowed her eyes as she looked at his cheeks. "Is it the sky and the grass, meeting on the mountains?"

His mouth dropped open. The silence stretched out.

"What are you saying?"

For the first time, Ava heard a dangerous note in the general's tone.

"Can you wait a day?" she asked the warrior.

"Yes. If the chance is to meet with the Commander of the Rising Wave, it would be foolish to do otherwise." But the look he sent her was suspicious.

Ava turned to the general. "He agrees it's worth his while to accompany us."

The general looked between them and then nodded. "Tell him to make himself welcome. Make sure he knows where to get a meal. Be his guide here."

Ava thought it funny. She'd only been part of the column for three weeks, but she inclined her head and moved away, gesturing to the warrior to follow her.

"How do you come to speak Skäddar?" the warrior asked her, and she suddenly grew tired of not having a name for him.

"My name is Avasu." She touched her forehead and bowed in greeting. "I'm from the border with Skäddar."

"Huh." He inclined his head. "My name is Kikir." He watched her with interest. "No rude comment about me and mine stealing your goats?"

"No." She smiled serenely at him. They had reached Deni and Sybyl, and she waved a hand at the senior guards, introducing them.

"We should have the two of you fight each other in training, Avasu." Sybyl gave a slow, evil grin. "See if those Skäddar moves of yours are effective against a Skäddar warrior."

Ava smiled back. "I don't think fighting Kikir is what the general had in mind when she asked me to make him welcome."

Her weapons master, Carila, had taught her everything he knew—it was part of his agreement with her parents—and she'd assumed he'd passed on his Venyatux fighting skills.

But everyone's surprise at how good she was, and some of the more adventurous moves she used in her fighting style, had told her she'd made a mistake in not underplaying her skill.

She'd thought she'd need to prove her worth as a soldier, and instead found herself under scrutiny for being too good.

Too late to backtrack, she'd begun teasing the Venyatux relentlessly about how the border mountain folk were simply better at the fight than their cousins from the steppes—that the thin air and the long nights had given the highlanders the lung capacity and the time to be better than their fellow lowland tribesmen and women.

It had become a goodnatured rivalry, with Ava, the only self-confessed mountain girl, continually having to spar with whoever wished to prove her wrong.

If it had kept her skills nice and sharp, that was just a bonus to being accepted. The unit she'd been assigned to had chosen to treat her as a bright younger sibling, boasting about her to the other units and trying to put her in her place amongst themselves.

She had a feeling that Kikir might not be quite so willing to believe her lies. Especially if the fighting style Carila had taught her had no connection to the Skäddar.

"What is she saying?" Kikir asked.

Ava hesitated, then shrugged. She'd made a promise to herself that she was lying enough just by pretending to be Venyatux. She would not lie any more than she had to. "Sybyl wants me to spar with you. I was taught a fighting style that incorporates Skäddar elements. And I have been beating most of the lowlanders because of it. They want to see me fight a Skäddar warrior. And they are hoping you will win."

Kikir tipped back his head and laughed. "I agree."

"None of you get too excited." Ava couldn't help the humor that bubbled up in her voice. "We're riding hard today, to catch up with the Rising Wave."

"Now, now. We have to take a break sometime," Deni said, grinning. "We'll make time."

Ava translated for Kikir, and the wiry Skäddar clapped Deni on the back in enthusiastic agreement.

"You don't look too put out by this." Sybyl was watching her, her face tilted to the side. She seemed bemused.

Ava couldn't tell her years of being locked away, with no one for company, meant that she didn't mind having to fight if that's how she was accepted into the group.

The teasing, the jokes, they were like the sweetest sustenance to her after years of famine and drought.

"I'm not." She smiled at Sybyl, and she knew the senior officer would take it as a challenge.

"You're over-confident. It'll land you on your arse." But Sybyl was chuckling as she turned away.

"Who is that one?" Kikir asked, his eyes on Sybyl's tight, lithe frame as she trotted away from them.

"Sybyl is a senior officer, but you'll have no luck there. She has a partner." And while Iris would most likely laugh at the idea of someone trying to steal her lover, it didn't hurt to warn the Skäddar that he didn't have anything close to a clear field.

"The good ones always do." Kikir made a gesture of regret. Then he looked at her with a small spark of interest. "And you?"

She laughed. "I am a lowly soldier. And my heart is also in another's hands."

Kikir lifted his hands in a move that said, can't blame someone for trying.

"What do you want to do with the rest of the day?" Ava could see the column was traveling a little faster, now they had a goal. It was early afternoon, and they had at least four hours before the complex task of setting up for the night began.

"I don't need a babysitter. I'll come find you when it's time for a meal or for us to spar." Kikir's gaze followed down the column. "I'm interested in observing how the Venyatux do things."

He'd take the opportunity to have a good look at their weapons and organization, he meant. But the general had invited him to stay, and she didn't have the authority or the motivation to stop him.

"Fine. Just answer me one thing. Was I right about your patterns? And how do you apply them?"

"This again?" Kikir turned from his perusal of the long line of soldiers. "The markings are drawn in a special ink that takes a month to fade. I suppose your being from the border with Skäddar explains how you guessed the pattern symbolizes the meeting of sky and earth, at the very top of the mountains, but it also means pinnacle. I am the best warrior in Skäddar. I have reached the top of the peak. That is why I was chosen to make this journey."

Ava leaned closer to him, her gaze cataloging the way the pattern was constructed.

"It worries me, how interested you are in this pattern."

"Sorry." Ava lifted both hands and straightened. "I embroider. I like to learn new techniques."

"This would be too difficult to embroider." Kikir's lips quirked in amusement, as much, she guessed, at the thought of a soldier picking up a needle for fun, as for the idea of capturing his design in thread. "I will see you later."

He turned his horse and cantered to the very back of the column.

Ava lifted her face to the sun. It was something she did so often, the other Venyatux teased her that there must be a lot of cloud cover up high in the mountains.

Not clouds, she wanted to say, stone walls.

Even with her hunters lurking close by, she kept her eyes closed, let the warmth of the early autumn rays touch her eyelids.

She knew the men who had tracked her through Grimwalt and over the steppes had attached themselves to the column, just like she had.

She'd felt her workings of protection rise up in warning more than once.

As a result, she had worked a pattern of invisibility and obfuscation into her tent so she could sleep without fear of being found.

But right now, her cloak was silent. No one near her meant her harm.

She was free of her responsibilities, with Kikir off on his own.

She was on the outside of the column, so she rode into the stream of horses, people and carts, finding a sheltered spot beside a wagon pulled by yakkuna. The column may be moving a little faster, but it was still just walking pace for her horse.

She pulled out her sewing kit.

She always enjoyed a challenge.

CHAPTER 4

Luc and Dak rode toward the Venyatux column wearing the garb of scouts.

Perhaps if someone had looked carefully at the sword Luc carried, they would wonder how a scout came to have something worked with gold in the design on the hilt, but they would have to get very close.

They were stopped by the Venyatux foreguard, and Dak lifted the missive that was from the Rising Wave to General Ru, and one of the guards accompanied them to the head of the column.

Dak and Massi had insisted on Luc arriving in disguise, in case an assassin lay in wait for him amongst the Venyatux. And he couldn't deny it was a possibility, not when there had been more than one assassination attempt on him from within his own column.

He had agreed, but this trip, as far as he was concerned, was more because he couldn't wait until tomorrow to learn if anyone amongst the Venyatu contingent had seen Ava.

A possible way for her to come to him would have been through Grimwalt and into Venyatu.

Given the dangers for her in Kassia, he thought it was a route she would prefer.

Someone may have seen her.

She may even—although he forced himself not to hope—be here. Among them.

The sun was low on the horizon, and the column had halted, setting up tents and lighting campfires.

The smell of cooking and the low murmurs of people talking was so similar to the Rising Wave, it felt as if they were back there.

Except for the yakkuna.

The beasts were quintessentially Venyatux, their gangly, spindly legs tucked under them as they sat, big teeth yanking at grass.

"Commander." General Ru recognized him as soon as they dismounted, standing in front of her large tent with arms crossed.

"General." Luc touched his forehead and bowed, and the general did the same.

"You come in disguise?"

Luc twisted his lips. "There have been a few attempts to assassinate me, and my lieutenants urged me to take precautions."

General Ru barked out a laugh. "Ha! Yes. It is ever the same with lieutenants. What would we do without them, eh?" She gestured them toward the tent's entrance. "Let's talk."

They stepped inside, and the general plucked the missive from Dak's hand.

"Does it have anything written on it at all?"

Luc smiled. "It does, but nothing important."

Ru set it down and then gestured to the cushions on the floor so they could sit. "So, do I call you the Turncoat King? Or are you still Commander?"

Luc noticed Dak stiffen.

"The Turncoat King is a name our enemy has decided on for the Commander. We do not use the words of our enemy."

Ru's eyes danced with mirth. "And yet, it has a ring to it."

"The general is baiting you, Dak." Luc tried to find a comfortable position on the cushion, and failed. "Let's talk about joining the columns." Because while this lighthearted teasing from the general was all well and good, Luc could see the deeper meaning.

The general was not going to be subsumed by his own command structure.

He needed the Venyatux. There would be no victory without them. And the general knew it.

"Let's," Ru said, giving a quick, decisive nod. "That will save time."

"Moving forward together as a single column makes sense. It will be good for the soldiers on both sides to get to know each other. They'll need to have a sense of each other when we fight side by side." Luc shifted and nearly slid off the cushion. "But we each command our own people, as if there are two columns, not one."

Ru sat straight on her cushion, obviously completely at ease. "I like you, Commander. You are quick to grasp things, excellent at strategy. Agreed. We each control our own people. But we need to be clear on what each of us wants out of this war. We should think about what the best outcome is for both of us and discuss it over the next few weeks as we march toward Fernwell."

Luc inclined his head. This was a delicate point he had been wondering how to raise. "Agreed." He gave up on the cushion, and rose to his feet. "Have you had many people joining your column as you've crossed from Venyatu into Kassia?"

Dak sent him a dark, forbidding look, but Luc ignored him.

"I wouldn't be informed of something like that unless my lieutenants were concerned about the individual, but I'm sure we have had some late-comers. Why do you ask?" Ru had gone still for a moment, and then rose to her feet, eyes narrowed.

Luc hesitated, then chose to go with the truth. "Because I am expecting a friend to join me, and she was coming from your direction. I'm worried about her, and was hoping she had found the safety of your column."

Ru stared at his face for a moment and then gave a nod. "Apologies for my suspicious nature. We did have someone join our column today, and I wondered if that was who you were referring to, and how you could know about it without having a spy amongst us."

"Who joined the column?" Dak asked.

"A warrior from Skäddar, with a message. I asked the Skäddar to watch the border with Jatan for us, and tell us what was happening between them and the Kassian. The warrior they sent with the answer has agreed to stay to meet with you tomorrow. Would you like to talk to him now?"

"We could greet him, at least, and make a time to meet tomorrow," Dak said.

Luc knew he should be interested in this information. At least energized by the idea of the Skäddar agreeing to assist them, even just as spies, but all he could think of was he was no closer to knowing where Ava was.

"You are worried for your friend?" Ru had been watching him, Luc realized.

He nodded. "She is taking longer to reach me than I thought she would."

"Ah, well. Perhaps she has joined us. If so, you will find out about it tomorrow, when our columns merge." Ru walked them out of the tent and looked like she was going to join them in meeting the Skäddar, when she was approached by a lieutenant, who whispered something urgently in her ear.

"I'm afraid I have something to attend to, Commander. Senca here will take you to the Skäddar warrior, and find you a place to sleep if you wish to spend tonight with us."

"Thank you." Did they want to stay here overnight, Luc wondered? It was a three hour ride back to the Rising Wave, and here he could keep his eye out for Ava.

"You want to stay?" Dak asked, and he sounded resigned.

"Let's see," Luc said, trying to fight the compulsion. He knew it made no sense, and yet, he couldn't let it go.

The guard assigned to lead them to the Skäddar warrior paused to speak to someone in low tones. When he turned back to Luc and Dak, he was grinning.

"The Skäddar warrior is this way. He's sparring with one of our best fighters and we're hoping he wins." His smile widened as he led the way.

"Why are you hoping he defeats one of your own?" Dak asked.

"Because she's from the mountain border with Skäddar, and has been teasing us steppe-dwellers about how the highlanders are superior. It will be very good to see someone land her on her arse."

"None of you have been able to?" Dak lifted his brows.

The guard gave a grunt. "Not yet."

Luc could tell they were close to the sparring match. The sound of cheers and whistles started up, and ahead of them was a circle of soldiers, all looking inward.

The guard led them around the side, to where the crowd wasn't as thick.

The sun had almost completely set, so two torches had been driven into the ground to illuminate the fighting ring, and the opponents were already circling each other.

The man was obviously Skäddar. Luc had met only a few of the northern dwellers before, but they all had markings on their faces like this one.

The Venyatux highlander was much smaller than her opponent, and had her back to them.

Luc felt the air freeze in his chest and throat as he recognized her hair first—a little longer than it had been since he'd last seen her a month ago but still much shorter than everyone else's.

Ava.

She ducked as the Skäddar swung his fighting stick at her head, and the vicious, no-holds-barred move forced a sound out of the back of Luc's throat. Shock and anger seemed to deafen him, a roaring in his ears.

Ava spun, but her attention was on keeping from being struck down, and she never looked his way as she grabbed the bottom of the Skäddar's jacket, twisting it in her hand and using it as leverage as she kicked up her legs and swung herself behind him.

He staggered, off-balance, and she chopped at his neck with the blade of her hand.

He stumbled forward with a roar, and in the moment when she had nothing to do but watch her opponent stagger toward the crowd, her gaze met his.

For the first time since he'd seen her, she stopped moving, no longer the fluid, quicksilver adversary she had been.

The Skäddar managed to stop himself before he ploughed into the spectators, and turned.

Luc realized the moment he saw she was distracted, the sudden acceleration as he leaped toward her, stick raised.

He shouted her name and she snapped back to the fight, too late to avoid the onslaught but quick enough to slide her body to the side, so the blow landed on her upper arm.

The wooden sparring knife she had been holding dropped from her grasp, and she staggered to the side. Even then, her gaze returned to his face.

The crowd had realized something was happening, because a few started to murmur, and one to shout out a question, but the Skäddar was caught up in the fight, not able to read the change in circumstances.

He spun to get momentum, stick raised, to hit her while she was off-balance, and Luc leaped, grabbing the stick out of his hands and knocking him to the ground.

He stared down at the Skäddar for a moment, the rage, the desire to kill, riding him so hot he almost gasped for breath. But he pulled back his temper, and instead snapped the stick in two with his hands.

The Skäddar had been about to shout at him in outrage, but the look on Luc's face had dried those words up.

Luc deliberately turned his back on the warrior, to find Ava standing, staring at him.

She was holding her injured left arm. "You are here. You came to find me."

"I did." He dropped the two pieces of the Skäddar's stick, scooped Ava up and turned, found every eye was on them, mouths agape. "I will always come to find you."

Even Dak was staring at him, wide-eyed.

He didn't care. He had everything he needed right in his arms.

He shoved his way through the crowd and into the now dark camp. "Where to?"

She lifted an arm and pointed, and he blundered through the tents, avoiding the ropes, until he reached a patch of ground that seemed to be empty.

"There," Ava murmured to him, but he couldn't see anything where she was pointing, and he carried on walking out onto the plain.

He knew this place. It had once been his home, long ago.

He would win it back. And he would win Ava, too.

CHAPTER 5

"I was almost afraid to go looking for you tomorrow." Ava brushed a finger down Luc's chest, her voice still a little breathy.

Luc shifted on his cloak and cupped a hand to her cheek, rubbed his thumb over her cheekbone. "Why afraid?"

"Because it has been two months since we said goodbye, and I didn't know whether you would be glad to see me, or not."

"Ava." His hand stilled. "I don't think I could have made it any clearer that I wanted you to come. That I will always want you, and if you don't come to me, I will come to you."

She gave him a wry smile and lifted naked shoulders. "Doubts crept in."

"Never doubt when it comes to me. I will never not be happy to see you."

She leaned forward, pressed herself against him, and wondered if that was true. If he knew everything about her, he may not be so hasty to say that.

But some secrets were hard to let free.

Beneath her, Luc went still.

"Someone is coming." He handed her her clothes, and she took them and scrambled up so he could stand as well.

They dressed silently, and Ava tensed a little when she swung her cloak around her.

Whoever was looking for them didn't mean her harm, exactly. But they weren't feeling friendly toward her.

"Do you think it's an enemy?" she asked Luc, glad he still had the handkerchief she had given him as protection.

When they had started kissing, started undressing each other in desperate, jerky movements the moment they were far enough away from the camp, she had been delighted to find it tucked into his shirt.

He had stuffed it back as she watched him dress. It pleased her immensely. Although it was possible the protective working had slowly degraded.

She had no sense of how long her work lasted, but she had something new she had been making for him. Something better than a handkerchief.

He shook his head. "My lieutenant, Dak, is my guess." He drew her close to him, tucking her under his arm in a move so protective, Ava looked up at him.

She hadn't woven a working into Luc's handkerchief that included protection of her, so Luc must know his lieutenant didn't like her.

And yet, the man had never met her.

She braced herself as he appeared out of the darkness; for what, she wasn't quite sure.

"I was worried." Dak spoke to Luc, but his gaze was on Ava. "They say you're from Venyatu, from the border with Skäddar. But you told Luc you were from Grimwalt."

"I lied to get into the Venyatux column. I was being hunted by two men from Grimwalt, and I needed the Venyatux to take me in quickly and without suspicion. My weapons and defense master was from the Venyatux highlands, so I told them I was from his home region. It was the only place in Venyatu I could speak about confidently."

"Who was hunting you from Grimwalt?" Luc asked, stepping away from her a little so he could face her.

"I'm not completely sure but I think . . ." She realized Dak was still glaring at her, and her words trailed off.

"We need to smooth things over with the Skäddar and the Venyatux here, Luc. This is going to complicate things." Dak shifted, looking away from them both, back toward the camp.

Ava could see the dance and leap of the campfire flames, and hear the laughter and conversation drifting over to them on the evening breeze.

She felt her heart squeeze, because Dak was right. This was going to complicate things.

She'd thought she'd sneak through the Rising Wave and find Luc quietly. Secretly. Perhaps keep up the pretense of being Venyatux, with his knowledge.

But she realized that was a foolish strategy. He was the Commander.

There would be no way to hide a relationship with him.

And if General Ru ever found out who she really was, she would assume Luc had known Ava's secrets all along.

His reputation would suffer and he and her new friends would be hurt at her betrayal.

"Dak's right." She said it quietly.

Dak turned sharply. "So what do you suggest?"

There was more than a little venom in his tone.

"I didn't stop the fight and carry myself off," she reminded him mildly. "That was someone else."

"So it was." Luc pulled her close again and kissed the top of her head. "I'll face up to my transgressions. Let's go."

"Let's go?" Dak drew himself taller. "What do you mean? How can we explain what's going on here? I don't have a clear idea myself."

"I have a suggestion." Ava thought of the general's hard, blank eyes from this afternoon. "Can we skirt around the camp and approach the general's tent without passing too many people? I'll speak to her alone."

"Alone?" Luc frowned. "I'll come with you."

"Let me talk to her first. I'm the one who has wronged the Venyatux, and I need to apologize to the general. Let her decide how she wants to handle things. I don't want my lie to affect your alliance with this column." She didn't know if this was the right course, but it was the one way to protect Luc from all the baggage she dragged around with her.

So she would do it.

"That sounds . . . sensible." Dak glanced at her sidelong. "We can get you to the general's tent."

She nodded. She had a scarf in her pocket that would help her get to the general's tent on her own if she wanted to, and no one would stop her, but that was not something she would ever say.

She and Luc followed Dak, hands entwined, and she realized Luc didn't seem worried at all.

She looked up at him and gave him a smile as she squeezed his hand.

This was more than she'd dared dream while she'd been planning her revenge at her grandmother's house, while she'd been racing through Grimwalt's forests, and while she'd been traveling in the Venyatux column.

She wanted to carry on walking, Luc's hand in hers, until everything was behind them and the world lay before them, with no responsibilities or cares.

Her mother had told her over and over that the truth about herself, both who her family was and what she could do, would be nothing but a danger to her.

Speaking the words of what and who she was had caught in her throat the few times she had been tempted to utter them. She had a sense of inevitability about telling Luc at some point, but she was greedy for more time with him before that day.

She would manage this.

She hadn't asked how his side and chest were. She had traced the wounds she had stitched with feather-light fingers as they made love out on the plain, and she had not found so much as a ridge of skin.

It was as if he had never been shot by an arrow and stabbed.

She glanced at his forearm, but she guessed that wound, too, where he'd been slashed with a sword, was probably also gone.

He must wonder about that.

He had already asked her once, before they'd been captured a second time by the Kassian. And she was sure, when they had time and privacy, he would ask again.

She would have to think carefully how she answered.

Dak had led them through the tents with an amazing sense of direction, and Ava felt a tingle at the thought.

There was more than one kind of magic.

She'd thought since she'd met him that Luc had something about him, too.

Something . . . more.

"We should announce ourselves, before someone takes us for the enemy," Dak said, stopping a short distance from the general's tent.

"Stay here. I'll call you when I've spoken to her. I've been translating for the general since the Skäddar arrived, and I'll be able to gain entrance." That was all true, but the reason she would be able to gain entrance had nothing to do with the small job she'd done for the general earlier that day.

She doubted the Venyatux military leader would even remember her.

Luc released her reluctantly. "Shout if you need help."

She nodded, reaching into the pocket of her cloak. As she walked away she heard Dak's harsh whisper.

"Help her how? We're surrounded by the Venyatu."

She thought she heard Luc sigh in response.

His friend was obviously worried about him. Nervous about the woman who had captured his attention.

She couldn't blame him. Not completely.

She was deep in the long shadows now, and she wound the scarf around her neck. When she reached the general's tent, she called a soft greeting.

"Enter." The general's sharp answer had her guards turning, suddenly realizing Ava was right beside them as she pulled the scarf away.

She stepped into the tent before they could do much more than gape, but she saw the instant of recognition in their eyes, and they settled back into place.

They would assume she had come to pass on information she'd gleaned from the Skäddar warrior.

That suited Ava just fine.

The general started at the sight of her and stood. "Who are you?" She frowned, and then snapped her fingers. "The translator! Come here to tell me . . . what?"

"Nothing to do with the Skäddar, I'm afraid." Ava bowed her head.

"What else could you tell me?" The general sat back down on a cushion and waved at one for Ava to do the same.

Ava lowered herself down, and drew her cloak even closer around her. "It's a bit complicated, I'm afraid."

CHAPTER 6

Ava took a long time in the general's tent.

So long, Luc began to move toward it, worried for her.

Dak swore, then got into step with him.

"I don't recognize you," he said.

Luc tilted his head. "Is that so?"

"Could she have enspelled you? She's from Grimwalt, and they're more likely to have magic than most."

Luc quirked his lips. He had wondered that himself, a time or two. And found he didn't care. "Have you ever heard of a spell that lasted two months?"

Dak didn't respond.

The guards from the general's tent were far more alert to their approach than he'd seen them be for Ava's, but then she had been traveling with the Venyatux for weeks now, and they knew her.

"Let them through." The general's voice floated from inside the tent, and the guards reluctantly parted.

Ava sat on the cushion Luc had been on earlier that evening, as comfortable and relaxed as the general.

"So. This is your friend you were worried about." The general's gaze was sharp on Luc's face.

He nodded.

"Well. She has told me the story of how you met in Kassia. I had heard you'd been captured, but when you sent me a missive from the Rising Wave three weeks ago, I assumed it was false information."

"Someone in my column was working for the Kassian. I trusted him, and it led to two deaths and my capture." Luc still thought sometimes of the look on Derek's face as the Kassian had thrown back the cloaks they'd used to disguise themselves.

It hadn't been triumphant, or even gleeful. It had been full of shame.

He wondered what had happened to the young soldier. Luc had never seen him again.

He must remember to ask Dak or Massi about it.

"Escaping from a northern Kassian fortress can only add to your legend," General Ru said. "You should not keep it a secret."

"Those in the Rising Wave know what happened to me." Luc lowered himself beside Ava, careful not to sit on a cushion. "It isn't a secret."

"Good. It's not well known among the Venyatu but that will change when I tell my officers that Ava was my spy, and was also caught. That she met you in the fortress dungeon and you escaped together. She left you to work her way through Grimwalt to Venyatu."

"But that isn't true." Dak looked between Ru and Ava.

"No, but it suits both Ava and I for it to be considered true." The general smiled a strange smile as she glanced at Ava.

"Why?" Dak was blunt, but in truth, Luc wondered, too.

"Because Ava can be a good liaison between our columns. She's been accepted as Venyatux here, and yet she is the lover of the Commander of the Rising Wave. That is all positive, as far as I am concerned."

"That can't be the only reason." Dak shook his head.

"It isn't. But Ava has explained her situation to me, and asked me to do this, and I have agreed to it." General Ru looked smug.

Ava had promised her something. Or offered her something. Luc didn't know what she had to offer, but he was sure of it.

"Ava?"

"I have made friends here over the past weeks. Friends I will be sorry to lose when they discover I've been lying to them." She looked up from her lap at last. "And it is much safer for me to be a Venyatux in the Venyatux column than the Grimwaldian ex-prisoner of the Queen's Herald."

Given the Kassian spies he knew must still lurk in the Rising Wave, that was very true. But . . . "There is another reason you aren't telling me."

She hesitated, looked over at the general, and received a nod. "The general would like my help negotiating a trade agreement between Grimwalt, Venyatu and the Skäddar. That is the price the Skäddar have asked for in return for spying for us on the Jatan border."

"How can you help with that?" Dak's tone bordered on disrespectful, and Luc felt a sharp pain in his chest that the man he considered his brother was so hostile to his lover.

"Because my parents were Grimwalt's trade emissaries before they were murdered by the Kassian. I have some influence in the Grimwalt trade department."

"And there you have it," General Ru said. "The benefits to us both are very clear."

Luc took Ava's hand. "You're going to continue to pretend to be Venyatux?"

She nodded. "You haven't told many people in the Rising Wave about me and how we met, have you?"

He shook his head. "Only Dak, and my other two lieutenants. They will keep your secret."

He looked over at Dak, and his friend gave a slow nod.

"Then it's settled. I will have to call my own lieutenants together and lie to them a little, but sometimes leaders must consider the greater good, mustn't we, Commander?"

"Unfortunately." Luc had a feeling he was being laughed at, but he didn't have it in him to care.

"It is so late, you will surely stay the night?" General Ru rose up. "I will get someone to show you to our guest tent."

Luc got to his feet. He would be staying in Ava's tent, but he didn't need to say that here.

"Thank you, General." Ava touched her forehead and bowed.

"I met your grandmother once," Ru suddenly said to her. "You are not in my debt."

Ava seemed to pause, and Luc wondered what she saw in the general's eyes before she gave a final nod and turned away to lead them out of the general's quarters.

A guard appeared to take them to the guest accommodation. Ava glanced at Luc and he sent her a quick smile.

She smiled back, falling into step with him until they stood outside a large tent big enough for at least four.

The guard left them at the entrance.

"You're not sleeping here, are you?" Dak asked.

"No."

"I'm supposed to watch your back, Luc. I can't do that if I don't know where you are."

"My tent is close to where you found us earlier. He'll be safe with me."

Ava's tone was earnest. She was trying to appease Dak, and Luc decided if his friend didn't start at least pretending to accept Ava, he would have to beat some sense into him.

"It doesn't matter anyway. He'll go with you, however much I object."

"I just want a little time for myself." Luc put a careful hand on Dak's shoulder, because he felt like hitting out at him, rather than making peace. "No one will know where I am. I'll be safer with Ava than in the guest tent, surely?"

Dak shrugged gracelessly, and Luc turned away from him, unwilling to show his frustration and anger.

Ava continued to look at Dak for a beat, and then she turned, too, took his hand and led him into the darkness.

THE DAWN LIGHT FILTERED THROUGH THE THIN CANVAS OF HER tent, and Ava tilted her head to look up at Luc. She was tucked up close against him, and filled with a warmth and joy she realized she may have never felt before.

They had spent only three nights together before now, and they had either been prisoners or hunted for every one.

This . . . this was a gift.

"Have we ever not had to run for our lives when we've been together?" Luc's voice was a rumble in her ear.

She smiled against his chest. "I was just thinking the same." She stretched against him. "Although I do have to get breakfast and go, because I'm on guard duty this morning."

He stilled beneath her. "You're going to continue with that?"

She met his gaze. "It might be possible to pull back on that a little when the general's story about me starts to circulate, but for now, yes, I'd better keep to my schedule."

He regarded her with serious eyes. Ran a hand down her naked back. "Was helping negotiate the trade deal all that the general wanted from you?"

Ava nodded, but her fear at the general's parting comment was a tingle against her lips.

If General Ru knew her grandmother, she just might know who her relations were on her father's side.

It wasn't common knowledge. Her father was the Kassian queen's much younger half-brother, and he had disavowed his connection to the throne twelve years ago.

But the general came across as someone who would be well informed.

And if she was, and if she told Luc, every hesitation, every delay now, would make the moment he discovered the truth worse.

It might be the end of them.

The thought of that was a dark, endless pit in her stomach, a pain in her heart. And she bargained with herself that she would find a better moment.

And knew she was a coward.

She laid her cheek against his chest so she wouldn't have to look in his eyes. "The general wanted me to use what influence I have with the

Grimwalt Council to advance Venyatu's interests as well as approaching the trade department with the Skäddar's request. I promised to use whatever goodwill I have there because of my grandmother and my parents. The general seems to think that is a good bargain. I'll keep my word and try my best to help. It's a good bargain for me, too."

"You never considered telling the Venyatux the truth when you reached the column?" He pulled her up on top of him, and she pressed a kiss to his neck.

"I was being trailed by at least one, but I think two, men from Grimwalt. I couldn't risk being turned away." She thought of the tug on the working in her cloak the few times her hunters had been near her, searching for her among the tents, and shivered.

"I remember you saying that last night. Why were they tracking you?"

"More than tracking. They want me back in Grimwalt. I wouldn't go to Taunen at the Speaker's request. The last time I refused, the messenger and another man came to my grandmother's estate and tried to kidnap me. We chased them off, but I don't think they went back to Taunen, they waited and followed me when I left to find you."

"Why wouldn't you go to Taunen?" He tangled his fingers in her short hair.

"Because it would have taken me another two weeks at least, and I refused to delay leaving to join the Rising Wave that long."

"Good choice." He kissed her, his hands tracing her sides to grip her buttocks.

She had to go soon to start her shift on guard duty, but she would skip breakfast for this. She would do without a lot of things.

She wouldn't be giving him up.

And his friends would just have to deal with it.

CHAPTER 7

Luc started dressing after Ava left, pulling on the shirt she had pressed against his chest before she crawled out of her low tent.

"I've been working on this for you." She smoothed it out over his torso and down his arms, and gave a pleased nod when it seemed as if it would fit. "I hope you like it."

She hadn't waited for his response, scrambling out and striding away.

Her tent was too thin for the coming winter, he noted. Too thin and too small.

A traveling tent, he realized. Something she had strapped to her saddlebags.

He would have to convince her to sleep with him from now on.

He laced his boots and grabbed his jacket, shrugging it on as he rolled to his feet.

"There you are." Dak sounded a little frantic. "You popped up out of nowhere."

Luc shrugged. He was tired of Dak's bullshit, and he refused to let his good mood be soured.

"New shirt?" Dak extended a hand and touched the embroidered edge of his sleeve.

"Ava made it for me." He hadn't paid much attention to the stitches, but he saw now the intricate pattern of swords and waves done in pale blue and yellow. "Sewing is her thing."

"It's exceptional." Dak hunched his shoulders. "Let's get something to eat." He pointed to the rising smoke of a campfire and Luc realized he was starving.

"I apologize." Dak didn't look his way as he spoke.

"For?" Luc did not feel like making it easy for his lieutenant.

"For my hostility toward Ava. It wasn't fair of me."

"No, it wasn't." Luc was silent for a beat, and then loosened the tension from his shoulders. "Just treat her with respect, that's all I ask of you. She doesn't deserve anyone's contempt. Quite the opposite."

They had moved between the tents to arrive at a campfire, and Dak simply nodded his head instead of answering.

Everyone turned to look at them.

"You're the messengers from the Rising Wave?" one of the soldiers asked, and handed them each a bowl.

"We brought a message for the general. I'm Luc Franck, and this is Dak Xaven."

"Luc Franck." One of the other soldiers twisted around to look at them. "The Commander?"

"Some people call me that." Luc took his bowl to the pot sitting over the fire and spooned in some thick, fragrant porridge.

"Wasn't there something to do with you and Avasu last night?" The woman who'd handed them the bowls asked.

They had everyone's attention now. Even people who weren't sitting around the campfire.

"Ava . . . su and I escaped the Kassian together. We have known each other for some time." That was a lie, they'd known each other less than a week, as his lieutenants were quick to point out, but it had been enough for him.

Enough for her, too.

He smiled at the thought.

"She walked away without winning her fight when she saw you." The soldier who spoke sounded grumpy. "I had a lot bet on that fight."

"She didn't lose it, though." Dak spoke for the first time. "Or do you consider someone leaving the ring as a concession to defeat?"

They started discussing the rules of the sparring ring, and decided because it had simply been a friendly sparring match, a training exercise, and Ava had been interrupted by someone of much higher rank, perhaps it was a draw, and they could organize a rematch.

They seemed to be a lot more cheerful by the end of the conversation.

"How did Avasu come to be captured by the Kassian with you?" the soldier who'd recognized his name suddenly asked.

"I think that is hers or the general's story to tell, not mine." His words caused sidelong looks. He finished his breakfast and crouched by the small barrel of water placed beside the fire for clean-up, rubbed it clean with the cloth, took Dak's and cleaned his, too, and then rose up.

"We'll see you later at the Rising Wave," Luc said to the group. "Thank you for your hospitality."

The men and women responded with enthusiasm, and Luc walked away, pleased with the camaraderie he sensed.

"The general may have been right about Ava's ability to tie the two columns together. I thought that was the weakest of the reasons she gave last night, but seeing what happened over breakfast, I think she was right." Dak buttoned up his jacket, and for the first time since last night, Luc relaxed.

Things would be all right.

His friends were his family. They had gone through more together than anyone should, and they had come out of it stronger and closer. He had fought for them over and over.

For them to turn their back on him because of his love for Ava would be very hard to accept.

AVA BOUND OFF THE THREAD AND TUGGED IT TIGHT.

"What's that?" Tras, the guard on duty with her, had gotten used to her working on something as they waited for the lieutenants to come to them with their orders for the day.

"A gift for the Skäddar." An apology, really. For leaving him in the middle of a fight. She smoothed it over the saddle leather in front of her, and eyed it critically.

"Those are the patterns on his face along the bottom edges." Tras nudged his horse closer to look more carefully. "Is that a scarf?"

"It gets cold in Skäddar."

Tras made a non-committal sound beside her and she realized the wait for the lieutenants was over. They were approaching. She folded the thin, soft scarf in half, rolled it up tight and shoved it into her jacket pocket before she raised her eyes to greet Raun-Tu and Heival.

They were watching her with interest.

"You don't sew while you're on watch, do you?" Heival asked.

"Only while I'm waiting for orders, or when I'm on my own time."

Raun-Tu gave a grunt of dismissal, uninterested in her embroidery. "You were a spy for the general."

"She mentioned it?"

"She did." Heival looked unamused. Her hair was tightly braided today, and she flicked it over her shoulder in irritation.

"I was not authorized to tell you." Ava lowered her gaze. "You would be the first to agree."

"That is both true, and annoying, at the same time." Heival suddenly smiled. "And at least it makes this nonsense of yours that highlanders are better fighters than the steppe-dwellers finally make sense. You're obviously highly trained."

"You were a spy for the general?" Tras sounded outraged. "You never told me!"

"Nor could she, on orders of the general." Raun-Tu's tone was harsh, the stocky lieutenant looking between them as if to assure himself Ava really hadn't said anything to her fellow guard. "But you forced the general into revealing who you are with your display last night. Very undisciplined."

Ava stared at him for a moment. She hadn't considered this. That she would be thought rash and impulsive for the way she'd gone off with Luc the night before.

She *had* been rash and impulsive.

And she would do it again without a second thought.

She bowed her head. "I had not seen my heart's choice in nearly two months. I had prepared myself for sneaking over to him when we reached the Rising Wave tonight, and reuniting with him in secret, but he had the same idea about me, and when I looked up during the fight and found him standing there . . ." She shrugged and lifted her hands.

Every word of it was the truth.

"That's romantic," Tras said. He had a look in his eye that said he could barely sit in his saddle he was so eager to go off and spread the news. Unfortunately for him, their shift was just beginning.

He ended up peppering her with questions throughout the morning, as the camp packed up and began to move like the behemoth it was.

She deflected most of the questions, and was tired of the topic by the time it came to break for lunch.

They went their separate ways, he to his unit's campfire, her to hers.

"Avasu." Deni was standing by the horse station when she drew up.

She slid down and looked at his face. He seemed concerned, rather than angry.

She suddenly realized her error from last night.

She had bargained with the general to protect Luc from her own demons and baggage. And she would do it again. But she should have tried to find a way to protect Deni as well. He was her friend. One of the first friends she'd had in years. She didn't want to lie to him.

She decided she wouldn't lie to him.

"I looked for you," he said. "When the messenger from the Rising Wave carried you away I was worried."

"He wasn't a messenger from the Rising Wave." Ava reached out and grabbed Deni's hands. "He's my lover, Deni. The one I told you about who has my heart. And he is the Commander of the Rising Wave."

Deni's hands jerked beneath hers. "How can that be?"

"You'll hear a story today about me being a spy for the general, and how I was captured by the Kassian and imprisoned in the same dungeon as the Commander, and how we escaped together two months ago."

"A story?" Deni watched her, and she saw he understood what she was saying.

"A story. Some of which is true. Some of it . . . less so. But it is the story the general has told her lieutenants. I want you to understand that some day you might hear a different story. Don't be surprised when you do. Know that this story is the one that works for now. It is the one that will keep the most people safe." And if she had her way, the real truth, the one she was hiding from Luc, would never come out.

Deni turned his hands over to grasp hers. He squeezed. "That is all I need to know. The general has already told her lieutenants this story?"

"Raun-Tu and Heival have already dressed me down about it this morning."

"Dressed you down? What for?"

"For forcing the general to reveal my identity because I couldn't control myself at the sight of my lover. My going off with him was very public."

Deni suddenly laughed. "The look on the Skäddar's face when you just left the ring. Like you didn't care."

She shrugged. "The moment I saw Luc, I didn't care."

Deni laughed again, and clapped her shoulder. "Come eat. You can tell your story to the rest of the unit."

She glanced at him, to make sure he understood what she'd tried to say earlier, and he gave the tiniest nod.

When they reached the circle, she saw the Skäddar, Kikir, was sitting with them, and she slid into the open space beside him.

"I have something for you."

He turned cold eyes on her. "If it's the offer of a rematch, forget it. I don't fight people who leave the ring before time is called."

"I am sorry for that. But my heart's choice had come to find me. He and I have been parted for two months, and I had not expected to see him until later today in the Rising Wave column. I was overcome and I apologize." She dug into her pocket and held out the soft, fine scarf, bought from one of the small stalls that set up shop on days when they reached their night's destination early enough.

She'd bought four of them, all plain, undyed cotton, as smooth as bird's down.

He stared at it, and then took it carefully.

"How could you do this in just one day?"

"I worked on it all yesterday afternoon and finished it this morning."

He smoothed it across his palm and then wound it around his neck.

"You match," Sybyl said, moving her finger between his face and neck.

"This is intricate work." Kikir smoothed his fingers over the ends, the only place she'd worked the design. "I never thought it could be duplicated on cloth."

"I'm glad you like it." Someone had handed her a piece of flatbread and a bowl of stew, and suddenly starving, Ava dug in.

"So what's this about your heart's choice, Avasu? Surely love couldn't draw a highlander away from the fight?" One of her unit, Nabi, poked at her. Most of the teasing was goodnatured, but with Nabi, she sensed an edge.

"Love can do many impossible things," she answered.

All around her, her unit members scoffed and laughed.

"That's the most poetic I've ever heard you," Sybyl said. "And word from on high tells me that you are not some poor little herder girl from the highlands, but in fact a spy for General Ru, who got herself captured with the Commander of the Rising Wave."

Ava looked up at her, unable to hide her surprise. Sybyl was helping her. Telling the story as her superior officer. Making it easier.

"And fell deeply in love with him," she said, and tapped her heart with two fingers and then brushed her hand downward.

"It seems the feeling was returned." Deni got into the teasing game, too. "The way he pushed Kikir here aside and carried you off."

"I know." Carrie, one of the members of her unit, pretended to fan herself. "That was not something I expected to see in a sparring match."

"He broke my good stick." Kikir sounded affronted, but Ava thought there was a thread of laughter in his tone now.

She had not worked any magic into his scarf, but she had hoped he would forgive her as she finished it off this morning. Was that enough to create a working and influence this change of attitude since he put it on?

Then she realized what language he'd just used. "I thought you needed a translator. Your Venyatux is completely understandable."

Kikir shrugged, his eyes gleaming. "I might speak a word or two."

"This is a day for uncovering secrets, it seems," Carrie said, and Kikir winked at her.

Ava ate her meal and wondered whether Luc and Dak had reached the Rising Wave already.

The Venyatu would reach the column by tonight, and she would finally be among his people.

Carrying her secrets and her lies.

As she called goodbye to her friends and mounted up for the second half of her shift, she wrestled with the right thing to do.

And came no closer to an answer.

CHAPTER 8

"Here they come." Revek shielded his eyes against the setting sun as he looked at the dust cloud headed toward them.

They would be here within the hour, Luc thought with satisfaction.

Ava would be here within the hour.

He had arranged his tent so that they would have privacy, rather than the open plan space he'd had before, where he'd meet with his lieutenants to plot and plan, with no screen separating his bed from the strategy table.

Two Venyatux scouts appeared out of the murky brown of the dust, riding without too much urgency.

"Welcome to the Rising Wave," Massi called to them, and they pulled up with a smile, their gaze going to Luc.

"Commander." They both thumped their chest and bowed their head in a formal greeting.

"Welcome." Luc inclined his head in response. "I didn't lose you any money last night, did I?"

One of them laughed. "It's been declared a draw. Everyone walked away none the worse for it, and we got the entertainment of your arrival, so we are all considering it a win."

"What's he talking about?" Massi asked, and Dak barked out a laugh.

"Luc made an entrance last night. He carried his girl off while she was in the middle of a sparring match."

"We were wondering who had stolen Avasu's heart," the other scout said. "We couldn't think who could have won someone so fierce, but the Commander of the Rising Wave certainly was not on our list."

"You have word from the general?" Luc asked, because he could see Massi was about to ask more questions about Ava, and he had not seen his lieutenant all day, and hadn't had a chance to update her on anything, other than to let her know Ava was in the Venyatux column.

"We'll draw up parallel to you, and set up for the night, if that suits you?"

Luc agreed it did, and Dak rode back with them to show them the best place to settle in.

"Well?" Massi asked when they were gone. "You made an entrance?"

"I'm most interested to hear this as well." Revek turned on his saddle, his face alight with mischief.

"Dak and I were going to meet with a Skäddar warrior who'd come to talk terms about spying on the Jatan for General Ru, and it happened he was sparring with Ava."

"Avasu, you mean," Massi said.

"The Venyatux call her Avasu." Luc shrugged.

"So she was sparring with the Skäddar, and you came upon her, and . . . ?"

"And she saw me, and abandoned the fight, and I took her off to be somewhere private." He smiled at the memory.

"You grabbed their girl, and carried her off into the night?" Massi asked.

"I grabbed *my* girl," Luc corrected. "And carried her off into the night."

"And there was money on this fight, for some reason?" Revek asked.

"The Venyatux like a wager." He hesitated, but he had to tell them the lies the general had agreed to last night, so the story was not muddled. "You will hear that Ava is Venyatux, from the highland border with Skäddar, and that she is a spy for General Ru."

Massi's mouth dropped open. "Is that true?"

He shook his head. "But she was in danger, someone was following her out of Grimwalt, hunting her, and she pretended to be Venyatux to get into the safety of the column. The general knows the full story, and has agreed to pretend Ava was her spy and met me when we were both captured by the Kassian."

"Why would General Ru agree to that?" Revek asked.

"Because Ava can help her with the Skäddar. Her parents were trade emissaries for Grimwalt, and she has some influence there. The Skäddar have agreed to spy on the border with Jatan and pass on information to the Venyatux in exchange for help with a northern trade alliance which includes Grimwalt. Ava will advocate for it with the people she knows."

"You were busy last night." Massi's tone was neutral.

"I was." He kept his tone just as neutral. "I'm looking forward to introducing you to Ava."

"Who we have to pretend is Venyatux." Revek lifted an eyebrow.

"Who you have to pretend is Venyatux. It will keep her safe in the Rising Wave, as much as it helps her with the Venyatux."

"And what if others have heard us talking about her being Grimwaldian?" Revek asked.

"Who would have heard? We've only ever discussed her in private."

Revek shrugged. "You never know."

"Well, then say it was the story Ava gave to the Kassian in the hopes they would go easier on her, thinking her from a neutral country, rather than their enemies, the Venyatux."

"That will work." But Massi was looking at Revek strangely. "I doubt it will be necessary. I haven't spoken of her to anyone but the four of us."

Revek nodded. "Just covering all possibilities."

The first line of the column appeared, the yakkuna pulling wagons containing tents and supplies, the soldiers ranged on either side of them.

The Rising Wave was almost doubling its numbers, and Luc felt a surge in pride and optimism. "We did it, Mass. We pulled it off."

Massi leaned into him, elbowed his side. "More you than us, but yes. We've got the makings of a formidable army."

He laughed. "The makings of one? I thought we had one."

"We don't know how well they can fight," Revek reminded him.

"We'll see soon enough. And if they need improvement, we have some time before we make it to Fernwell, if we don't meet with any resistance."

"They have to be willing to improve." Revek sounded like he didn't think they would be.

"Ava can help with that. They see her as one of their own."

"Even though she isn't," Revek said.

"She is as far as we're all concerned, from now on." Luc turned to look at his old friend. He had been different since Luc had returned from his capture. Negative. Always quick to assume every obstacle was impossible to overcome.

"So we're starting out with lies." Revek tilted his head in challenge.

"Just like old times, my friend," Luc reminded him. "Just like pretending to fight for the Kassian, and then betraying them on the battlefield, or had you forgotten you fight with the Turncoat King?"

Revek held his gaze for a beat and then looked away. "Of course not."

"Is there something you want to tell me? Is something wrong?" Luc had wanted to ask this a few times in the months since he'd returned.

"No. I'm just tired. I want this to end." Revek shrugged. Gave a lopsided smile. "Not all of us have met our heart's choice and had a grand adventure with her, you know."

"Or him," Massi reminded him. "Maybe there'll be a handsome Venyatux in that column who will carry me off somewhere private."

"Shut up," Luc told her, and then rode forward to meet the column and find Ava, while Massi's laughter rang out behind him, warming him through.

CHAPTER 9

Ava stood, hesitant, her tent in her hand.

Did she put it up? Or assume she would spend the night with Luc?

She didn't know, and felt foolish standing there, debating with herself.

With a huff, she set the tent up anyway. Stored her things there.

She had been off duty since late afternoon, as they approached the Rising Wave.

She had looked for Luc, but she guessed he was busy working on the logistics of merging two massive armies, and she didn't ask for his whereabouts.

She missed him.

Wanted the closeness they'd had this morning.

But she would have to meet his other friends, the lieutenants he'd been through the Chosen camps with, and they might treat her with the same suspicion as Dak.

Again, she huffed. So what?

She had faced harder obstacles than that. The Queen's Herald, for one.

Although she didn't care what her cousin thought of her, and she did care what Luc's friends thought. They were important to him.

With a sigh, she shrugged her shoulders to loosen them, pulled on her cloak, and started walking through the camp toward the Rising Wave.

She was hailed by friends as she wound her way between tents and the campfires that were being lit as the sun set.

She waved back but didn't let herself get distracted until Deni called to her from a campfire, and as she turned toward him, she felt her cloak tingle.

Someone nearby did not mean her well.

She stopped to look around more carefully, relaxed a little when she saw Nabi was sitting with the group.

She already knew he didn't like her.

"Have you eaten?" Deni asked.

"Not yet." Maybe she should. She had no idea whether Luc would have eaten a meal yet or not.

She drew closer, and the working in her cloak intensified its warning.

She looked at each face, and decided it might be someone watching from a distance, not one of the people sitting around the fire. Even Nabi didn't dislike her this much. That prize went to whoever hunted her.

She forced herself not to look around. Not to give away that she knew he was watching.

"Off to find the Commander?" Deni asked her.

"Yes." She took the bowl he handed her with a smile.

"Looking for more luxury than we can give you?" Nabi sneered from the other side of the fire.

When she looked up, she kept the look of amusement firmly in place, although her feelings had turned to irritation.

Nabi was a problem.

It suddenly occurred to her that her rejection of his offer of bed sport, shortly after she'd joined the column, had clearly not been well received, no matter that she had done it politely and firmly. He'd managed to persuade a number of women to invite him to their tents since then, and he'd been nothing but trouble to all of them afterward.

"Well, possibly more luxurious than my traveling tent," she agreed with him.

"If you think a foreigner is better than one of your own." Nabi's tone was ugly enough to attract the attention of others.

"The Commander is certainly the best one for me. And our people agree, it seems, given the size of our army here to join him." Ava scooped the last bite of stew out of her bowl, and stacked it with the other empties in the bucket beside the fire.

She didn't look Nabi's way as she waved goodbye to Deni, but he didn't notice. He was watching Nabi, his face set in disapproval, and Ava left them all to it, weaving through the small knots of soldiers chatting after their meal, and skirting around games of boules and pins.

She crossed the narrow space between the two columns and stepped into the almost identical tent world of the Rising Wave.

People sat around the fire, relaxing at the end of another day's travel, although there was a sense of excitement in the air here she assumed came from the arrival of the Venyatux.

A few people looked at her curiously, but no one stopped her or challenged her right to be there.

Her hair was not in the Venyatux style, and both sides had very similar clothing, so she guessed there was no reason to suspect she was a stranger.

She headed toward the largest tent in the column, set at the very heart of the Rising Wave.

She frowned as she walked toward it. Luc should not advertise his location so obviously, if this was in fact his tent.

At least there was open space around it, so whoever approached would be exposed and could be—

"Halt. Who are you?"

Her cloak told her the woman blocking her way meant her considerable harm.

Ava considered her carefully. This might be one of Luc's friends. One of his lieutenants. "My name is Ava. I'm looking for Luc."

"Luc's been with Ava since late this afternoon. Try again." The woman pulled out a knife, as long as Ava's forearm.

Ava lifted both hands. "But he hasn't been with me."

A man roared out an unintelligible shout to the left of them—a feral, out-of-control sound—and as Ava turned to look he ran toward her, pulled back his arm, and threw something at her.

She leaned to the right, and a long metal object flew past her, so close she felt the air of its passage brush her cheek.

The man was running full tilt now, and he roared again as he leaped the last few steps toward her, hands outstretched.

Ava crouched down, and he flew over her head.

She wondered if she could have avoided him without her cloak.

She had not added any workings to the clothing she wore during her sparring. She wanted to be seen as competent but not outstanding. She wanted to rely on her own abilities.

She hadn't realized how well Carila had taught her until she'd won almost every session she'd fought.

More than half of the Venyatux in the column were volunteers; learning to fight in daily training.

They were farmers, herders, tradespeople.

Whereas she had been taught by a weapons master, and had practiced what she'd learned every day, even when she'd been imprisoned.

Sybyl had started pairing her with more experienced opponents, some the size of the man attacking her now, and she had lost a few times, but she'd enjoyed the test to her skill.

Since joining the Venyatux, she had never had to work so hard, and in the last two weeks, she knew she was fighting better than she ever had before.

Even without her cloak, she had confidence in her abilities. But with it?

She didn't think she would go down easily, even against the giant of a man coming after her with deadly intent.

She had layered protection after protection into the heavy brown fabric that swirled around her. Even though she still didn't know what her attacker had thrown at her, it didn't seem to matter she hadn't specifically warded against it—she hadn't been touched by it.

If she could manage to stay unharmed for long enough to convince these people she was no threat, she might walk away from this.

She hoped.

They were Luc's family, after all.

"Revek!" The woman who'd drawn the knife on her turned to the man who was picking himself off the ground. "What are you doing?"

He was still on his knees and he blinked at the woman for a moment, as if he didn't know where he was.

"You try to kill all of Luc's visitors?" Ava asked in the moment of silence.

The woman turned her attention back to her.

Ava saw her take note that she still had no weapons in her hands.

"While I appreciate you want to protect Luc, you might find it a little difficult to explain how you came to kill his . . . friend . . . when she came looking for him." She opened her hands for emphasis and held them out, palms up.

The berserker who had attacked her finally found his feet again, and he lunged at her, quiet now. No more shouting, just deadly focus.

He must have drawn a sword while the woman and Ava sized each other up, and he swung it at her head.

She slid down, right leg extended, left knee bent so she sat on her left heel. She shifted her weight to her right foot, propelled herself with her left leg, spinning, so her left foot swept behind her attacker's knee and he fell. Again.

Silence forgotten, he roared in frustration, and flipped up to his feet, more agile and fit than he looked.

"Avasu!" The shout from behind her made her turn a full rotation to check what was happening around her.

People stood in a circle, and the person who had shouted her name was Venyatux. She vaguely recalled him. One of the soldiers she'd sparred with when she'd first joined the column.

He was grinning, not understanding that this was deadly—not a sparring match at all.

"I'll take bets, if you're brave enough," she heard him taunt the Rising Wave soldiers as she turned back to her attacker. She thought she saw a flash of hesitation in Revek's expression as he, too, saw she had no weapons, and she took her opportunity.

"I don't want to hurt anyone."

As soon as the words were out of her mouth, she realized she had made a mistake. It was as if a lever had been pulled. There was no other word for the sudden fury that came over him.

He threw his sword to the side and came at her with his bare hands, like a battering ram, but whatever working she'd embedded in her cloak helped her not be there when he grabbed at her.

He would have had her without it. No question.

It made her feel exposed. As if she was giving away clues to her darkest secrets.

Perhaps she should simply run away.

That was the least dangerous for everyone involved.

She could find Luc later, have him introduce her to his lieutenants. There would be some embarrassment, perhaps, but no one would be hurt.

"Revek! Stop!"

She had completely forgotten about the woman, but now she noticed her circling the two of them. The woman looked over her shoulder, hailing someone in the crowd, and Ava heard her tell them to get Luc.

The crowd had grown, she noticed. To run would look weak to everyone here. And she needed to look strong. And for the Venyatux to look strong.

She sighed.

Revek had stumbled when she'd dodged him, but he was facing her again.

"We don't need to do this. It's not going to end well, no matter who wins."

Like before, her words seemed to snap something in him, and he charged again. But this time, when she ducked to the side, her cloak swirling, he managed to get hold of the fabric in a bunched fist and rip it off her.

It seemed to burn him, because he let it go with a cry, and Ava watched as it fluttered to the ground.

Now, she was in trouble.

Talking had so far done nothing but further enrage him, so she kept quiet as the fight became life and death for her.

She began to strike out. There was only so far she could go to not hurt him, while he was trying to kill her, and she had reached that point.

She went for the places Carila had taught her. The throat, the back of the knee, the pressure points; getting in lightning strikes when she could, keeping out of reach when she couldn't.

She felt the air stir past her sweat-slicked skin as he got better and better at judging her dodges, and then the blinding, white hot pain as he clipped her shoulder when she didn't dodge fast enough.

She would not last much longer. This man wanted her dead and he hadn't held back.

She was leaping back from a massive roundhouse swing when Luc stepped between them.

It was so sudden, she almost attacked him, her next move already clear in her mind. One moment she was facing her opponent, the next, Luc stood in front of her, facing Revek.

Revek reared back, as confused as her, and then went still.

"What are you doing, Rev?" Luc asked.

Revek shuddered, a full body vibration, and then rubbed a hand over his eyes. "She said . . ." He looked over Luc's shoulder at Ava. "She said she didn't want to hurt me."

Luc swore softly. "And that was enough to attack her?"

She wondered what was on his face, because the look on Revek's slowly changed from the red fury of the fight, to the drained gray of defeat.

He turned on his heel and walked away.

Luc turned slowly to face her, his gaze on her face. "Those words are a trigger for him. I'm sorry he attacked you after you said them but—"

"He had just tried to take my head off with a sword when I said it." Ava was in no mood to hear excuses for his friends. "He was already attacking me." She turned away, found a wall of people in front of her.

For a moment she just stared blankly at them, chest heaving. Sweat had stuck her short, shorn hair to her forehead and cheeks, and she pushed it back with her arm.

She remembered her cloak and turned back, found Luc had picked it up and was holding it out to her.

The woman who had originally blocked her way had appeared again, and was standing behind Luc.

"Thanks for starting this," Ava said to her. "And for all your help." She pulled the cloak from Luc's fingers as he turned his head in surprise to look at his friend, held it close to her chest, and pushed her way through the crowd.

As she went, the Venyatux rubbed her shoulders, as was their way, to show pride and congratulations, and around her, she heard arguments about who had actually won.

It was the second time Luc had stopped a fight, although she had no complaints about either time.

Revek was bigger than her in every way. If he'd managed to land more than a glancing blow, she would have gone down. And she didn't know if she'd have been able to get back up again.

As soon as she was free of the spectators, she settled the cloak around her again, pulled her scarf out of a pocket and wrapped it around her neck.

She slowed down, careful to avoid bumping into anyone, keeping to the shadows.

She didn't think the see-me-not working she'd embroidered into her scarf was true invisibility, but she had found people's eyes seemed to pass over her. As long as she didn't make a noise or get in their way, she went where she liked without being noticed.

When she reached the edge of the Rising Wave, she suddenly stopped.

Where was she going?

Back to her tent to lick her wounds?

It felt like a defeat.

Like Luc's friends had won and she was the one in retreat.

She turned back the way she had come, and saw Luc striding down a narrow walkway between tents, parallel to her own route, heading for the Venyatux side.

She pulled her scarf off, walked to intercept him.

"Looking for me?" she asked.

He stopped short. Stared at her. "Yes."

"All I did was go looking for you," she said. He opened his mouth and she lifted a hand to stop him. "Wait. I went looking for you, announced myself, and I was attacked. First that woman pulled a knife on me, and then Revek came at me with a throwing knife, a sword and then his bare hands. I don't understand." She passed a hand over her forehead, to push back her hair again. "I was just wondering how I was going to survive when you arrived."

"There's no excuse for it." Luc seemed lost. And angry. "I wanted to make sure you were all right before I go speak to them. Did he hurt you?"

Her hand crept up to her shoulder, which was throbbing, but less so now she had her cloak on. She had worked healing into it when she'd come off worse in a sparring match, and had been delighted it worked. She was just as delighted now.

"Your shoulder?" He stepped closer but she stiffened and he stopped.

"He clipped me, that's all."

"Where will you be? I've been looking for you all afternoon, and to find you like that . . ." He rubbed a hand over his face. "Please tell me where I can find you after I've dealt with Massi and Rev."

"I'm going to the bath tent. I need to soak for a bit after that. You can find me there." She gathered her cloak tightly around her for comfort, and started across the narrow divide between the columns.

"Ava."

She turned to look at him.

"I won't let this come between us."

She said nothing to that, simply turned and walked away. Because she didn't know if that was even possible any more.

CHAPTER 10

Luc watched Ava vanish into the darkness on the Venyatu side, and felt as if she had slipped from his fingers. She was right to wonder how they had stumbled into this nightmare.

His life since he'd broken free of the Chosen camps had been as he'd decided it. He had taken back control of his life, and had made certain no one would have power over him again.

This . . . whatever this was . . . left him feeling as if he was back in the dark, helpless days when he was at the mercy of those who actively despised him.

A movement caught his attention, and he turned his head as Dak stepped out between two tents.

"This is worse than the old days," he said, surprised at how steady his voice was. "At least then, you knew they hated you, and you expected them to make your life a living hell. This was done by two people I considered my family."

Dak shuffled his feet. "I'm a culprit, too, with my attitude toward her yesterday. But I swear I had no idea this was coming."

"We were just talking about Ava this afternoon." Luc shook his head. Turned toward his tent. "Where's Revek?"

He started walking.

"I'll find him." Dak melted into the darkness and Luc kept going.

When he reached his tent, which was more council chamber and meeting place than his bedroom, he found Massi standing outside the entrance, hands clasped together.

She jerked at the sight of him, then ducked inside.

He followed her in.

The crowd that had been there before had broken up, although there were a few small groups still left, haggling over the wagers that had been taken.

"I have no excuse." Massi wrung her hands together. "I only intended to play with her a little, Luc. I promise. And even saying that makes me realize how poorly that reflects on me."

"You wanted to *play* with her?" Luc said it slowly. "By pulling a knife?"

Massi's cheeks went red. "I don't know what came over me. All I've done is think about what happened, replay it, since you put an end to it. She told me who she was, so calm and normal, and I drew the knife. It felt good in my hand. The surprise on her face when . . ." She shook her head. "I wanted her to know I had the power to block her. That she couldn't just come into our circle without some sacrifice."

"Why would you want to play those games with her? Chosen camp games?" He was incredulous. This was what had been done to them. And he had promised it would never happen again.

And yet Massi had taken those lessons and applied them to his lover.

"When you say it out loud, I can see it clearly." Massi rubbed the back of her hand over her mouth. "I can see I was using what they did to us just like a bully guard and I'm ashamed. Ava would have been wary of me forever after that, even if Revek hadn't attacked her."

"You were trying to turn her against you. So I'd have to choose between you. Between my sister and my heart's choice." Luc walked over to one of the boxes they used as chairs, and sat down. Rested his head in his hands. "I almost don't care why anymore. What you did goes against everything we said we'd be."

Massi didn't answer, and when Luc looked up he saw she was crying. He had never seen her cry, not in all the years he'd known her.

Not through anything the Kassian had done to them in the Chosen camps.

He realized he felt cold. "Ava accused you of starting this, and then doing nothing to help her. So are you crying because you're sorry, or because you're sorry you got caught?"

Massi's flinch was like a body blow to him. Because she had been there with him every step of the way in the camps. Helped him when he was beaten and starved and tortured. Never let him down. Until now.

"I did start it. I didn't realize Rev was nearby and must have seen me pull the knife. It had to have triggered him. But I did try to stop it. I asked Finnian to call you, and I was looking for an opening to intervene when you arrived." She walked closer to him, but didn't sit.

"If you had put yourself between them, Rev would have stopped."

"Maybe, or maybe he'd have killed me. Should I have put myself in that kind of danger?"

Luc lifted his head and stared at her. Let the silence stretch out.

"What is wrong with me?" She slowly put a hand over her mouth and stared at him with shocked eyes over the top of it. "I didn't mean that, Luc. But truly, in the moment, I was trying to find a way to get through to him. Ava seemed able to keep out of his way, except that one time she didn't quite move fast enough."

"Her shoulder," Luc said.

Massi nodded. "There'll be a bruise, at least."

"This isn't helping." Luc got to his feet. "I said to Dak this feels worse than the camps, because there, I knew to expect betrayal and pain. That's how it was. But I didn't expect something like this from you. It hurts, Massi. Worse than when Derek betrayed me to the Kassian and got me captured. Because you and Rev mean much more to me."

"You're my brother." Revek spoke into the silence from the tent entrance, Dak just behind him. "I don't know what happened, Luc. I saw Massi pull a knife on a woman near your tent, and I just thought, another assassin." He stepped inside, and lifted a shaking hand to his mouth, rubbed it. "I don't remember anything but a blur of images and feelings after that until you stood in front of me."

"That's very convenient, Rev."

Revek's head jerked up to meet his gaze. "I'm not saying it because it's convenient, I'm saying it because it's true. I was lost. Like I used to get, in the camps." He looked down. "I haven't done that in years."

"So you're saying something just came over both of you, coincidentally, when Ava arrived." He lifted his brows.

"I didn't think she'd ever come." Massi finally sat in her usual place, but on the edge of the seat, as if uncertain she was welcome. "I knew you believed she would, but I didn't. I was glad about it. Because we're a family. A team. A force to be reckoned with. And now this woman from Grimwalt was just going to dance into our circle and be one of us? Take your time and attention? I told myself it wouldn't happen. And then it did."

"You aren't the only one who felt like that." Dak had been hovering near the entrance, but he made his way deeper into the tent. "I was rude to Ava last night. She tried to be friendly. Tried really hard. And I didn't give her a chance. And then I saw Luc's face as he turned away from me to go with her, and I asked myself, what was I afraid of? Luc has put himself on the line for me time and again, taken beatings for me. He created the Rising Wave so that we can take back our land and our identity. And I was behaving like a petty child. I barely slept, wondering if I'd damaged our friendship." He looked over at Massi. "And so I apologized."

"Dak apologized, and was able to repair what damage had been done. But you and Revek?" Luc looked over at them. "It will take time, and actions, rather than words, for me to trust you like I used to. Because you didn't just try to hurt her with words."

"I think I would have killed her, if I had managed to grab her." Revek spoke slowly. "I remember a blow. Is she all right?"

"She says she is." Luc let his gaze rest on his friend's face, even though he wanted to get up and walk out. Find Ava and make things right. "I don't know whether to believe her or whether she just said it so she could be rid of me sooner."

Massi made a sound and when he looked over at her, she met his gaze with eyes still glistening with tears. "I am sorry. I feel sick. Like some beast has ripped my guts out. Worse than I remember ever feeling in the camps. I want to turn back time and have my chance again."

"When I bring her back here . . ." He wondered if she would even agree, but forced himself to continue, "when I bring her back, I insist that you come and apologise to her. Even if she won't accept it, I want people to see you in here with the two of us, as if there's nothing wrong." It was politics. Something he didn't always like, but understood all too well.

"Most people thought the fight was a friendly sparring match, although it didn't escape me that some looked worried just before I stepped in." Luc looked back at Rev. "They might assume you got caught up in the moment, Revek. If you're asked, laugh it off. We can't have anyone thinking there's tension between the two camps. Especially from the top."

Massi and Rev nodded and Massi got to her feet.

"I'll go to the baths and come back later." She tried to catch his eye, but he was sick of her, suddenly. Sick of them all.

He stood. Thought perhaps he should say something more, and then realized he didn't care enough to. And walked out.

CHAPTER 11

Ava could have gone back to her tent after her bath and left Luc stumbling around looking for her in the dark, asking directions. But that would have been unwise.

It might occur to others that they had never seen her tent themselves.

Also, it wouldn't have been fair.

Luc hadn't done anything wrong, even though she felt as if he had.

She poked at the feeling, trying to understand why she was so angry with him.

It felt as if he had betrayed her, but he really hadn't. His friends had betrayed him and her, both.

She was calmer now that she was clean, her muscles eased by the hot water, but the heavy, sick feeling in the pit of her stomach hadn't gone away.

She wanted to resolve it.

She stepped out of the tent and found him already waiting for her.

He was turned slightly away, talking to a soldier, and his tall, muscular build made her heart hitch. He didn't look his usual self, though. There was a sadness in his posture, and when he turned to her as she walked toward him, she saw something in his eyes she didn't like at all.

She stepped up to him and put her arms around him, pulled him close.

He went still for a beat and then shuddered in her arms, his lips coming down to brush her neck.

She had plenty of questions for him, but here and now was not the time, so she fitted herself under his arm and they started walking.

He steered them toward the Rising Wave camp.

She forced herself to sound lighthearted as she responded to those who called out greetings, teasing her for being distracted two fights in a row.

There was an edge to some of the comments, though. Revek's focus on harming her hadn't gone completely unnoticed.

On the Rising Wave side, the speculation was more about their commander's interest in a woman, especially a woman from the Venyatux camp, and by the time they reached Luc's tent, even though she'd have preferred a different destination, she was happy to duck into the enclosing walls of thick canvas, away from curious eyes.

The interior was lit with lamps, and featured a table in the middle, maps neatly stacked to one side. Boxes surrounded it, clearly used as chairs, and toward the back a curtain hung down to shield his private quarters.

She turned slowly to take it all in, and found Luc watching her.

Before she could speak, Massi, Revek and Dak crowded behind Luc, and he stepped away from the entrance and walked over to her, drawing her close with an arm around her shoulder.

It drew the battle lines.

Luc and her on one side, his old Chosen camp friends on the other.

The gesture eased the last of the unreasonable hurt she'd felt.

"She's bespelled you." Revek looked surprised that the words had come out of his mouth and he snapped his jaw closed with a clink of teeth. He closed his eyes and breathed in, and then opened them.

"Want to start again?" Luc asked. His mild tone was deceptive.

Ava could feel the tension in his fingers as they gripped her shoulder.

“I apologize for attacking you earlier.” Revek’s fists were clenched.

Her cloak was still over her shoulders, and Ava could feel the tingle of danger.

“Commander?” A soldier poked a head in, took in the tableau, and reared back a little. “Sorry, I can come ba—”

“No.” Massi sounded relieved. “What is it?”

“The scout parties from the Kassian side have doubled since the Venyatu column joined us.” The soldier’s gaze landed on Ava, and she could sense the curiosity from him. “They’re coming closer, too.”

“Double our own patrols, then. I know it’s usually Massi’s task, but Dak, can you see to it right now?”

Massi’s lips thinned at Luc’s words, and Dak glanced between them before nodding and leaving with the soldier.

“You don’t trust me to run the patrols anymore?” Massi asked.

“I don’t trust you to come back and finish what I asked you to do.” Luc shrugged. “Am I wrong?”

Massi was silent for a beat and then gave a sigh. “No. I’m sorry, Ava. I shouldn’t have done what I did. I have no excuse.”

She also didn’t like Ava, according to the working in Ava’s cloak. But her cloak’s warnings seemed to be getting more sensitive, she’d noticed over the last few days. She had worked in a protection spell, layering it a few times against specific threats, but it had become so fined-tuned it was now a barometer of how people felt about her.

“Apology accepted.”

You can accept apologies graciously, her grandmother had always said. *Doesn’t mean you forget, or ever trust the same way again.*

Massi seemed surprised at how easy it had been. She opened her mouth, closed it, then opened it again. “Thank you. I look forward to getting to know you.”

Everyone turned to Revek. His fists were still clenched and he was looking down, but he slowly raised his head.

“I am sorry, too. You did nothing to warrant my attack. I don’t remember it, or why I started it, but I am sorry you came close to being hurt.”

Ava inclined her head. “Again, accepted.”

He nodded, then turned on his heel and walked out of the tent.

Massi looked like she was going to go after him, then stopped and turned back. "He wouldn't have done it if I hadn't been playing stupid games. It's my fault. It's been a shock, having him get lost in the rage after so long. I'll go make sure he's all right."

She walked out, and for a moment, there was nothing but silence around them.

"Thank you for accepting their apologies."

Ava turned to Luc. He was still focused on the tent flaps behind which Massi had just disappeared.

"They're your family more than your friends. And families can be difficult."

He glanced at her, and his mouth quirked.

"You've got that right."

Someone hailed a hello from outside, and Luc grunted in irritation before he walked over and lifted the flap.

Deni and General Ru stood together.

"Welcome." Luc drew the flap back and waved them in, turning to mouth an apology to her.

Deni gave her a quick, amused look, and then took up a guard's stance just within the door.

The general came deeper into the space, looking around just as Ava had.

"You have a lot of maps," she said with interest, and moved over to the table. She caught Ava's gaze as she crossed to it. "Avasu."

"General." Ava bent her head.

"Tell me about the fight you had outside this tent tonight."

Ava glanced at Luc. She would leave this to him to explain.

"Some of my people were joking about my taking Ava away from her fight last night, and they thought it would be amusing to spar with her again. Unfortunately, the soldier who entered the match with her was once in a Chosen camp, like many of us, and he suffered a relapse, his mind taking him back to the horrors of the days spent fighting for our lives against each other. He forgot he was safe and sparring against a friend. Ava held him off without harming him until I arrived to stop it."

There was silence as the general took in his words.

Ava glanced at Deni, and saw this was the first he was hearing of it. His face had hardened, and his gaze on Luc was no longer so friendly.

"If your people are prone to forgetting who is friend and who is foe, that is a problem." General Ru looked up from a map she had rolled open.

"I agree." Luc moved over to the table, and began to place weights on the edges of the map so the general did not have to keep holding it. "But to say they are prone to it is not true. It is one person, falling into a fugue state for the first time in years. I'll keep a careful watch on him, and I'll make sure there's no possibility of harm to your people."

General Ru said nothing as she bent her head over the map. When she looked up, Ava could not read her at all.

"Accepted, Commander. I will trust you to keep your word."

Luc held her gaze a moment, then nodded. "Our guards have reported an increase in the Kassian scouting parties." He pointed to the map.

"As have ours. But before we continue . . ." General Ru held up a hand, and looked over at Ava. "You are not authorized for this level of information." She glanced over at Luc. "I would like to bring in two of my lieutenants for this strategy session. Ava, you can fetch them, and then find something to do away from here until we're finished."

Ava saw the look in Luc's eyes—the quick flash of fury. She took a step toward the general, bowing almost from her waist.

"Certainly." She turned to Luc, her gaze fixed on him. She saw him struggle to rein in his temper, and then finally succeed. "Would you like me to find your lieutenants as well?"

Luc said nothing for a long, slow beat. "Thank you, yes."

She winked at him, making him blink in surprise, then turned and walked out, glancing a parting shot at Deni as she stepped through the door.

He was watching her with interest, putting the pieces together.

And there were a lot of moving parts to this, she admitted.

It was going to take a lot of juggling to keep everyone happy.

But the general was right. She couldn't stay to listen to high level strategy in her current position.

She was Luc's lover, not his lieutenant. And she was under the command of General Ru by her own request.

So she would play messenger, and wander through the camp, listening, and making friends.

Given what her life had been just over two months ago, that actually sounded like bliss.

CHAPTER 12

While they waited for their lieutenants to arrive, Luc offered General Ru something to drink, and called to one of the guards outside the tent for some food from the open kitchen nearby.

It arrived quickly, and the general ate with relish.

"I heard you say you had met Ava's grandmother once." Luc waited until Deni had stepped out of the tent to join his own guards at the entrance. He had wondered about that statement since the night before.

"I did. On a mission to the Grimwalt court. She was present as a representative of her region."

"She passed away while Ava was held captive." He could still hear the hitch in Ava's breath from last night, the clog of tears in her throat, as she'd told him.

"And I understand her parents are dead, too." General Ru put down her cup.

"Killed by the Queen's Herald."

General Ru gave a slow nod. "I can see why she is very determined to be part of the Rising Wave."

"And yet, she's chosen to remain with the Venyatux." He still didn't quite understand it.

"It was part of our agreement." General Ru shrugged. "But it is also more than that. She was alone for a long time, I think. And with us, she has found friends. Camaraderie. She doesn't want to lose what to her is something very precious."

Before he could respond, there was a hail from outside, and Dak and Massi came in, followed by two of the general's four lieutenants.

No one made mention of Revek's absence, and Luc preferred it that way.

"The enemy is no longer content to watch us from afar," Dak said as they crowded around the map on the table. "They've increased their patrols, and they're coming closer."

"Agreed." The Venyatux lieutenant who had introduced herself as Fervanti tapped the place where the two columns were currently camped. "I don't think they're taunting us by coming so close. I think they're trying to work out how many of us there are and where we're all from."

"Because they want to know who might still be coming." Massi nodded. "I hope they caught a glimpse of the Skäddar. That would give them a fright."

"Who *is* still coming?" Kurvin, another of General Ru's lieutenants, asked. He was a wiry man in his early thirties, although the long brown braid falling over his shoulder was liberally threaded with silver.

"We are hoping to collect more Cervantes as we move through the plains."

"Have you opened a line of communication with the Jatan?" Fervanti asked.

"We tried." Massi put her hands on her hips. "They weren't interested in even an exchange of information, even though it would have been beneficial to us both."

"That's their way." General Ru leaned over the map. "They don't like cooperating with others."

"As long as their way is to wage war with the Kassian to the north west, I'm happy." Luc had never expected the uprising on the Jatan border, and it had given him months to gather his Rising Wave. Months he would never have had otherwise. "They've helped us enough, just by taking on the Kassian and focusing their numbers and strength away from us."

"But by now, the Kassian must know how big our combined army is." General Ru tapped a considering finger on her chin. "Even if they've withdrawn some of their forces from the Jatan border and diverted them back to Fernwell, the Queen's Herald will soon have to decide whether to come out to meet us before we reach Fernwell, or whether to prepare for a siege. He has to."

"Agreed. So the question is, how many of his forces has he moved away from Jatan, and where will they choose to meet us?" Luc stared at the map, and tapped at a point on the Bartolo River, just north of the city of Bartolo. "Here would be a good place to get us. Crossing a river that wide is hard enough without dealing with an attack."

General Ru nodded. "If they're good strategists, they'll definitely be looking there."

"So we have to send scouts ahead to keep watch at that point. And wherever else anyone here thinks will be a good ambush spot." Luc studied the map and the path they would need to take to Fernwell. Once off the plains, with its clear view in all directions, there were a lot of places where they could be surprised.

"Will they definitely ambush us, not simply attack?" Kurvin asked.

"It's certainly possible they could choose a straightforward attack. And they're arrogant enough to think they could best us without the element of surprise." Luc pointed to Dak and Kurvin. "You two, find places that would suit a front-on attack, Massi and Fervanti, you find places where an ambush is more likely. General Ru and I can look over your suggestions, and then we can put together small parties to go ahead to those places, keep hidden, and see if the Kassian look interested."

He realized belatedly that he'd just ordered the general's staff around, and he looked over to her and gave a bow. "If that makes sense to you, General?"

She looked at him with a glint of laughter in her usually unreadable dark eyes. "I agree. Let us meet tomorrow to discuss this." She took a final handful of the sweetened nuts from one of the bowls the cooks had brought in, and wished them all a good night as she left.

"Where are you going?" Massi lifted her head from the map as Luc followed close on her heels.

"To find Ava." He waited for her to make a comment, but although her lips thinned a little, she nodded, and he stepped out into the night, fragrant with woodsmoke and roasting meat, and soft with low laughter and conversation.

Someone called a hello to him, and he responded in kind. As he moved through the erratic pathway created by the tents, he realized that for the first time since he'd left Ava near the Grimwalt border two months ago, he finally felt at home again in the Rising Wave.

AVA STUDIED THE KNITTING, GETTING ON HER KNEES AND shuffling closer to the fire for better light.

"How do you twist the stitches?" she asked.

The Cervantes soldier she had befriended, Raelene, joined her, and held up a small wooden needle that instead of being straight, curved up on both sides. "You transfer the stitches to this, hold it in the back or front."

She took the knitting from Ava's hands and showed her.

There was magic in this. Ava could feel the tingle in her fingertips as she tried it herself. "Thank you for teaching this to me."

"My pleasure. I like the embroidery you've shown me." Raelene smoothed the shirt she'd been repairing over her knees.

Ava studied the tent and horse she'd embroidered for Raelene onto either side of the collar.

She was getting better. Quicker.

Every now and then she was overcome with a spike of fear that someone would notice her sewing and she would be punished, and then she would remember she wasn't in the fortress any more and no one was going to stop her. Sewing was allowed.

It was considered mundane and boring by most.

She had been teased about her interest in it by her fellow warriors more than once.

She simply smiled and wondered what they would say if they understood what she was capable of.

"Did the Cervantes live in tents before the Kassian invaded?" she asked, tracing the tent with a fingertip.

"No." Raelene folded the shirt carefully, keeping the collar visible so she could continue admiring it. "We lived in villages just like everyone else. The Kassian burned a lot of them down when we wouldn't hand our children over to the camps voluntarily, and after that the only way we could keep the children safe was to keep moving. They still found us. Took our babies. But not as many as if we'd stayed put."

"So the tent and the horse are symbols of survival. Of protection."

"Yes." Raelene's smile wobbled a little.

Ava was sorry now she hadn't asked her question while she was doing the embroidery. She could have woven survival and protection into the shirt. Instead, she had been happy to sit by the fire, talking to someone who sewed and knitted, discussing various techniques.

As she asked where to get supplies to start knitting herself, and said her goodbyes, she made herself relax.

She didn't have to always include a working. She could do something just because it was beautiful.

Perhaps the last few years had focused her too much on weaving magic into whatever she did, because it had to be done in secret and could so seldom be done at all. And if she were caught, it would mean torture or death.

Everything she'd embroidered in captivity had to be worth the risk.

But she didn't have that hanging over her anymore.

And now she could try other things. Knitting.

She felt a buzz of excitement at the idea of giving it a try.

She might even be able to infuse the very fabric with a working, rather than stitch on top of it.

A working that would be completely invisible. In the actual weave and twist of the stitches themselves.

The stores managers and free traders kept to the back of the Rising Wave column, out of the way, and she made her way through the tents toward them.

In the weeks she had been with them, Ava had made connections with the traders on the Venyatux side, but she hadn't seen any wool or knitting needles among their wares.

Then again, she hadn't been looking. Perhaps she just hadn't noticed.

Raelene assured her she could find supplies on the Rising Wave side.

When she reached the traders' area, she found she was far from the only one looking to buy or trade this late at night.

The tents had crowds in front of them, and quite a few people were from the Venyatux column.

There was obviously an interest in seeing what new items were available. And probably a fair crowd from the Rising Wave were over on the Venyatux side, too.

While she stood, looking for the most likely stall for what she needed, she felt the sudden, quick flare of warning from the working embroidered into her cloak.

She turned slowly, trying to find where the ill-feeling was coming from, but it was difficult to see over the crowds, and she was hemmed in.

"What're you looking for?" A girl tugged at her cloak.

Ava turned sharply to look, but there was no danger from this direction. The girl was about fourteen, slender, with huge eyes in a narrow face.

"I want to knit," Ava told her.

"We have what you need. The best yarn."

Ava followed her around the back of a small tent which had a sizeable crowd in front of it.

"How come I get special treatment?" she asked.

"Because I saw you earlier. You're the Commander's lady, aren't you?"

"Yes." She hadn't thought about this. That her relationship with Luc would elevate her in the eyes of those in the Rising Wave.

"We honor the Commander's lady. It will be our pleasure." She gave a cheeky grin before she slid between the flaps at the back of the tent, then stuck a delicate hand out and waved Ava in.

Inside was gloomy, lit only by a single lantern, but the smell in the air . . . it was of lanolin and the earthy, almost musty scent of vegetable dyes.

Pieces of fabric were folded and stacked on top of each other, the colors mostly plain—black, cream or gray.

The wool, on the other hand, was in baskets, rolled into balls of every hue. Greens, blues, reds and browns.

Ava crouched down to touch them, scrunching them in her fist, delighted by the squishy feel of them.

This tactile heaven was something she'd never even thought of, all those months in a cell, hiding her needle and thread.

"What's your name?" she asked the girl, who was hovering over her shoulder.

"Lettie."

"Lettie, what's your softest wool? The type that feels the best against the skin." She turned to look up at the girl, saw her worrying her lower lip.

"Some are a little bit scratchy, but this one always feels good. I've never had anything made from it though. Mother says it's too expensive." She held out a plain cream hank. "It's made from the goats up near the Skäddar border, in the Venyatux mountains. But then, you're from there, aren't you." Her face fell. "You probably already have this yarn. It's probably not special to you at all."

Ava took it, rubbed it between her fingers. It sang to her, the texture, the feel. She lifted it to her cheek and brushed it against her skin.

"No. I don't have any." She held it closer to the lantern. "It's not dyed."

"It's even more expensive if it's dyed, so we just got the undyed type. And we haven't been able to sell it yet."

The girl was charmingly honest.

Ava asked the price, and realized she was going to have to find out how much she'd earned as a guard for the Venyatux, because this purchase would wipe out the rest of the coin she'd brought with her from Grimwalt.

She managed to get a pair of needles and a cable tool thrown in with the wool, and walked out with it in a little hessian bag.

Lettie was grinning as she let Ava out the back. "You are nice."

Ava smiled back. "Because I bought your expensive wool?"

"Because you didn't try to get a discount, even though you're the Commander's lady." From the look on the girl's face, she couldn't wait to find her mother and tell her the good news. "What are you going to make with it? Something for the Commander?"

"Maybe."

The girl nodded sagely. "That would be a very good use of our best wool."

If she had any left, Ava decided, she would make the girl a knitted cap, like she'd seen the Skäddar wearing. It pulled over his head to his ears, and while it was plain, she thought the twisted stitches Raelene had shown her would look very good on it. And it would be quick to make.

She waved a goodbye and started back toward Luc's tent. Did she want to spend the night there, or should she persuade him to come back to her tent?

The problem with that was if he was needed, they would never find him. The magic she had worked into the canvas would make sure of it.

And when people couldn't find something that should be there, they might start to wonder.

Her mother had drummed into her to keep her magic secret.

She wouldn't even discuss her abilities with Ava, which meant Ava didn't know how powerful she was in comparison to her mother and grandmother, whether everyone with a skill with the needle could do what she did, and what her boundaries were.

Or even how many like her there were.

Her mother's fear was because of the risk to her. The temptation she posed to those who would force her to do mischief for them. Who would lock her away and make her workings their own.

That fear, though founded, had not helped to keep her safe.

Both Ava—and she later discovered, her mother—had been captured anyway.

Her grandmother's skills had been known only in Grimwalt, as far as she was able to tell, and only to a select, trusted few, who commissioned workings from her.

Her grandmother had never discussed it with her, but Ava had the impression that it was something only shared with those she trusted.

But her father's view had been that none were to be trusted. Friends fell out, lovers betrayed you, and when it came to power, all could be bought, for a price.

Her father had said more than once she must never talk about her magic when they were in Kassia, as she would be taken by the Queen and never seen again if her family's abilities were known.

That was the Kassian way, perhaps. To fear those whose power you didn't understand.

It had certainly been the case with the Cervantes.

They were such fierce, amazing warriors, the Kassian had taken their children and tried to raise them as a dedicated army for the Kassian cause.

And coming toward her, his body moving in a way she still believed had its own power and magic, was the reason that plan had failed for the Kassian.

Her heart's choice, a Cervantes warrior from a Chosen camp who had snuck over to the Venyatux army on the eve of battle for the Kassian, made a deal, and then, the following day on the battle field, had turned on his masters, safe in the knowledge the Venyatux would not attack.

The Turncoat King.

"There you are." Luc smiled at her.

She let his smile warm her, and slid her arm around his waist. "You and the general all finished?"

He shook his head, but he steered her back toward his tent anyway. "The lieutenants are doing some work in there, but we can reclaim it for ourselves."

"Would you like to come to my side?" she asked. She would just have to sleep lightly, and listen out for someone calling for him, if he was needed.

"I'm expecting reports through the night. The Kassian scouts are venturing closer and closer, and it will be better if I'm in the main tent. Do you mind?"

She did, a little, but she shook her head.

She steeled herself for unfriendly looks from Massi as they returned to the tent, but she was simply ignored, which suited her fine.

Dak made an effort to be pleasant, and Revek was nowhere in sight.

It was a better end to the situation than she'd feared earlier.

The Venyatux lieutenants were much more interested in her, though. She mainly dealt with their colleagues, Raun-Tu and Heival, who gave her her orders each day, and she was sure she would be the topic of conversation the next time all four lieutenants got together.

She left Luc talking to them and disappeared behind the curtain to find a big bed of straw with thick covers, a wooden trunk and nothing else.

Her lover traveled light for the commander of a rebel army.

She wondered whether they had been allowed any possessions in the camps, and thought probably not.

She took off her cloak and boots, settled onto the bed and began casting on her yarn.

She already knew Luc's dimensions from the shirt she'd made him, and she was happily a few rows in, thinking about the pattern she would weave with the cable tool, when the talk ended in goodbyes and plans to meet the following morning.

She would have to make sure to be out and doing something else.

She looked up when Luc stepped behind the curtain. He raised a brow at her, curled up against the pillows, knitting in hand.

She grinned, put the knitting down, and crooked her finger.

He walked closer slowly, and she watched him through lowered lashes.

"Alone at last?" she asked.

"Alone at last." His voice was slightly rough. "You're finally where you were meant to be two months ago." He crouched beside her.

"I can't regret going home. And I put plans in place . . ." She hesitated, unsure how much to admit about her plans of vengeance.

"Plans against the Queen's Herald?"

She nodded. "Plans that will likely get him killed by the Queen's own hand, rather than my own." She worried her lip. "Is that cowardly of me? I probably won't be there when it happens."

"And how will you get the Queen to kill her own nephew?" He sat back on his heels.

"By making him admit he has plotted against her." There were so many variables. She may not have gotten it right, but even at its least effective, her plan would do some damage.

"And how will you do that?" He had hold of her arms, his gaze on the place where her neck met her shoulder, and she couldn't resist tilting her head to give him access.

He brought his lips down as she whispered: "I plan to use his own vanity and insecurities to get him to confess." She swallowed as she felt the edge of his teeth.

"Perhaps you can tell me how another time."

"Another time," she agreed, and arched back against the pillows. And decided she needed to stitch a working into the curtain between the bed and the main tent that muted all sound.

CHAPTER 13

"You probably don't have to do scout duty anymore." Deni glanced back at her as they rode toward the head of the column.

The rising sun was in her eyes, and Ava had to shield them to return his gaze. "What should I do instead?" she asked.

"I don't know. Wander around making friends with the Rising Wave."

She laughed. "You heard that part of the bargain, did you?"

"I asked the general for the details of your agreement. I don't think she told me everything, but she did say you were to be a liaison." He slowed to let her catch up, and they broke free of the front wagons and sped up as the plain opened in front of them.

"I can only be a good liaison if I'm respected, and wandering around chatting to people all day would not accomplish that."

"True." Deni lifted up on his saddle and hailed the small group of riders coming toward them. "What news?"

The leader of the scout party they were relieving pulled up her horse and it danced beneath her, knowing full well a meal and water lay up ahead. "Same as yesterday. We saw four parties, and usually we're lucky to see one. And they were much closer. We could hear them shouting something one time, but when we moved toward them they rode away."

"So it's likely they're trying to collect information. They aren't looking to attack." Deni had to move his horse out of the way of the scout's twitchy mount.

The woman nodded her head. "They didn't even point an arrow in our direction." She finally gave her horse its head, and the group of three galloped away, one of them whooping as they went.

"Are we coordinating with the Rising Wave?" Ava asked as they began to trot forward.

"They're taking the west side of the combined army, we're checking the east side." He looked over at her, as if he wanted to ask something, but then shook his head, and they rode in companionable silence, heading toward the low scrub and trees.

"Why do we get the bushes, and the Rising Wave gets the open plain?" Ava asked. The section they were covering was a strip of tangled brambles, bushes and low trees. She couldn't tell how deep the vegetation went, but it looked almost impassable.

"Do you see that?" Deni pointed, and she caught a glimpse of a horse before it disappeared among the gold and orange leaves.

They slowed, and then came to a stop just before the vegetation became more dense.

"Do we go in?" She suddenly wished she had made something for Deni with a protection worked into it.

She pulled out a scrap of fabric and embroidered a few tiny stars onto it, working as fast as she could as she hummed.

"What are you doing? Are you . . . all right?"

She looked up to see him staring at her in absolute astonishment.

"This is for good luck." It wasn't as good as if she had time and the ability to concentrate completely, but it would be better than nothing. She leaned across and tucked the long, narrow scrap down the neck of his shirt.

He batted her hand away, but didn't try to pull the fabric out.

She gave a nod of approval. "Keep it against your skin."

"Avasu, this is not normal."

She shrugged, and smiled at him, hoping it looked easy and lighthearted. "Just indulge me. My grandmother swore by it. And what can it hurt?"

He shook his head in disbelief, but she didn't care if he thought her mad. The working would protect him either way.

She looked back at the column, lumbering in its slow, steady way south east across the plains, and then back into the scrub.

"Have they ever come this close before? I mean, they could fire an arrow from where we caught sight of them and actually hit someone."

Deni shielded his eyes as he looked between the trees. "When they said the Kassian were getting closer, I didn't realize it was this close. But maybe this one just strayed too close by mistake. I haven't seen them again."

She hadn't either, and her cloak offered no warning.

"What do we do?"

Deni thought about it, like her, looking back at the column and then into the trees again.

"Let's go to where we saw whoever it was. You never know what you might find."

He took the lead and she followed him, making herself as small as possible in the saddle as the denuded branches of large bushes scratched and grabbed at her cloak and hair.

"This is hard going." Deni stopped to unhook a sharp stick from his hair. "I don't see them moving through here easily. Perhaps they thought they'd be safe to watch from here, because we wouldn't patrol within the scrub."

"They'd have been right." Ava tucked her cloak tight around her, and winced when some of the threads were hooked and damaged by tree limbs.

She smoothed over some of the ripped stitches, and wondered whether the protections she'd sewn into the cloak would still work.

"Here." Deni's voice led her into a small clearing, and she could see the snapped twigs and branches, the churned ground. More than one person had waited here for a while, and their horses had gotten testy about it.

She looked out toward the column, and she could just see it through the foliage. "This is where they were when we spotted them."

Deni nodded. "They're long gone now."

She saw the point the spy or spies had taken out of the clearing. Cocked her head in that direction in question.

"I don't know what good it would do us." Deni hesitated, then gave a nod, pushing her horse aside with his own so he went first through the narrow gap in the vegetation.

Ava ducked as branches whipped back, and only just glimpsed the arrow flying over her head.

Deni's horse reared up as another arrow flew, trying to back up and finding Ava's mount in the way.

It turned, forelegs kicking out, and panicked, Ava's horse bolted in the only direction that was open, the narrow path ahead.

Ava swallowed a cry as branches struck her in the face, and then pain exploded in her forehead and she was flung off.

She lay still for what felt like a long time, listening to her horse's panicked path through the underbrush, and then finally opened her eyes.

A man stood over her, and there was someone else near her feet.

"Did the other one get away?" The man above her turned his head as he asked the question.

"Yes. Could you have shot any worse, Nedar? He was right in front of you and you missed him completely."

"My aim was true. I don't know what happened. He moved at just the right moment." Nedar's voice was defensive. "It happens sometimes."

"Well, it's a huge fucking pity it happened now. Because he's off to call in reinforcements and we're not exactly able to make a run for it." There was deep bitterness in the man's voice.

"What do you want me to do about it, Cassak? It's not my fault we're hobbled. I didn't want to come so close, if you remember."

"Did I? We were *sent* here, asshole." The bitterness increased. "And we spent too long here looking for that fucking message. Which we didn't find." He made a choked sound and she heard what sounded like a boot kicking a tree trunk. "What about her horse? Do you think you could go after it?" Cassak finally came into view, looking to the left, and Ava listened for sounds of her horse in the underbrush, but there was nothing to hear over the persistent thump in her head. Every beat was like a spike driving through her brain.

With careful fingers, she touched her forehead, felt the large bump on her forehead.

Above her was the offending branch. Far thicker and sturdier than the others had been.

“You finally awake, scout?” Nedar leaned down.

She nodded her head slowly, and winced when the pain of the movement overwhelmed her.

“I know the feeling.” The other man, Cassak, touched his own forehead, and she noticed there was blood along his hairline and a dark bruise blossoming above his eyebrow.

So they’d come to grief here, too.

She curled on her side and closed her eyes, too dizzy to do anything else.

She didn’t think she’d lain there more than a minute before she was woken by someone shaking her by the shoulder.

“We’re going to need you alive and able to walk if we’re going to use you as a hostage.” Nedar’s bow was slung over his shoulder, and his arrows rattled in their sheath.

He was the one who’d shot at them. Except his arrows had missed.

She smiled and closed her eyes again.

“She’s out of it. She doesn’t even realize she’s in enemy hands by the looks of it.” Nedar didn’t lower his voice, and the noise of it was like hammering in her brain.

She lifted a hand to cover her ear.

“Just make sure she doesn’t die, Nedar. Don’t let her sleep. We can’t bargain with a dead woman. Her horse is long gone, so is mine, and the only one we have left is caught in the thorns.” He sounded like he was about to scream.

She hoped he didn’t, her head couldn’t take it.

Rough hands grabbed her and lifted her up into a sitting position, and she felt the rough bark of a tree against her neck and hair.

White light exploded across her vision for a few seconds, and she leaned to the side and vomited.

When she was done, she closed her eyes and tilted her head upward, resting against the tree trunk.

She could hear the men bickering close by, and she finally worked out the long mane of Nedar's horse had been caught in a bramble bush, and they were trying to work it free.

They had also been sent to pick up a message from a spy in the Rising Wave column, and they hadn't been able to find it.

Cassak thought the spy hadn't been able to leave the message for some reason, and Nedar thought they'd been given the wrong location.

Both agreed they couldn't look for it any longer, though. They had to go as soon as the horse was free.

It didn't sound as if the horse was cooperating, though. It stamped and tried to throw back its head, then panicked all over again as the brambles kept it in place.

She took stock of her injuries while they were distracted.

She had worked a healing into her cloak, but she wasn't feeling any better, even though she was gripping the fabric with both hands. It might be that her healing spell had been damaged by the sharp branches.

She needed to remember to work something into her shirts after today, if she somehow escaped. She needed something closer to her skin.

She was always getting others to wear her protections close, but she had put so many layers of protection into her cloak, she'd gotten complacent.

The fight with Revek last night should have been a warning. Once he'd taken her cloak off her, she had been without a shield. But that had only been last night. Less than twelve hours ago.

She hadn't had time to process everything it meant. And she'd had other issues to deal with.

Still, she was paying the price now.

"Here." A leather water skin was dropped onto her lap, and she lifted it with shaking hands and sipped at the water carefully, resting a little after each swallow.

"Careful." It was ripped from her grasp, and she realized she had tipped it to the side and water was spilling onto her cloak.

She rubbed her fingers over the wet patch and found a snarl of ripped threads.

She needed to craft new protections.

Even hastily thrown together ones seem to work well enough in the short term. She assumed their power would dissipate quickly, but she didn't need them for long.

She dipped her hand into her cloak pocket, so used to the motion she kept her eyes closed. She worked her needle free from where it was woven into the fabric of her pocket for safekeeping. She always kept it threaded with dark brown thread, the same color as her cloak, to make her workings easy to overlook.

She smoothed a hand over the fabric, finding a place with no embroidery on it, and an obvious tear. She lifted it up in front of her and finally opened her eyes.

"What are you doing?"

She jerked, heart racing, to find Nedar watching her.

"Repairing my cloak. It got ripped by the branches."

He narrowed his eyes at her. "That's a strange thing to do now."

She shrugged. "I'm not doing anything else. I have the means. Why not?"

"You don't seem particularly frightened for a prisoner of war." Cassak spoke from across the small clearing, working a thorn studded branch out of the horse's mane, and she winced as she turned her head a little to look at him.

"I'm in too much pain to care." She kept her voice flat and matter-of-fact.

Neither man responded to that, and she started working a healing spell into her cloak, using the symbolism of repairing the tear to repairing the damage done to her. It took her much longer than usual. She kept needing to rest, and her mind kept floating off, untethered, and she would realize she hadn't focused on what she was doing for a while.

When she was done, she was unhappy.

It was not her best work by any measure, and she started again. She was a little better the second time, embroidering a bed to symbolize rest and recovery. When she was done, she felt better still, and she realized she was piggybacking on the incremental improvement of each working.

She could inch her way to healing herself completely.

She was on the fourth working when she finally felt well enough to take more notice of her surroundings.

The two Kassian spies had been talking to each other in low, urgent voices as they calmed their horse and slowly worked it free of its snares, but she had stopped listening to them when she'd started working her healing spell.

Now she could concentrate, she heard the huff of their horse as it finally stepped free of the bush.

"I can hear them," Nedar was saying, and she could hear both fear and relief in his voice. "We got the horse free just in time. Who's going to talk to them, me or you?"

"Me." Cassak rose from a crouch, and caught Ava looking at him.

She kept her face blank and closed her eyes again.

"She's still barely awake," he said. "But she's breathing, and that's all we need."

"We can't carry her. She's small enough, but you're injured and I need both hands to use the bow."

"We could put her on the horse," Cassak suggested.

"We could." Nedar paused. "We might have to tie her on. She can barely sit up against the tree, let alone in a saddle."

Cassak swore. "The rope was in my saddlebag, and who knows where my horse is now. Probably back at camp."

"If it got back to camp, they might come looking for us," Nedar said. "That would be helpful."

Cassak grunted in response. "Let's assume no help is coming and we have to save ourselves."

"Ava!" Luc's voice cut through Nedar's response. He sounded close. Ava's eyes opened, and she saw her captors had frozen at his shout.

That didn't last, though. Cassak was suddenly beside her, hand over her mouth.

"Don't come any closer or your scout is dead." The timbre of Cassak's voice was a little uneven, and she could feel his fear in the tight grip over her mouth and chin.

"What do you want?" Luc called.

"To get away without being followed. We lost one of our horses and have some injuries. Give us a horse and an hour to get away, and we'll leave your scout to walk back."

"What's stopping you from taking her back with you as a prisoner?" Luc asked, and Ava realized her mind must have truly been clouded that she hadn't thought of this herself.

Cassak was quiet for a moment, and she wished she could see his face.

"We want to get away, and she'll slow us down."

She also remembered he was injured. Suddenly realizing his hand was resting on her shoulder, she tried to shrug him off.

She wasn't sure if her working would heal him, but she didn't want to take the chance. He was far less likely to try and take her back to the Kassian camp if he was still injured.

He put his hand back down, and she struggled even harder against him, twisting and fighting.

"What's wrong with you?" he hissed in her ear. "Cooperate and we'll all get out of here alive."

"Here." Nedar crouched on her other side with a piece of cloth in his hand and gagged her.

Then Cassak and him both held her hands in front of her and tied them together with another piece of cloth.

"Stay put, or I'll put an arrow through your leg." Nedar stalked away, and grabbed his bow from where he'd hooked it to his saddlebag.

"He means it," Cassak warned her, and she gave a reluctant nod.

They stood in front of her, their attention wholly focused on Luc.

She didn't mind, as long as they didn't feel the need to look back and see what she was doing.

She'd dropped her needle and thread onto her lap when Nedar had tied her hands, and she picked it back up again.

It was difficult to sew with her hands bound together, but not impossible. She worked slowly and carefully, using the working she had sewn into her tent. Making her cloak impossible to see.

She wished she had her scarf with her. All she would need to do was pull it out, although she thought it only made her difficult to concentrate on, easy to overlook. She had never assumed it made her truly invisible. She would need something to cover her entire body for that.

When she was done, she lifted her hood and drew up her knees, awkwardly tucking her cloak around her with her bound hands. She bend her forehead to touch her knees, arms tucked against her body, and hoped her cloak covered her completely.

Then she kept very still.

Cassak and Nedar had moved forward a little, and she tuned back into the negotiation they were having with Luc.

She heard the sound of a horse trotting into the tiny clearing, and risked looking up. It stopped and then moved back when it saw strangers blocking its way.

"No, no, no." Nedar leaped forward, grabbing hold of its reins, and it jerked in panic.

Cassak moved forward to help him, and they finally got the horse under control.

"You've got your horse, now give us our scout." Luc's voice was so close.

Just beyond the tangle of bushes.

"That wasn't the deal. Stay back or we'll hurt her." Cassak sounded panicked.

Nedar shot him a look and made a gesture with his hand she guessed meant *shut up*. "We're taking her with us," he called out. "Give us an hour and then you can come find her."

"If you hurt her, there isn't a place you can hide from me." Luc's voice was calm now. It was a promise, not a threat.

Her two captors glanced at each other, and Ava realized they sensed something off about Luc's very personal reaction.

"You do that for all your scouts?" Nedar asked.

"Why do you think every single Chosen turned and fought with the Commander against the Kassian two years ago?" Luc's voice had gone soft. "It's because we fight for each other, and have each other's backs, no matter what."

It was a good save on Luc's part.

Ava saw Cassak visibly swallow.

"Don't follow us, and you won't have to hunt us down anywhere. Because we'll leave her nice and safe for you to fetch."

That was her cue.

Ava bent her head again, hunching low.

She heard Nedar helping Cassak up onto the horse's back, and then knew the moment they realized she was gone.

All sound stopped.

Cassak sounded slack-jawed with shock. "Where—?"

He grunted in sudden pain, and she guessed Nedar had hit him to stop him saying anything out loud.

Nedar swore under his breath, dragging the word out softly and then she heard the jingle of his stirrups as he mounted his own horse. "An hour," he called out. "Any sooner and she gets hurt."

He led the way out, and Cassak followed after him.

As soon as they were out of sight, she lifted her head and started unpicking her invisibility stitches.

Luc must have been moving so quietly, she didn't realize he was in the clearing until he'd passed her. His face was focused, his body fluid as he ghosted through the small space and disappeared between the trees, following her captors.

Damn!

He hadn't seen her.

She frowned. Her head hadn't been down. And he still hadn't seen her.

She refused to believe he wouldn't have been paying attention to everything around him.

Which meant—

She went absolutely still when she heard a rustle of leaves, and then a small group of five soldiers stepped into the clearing. They were a mixed bunch; Rising Wave and Venyatux.

Deni was among them, and a Venyatux soldier she had sparred with before, Taira.

"This is where they must have been holding the Commander's friend." One of the Rising Wave soldiers looked straight at her, and she waited for him to call out or notice her, but his gaze moved on.

He had looked straight into her eyes and he still hadn't seen her.

He had a bulky frame, a maturity of stature, that told Ava he was older than the rest of the group. He had an insignia on his leather vest that spoke of some kind of rank.

"Quiet," Deni hissed. "If they hear us, they promised to hurt Avasu. As it is I'm worried about them hearing your Commander."

"They won't hear him." The ranked officer shook his head. "Truth is, there is no one I know who moves as quietly as that man."

"How does he do it?" Taira asked.

"All Cervantes move quietly. It's in our blood. But he's the best I've seen. Still, he's already been caught by the Kassian once, so I wish he'd let us go with him." The unit commander lifted his shoulders.

"He asked us to wait, and I have to trust he has Avasu's best interests at heart." Deni spoke softly.

"I've heard she's enspelled him." The woman who spoke was Rising Wave.

Ava's focus fixed onto her.

"Who's enspelled him?" Taira scoffed.

"Your Avasu." The woman rubbed the back of her neck, her gaze darting around the clearing.

"Who told you that?" Deni asked.

"Yes, who did tell you that, Haslia?" The ranked officer asked. "I've heard that rumor and I've been trying to work out where it started."

"It's because Haslia shares pillows with Revek sometimes," the remaining Rising Wave soldier volunteered. "I thought she got the story from him."

Haslia shook her head. "I didn't start it. And I didn't hear it from Revek." She slowly turned in a circle. "Do you feel eyes on you?" She spoke in a whisper.

"Don't change the subject. You're the one who tells it the most. I think you did start it," the soldier who'd mentioned the women's connection to Revek said. "The story I've heard that has more weight, though, is about his sword."

"What about his sword?" Taira asked.

"Enchanted," the soldier said.

"Enchanted?" Taira scoffed.

"Have you seen it?" The soldier's face was earnest. "It's got a gold pattern on the hilt. It's like nothing I've ever seen before. He got it in the dungeons of the Kassian fortress where he was held prisoner. Found it there and used it to fight his way out."

"Why does anyone think he's been enspelled or carries an enchanted sword anyway?" Deni asked. "Has he been behaving strangely?"

"He was always a good fighter," the soldier said. "The best, really. But now . . ." He lifted his shoulders. "There have been three assassination attempts on him since he got back to the Rising Wave from Kassia, and he's stopped every one of them singlehandedly. It's like he's got a magical edge."

"And that's a bad thing?" Deni asked.

"Magic isn't the way to fight a war," Haslia said. She had relaxed a little and Ava focused on her again.

As soon as she did, Haslia began to fidget.

"If magic's given, it can be taken away. Or perverted. What can be made strong can also be made weak."

"I see the Commander out on the field every day, training." The officer gave Haslia a long look. "There's no sorcery involved. Just hard work." He narrowed his eyes at her. "And I'll tell you now, Haslia. If I hear another word about the Commander's heart's choice using spells on him, I'll assume you aren't busy enough, and give you more to do."

"Beside, you're saying that he's been enspelled since he got back from Kassia, but he and Avasu only met up again two days ago, after two months apart," Deni said. "She's been traveling with us a lot of that time. Are you saying she's such a powerful spell caster she can work a spell that lasts two months?"

Haslia shrugged. "I didn't come up with the story, despite what Fredrik says." She sent the other soldier a dark look. "And I won't repeat it again."

Frederik pointed a finger at Deni. "I hadn't even thought of that, but you're right. How could he be enspelled by your scout all this time they've been apart? A magical working only lasts a few hours."

"Says who?" Haslia scoffed. "What do you know about it?"

"What do *you* know about it?" the officer asked.

"Enough to know with so few spell casters around, we don't really know what they can do, do we? And if I could cast spells, I'd be sure to downplay how long they last. Wouldn't you?"

"This story has been swirling around since your Commander escaped the Kassian?" Taira asked.

"Yes. Since a few days after he got back." Frederik folded his arms and looked over at Haslia.

"So he told everyone he'd escaped with Avasu?" Taira frowned.

"No." The officer drew the word out. "That's a good point. Only someone who knew he'd escaped with a woman would be able to make up a rumor about a woman enspelling him."

"Like Revek," Frederik said.

"Or like the Kassian themselves." Deni's voice was low.

Haslia stopped looking around, as if for escape, and slowly let her gaze travel over each of them. "What, I'm a spy now because I passed on a rumor? I won't repeat the stupid story again, all right?"

"I want to know who told it to you if you didn't make it yourself." The officer took hold of her arm.

"I can't remember." She jerked her arm away. "I might have been a little dramatic in retelling it, and bringing it up too often, but I won't do it again. I promise."

A sudden rustle of leaves and branches made everyone, including Ava, turn to the left.

Her horse stepped through the trees, and Taira blew out a breath in relief. "Avasu's horse. That's something."

"You take it back to the Venyatux, Haslia." The officer caught hold of its reins and handed it to the woman. "The rest of us, let's go after the Commander."

They disappeared into the trees, and Haslia was left standing beside the horse, staring after them.

Her face was blank. She took one last, slow look around the clearing before she led the horse out, her gaze passing over Ava again.

Well.

Ava sat very still for another long beat.

She hadn't heard the rumors they were talking about—how could she when they'd only just joined the Rising Wave?—but she could hear the voice of her cousin in them.

Oh, yes. There were Kassian spies in the Rising Wave, and they'd been salting the earth in anticipation of her arrival.

It sounded as if a counter-narrative had risen up as well, though, based on Luc's sword.

She vaguely remembered him grabbing it from the dungeon beside her mother's tomb.

How frustrating to whoever had started the enspelled-by-a-witch rumor when the magic sword story began to take hold.

And how interesting that Haslia occasionally shared pillows, as the Cervantes put it, with Revek.

That woman needed watching.

CHAPTER 14

Luc moved as fast as he could.

He didn't trust the word of the Kassian spies. He would certainly not trust them at their word with Ava's life at stake.

He could hear them talking in low, urgent tones up ahead, two men, by the sound of it.

He hadn't heard Ava's voice once.

From behind him, something crashed through the undergrowth and he went still.

So did the two men he was following.

Someone had come after him, when he'd specifically told them to wait.

He used the fact that the two Kassian up ahead had stopped and kept moving forward, making up ground.

The flick of a horse's tail through the leaves slowed him, and he edged to the side, looking for a good view of the pair.

"Is it her?" One of them whispered. "Stumbling around? She hit her head hard enough she might be disoriented."

"Maybe. Or maybe her friends decided not to wait on our word. I wouldn't have." The other man's voice was just as low.

"If it's her, we could grab her."

"We can barely get through the bush here with the two of us, Cassak. We just keep moving forward, and be thankful they'll find it just as hard as we are."

Was the 'her' they were talking about Ava?

Luc crouched down, shuffled closer.

The men had gotten off their horse, and he could see why. The going was impossible, too many low-hanging branches blocked the way.

They were moving slowly, and there was no sign of Ava anywhere.

So they didn't have her.

And she was badly injured. Deni had shouted something about her being knocked from her horse when he'd come racing toward the column, waving his arms.

Luc turned away from the spies, immediately dismissing them in his mind, and started going back the way he'd come.

The sound of leaves crunching beneath a pair of boots had him going still.

So someone *had* followed him through the bush.

He pressed up against a tree, deep in shadow, and caught sight of Revek pushing his way through a tangle of branches.

His face had been slashed by sharp twigs, and he smeared some of the blood over his cheek with the back of his hand.

He nearly didn't see Luc, but he was a Chosen, too, and he stopped dead after a few steps.

He turned to look, and seemed to relax.

Luc stared at him.

His trust in Revek had begun to erode the first night he'd returned to the Rising Wave after escaping the Kassian fortress with Ava.

That night, he'd nearly been killed on Revek's orders.

His old friend had sworn it was a mistake, but he knew there was something wrong with what had happened.

The attack on Ava was just another reason to be wary.

Revek's face stilled.

A look of hurt flashed in his eyes.

"Attack?" he mouthed.

Luc shook his head. "They don't have Ava."

Revek blinked. "Where is she then?"

Luc shrugged. Turned and started back the way he'd come, but Revek's hand grabbed his shoulder.

"You're letting them go?" Rev's whisper was directly in his ear.

"They don't have Ava, so yes. She's hurt. I need to find her."

"You do that." Revek sounded bitter. "I'll go after the spies. It'll be good to find out what the Kassian plans are."

Luc inclined his head. "Good."

Revek said nothing, and as Luc moved ahead, Revek's hand disappeared from his shoulder.

He left his lieutenant to it, carefully retracing his steps, looking for any sign of Ava.

What he found was some of the soldiers who'd been with him when he'd negotiated with the Kassian spies for Ava's life.

"They slipped passed you?" Rafe sounded disbelieving.

"No. Ava managed to escape them. They don't have her." He inclined his head the way he'd come. "Revek's gone after them, I'm looking for Ava."

"Where did Revek come from?" Rafe asked, surprised.

Luc frowned. "I don't know."

"If you want to split up, some can help me, some can help Revek."

"Taira and I will help you look for Avasu," Deni said.

Rafe met Luc's eyes and nodded, then he and the young soldier with him moved on, following the path the Kassian scouts had forged through the undergrowth.

"Spread out," Luc told the two Venyatux. "She's injured, so she may be unresponsive. Call out when you find her."

They nodded, and Deni went right, Taira left, and Luc moved back the way he'd come, to see if he could pick up a trail from the clearing where they'd held her.

As he stepped into the tiny space, the hairs on his neck began to prickle, and a feeling swept over him that he'd known before, from the Chosen camps.

Someone was watching him. Even though he couldn't see them, he felt their eyes on him.

He turned slowly, pulling out his sword, although the vegetation was so dense, he wouldn't be able to get in a full swing.

The feeling slowly faded, but that didn't comfort him.

His heart sped up, and he fought back the memories of sitting for hours, never sure who was behind him.

That the Kassian guards running the camps meant him harm was a given. The timing of when that harm would come to him, though, that he could never predict.

He had long ago worked out it hadn't mattered what he did.

Comply. Rebel. Pretend respect, or show his true contempt.

They'd already decided what they were going to do. And they deliberately kept it inconsistent, to mess with everyone's heads.

They'd thought it would break the Cervantes children they had stolen. That they would end up needing order and consistency, and cling to it when it was finally offered to them.

Become good little soldiers for the Kassian cause.

It hadn't worked on Luc. And he had made sure it hadn't worked on as many fellow camp prisoners as he could reach.

He had wondered if it was someone with magic who had watched him all those years ago. Made invisible by a spell.

He wasn't the only one who had felt it, but most had convinced themselves they had imagined the watcher. And perhaps it truly had been a figment of their imaginations. A shadow monster born of exhaustion and fear.

But he would swear it was the same sensation he'd felt moments ago.

And if he was right, that meant there was a magic user in these trees, watching all over again.

He forced himself to let it go.

That wasn't important right now. Ava was.

He could think about this later. Not that he would have any way to truly know, one way or the other. Which was all the more reason to let it go.

He took one last look around, but the sensation had passed and he sheathed his sword. The moment it slid home in its scabbard, Ava rose up from the shadows, out of nowhere.

As if she had stepped from the Otherworld itself.

Ava didn't think it was a coincidence that Luc had put his sword away the moment she had taken her eyes off him to unpick the last of her working.

When he had first stepped into the clearing and suddenly gone still, he'd looked lethal.

Ready to engage in battle.

She had hidden at the sound of someone returning, crouching deep in the shadow of the tree, and when she had seen it was Luc, moving in that quiet, predatory way of his, she had been about to rise up, call out to him, when he had stopped dead.

And then suddenly, his sword was in his hand, and he was turning, looking for some threat he obviously sensed. She had the feeling that if she had moved at that moment, he would have cut her down before she could identify herself.

She closed her eyes, trying to listen for whatever or whoever it was he sensed, but there was nothing to hear but the whispering of leaves and the quiet, steady breath of her lover as he stood ready to kill.

And then she glanced up to see he had relaxed somewhat, sliding his sword back into place, and she made a hard, hard decision and ripped out the last of her stitches, got to her feet and stepped into the light.

"Ava." He stared at her, dumbfounded. "Was that you watching me?"

She stared at him, lifted her bound hands, and pulled the gag from her mouth. She cleared her throat. "I heard someone come into the clearing, but I hid because I didn't know it was you, and then you had your sword out, so I kept still, and . . ." She suddenly understood, and the realization roared over her like a gale, like the hard storms she'd battled through the Grimwalt mountains on her way home just a few months ago.

She gaped at him, and her mouth tried to form words. "It was me," she whispered. "Me you thought was a threat."

"How were you not here, and here at the same time?" He stepped closer to her, and she realized that his sword was in his hand again. Had been there since she emerged from the shadows.

He stared down at it, unable to reach for her while he held it, and slowly slid it back into the scabbard strapped to his back.

"I worked magic into my cloak," she said, as softly as she could while still making herself audible to him. "I needed to hide from the Kassian spies, so while their back was turned, talking to you, I worked an invisibility spell into my cloak, and when they turned around to grab me, they thought I was gone."

It felt as if she was shredding her clothes to stand naked in front of a jeering crowd. That some terrible fate would befall her the moment the words were out of her mouth.

She had never revealed anything like it to anyone, ever.

She realized she was panting, as if she'd run a long, long way. She held out her bound wrists to him. "Will you cut me loose?"

He started, and then pulled a knife from his boot, sliced through the binding. He took her gag, too, and cut it off her where it hung around her neck.

"Tell me," he whispered. "Tell me how."

He looked like he was fighting a war with himself. Like he wanted to pull her close and push her away at the same time, and she drew herself straight, and took a step back.

"I don't know how." She lifted her shoulders. "My mother and my grandmother could do it, too. That's why the Queen's Herald had me and my mother locked up. He wanted me to work magic for him, and I wouldn't. I thought I'd outsmarted him, but instead . . ."

"Instead, he took your mother and forced her to do it. Most likely with the threat of harm to you."

She gave a nod.

"And this?" He plucked at his shirt.

"A working of protection." She lowered her eyes. "That no harm should come to you."

"Avasu!" Deni's shout made them both jerk. "You're all right."

She turned, rubbing at her wrists. "Yes." She tried to smile at him. "It's good to see you, my friend."

Deni rubbed the back of his neck in embarrassment. "Sorry for leaving you, but my horse bolted when we surprised them. Thank goodness we did, or they may have shot a little straighter."

Before she could respond, the sound of shouting came from up ahead, and then she heard Revek's voice call Luc's name.

"I'm needed." He put out a hand to clasp Deni's shoulder. "Keep her safe for me."

He was suddenly gone. He hadn't looked at her. Hadn't even spoken to her directly.

Her eyes were suddenly hot and a tear ran down her cheek.

"Don't worry, Avasu. He's the Commander. He'll be fine." Deni patted her back, and then Taira joined them in the clearing, and they helped her out of the thicket, onto the open plain.

She was almost completely healed, but she let them support her as if she was still injured, and somehow, that didn't feel like a lie.

CHAPTER 15

Ava.

It had been Ava's eyes on him.

As he ran toward Revek and the others, Luc tried to balance the horror he'd felt earlier with the knowledge that this time, the eyes on him had only meant him well.

It was hard.

He admitted to himself that he was relieved to have an excuse to leave Ava with Deni, to think things through without looking at the pain and vulnerability he'd seen on her face.

He could hear a fight up ahead, and it sounded as if there were more combatants involved than there should be.

He burst through the thicket and saw Revek, Rafe and the young soldier in a fight for their lives with five Kassian soldiers.

The two spies had been joined by three others.

An arrow whistled past him, and he looked up to see the archer staring at him in disbelief, bow still raised, arm still back.

That no harm shall come to you.

That's what Ava had told him she'd worked into his shirt.

Someone screamed a war cry, and he was suddenly engaged, fighting up close with his sword.

The tight space and enclosing bushes made everything harder, but he managed to get in a killing swing.

He looked up as his opponent went down, saw the archer aiming for Rafe, and made the decision to trust in his lover.

Trust her with his life.

He leaped in front of his unit commander, swinging his sword at the nearest Kassian spy, and the arrow fletch scraped the side of his neck as it shot past and disappeared into the bushes.

The archer turned his horse and gave a shout. One other Kassian managed to swing up onto their mount and the two urged their horses out of the clearing.

Two men lay dead, and the one Luc had just swung at lay injured at his feet. But he wouldn't last long.

Luc saw he'd hit an artery, and the spy was losing blood too quickly.

Breath heaving in and out of his chest, Rafe bent over, and spat out some blood. "Just took a fist to the mouth," he said, waving Luc away. "It's Revek who got shot."

Sure enough, his friend had an arrow sticking out of his left shoulder. He looked gray, and was down on one knee.

"Frederik?" Rafe turned to look for his underling, and Luc saw the young man slowly get to his feet, a slash across his cheek.

"That arrow." Frederik's eyes were wide. "I thought you were shot for sure, and then you moved just at the right moment."

"You think the Kassian created those camps for the Cervantes just because, boy?" Rafe asked. "They wanted us because we are the natural fighters they wish they were themselves."

Luc pulled a cloth from his pocket and wiped his sword down, slid it into its sheath, and noticed Frederik's eyes were on the weapon the whole time.

"How bad?" he asked Revek.

"Not bad." Rev wouldn't look at him. Instead, he breathed in and then gave a shout as he ripped the arrow from his flesh.

Frederik turned to look at him, wild-eyed.

"Rafe, help me get him into the open." Luc didn't bother going back the way they'd come in. It was a circuitous route that would take too long. He slung a shoulder under Rev's right side, and Rafe took the left. Frederik went ahead of them, holding branches back to make the going easier, and they eventually stepped out into the open.

Blood was flowing from Revek's wound in a steady, relentless flow.

"He should have left it in until we got him to the healer."

"Yes." Luc sighed. "But he can't bear having anything piercing his skin."

It would do no good to blame Revek for this. He was how he was for good reason. And Luc had yet to find a way to help him.

He thought time would do that, but as the last few days had shown, that hadn't happened.

A short way down from where they emerged, Ava stood with a patrol unit.

Luc saw her turn in their direction, her face shadowed by the hood of her cloak.

Was that worked with protections, too?

As they moved toward the group, Rafe shouted for a horse to carry Revek, and everyone sprang into action.

As Rafe rode off with him lying across his saddle, one of the Venyatux lieutenants, Raun-Tu, rode up, braided hair flying.

"Will you come speak to the General?"

Luc felt a stab of guilt at the relief the request gave him. More time away from Ava to gather his thoughts.

He nodded, moving across to the trees to untie the horse he'd left when he'd gone into the bush to find Ava.

"I'll see you later," he murmured to her as he passed her, letting his hand brush along her shoulder.

She looked up at him, and he thought she might have been crying. It shocked him into a stumbling step, but didn't stop him.

She gave a nod, but as he swung up into his saddle and followed Raun-Tu, he had the same hollow sensation in the pit of his stomach he had the night before when she had walked away.

He might be the one leaving this time, but he was still the one with something to lose.

CHAPTER 16

She had ripped away the veil, and it had gone about as well as her mother and father had always warned her it would.

Ava pulled herself gingerly up onto her horse and started back toward the twin columns.

She felt sick to her stomach, and frightened.

Luc had the power now to reveal her secret to others. To put her in more danger than she'd ever been in before.

She had given him that power.

And yet, she still had hope in her heart that he would not do anything to hurt her.

Did that mean she'd won? Had managed to keep true to herself no matter the hard lessons being a prisoner for two years had taught her? Or was it naive and stupid? Trusting too much, too soon.

She gave a bitter smile.

She would learn soon enough, and could do nothing about it now.

"You don't look so good." Taira came up beside her. "Deni said you were knocked out cold by that branch."

She gave a nod, more than happy for her demeanor to be put down to her injuries.

They had just reached the Venyatu column, still lumbering forward at its slow pace, when they were hailed by Raun-Tu, who came galloping down toward them.

When he pulled up beside them, there was a glint of speculation in his eyes. "Avasu, are you well enough to report to the healer's tent on the far side of the Rising Wave column? The young soldier who went in to help you has had his face cut open, and the Commander says you are the best person to sew it up."

Ava simply nodded, refusing to allow any emotion to show on her face. She turned to find the best way through the Venyatu column to the Rising Wave beyond.

Why had Luc suggested that? Because he believed she could heal his friend, or to see what happened to the wound? What magic she could work.

She hated that she was suspicious of his motives.

"If you're sure you're up to doing it, I'll come with you," Taira said, watching Raun-Tu's back as he galloped off again. "I liked Frederik. You know he believes some crazy story about the Commander's sword?"

"I've heard something about it." Ava didn't want to hear the story again. It might lead to Taira bringing up the other story. About the witch who enspelled the Commander of the Rising Wave.

"There's one about a witch, too." Taira kept her eyes ahead, and Ava's stomach sank.

"A witch?" She couldn't help that her words sounded dead, even to her own ears.

"Who escaped with the Commander and enspelled him." Taira glanced at her.

"Me, you mean?" Ava asked, and then found a spark of anger inside her. This defeat was the Queen's Herald—her cousin's—intent, and when had she ever, ever not fought him? With everything in her.

"Where did this story come from?"

Taira shook her head. "Unknown. But obviously ridiculous. I just thought you should hear about it from a friend rather than anyone else."

Ava forced herself to laugh. "They must be talking about another woman, because I've only just seen him again after two months."

"That's what Deni said!" Taira laughed, too, although Ava thought it sounded genuine.

By the time they'd found the healer's tent, set up a little way away from the moving column beside a large cart, Ava had made a decision about how she was going to proceed.

She had a gift. But that didn't mean she had to expose herself to harm.

So she would do what good she could, while keeping her secrets to herself.

She couldn't think of the way she'd exposed herself to Luc. There was nothing she could do about that, except react to the consequences.

Whatever they may be.

She took out her silver needle, and her own thread when the thread the healer offered her was too thick.

She knelt down and had Frederik lie back on her lap, angling them both toward the sun so her arm didn't create a shadow.

She forced herself to concentrate as she sewed.

This would heal well—very well—and there would be a beautiful scar. Straight and fine, but there. Proof of an injury received in a fierce fight.

There would be no cause to wonder how it disappeared. Because it wouldn't disappear.

She kept that in her mind as she worked her needle in and out of his skin.

"You look fierce," Frederik told her, voice a little hoarse. "Like you're fighting."

"Maybe I am." She was fighting her perfectionist nature. The compulsion to make things whole.

But she was going to be careful, and protect herself, whatever Luc's motivation for putting her in this situation.

She leaned back, and Frederik sat up.

"That *is* good work." The Rising Wave healer, a woman in her late fifties, with short, thick white hair held back from her face with a headband, studied his face. "Can I call on you again?"

Ava nodded, but she would have to keep a check on Frederik. Make sure his scar didn't disappear.

And if it did, she would have to tweak her response the next time she did this.

There was a groan from inside the tent, and Ava realized it was Revek.

"How bad is he?" she asked.

"He shouldn't have pulled out the arrow. That's my job." The healer's annoyance was clear. "He's lost a lot of blood. When I've finished with the clotting poultice, perhaps you can sew him up, as well? Your handiwork is far superior to mine."

Ava gave a slow nod. "If he lets me. He's suspicious of me."

The healer gave a snort. "He'll do what the Commander says."

Ava didn't think Luc would force Revek to deal with her, but then again, he did know what she could accomplish when it came to arrow wounds.

So perhaps, for the sake of his friend's recovery, he would try to force the issue.

"I'll help if he agrees." She looked over at the march of soldiers, the roll of the wagons. "What will you do when they pass you?"

"We'll put everyone into the cart who isn't able to ride or walk on their own, and start moving soon. Revek should be all right to travel in a bit."

Taira had been talking quietly to Frederik, but she stood, squinting up at the sun. "I'm back on shift this afternoon, so I have to go."

"I'll come along." Ava didn't know where she stood with regard to her own shift.

She was fully healed now. Her cloak had done its job. So she would find Deni and get her orders.

"I might come find you tonight," the healer said as Ava swung up into her saddle. "Revek should be ready to be stitched by then."

"You'll find her with your Commander, not on our side," Taira said with a grin.

Ava nodded, but she didn't think that was true any longer. And for tonight, at least, she liked the idea of the quiet privacy of her hidden tent.

Luc had eagerly taken the opportunity to put some space between them. She suddenly realized she wouldn't mind doing the same.

CHAPTER 17

"Is it enchanted?"

Luc looked up from cleaning his sword to see Frederik standing on the other side of the campfire, eyes gleaming in the firelight.

"No." He wiped the blade down one last time with the oiled cloth and then slid the sword back into its scabbard.

"They say it is." The young soldier stepped closer and then sat down.

Luc's mouth twisted in a wry grin. "Who's they?"

Frederik lifted his shoulders. "The other soldiers. The stall traders. Sometimes the cooks." He turned his head to look at Luc. "Rafe says you're as good as you are because you're Cervantes, and you train hard."

That wasn't completely true. Luc stared into the flames. He had taken a chance on Ava's protections. Run in front of an arrow.

They hadn't let him down.

"Listen to Rafe." Luc stood. He had been avoiding Ava, but suddenly he needed to speak to her. Work out what had happened today.

The crawling sensation of invisible eyes on him had faded, and he couldn't blame her for hiding as she had. He *wanted* her safe. Was glad she'd been able to get away from the Kassian scouts.

They needed to talk about her abilities.

Speaking of which . . . "Did Ava sew your cheek?"

Frederik turned his head so the firelight illuminated the left side. "Yes. The healer says she's never seen such a neat job."

Luc crouched down to examine it. It looked perfect. And like it was already healing. "We're lucky to have someone with Ava's skill."

He suddenly realized the position he'd put Ava in by making the request to Raun-Tu. He hadn't spoken to her about it.

Before he knew for sure she could create magic with her needle, he would most likely have mentioned her ability, but as of this morning, he knew the risk she took.

It wasn't that spell casters were reviled. They were held in awe, but also suspicion.

Rare power did that.

They were also considered prizes to be won or stolen.

And isn't that exactly what had happened to both her and her mother?

No wonder she hadn't wanted to say anything about it.

He remembered demanding she tell him what she'd done to him before the Kassian forces had caught up with them again after their escape, and the trapped look that had come over her.

He straightened, and strapped his scabbard to his back. "Good night, Frederik. You fought well."

The solider tapped his chest with his fist in gratitude. "If you're looking for your lady, the healer called her to stitch up Revek."

Luc changed direction with a nod, hoping his face didn't show his surprise.

Ava was only a few rows of tents away from him.

He hadn't asked her to sew up Revek earlier, because he didn't want her anywhere near his friend after the fight they'd had.

He didn't trust Revek with her.

He increased his pace, found the white tent they always used for the injured set up beside the healer's large cart.

Ava waited outside next to the fire burning in front of the tent's entrance.

"Good. Luc. I need help bringing Revek out closer to the light." The healer, Dorea, turned as he arrived, ducking into the tent ahead of him.

Ava watched him from her place beside the fire. She had a pouch out on her lap, and he saw thread in her hand.

"Ava." He crouched in front of her.

"Luc!"

He turned to look through the open flaps of the tent, and saw Dorea standing with her hands on her hips.

When he glanced up at Ava, there was a gleam of amusement in her eyes.

He rose up, suddenly not as irritated with Dorea as he had been.

If being scolded by her eased the taut stretch of tension between him and his lover, he would accept it.

Revek lay on a couple of pallets, with pillows packed around him for comfort.

He looked flushed, and Luc could see the sweat on his forehead and his bare chest.

The arrow wound was high, right in the crease of his collarbone and his arm.

"You want your lady to sew me?" Revek asked, and there was rasp to his voice.

"I didn't want her to, no. I don't trust you around her. But Dorea thinks she's the best person to do it, so if you promise not to attack or insult her, I'll allow it."

Revek blinked in shock. "You're worried about what I'd do to her?"

"What do you think she'd do to you?" Dorea scoffed. "Hold you off for ten minutes again while you tried to kill her?"

Luc hadn't realized Dorea knew what had happened, and neither, by his slack expression, did Revek.

"She's enspelled him." Revek said to the healer, pointing at Luc. "She's made him . . ." He trailed off.

"Made me faster? Made me stronger? Made me more accurate?" Luc kept his words quiet.

"What can be given, can also be taken away, or corrupted." He spoke the words as if he were repeating something he'd heard, not something he believed himself.

"So you do share pillows with Haslia."

Luc turned to find Ava standing at the foot of the bed.

"She told a similar tale while she was in the woods today. Her unit commander seemed to think she'd started the rumor herself, and the others agreed with him. Although one of the group thought maybe you'd started it, and she was merely repeating what she'd heard while her head lay on your pillow."

Revek was looking at her in shock. "She made it up?"

"According to Rafe. She's certainly the only one repeating it, keeping it alive. Other than you. Either you heard about me from Luc and decided to make my life as difficult as possible when I made it to the Rising Wave, or Haslia is in touch with the Kassian who captured Luc in the first place. Because the Kassian soldiers at the northern fortress are the only other people who know what happened."

Luc forced his gaze away from Ava, and turned to look at Revek. His friend looked . . . ill.

"I never told anyone. I . . ." Revek rubbed his forehead. "I never meant you harm and I didn't try in advance to make your life difficult. No one pays any mind to that story, anyway. They like the one about the sword better."

"Now that's cleared up, Luc will help you stand up so we can take you out to the fire. Ava needs the light to work by." Dorea patted Luc's shoulder, and when he glanced up at her, he saw her lips suddenly form a thin line.

"Can I help you, Haslia?"

Luc turned, to see a soldier who he'd noticed sitting with Revek before, eating meals with him around the fire. She stood in the tent's opening.

He didn't know how he was sure, but the way she looked at them, he knew she'd been eavesdropping.

"I just came to see how Revek is doing." She smiled, and Luc felt the buzz of sensation he'd experienced for a while now when meeting certain people. A warning bell that rang in his head. He associated it with a need to be cautious.

The last two assassination attempts, he'd felt its hard tug moments before the attacks.

Haslia might be smiling, but she was not happy. And she didn't like them. Or, at least, she didn't like him.

She walked boldly into the tent, and brushed past Ava to crouch down beside Revek.

Ava flinched back, drawing her cloak closer around her. "Thank you for taking my horse out of the woods this morning." Ava's gaze was fixed on the young woman. "Taira told me you led her out."

Haslia arched a brow as she turned to look up. "Taira seems to have told you a lot of things." She shrugged. "I was coming in to ask after Revek when I heard you talking about me."

She patted Revek's chest with a delicate hand, then cupped his cheek and ran her thumb across his cheekbone.

It seemed deliberate, rather than affectionate, and Luc edged closer, feeling as if he needed to protect Revek, although his friend was looking at her as if she was as precious as the freedom they had all won.

"Taira told me you said I'd enspelled the Commander." Ava was watching Haslia carefully. "How did you come by that story?"

Haslia slowly got back to her feet, lifting her shoulders. "It's just a story. I promised Rafe I won't repeat it again." She gestured to Revek. "He's always saying it. Why shouldn't I?" There was an edge to her voice, accusing and plaintive.

Luc registered Revek's shock. He seemed blindsided by her sudden hostility.

"I never—" He trailed off and then began to cough, turning to the side and gasping for breath.

When the coughing fit was over, he stared at her, blank eyed.

After a moment's silence, Haslia lifted her chin. "Well, you do say it. Everyone's heard you. And you're obviously fine." She turned on her heel and walked away.

"Haslia." Revek lifted the arm on his uninjured side as if to grab her back, and then let it drop down. He closed his eyes. "I don't remember it that way."

"Whatever way you remember it, the consequences to Ava are very real, rumor or not." Luc wouldn't let him off the hook for this. Not after the way he'd attacked her last night.

Revek closed his eyes again, and his skin seemed to lose color in front of Luc's eyes. "I'll let her sew me."

Ava laughed, the sound exploding out of her. She put her hands over her mouth, as if even she was surprised by her reaction. "You'll martyr yourself to me as penance?" She shook her head. "If you don't want me to sew you, that's no skin off my nose, Revek. I'm doing this because Dorea asked me to. Not to punish you." She turned away in disgust and followed Haslia out.

"I never . . . say or do the right thing where she's concerned." Revek shifted on his pallet, the movement labored.

"Well, I'd say boohoo to you if you didn't suddenly look so bad." Dorea bent over him, and Luc thought she looked worried. "You can do better than this poor me attitude, Revek, but right now, I'm giving you some slack."

Luc studied him. "He is getting worse."

Dorea sent him a warning look. "He needs his open wound sewn up." She placed a hand on his forehead. "And he needs something to bring down his fever." She crouched lower and slid her arm around his back.

Luc mirrored her, taking most of Rev's weight as they lifted him up.

Revek couldn't hold himself up, and Luc ended up carrying him to the fire.

Ava was there.

He'd assumed she'd stalked off in disgust at the lot of them and he'd have to go find her, but she was sitting cross-legged by the fire, a pillow on her lap.

"It's easier if you lay him down here." She patted the pillow. "I can see better that way."

Luc tried to catch her eye as he set Rev down, but she was already focused on the wound.

Revek's eyes had closed, and Luc didn't know if he was semi-conscious, or simply blocking out an ordeal the best way he knew how.

He stood, at a loss for a moment, and then found a place to sit where his shadow wouldn't fall over them.

"The wound is clean," Dorea said to Ava. "I disinfected it just a few minutes before you arrived."

She nodded, and began to work.

Unable to look at the needle digging into flesh, Luc studied her face.

She seemed to be saying something under her breath with each tug of the needle.

He was too afraid of distracting her to ask what it was, but it sounded like an incantation.

"Do you hear her?" Dorea asked him quietly. She'd been standing on the other side of the fire, watching, but must have gotten tired of being on her feet and come to sit down.

"No. What's she saying?" His voice was close to a whisper.

"She's saying *healthy and a beautiful, straight scar* over and over."

Luc frowned as he looked up. "That's all she's saying?"

"Like a mantra. I do it myself sometimes. Talk to myself as I'm working with patients. Telling them they're going to pull through." She shrugged. "Not sure if it works, but it can't hurt, can it?"

"No." But Luc rubbed his forearm, where once the skin had been cut open to the bone beneath. Now it was smooth as the day he'd been born.

If this was the result of Ava saying a mantra, then it had worked all too well.

CHAPTER 18

"Is it my imagination, or has Revek got considerably worse?" Ava glanced over at Luc and Dorea, and Dorea rose up to come crouch beside her.

"His fever is higher. He's more listless." The healer felt for the pulse in his neck.

Ava had been aware for a few minutes that he had slipped into unconsciousness, and while that might be best for him, to manage the pain sewing his wound caused, she didn't like how hot and dry he felt beneath her hands. And how hard it seemed to be for him to breathe.

"There's something on his cheekbone. Oil of some kind. I can see it glistening in the firelight." She was sitting directly behind him, with his head and shoulders in her lap, and the gleam of it in the firelight had caught her eye.

She often grew tired when she worked, especially if she worked in magic. The precision needed, and the focus, sapped her energy. But she was already exhausted and she had only sewn half of Revek's injury. It felt as though something was working against her. Taking the work she was doing to imbue healing into him and dissipating it as fast as she created it.

"What are you saying?" Luc was suddenly crouched on her other side, his gaze on his friend. "That there is something wrong with the oil? Something doing him harm?"

She looked at him carefully. She really was only going on instinct here. Just as she'd been forced into doing in so many other ways. And she wasn't sure of her ground. "I don't know, but the way Haslia swiped her thumb across his cheek, and the way he seems to have worsened since . . ."

Luc lifted his head from his friend's face, met her gaze. "I agree. I thought there was something strange about it at the time."

"I'll get a warm, wet cloth." Dorea strode into the tent and came back in moments, wiping Revek's cheek. She turned the cloth and wiped again, then, in a sudden, violent move, threw the cloth into the fire.

It flared up for a moment, the water spitting in the intense heat, and then they all saw the flame turn green before it burned away to nothing.

Revek drew in a rattling breath, the deepest one since Haslia had left the tent.

"I think his color is already looking better." Dorea looked over Ava's head at Luc.

"I'll go find Haslia. Find out what she has to say." Luc got to his feet, his face as grim as Ava had ever seen it.

"Wait." Ava hoped it would go faster now whatever had been fighting her had gone. "Let me finish, then we can help Dorea get him back on his bed. I'll go with you to look for Haslia."

She tugged the thread through, for the first time without resistance, and thought about healing again, and a straight scar.

"You got your orders, boy." Dorea snorted out a laugh. "And the lady is right. I can't carry him in on my own."

Confused, Ava looked up, and saw Luc watching her with a wry expression. "What?"

"Nothing." He suddenly grinned. "I'll wait for you."

She focused on finishing up, tying off the thread and looking over her work critically before she eased back and stood, stretching out her stiff legs.

While she'd been sewing, Luc had found two guards to help carry

Revek back inside, so she tidied away her things and was ready when Luc emerged from the tent.

"You look tired." He stood in front of her, and lifted a hand to cup the back of her neck.

She nodded, unsure whether to tell him about how she felt something had sapped her strength while she worked on Revek.

He waited for a response, and then stepped back and let his hand fall away. "I want you to be able to speak freely to me."

She thought back to his reaction earlier today. "And I want the same of you."

He inclined his head in acceptance of her rebuke. "We need to talk. But first, I need to deal with Haslia. I cannot have a spell caster with ill-intent in my camp."

She felt a quick hitch in her breath at that. He knew what she was now. Did intent matter? A spell caster could be as mercurial as anyone else.

But she said nothing, and they made their way into the jumble of tents around them.

She loved the haphazard nature of the column.

She had seen the Kassian mobile forces, with their straight rows, and she thought Luc had it right to let his soldiers place their tents wherever they wanted.

It was harder to find people, easier to get lost.

All of this would make infiltrating the column difficult on their enemies.

Luc questioned the small groups huddled around fire pits or sitting in front of their tents, playing stones, and their answers led them to a large tent near the baths.

"Have you seen Haslia?" he asked two women who were wrapped in blankets, sitting close to a small fire with a pot over the flames.

"She returned to the tent less than an hour ago, Commander." One of the women stood respectfully. "I can call her for you."

She stepped into the tent, then came out almost immediately. "She's not here."

"I didn't see her go." The other woman stood as well.

"She's taken everything. Her pack, her bedroll." The woman peered back into the tent. "Look, she left through the back. The rear pegs have been pulled up."

Sure enough, the back canvas was flapping loosely in the gentle breeze.

Ava moved to the back to see the path Haslia would have taken and Luc came to stand beside her, looking at the criss-cross of paths through the tents out to the plain.

"She was supposed to have left something in the bushes for the Kassian spies." Ava spoke quietly. "I don't think it was a coincidence that she was with the group who came to look for me. The scouts said they'd only come so close to the column because there was a message to pick up from a spy, but it wasn't where it was supposed to be."

"I ordered everyone to keep close to camp last night, because of how close the Kassian scouting parties were coming. I didn't want anyone taken prisoner or killed. We thought the Kassian were trying to get a better look at the Venyatux column, and maybe they were, but the result was Haslia would have found it difficult to sneak out."

"So she thought she could do it under the guise of helping to rescue me." Ava nodded. "She could have left a message when she was with Deni and the others. She went back to the column with my mount before you killed the spies, so as far as she was aware there was still a possibility they'd come back for it."

"It's worth a look." Luc studied her carefully. "I'll get Rafe to come with me, show me the path they took. You were badly hurt this morning and you look exhausted. Go rest."

"You should put a guard on Revek," Ava said. "She wanted him dead for a reason. She would have already planned to run before she came to the tent to see him. She was flustered to find us with him, but she risked casting her spell anyway. I think Rafe and Deni questioning her about the story she was telling frightened her enough she decided it was time to go, but she was worried Revek would tell you something, or reveal something once it was discovered she'd gone, that made her decide to kill him."

"And kill him in a way that looked like a result of his injuries." Luc swore softly. "If you hadn't seen the oil on his cheek . . ."

Ava lifted a shoulder. "It was more than that. I could feel something wrong, something pulling away the healing I was casting into the stitches."

"That's why you're so drained. You were fighting for Rev's life." He stepped close. "You didn't want to tell me what was wrong before, because you'd have had to admit you were spell casting. And you thought that would . . . upset me."

"Upset you again," Ava clarified.

He turned away. "The way I reacted this morning is not something I'm proud of. In the camps, there was someone watching us sometimes, eyes that we couldn't see. I think they had something like your cloak on them. Would they need to have been like you, or just have a cloak someone like you had worked?"

Ava turned back toward the healer's tent, because she wasn't sure Haslia wouldn't pretend to have run, and stayed around until she was sure her victim was dead.

"I think they would just need a cloak that was worked with invisibility. But I'm not sure how long the casting would work."

"How long do yours work?" Luc asked.

She shrugged. "I add new things all the time, so it's difficult for me to say. How long did the protection I gave you on that handkerchief work?"

He sucked in a breath. "I think it still does."

She tilted her head from side to side in a maybe gesture. "The shirt you're wearing is a stronger version of it, so that's what would have helped you today. I don't know what strength would be left in the handkerchief."

"And the workings you did in my skin?" His voice was almost inaudible as they traversed the camp.

She glanced at him guiltily. "I didn't know how that would work." She hunched her shoulders. "Theoretically it shouldn't have worked on skin at all, but I knew from when I stitched myself," she touched the place above her eye where her cousin had struck her with the pommel of his sword, "that I could make the skin smooth again, if not scar-free."

"What happened there?" He stopped and reached out a hand, rubbed a fingertip over the skin above her eye.

She took hold of his hand, moved it to the correct place. He peered closer.

"There's no sign anything was ever there."

"The Herald struck me, and split the skin. I'm glad there's no longer a sign anything was there." She wanted no reminder of what her cousin had done to her. "Perhaps by the time the working fades, the magic is no longer needed because the scar is gone."

They had reached the healer's tent. Dorea was sitting by the fire, sipping from a cup.

"How's he doing?" Luc asked.

"Much better since we wiped that filth on his cheek away. Did you find that woman?"

"No. She's packed her things and disappeared. But she might still be hanging around, watching to see if Rev is dead."

Dorea sucked in a breath, as if the possibility hadn't occurred to her. "What do we do?"

"We set guards, and keep a lookout for her."

While they talked softly about the arrangements, Ava moved into the tent, saw that Revek was asleep on his pallet.

His color was good, his breathing even.

She sank down beside him to get a better look at her working.

As she sat on her haunches, the tent wall beside her moved.

She waited, keeping absolutely still, as the canvas was lifted a little.

She slid her knife out of her boot. If this was Haslia coming back to finish the job, she would be getting a big surprise.

A hand snaked through the gap, and she focused on it, waiting for Haslia to wriggle through, when the hand flicked something in Revek's and her direction.

And then suddenly, she was on fire. Or her cloak was.

She felt a pitching sensation, as every protective working she'd embroidered into the fabric pulled hard in warning, and she stumbled to the side, fetching up against the wall of the tent.

Flames flickered from her hem upward, and the canvas of the tent caught fire.

She must have made some kind of noise, because Luc and Dorea were suddenly inside with her.

She saw the horror in Dorea's eyes.

"Ava. Look at me." Luc was in front of her, reaching for her. He stopped, lifting his hands to shield his face from the flames."Undo your cloak." He coughed and choked on the words.

She staggered toward him, her hand going to her throat. She fumbled with the tie and then stepped away, letting the cloak fall from her shoulders and flutter down to the ground behind her.

As soon as it was off her, she could feel the heat scorching her cheeks. "Revek." She turned to look at him, but while she'd been concentrating on Luc, the two guards who'd helped carry him inside after she'd stitched him were carrying him out again.

The fire had taken hold of the tent now, and the back was an inferno.

Dorea darted past her, heedless of the flames.

"Ava." Luc grabbed her and swung her into his arms, and she realized she had just been standing as the world burned down around her.

She couldn't understand why.

Luc set her down and then ran back into the tent.

She looked after him, saw Dorea was still inside. The healer had loaded herself up with leather satchels, hanging them from her shoulder, and was trying to drag a wooden chest out.

Luc tried to pull her out, and then lifted her into his arms and ran out with her as the tent collapsed behind them.

The healer was sobbing as the flames leaped high, her face turned toward the bonfire.

Ava caught sight of someone standing just beyond the flames, hidden by the long shadows the light created, watching.

Then they were gone and soldiers were suddenly swarming around, shouting as they threw sand on the conflagration. An out-of-control blaze was deadly in a tent camp.

They had it under control in moments.

"What happened?" Luc's voice was hoarse with smoke. He had set Dorea down and turned from the flames to look at her. She saw the fury in his eyes.

Ava looked at the smoldering mess and felt the loss of her cloak like a knife to her heart.

If she hadn't layered on so many protections, she reminded herself, perhaps neither she nor Revek would be alive right now, but to have to start again . . .

"I was sitting beside Revek, checking his wound, when I saw a hand come through the bottom of the tent. I thought it was Haslia, and I drew my knife, waiting for her to wriggle through. Instead, the hand did a kind of flick toward where Revek was lying and suddenly my cloak was on fire."

"It was definitely Haslia?"

She slowly shook her head. "I thought it was her, but I never saw anything but the hand. It could have been anyone. It's most likely to be her, though. If she was lurking, waiting for confirmation that Revek was dead, and found out he wasn't . . ." She lifted her shoulders.

"Death by fire is a very direct attack." Dorea spoke from behind her, and Ava tried not to start in surprise.

Her cloak would have warned her someone was there, she realized. She hadn't understood how much she had come to rely on it.

It made her defenseless. Made her feel off-kilter.

She needed to remedy that right away.

The cold, hard anger at the destruction of something so precious and useful to her spiked in her chest, and she bowed her head to get it under control.

Behind her, Dorea began to sob again, and she remembered she wasn't the only one who'd lost something important and precious in the fire.

"How much did you manage to save?" She held out her hands to take Dorea's in her own.

"Some of the common ointments and most-used remedies. The precious, rare things, they were in the wooden chest."

"Maybe it survived the fire." The flames were gone now, and there was nothing but the stink of burned hemp and the gentle drift of ash.

"Maybe." The healer didn't sound very confident.

A Venyatux solider hailed them, and Luc stepped forward, had a low conversation with him.

He would be busy now. Sorting out this mess, telling the General about the attack.

She had things to do, too.

First priority would be to buy a new cloak, only she'd run out of money last night when she'd bought wool from the traders.

She realized the Venyatux soldier had gone and Dorea and Luc had been talking in low voices to each other.

She forced herself to pay attention. She had a headache—a low throb behind her eyes.

"Haslia is the most likely culprit, but it's not impossible she instructed another spy to finish the job for her." Luc's lips had formed a grim line. "We can't let our guard down." He glanced over at where Revek lay, half-aware. "I'll have guards standing guard over Revek until he's able to remember whatever it is Haslia doesn't want him to tell us."

He watched his friend for a long moment, and Ava wondered if he was worried Revek had betrayed him in some way. Deliberately kept whatever secrets Haslia had shared with him.

Others may wonder the same about Luc if all her secrets were laid bare, she knew.

So she had better make sure that never happened.

CHAPTER 19

"I have an embarrassing question for you." Ava slid beside Deni, crouching in front of the campfire.

"You need me to explain *that* to you?" Deni lifted his brows, eyes dancing in jest.

"Ha ha." She elbowed him in the side, and he had to put out a hand to stop himself falling over. "My cloak has been burned."

Deni's gaże sharpened immediately, and he looked her over from head to toe, sniffed. "I thought I smelled ash. How?"

She leaned close in to him. "Luc is discussing it with the General now, but it looks as if Haslia was a Kassian spy. She tried to kill Revek tonight, and then when it didn't work, either she or one of her fellow spies tried to burn him. I got in the way."

"Are you—?"

"I'm fine." Ava sent him a lopsided grin. "Bashed on the head, taken captive and then set alight all in one day. I'm ready for bed, I can tell you that much. But I have no money left to buy a new cloak. Am I owed any for my duty here?"

"You are, but it isn't given out on the road. What you can do is get a letter of credit from Raun-Tu or one of the other lieutenants, and then take it to a trader. They have to honor it, and then they collect the money at the end of the journey."

She sighed in relief. "Thank you."

"It won't be much," Deni warned. "Do you have money from all the fights?"

She frowned. "Fights?"

"The sparring sessions, where everyone was betting."

She shook her head. "I didn't bet in those." She didn't even know how that would work.

He frowned. "You should have some money from that. I'll speak to the others. It isn't right everyone won except you."

She hadn't thought about it until now. And she wasn't able to care very much, either way. As long as she could buy a cloak, she'd make do.

For a moment, she let herself rest in front of the fire, let it warm her. Her eyes stung when she closed them, and it would be too easy to simply lay down right here and sleep.

She forced her eyes open. "Are the trader stalls open tonight?"

"They'll be closed now. It's late." Deni stood, and held out a hand for her to take.

She accepted it and he hauled her to her feet.

"Go to bed, Avasu. You're off duty tomorrow. Take the time to shop and buy yourself a new cloak. Spend a restful day walking slowly with the column. You took a bad blow to the head this morning. I don't know how you're still standing now."

She was only fine because of her cloak. Because of its healing spells. She felt the loss of it again.

She gave a nod. "I'll take your advice."

He patted her back, and she walked away through the tents, and then stopped.

Should she speak to Luc before she disappeared into her tent?

She let her feet guide her to the General's headquarters, and walked up to the guards at the entrance.

"Is the Commander in there with the general?"

"Yes." The guard who answered had been on duty the night Luc had come to the Venyatux column, and she had come with him to speak with the general. He knew why she was asking.

"Tell him I asked after him, but I'm going to bed now."

He flashed her a grin. "I will."

She smiled back her thanks and walked away.

She wished she could lie down in his arms, like they had the night before, but there was more than just his friends between them now.

Her own magic sat in the way like an ungainly yakkuna.

And she didn't have the concentration, or the strength, to argue about it now.

"Ava."

The hissed whisper woke her, and then the exclamation of surprise as someone blundered into her tent.

Not someone.

Luc.

She dragged herself to the opening, found him clutching his shin. "You all right?"

He glared at her, then shook his head. "Can I come in?"

She nodded, holding the tent flap open for him so he could see where it was.

He crawled past her, and as there was only room to lie down in her small traveling tent, he stretched out, with his head on the blanket she rolled up to serve as a pillow.

With a sigh, she crawled after him, fitting herself against him in the darkness.

"You're hard to find." His murmur in her ear made her shiver.

"That's the point." She couldn't resist nuzzling him back. "I know there's someone here looking to hurt or abduct me. I couldn't risk them catching me while I slept, but I needed to be able to actually sleep without fear. So I stitched an invisibility working into my tent."

"The same thing you did this morning, on your cloak?"

She hesitated. This was the issue between them. But he was here. Talking to her about it. She needed to trust that.

She made herself relax. "Yes. Doing it for the tent helped me work it quickly and with confidence this morning. It worked better than I thought it would."

"You don't know how well something will work until you try it?" He seemed surprised.

She shrugged. "No one taught me, I've learned as I've gone along. This morning, I thought I'd have to cover myself completely in the cloak to be invisible, like I am in the tent. But neither you nor the Kassian scouts could see me, even when I was looking right at you, with my face exposed."

Luc held himself still. "A Grimwaldian had that same working in their cloak when I was in the camps. They would watch us. I could sense them."

She was silent, lifting a hand to run it down his arm in sympathy. "It wasn't necessarily a Grimwaldian. It could have been a Kassian, or anyone. All they would need was the cloak."

He sucked in a breath. "Something like that could be commissioned?"

She lifted her shoulders. "All I know is my mother was kidnapped twice in her life. Both times her abductor intended to force her to work spells into garments. The first time was before I was born, before she married my father, and the experience traumatised her for life. She refused to teach me the skills she'd learned from my grandmother, because she wanted to keep me safe by making me a poor target. And then I was abducted anyway. So she and my father came to rescue me, and she was taken again. And I think, to keep me alive, she did what she had spent her life dreading—working spells into fabric for an evil man."

It was his turn to comfort her, his big hand running up and down her back. "How many of you are there who can do this?"

She shook her head. "I don't know. I don't know if I'm doing the workings right—if there even is a right way. My grandmother could do it, I know that. She was revered in Grimwalt because of it."

"Her skill was known?" Luc asked.

"Her housekeeper told me that her pieces were sought after, but easy to identify. She worked only in black silk, and in a particular style. So while observers might not know what the working in the garment was, they knew it was a piece by her, and the wearer had some kind of protection."

"The cloak we found wrapped around your mother's body . . ." Luc spoke slowly, as if working something out.

She nodded. "That used to be covered in black silk embroidery. The Queen's Herald must have thought the thread itself was magical, and forced her to unpick it to work whatever it was he wanted her to do." It also had the effect of stripping away her mother's own protections, working by working.

"So there could be other items, made by your mother under duress, that are in the hands of the Queen's Herald?"

"There most definitely are. Although I would hope my mother would have worked some surprises into them, or made sure they had a short lifespan."

"And he tried to make you do this, too?" There it was, the low, hot fury in his voice she'd heard earlier when the tent had burned.

"He tried. I refused at first, and then I agreed, and worked something very nasty into what he gave me. He only wore something I'd made for him once, and never again."

"What did you do?" The rumble in her ear made her shiver.

"I worked in the suggestion that he stab himself."

Luc went still. "Did it work?"

"He has a scar on his left side to this day." She thought back to the incident. Her cousin screaming as he unsheathed his knife and stabbed himself, calling for his guards to pull his new coat off him.

Luc breathed out. "I'm surprised you're still alive."

"He hit me with his sword. That's when I had to sew the skin above my eye. But he didn't dare kill me. He was hoping to wear me down over time. It cost him relatively little to keep me alive. If I was dead, he had no chance of using me to benefit him." She shrugged. "Then he must have kidnapped my mother. And then my being alive was how he forced her to work for him."

The rage of knowing her mother had been in the dungeon below, while she walked around and around her small cell in the tower above, swept over her in a wave. She tried to push it down, but like the ocean, it would not be stopped.

She could hear herself keening, trying to cry as silently as possible.

She felt Luc's hand, soothing her, rubbing her, as he crooned to her just like he had when she'd first discovered her mother's body, and she was struck again that he seemed easy in the role.

"Did you ever soothe babies?" she asked, when her throat was no longer so tight.

He nodded. "When I was in the camps."

"It shows. You have a well of patience and empathy that I've never seen in any of the Kassian soldiers I've been forced to interact with over the years. You are better for it. Stronger for it." She wiped her tears away. "What happened to the babies?"

"Some grew older, fought with me. Some were returned home." There was satisfaction in his voice. "When I turned on the Kassian, my first order of business was to liberate the camps. I knew betraying the Kassian army on the battlefield would lead to repercussions for any Chosen still under their control."

"So you destroyed the camps?" She hadn't heard anything about his exploits while she'd been imprisoned. About his amazing revolt against the Kassian two years earlier. About the liberation of the camps. And the battles he and his Rising Wave had fought since, gaining more and more of the north west, the land that used to belong to the Cervantes.

"They are gone. And Cervantes is under our control again."

He was marching to Fernwell, the Kassian capital, to make sure it stayed that way.

She would do everything in her power to make sure he succeeded.

She turned in his arms, facing him, and kissed along his jawline, until, with a growl, he captured her lips with his, and for the second time in two nights, she made a note to work a silencing spell into the canvas.

CHAPTER 20

The guard sent to find him ended up resorting to calling his name softly as he searched for Ava's tent.

Luc forced himself out of the warm cocoon he and Ava had made, and pulled on his clothes in quick, economical movements.

"They won't find us." Ava sat up and spoke through a yawn.

He still found that strange, and difficult to accept. But he nodded as he pulled on his boots. "I'll see you later." Because sending a guard to find him was something Dak or Massi would only do if it was urgent.

He leaned across and kissed her, first on the lips, then on the forehead, to remind her they were still together. That while the threads that bound them may be a little frayed, they were there nonetheless.

Then he crawled out of the tent. When he rose up, he was relieved to find the guard facing away from him.

He moved silently to the left and walked out between a few tents from which he could hear gentle snores.

"You were looking for me?"

The guard yelped in surprise. "Sorry, Commander, I didn't see you there."

It was dawn, the sun was just a faint line of light on the horizon, so Luc put a finger to his lips. "They need me at the main tent?"

The guard nodded, his shoulders relaxing as Luc followed him through the Venyatux column.

"It's not Revek, is it?" It suddenly occurred to him that this might be bad news about his friend, rather than an operational matter.

"I . . . don't think so." The guard shook his head. "I think a trader caravan has been spotted."

Luc relaxed and waved the guard off.

When he got to his tent, Massi and Dak were there, along with two of the General's lieutenants, Heival and Fervanti.

"A caravan?" he asked.

Massi nodded. "Coming from the west border of Grimwalt, perhaps, or the north west of Kassia."

"If it's from Grimwalt, that's a change. They closed their borders." Luc frowned down at the map, where Massi had marked where the caravan had been spotted.

"I know we didn't like it when we first heard they'd decided to cease trade, because it seemed like they were withdrawing from responsibility in the region, but at least they weren't providing aide to the Kassian. If they've started again, it might be a very bad sign."

"They never closed their northeast border," Fervanti said. "Trade between Venyatu and Grimwalt has never stopped."

Luc nodded. "I guessed that. And through Venyatu, with other countries to the east as well, I'm sure." He poured himself some water from a jug on the table, and then looked around at the group. "We have to go investigate. Find out if they've opened their borders again."

Massi nodded. "And maybe get some supplies we're running low on."

Luc conceded that with a nod, and Heival coughed.

"We would like to do the same when it comes to sourcing some supplies we are running low on, so I suggest that we let the store masters coordinate any purchases, to prevent hard feelings if one side gets more than their share."

Luc glanced at Dak. "You'll manage that?"

His friend nodded. "Heival can direct me to who we need to talk to."

"That's if the traders are willing to part with their goods," Massi said.

"If they are traders, and not Kassian spies trying to engage us in an underhanded way." Fervanti crossed her arms over her chest.

"That's a possibility," Luc acknowledged. "We need to approach with soldiers ready for anything before we let the store masters anywhere near them. What's more likely is the Kassian have at least one spy in the caravan. We'll need to make sure no one speaks out of turn."

"Agreed." Heival nodded. "Raun-Tu and and I will put together a unit."

"Massi and I will meet you at the head of the column."

The meeting broke up, and he went outside to the campfire to find something to eat before saddling his horse.

"Were you with Ava last night?" Dak stood beside him as he scooped up hot, spicy meat with warm flatbread. "We were worried when we couldn't find you."

"I was." Luc glanced at him. "I'll let you know next time." He hadn't said anything before he'd gone looking for her because he hadn't been sure of his welcome, and when she'd let him inside her tent, he'd been so relieved he hadn't wanted to give her even a moment to change her mind.

"Did you check on Revek?" he asked.

Dak nodded. "He woke up when he heard us arrive to visit him, and we stayed until Dorea shooed us out. He seems a lot better."

"We'll have to question him later." Luc felt the ball of cold suspicion and anger ignite again in his gut. What had Revek known about Haslia? He was one of the most suspicious people Luc knew. His time in the camps had made him close to paranoid, and yet, a Kassian spy had been sharing pillows with him.

It seemed unbelievable.

Dak grunted in response. "Maybe Massi shouldn't be there."

"Where shouldn't I be?"

They both turned, found Massi standing behind them, eyes narrowed.

"To interrogate Revek." Dak spoke bluntly.

Massi closed her eyes. "You're wondering about Haslia? About how much he knew?"

"Have you ever known anyone as cautious as Rev? And he misses a Kassian spy right under his nose?"

Massi sighed. "She cast a spell on him, didn't she? Something to make him sick?"

Luc tilted his head. "She rubbed an oil on his cheek. Ava noticed how sick he was suddenly getting, noticed the oil and got Dorea to wipe it off, and that's when he started to improve."

Massi hunched her shoulders. "She saved his life."

Luc said nothing. He didn't need to.

"If Haslia enspelled him to try to kill him, maybe she befuddled him with spells to stop him realizing what she was." Massi's mouth formed a stubborn line.

Luc gave a reluctant nod of agreement. It was possible.

"I heard Haslia was the one spreading the stories about you being enspelled by a woman." Dak rubbed the back of his neck. "Rafe started getting suspicious of her yesterday when she overstepped a bit. I'm assuming that's why she decide to cut her losses."

"Yes." Luc swallowed the last of his breakfast. "And then either she or one of her allies tried to burn Revek alive when her first spell didn't work. And Ava saved him again."

He went cold at the memory of Ava standing frozen, cloak alight, tent burning around her, and suppressed a shudder.

As he went to saddle his horse, he thought about what Ava had said last night.

Anyone could have a cloak like hers, if they had the money or the connections to get hold of one.

But he knew now he could sense someone hiding behind such a spell casting, and that gave him some comfort.

Also, he'd only sensed it in the camps, and when Ava had been hiding.

Something like that working in a cloak was rare. Someone with Ava's ability was rare.

No wonder the Queen's Herald had kept her locked away.

And now her cloak was gone, he recalled. Destroyed.

As he and the others galloped across the plain toward the traders' caravan, he wondered if they had a cloak for sale there, and if he could buy one for her as a gift.

"Don't say anything about Ava to the traders," he called to Massi as he came up alongside her.

She nodded in understanding.

Because there was no way the Kassian wouldn't have at least one spy in this caravan.

They would all have to be careful about everything they said amongst the traders, but now he knew her value to the Queen's Herald, Luc would not let a single word about his heart's choice be spoken.

CHAPTER 21

"It's because the weather started to turn cold nearly a month ago." The third trader she'd approached said the same thing as the first two who had no cloaks to sell. "Our journey hasn't come near a town in a long time. On purpose. So there's been no way to stock up." The merchant lifted her worn, wrinkled hands.

Ava nodded and turned away.

"You could look over at the trade caravan they intercepted early this morning."

Ava turned back at that.

The woman gestured up ahead, her braid of gray hair swinging across thin shoulders. "They're allowing some of us to go out there later, to see what we can buy. Stock up. That's why the column isn't moving yet. We need supplies, and this might be the quickest way to get some."

Ava hadn't been on duty today, and while she knew something urgent had come up for Luc to be roused from her bed so early, she hadn't heard what it was. She had wondered why, even though they had all packed up, they weren't moving.

"A trade caravan?"

"From Grimwalt, or northeastern Kassia, I heard."

"Can anyone go?" She had seen for herself that the Grimwalt border was closed, but she knew of at least one caravan of traders who had planned to slip out of the country on a backroad to journey to Kassia's capital, Fernwell. She had entrusted her revenge plan to them, so perhaps she should take heart that this group had gotten through. It meant it was likely the one that was set to leave two days after she had was also on its way.

"You have a horse, don't you?" the trader asked.

She nodded.

"Well, I'm Carys, and I could use a horse in case I buy more than my allocated limit on the cart they're taking us over on. If the General and the Commander say it's safe to go over and trade, we're to meet at midday and be escorted across. If you want to ride beside the cart as my helper, you can come along and look for a cloak, and carry whatever I can't fit in the cart back with you."

Ava bowed her head in thanks.

"Mind, they won't take your letter of credit over there, though. So you'll need to get your hands on actual coins."

She hadn't thought of that. "Thank you. I'll go see what I can do, and I'll meet you at midday."

Money had never played a big role in Ava's life. When she'd traveled with her parents, everything had been provided for her. Then she'd been held prisoner for years, and again, had no use for money.

That was no longer the case.

She hadn't worried about it up until now, and that was a mistake. One she wouldn't make again.

She walked through the camp, looking for Deni, but when she couldn't find him she guessed he might be with the General or the lieutenants, looking over the trade caravan for security risks.

Of course, the likelihood of there being a Kassian spy amongst the traders was high, so she would have to keep strictly in character as a Venyatux junior soldier.

She shivered as a chill wind picked up, and fingered the cuff of her shirt. Underneath, on the inside where no one could see it, she had embroidered some protections before leaving her tent this morning. Also on the inside of her collar, and on the cuffs of her trousers.

It wasn't close to what she'd created with her cloak, but it eased her fears a little and made her feel more secure.

She wandered past the carts. The yakkuna bellowed to each other and ripped out the last of the summer grasses while they waited for their drivers to give the signal to walk.

Deni was nowhere to be found, and in the end, she decided to go and help Carys anyway. Perhaps she would find Deni on guard at the caravan, but even if she did, there was no reason to think he'd have enough coins on him to lend her.

They set out at midday, a cart full of excited traders, surrounded by soldiers from both columns, and a few off-duty soldiers like herself, who had been pressed into helping provide extra carrying capacity.

"Be warned, no talking about column business. Assume every word you speak will end up in a Kassian ear, and conduct yourselves accordingly." The officer commanding the escort unit had already said it once before, but Ava didn't mind him repeating it.

What he said was true.

They reached the caravan after twenty minutes, and Ava thought the whole caravan looked nervous.

Perhaps that was natural when faced with a massive army intent on the overthrow of the ruling order.

Ava slid off her horse and tied it to the cart before she followed Carys to where the caravan had set up tables in readiness to barter and sell.

Most of the tables were shaded by canopies extended from covered carts, and the traders sat in deep shadow.

Carys got straight into conversation with the first trader they came to, a woman selling shoes, and Ava drifted on, looking over tables of food and drink, and with more interest, wool and fabric.

A stack of thin boxes caught her eye and she froze. Then slowly walked toward the table.

Her boxes. For sale here, to anyone who had the coin.

Her revenge, being squandered.

She moved her gaze from the stack to the man standing behind the table. "What's in those?" she asked.

The boxes were all tied with twine, as they had been when she had given them to Velda, with a short description of the design written on the side. All except the one on top. The twine had been cut on that one.

"Shirts," the man said. "The most amazing embroidery you will ever see."

"Is that so?" Her fury climbed higher. So high, her hands shook as she pulled a scrap of fabric and her needle and thread from her pocket. "Where did you get them?"

For a moment he hesitated, shifting a little under her gaze. "From a source in Grimwalt."

"Fine embroidery isn't a high priority in a marching army." She kept her voice neutral.

He twitched again, peering at her out of the shadows created by the canopy. "I was going to sell them in Fernwell, but if someone here wants to buy one . . ." He shrugged. "A sale's a sale."

"A sale's a sale," Ava repeated as she bowed her head over the fabric, working in quick, sure movements. "Can I see the work? I'm a fair hand at embroidery myself."

He seemed reluctant, suddenly. "Well, don't touch, mind. The fabric is very fine, and I need to keep it clean."

If anyone had touched those shirts . . . Ava had to breathe in deeply. They would be ensnared.

But she would first have to be sure.

The trader picked up the top box and lifted the lid, and there was her final work. The piece meant for her cousin. The shirt of blue and green feathers, thickly embroidered at the cuffs and hem, becoming less dense toward the top, with just one, single feather embroidered into the left shoulder.

"See?" The trader held the box in both arms and shuffled back so she couldn't touch. "The artisan who created these is in a league beyond any I have ever seen, so if you are able to match—" He peered at the scrap of fabric she held out to him, and closed the lid with a snap, put it back on the pile, and snatched the fabric from her.

She held her breath.

She never knew how her spell casting would work, although she had twice worked something similar to this. Once in the dungeons of the fortress where she'd been kept, and once when she had needed to rescue Luc while they were on the run.

It had worked both times, but this was more ambitious than those had been.

"This is good, especially in the time it took . . ." He looked up at her, eyes suddenly a little unfocused.

"I am very happy to help you take these boxes back into your cart." Ava gathered as many as she could into her arms. "It wouldn't do to have stock meant for Fernwell out when you don't intend to sell it to the Rising Wave."

The trader blinked. "Thank you, you're right."

He took the last few boxes and Ava followed him around the back of the cart, and then climbed in after him.

"Where is a safe place to put them?"

He opened a wooden chest and stacked them inside.

"So tell me, really, where did you get them?" Ava sat down and the trader slowly sat on the now-closed chest.

"I was given them, didn't even have to pay!" He chuckled as if he had shared a rare joke. "A family I know." He lowered his voice. "Magical, it's whispered, although I'm not sure about that. The work is magical, that's probably where the rumor comes from."

"What family is this?" She had thought the magical quality of her grandmother's work was well known, and Velda, her grandmother's housekeeper, had brokered this deal with the trader. Perhaps it was something known more at the Grimwaldian court than by the general population.

"The Yngstras." He tapped his nose. "Very old family. Very well respected."

"Why would they give you such beautiful work for free? It must have taken a lot of time to make."

He leaned closer to her. "On condition they reached Fernwell, and one was sold to the Queen's Herald. Imagine! I don't know how they thought I could sell something into those circles. I never have before."

"So you decided not to try? Even though you accepted the shirts?" She bit down on her lip.

"There'll be no repercussions." His smile was sly. "I heard the

Yngstras are out of favor at the Grimwalt court. The new speaker of the court has made some changes in the last six months. Someone told me the only Yngstra left is on the run."

"Who told you that?" Because their information was very accurate.

"One of the court messengers. I told him I was waiting to receive something from my contact with the family. He warned me off. Told me that wouldn't be a good idea."

"But you did take them."

"When I saw what they were . . ." The trader lifted his shoulders. "Who could have turned them away? They're magnificent."

"And the messenger didn't try to take them from you?" She went cold at the thought.

"We left before he returned." The trader glanced at her sidelong. "Well. We deliberately left before he returned. We were just grateful they were letting us go even though the border is supposed to be closed. They gave some messages to one of the traders to deliver to the court in Fernwell, and told us to keep quiet about it, but I had a very real fear they'd take the shirts for themselves, and no way was I letting them go."

Perhaps he had touched the one with the flowers, Ava thought. That was the one she had instructed be sold first. It created a desperate craving to own it. Or one like it.

The first person to touch it would be the means by which the others would be sought out and snapped up.

Or perhaps the trader was just a greedy crook.

"Which trader has the messages from the Grimwaldian court?" Ava asked.

"Karl. He got paid well for it, too." He leaned closer. "Said he'll pay us for any information we overhear this afternoon from the traders from the Rising Wave." He winked.

"It's a pity you won't hear anything useful then." She would make sure someone knew about Karl and his messages before the day was over. "Do you want me to tell you how to sell the shirts to the lords of the court in Fernwell? And to the Queen's Herald?"

"You know how?" He leaned back, astonished. His fingers smoothed over the scrap of working she'd given him again and again.

She had imbued compliance into the willow tree she had embroidered on the fabric. So he would bend to her will.

"I do." Ava realized her hands were in fists, and she was speaking through clenched teeth.

She wanted to strike out at him, but she managed to fight the urge. She would surely win a better victory this way than knocking him down.

"What you do is find the address of a lord who is an attendee of the court, and you send the shirt with the flowers and leaves on it to the house, addressed to him, along with a bill for the shirt. Make it expensive."

"Even though he hasn't ordered it?" The trader frowned.

"Yes, even though he hasn't ordered it. You pretend he has." Whoever touched that shirt would want it, would have to have it. And would want to pay its worth, for bragging rights if nothing else.

"Make sure you put your city address on the invoice, so the lord can find you again, or send his friends your way. Because after seeing him in it, touching it, they'll want one of their own."

"I don't have an address in the city," the trader said. "I work out of the traders' market, and sleep in my cart."

She hadn't considered this.

"Then you'll need to find a shopkeeper willing to let you work out of his or her shop in exchange for a portion of the profits."

"Well, all of it will be profit," the trader chuckled, "but I don't need to tell them that."

"No, you can keep that part to yourself, make as much as you can."

The trader nodded. "And then?"

"And then the orders will come. And you sell the shirts, but be sure to make it clear there are a very limited number." She paused. "What were you told about the shirt with the feathers? The one you showed me."

"That's the one for the Queen's Herald." He rubbed a hand over his forehead. "It's only supposed to be sold to him. No one else. Of course, I never thought that would be possible."

"It's more than possible. You keep that one aside. Even if someone comes when there are none left but that one, and begs you to sell them a shirt, you don't do it. You hold your nerve. The Herald will covet one of his very own. And when he sends someone to you to buy one, you'll be able to tell them you have one left."

"And this will work?"

"Of course." She forced herself to smile. "And at the end of this, you'll be so pleased you were true to your promise, and you'll be reminded that integrity pays higher dividends than greed."

"So true. So true." He nodded sagely. "You are wise beyond your years."

"One last thing." Ava looked around the cart, saw there were plenty of garments stacked into specially built shelves. "Do you have a cloak you can sell me?"

"I have a few." The trader stood and began rifling through the stacks. "This is my best one." He flicked out an armful of gray fabric and it swirled into a cloak with a hood. "It's lined with brushed cotton, not silk, but it's warm."

Ava took it from him. Her old cloak hadn't had a lining. She liked this one. She could embroider it on the inside. Where the workings would be closer to her skin, and out of sight.

She glanced around for something to give him, thinking that handing over something, an item he could take in his hands, would be best. She saw a collection of buttons in a small bowl and scooped some up.

"You drive a hard bargain, but the wool is fine, and as you say, the lining is warm." She dropped the buttons into his hand.

"Well," he smiled as he closed his fingers over them, "a trader has to make a living. But you're right, the wool is fine. It will see you through winter."

"And you of course will be making a lot of money from those shirts." Money from her work. Although, truth be told, he could make a small fortune, and she would count it as a fair trade if her plan worked and her cousin put that shirt on.

More than fair.

That he had decided to renege on the bargain he had struck with her grandmother's housekeeper, Velda, made her feel no guilt at taking the cloak. He was lucky not to be bleeding.

"Well, it's been a pleasure doing business with you." Ava walked to the cart's opening and dropped down.

The trader followed, a little wobbly on his feet. "Likewise. It's been a revelation talking to you."

"Two more things before I go." Ava waited until he was beside her on the ground before she covered his hands, still clutching the scrap of fabric, with her own.

"Yes?" He blinked up at her guilelessly.

"Never, ever touch the shirts. Or allow anyone else to do it. You know they have to be pristine and the people you'll be selling them to will not tolerate a single snag."

"Of course." He sounded almost insulted. "Not a finger. Not even my own!"

"Good. And lastly, everything we've talked about is our little secret." She tapped her nose just as he had. "We wouldn't want any of this getting back to the Grimwalt court's messenger."

"No." He gave a low chuckle. "Not a word." He mimed sewing up his lips.

She pulled the fabric from his fingers, and grasped his shoulder. "Thank you again. You emptied my coin bag, but I think the cloak is worth it."

"Oh." He shook his head. Then smiled. "Of course it's worth it."

A few of the Venyatux and Rising Wave traders were gathered around his table, looking through the tunics he'd put out, and with another smile, he bustled over to them.

Ava watched him talk to them in a jocular tone.

He didn't look her way. She walked along the line of tables, but kept looking back at him, but he made no move to fetch the shirts and put them up for sale again.

She would have nightmares about the working she had just subjected him to fading over time and him going back to his original plan further down the road.

But she had no way to change that, unless she joined the trade caravan herself.

She considered it. Then forced herself to acknowledge that she might as well take the shirts herself, then. And she couldn't have even the smallest hint of involvement.

Her cousin would be wary. Especially now she had escaped.

He might even be expecting her to do exactly what she was doing.

Which was why she'd created such an elaborate plan in the first place.

She'd known it was risky.

She'd now done even more to mitigate that risk.

She'd have to leave it to fate.

And let her cousin actively seek out his own doom.

CHAPTER 22

Luc circled the caravan again. There were others doing the same, keeping a watchful eye both toward the caravan, and outward, scanning the plains.

He kept the hood of his cloak up.

He didn't need any word of the Turncoat King being seen alive and well to reach Fernwell, even though they must suspect he had made it back to the Rising Wave after his escape.

Suspecting wasn't knowing for sure.

Of course, Haslia knew, and she could confirm it to her Kassian masters.

Still, long ingrained caution ruled his actions, and he wasn't prepared to be foolish, just because it seemed likely they already knew.

They would know Ava was with him, too, if Haslia was a Kassian spy and had headed for Fernwell herself after running last night.

Hopefully later today he could talk to Revek, and find out what he knew. What Haslia had said to him.

He sighed, and then straightened in his saddle when he saw Ava walking to the end of the carts that made up the caravan, and then turn to walk back down the line of tables toward the cart that had transported the Rising Wave and Venyatux traders.

She had on a new cloak, and he suddenly remembered his own idea to buy her one.

She had obviously had the same plan, and used her day off to do something about it.

He altered course, aiming his mount toward the caravan, but keeping his speed to a gentle trot.

She must have heard the hoofbeats, because she turned and shielded her eyes to look in his direction, and like him, altered her course to walk toward him.

When they met in the middle, he reached down and swung her up into his lap, and chuckled at the surprise on her face.

"How did you do that?" She gaped at him.

He shook his head. "What are you doing here, lover? You must know the Kassian will have a spy embedded in the caravan."

"They do. His name is Karl. He's carrying messages from the new, and it seems corrupt, speaker of the Grimwalt court, to the Queen in Fernwell."

It was Luc's turn to gape. "And you found this out how?"

She pulled a piece of fabric from her pocket, and then jerked it out of his reach when he tried to take it from her.

"It's spelled." She shook her head at him. "Be careful." She tilted her head. "But I have to ask, why *did* you reach for it so readily? The trader I made it for did the same. He almost threw something aside to reach for it."

Luc frowned. "I don't know. I wanted to see it. Didn't you work that into it?"

"Not specifically." She tucked it away again. "I obviously wanted him to take it. I thought he would have to touch it to be affected by my working. So I didn't bother to make wanting to touch it a part of the spell, because by the time he had it in his hand, that would be unnecessary. And yet . . ." She narrowed her eyes. "Maybe it can somehow reach out to people, even if they haven't yet touched it. But I don't know how that would work. And how it did, when I never put it there to begin with."

"I don't know how any of it works." Luc realized he would need to be very careful of what he took from others in the future. Ava was teaching him the world was full of deadly things that looked completely innocent.

"The working I showed you was to create compliance in the trader I gave it to." She paused, as if thinking about whether to elaborate. "Remember I told you I had a plan for revenge against the Queen's Herald?"

"Yes. It's what kept us apart for so long."

She nodded. "I made him a shirt."

Now that he knew she had compelled the Herald to stab himself with a jacket she had embroidered for him, he had an idea of what she had in mind with the shirt. "How were you going to get it to him?"

"That's the thing. The trader my grandmother's housekeeper arranged with to take the shirt to Fernwell is part of this caravan." She glanced over at the line of carts, and Luc thought her gaze rested on a particular stall.

"That's him?"

She nodded. "He had put out the shirts I had made for sale to the Rising Wave."

Luc sucked in a breath. "That would have been . . ."

"Very dangerous." She nodded.

He was going to say deadly, but dangerous covered it.

"I made a working, gave it to him, and convinced him the shirts couldn't be sold at all until he reached Fernwell. I was able to tell him how to get the shirt I made for the Herald into his hands, and I found out how they managed to leave Grimwalt as a trading caravan when the border is closed."

"And?"

"And, they were let through on the sly so that Karl could deliver the letters to the Queen from the Grimwalt Speaker." She hesitated. "Apparently, I'm considered on the run, so I might not have any power to help the trade treaty with the Skäddar, as I promised I would."

"Don't worry about that now." Luc ran a hand down her back. "That is truly a future problem we will come to in good time."

She sighed, nodded. "Karl also offered the other traders money for any gossip or information they heard from the Rising Wave traders today."

"Which means he's more than just a mule. He's an active spy."

"Yes." The wind came up, blowing sand and dried leaves at them, and she ducked her head against his shoulder.

His horse shifted uneasily beneath him, and he tightened his grip on her and bent his head, closing his eyes against the debris and burying his nose in her hair.

He had never felt so comforted, although if someone had asked him what he needed comfort from, he would be hard-pressed to say.

The wind died as suddenly as it had sprung up, and he raised his head, saw the traders seemed to be winding up their business.

"Will that working you made still be effective?"

Ava looked up. "You want to use it on Karl?"

He nodded. "What could you get him to do?"

She looked away. Lifted her shoulders. "I think almost anything."

She was afraid her admission would frighten him. Would drive more of a wedge between them.

But he would not allow it.

"I'll come along, you shouldn't go in alone." Only he could accompany her. Otherwise her secret would be out.

"How about you wait outside, and only intervene if there's a problem?"

He nodded reluctantly. "Is there some way you can find out who he is before everyone leaves?"

"Yes. I came with a trader, Carys, and I'm sure she will know who everyone is by now." She turned in his lap, and he lifted her down.

When she looked up at him, her eyes were searching, as if waiting for him to flinch. "You sure you want to do this with me?"

He nodded, and then watched her walk the short distance to where the Rising Wave and Venyatux traders were gathered.

He had made her doubt him. And he would do what he had to do to win back her trust.

"I SEE YOU GOT YOUR CLOAK." CARYS FINGERED THE FABRIC AND gave an approving nod.

"I did. Thank you for letting me come as your helper." She took the bundles Carys had set at her feet and tied them to her mount. "Someone mentioned a trader called Karl. Do you know which one he is, and what he sells?"

"Ask Gregor." Carys sent her an evil grin. "He's already deep into his wares."

Ava turned, and saw one of the traders groaning, hand to his stomach. Wine flasks sat around him.

"A wine merchant?" She frowned. "We haven't been here long enough for someone to get that drunk, have we?"

Carys shrugged. "Probably went straight there and has been sampling the wares since."

Ava had a bad feeling about that.

She looked over at Luc, but he had been joined by Massi and Rafe, and wasn't looking her way.

She made her way to the captain who had escorted them over, and gestured to him to dismount from his horse.

He narrowed his eyes at her, but he knew who she was, and he reluctantly slid down.

She leaned in close to him. "The Commander has cause to be suspicious of the wine merchant in this caravan. And given how sick the trader who has bought from him is, I'm worried that he isn't drunk, but perhaps poisoned, or has been deliberately given something that is off."

The captain drew in a sharp breath, and then looked over at where Gregor was heaving up the contents of his stomach.

"Take the traders back, and get Gregor to a healer. Make sure no one touches the wine he's bought."

"I don't take orders from you." The captain glanced over at Luc.

"Then go confirm your orders with the Commander." She turned and walked toward Luc herself. She hadn't got two steps before the captain's hand came down on her shoulder.

"What you say makes sense. I'll speak to the Commander later."

She nodded and kept going.

Luc had managed to rid himself of his companions by the time she reached him, and she thought he would have done it on purpose, to keep what they planned between them.

"It's the wine merchant. The trader who did business with him is busy heaving up his guts right now, so I wonder whether he thinks to cause us some problems in other ways, too."

Luc looked over at the traders, and then slid off his horse. "The captain is getting them back to the column."

"I told him you had cause to be suspicious of the wine merchant, and that the wine might be off, or poisoned."

"Good." He turned to the caravan. The traders were packing up. "There's the wine merchant, at the front of the caravan."

She saw a large, bluff man with jowled cheeks and hard eyes, and pulled out the fabric she'd used earlier. Added a few things to it.

She didn't know if it would still work the same way or not, but she thought it safer to boost it.

"I can't sell you more than I already have. I have to have stock for Fernwell." He spoke to them before they'd even reached his table.

"Oh, well, that's a shame." Ava broke off the thread with her teeth and held out the fabric to him. "I was hoping—"

He reached for the embroidery, almost snatching it from her fingers. "A wine carafe leaning against a tree?" He looked up. "It would look good etched into my casks."

"It would. A distinctive symbol." She started stacking the few remaining carafes under her arm. "Where would you like me to put these for you?"

"Oh, in the cart. Thank you." He bent and lifted a basket full of bottles, and led the way.

Luc said nothing, following behind like a shadow.

Since he'd taken the fabric, the merchant hadn't even looked Luc's way.

She didn't waste any time once they were inside. It would look strange the longer they stayed here after the others had left.

"You have some messages for the Queen?"

He paused, and frowned, and then gave a shrug. "Yes."

"Can I see them?"

He hesitated. "I'm not supposed to show anyone. Not even supposed to look at them myself."

"Of course. We just need to check they're safe. We'll bring them back tomorrow morning, early, for you. The caravan will spend the night here, and go first thing tomorrow. And everything will be where it needs to be, safe and sound."

"That's a relief." He leaned across to the other side of the narrow cart and began unstacking boxes.

When he reached the bottom one, he lifted the lid, and amongst the sawdust packing, were two scrolls.

"We'll just make sure all is in order." Ava lifted them out, and in their place, she set two of the bottles from the basket he'd brought in.

As soon as the empty spaces were filled again, the merchant let out a breath of relief. He closed the lid.

"Keep this box out, so we can quickly put things back to rights tomorrow morning." Ava saw his thumb was moving back and forth over the fabric. She would have to leave it with him. But she didn't know whether the compulsion would fade over the night or not.

"It's a pity you aren't feeling well today." To her ear, it sounded clumsy, but she needed to keep him away from the others in the caravan tonight. "But you're right that a good night's sleep will probably do you the world of good."

"You're very kind." He stumbled to his feet as she tucked the scrolls under her cloak.

"I'll see you tomorrow morning, to give you a soothing remedy from our healer. But until then, I hope a good rest will help."

"Very kind," he repeated.

He was already drawing the canvas at the back of his cart shut when she jumped to the ground.

"I never thought you'd take the scrolls from him." Luc kept his voice whisper quiet. "I thought you'd ask to have a look at them."

"I thought we might alter them, if it looks feasible."

He shot her a grin. "Now that's a good plan."

The Rising Wave cart had already left, she saw. And her horse with it.

Luc swung into his saddle, and reached for her again.

His strength and agility were incredible to her.

She held tight to the scrolls and leaned into him as they started back. "We need to hurry. I'm not sure how long my working will last. I've convinced him he isn't well, so he won't mingle with the other traders, but we should really return these within a few a hours to be safe."

Massi and Rafe suddenly came up on either side of them.

"What were you up to, Luc?" Massi asked.

"I'll tell you when we're in my tent. Rafe, can you get word to the General to come as soon as she can?"

Rafe peeled away, galloping with a whoop into the dusk. Massi stayed with them.

Ava could feel her eyes on her.

"Where's your horse?"

"I lent it to one of the traders to help carry what she bought back to the column."

"And what were you doing—"

"Enough, Massi. We'll explain everything when we get to my tent." Luc's voice was harsh.

He still hadn't forgiven her for Revek's attack.

Ava ran her hand in circles on the small of his back and looked over at Massi. "You feel hurt, because before, Luc would have told you what he was doing, and you would not have to ask what was going on."

Massi said nothing.

Luc sighed. "It was spur of the moment, Mas. We had to act immediately. You'll know soon enough."

She gave a stiff nod and with a yip, gave her horse its reins and galloped ahead into deep shadows as the last of the sun's face dipped beneath the horizon.

The column began to light up—fires coaxed to life, lanterns hung from poles.

"It looks its best right now, just as the sun sets, when you can still see the shapes of everything, but they are softened by the shadows," Ava murmured.

"Truth be told, it always looks its best to me. Because I never thought we'd get so far, or be so many." Luc slowed his horse, as if to prolong their time together, before they reached the column, and the tricky conversations ahead.

"Thank you for keeping my secrets." She knew it might cost him dearly in the long run.

"I look after my own. And you are mine."

She believed him. "And I'll do everything I can to protect you. Because you are mine, too."

Unfortunately, she may not be able to protect him from herself, or the baggage she dragged along behind her.

CHAPTER 23

The General walked into Luc's tent moments after they did.

Ava could see curiosity in her eyes, and pent up energy in her movements.

She had brought Raun-Tu and Heival with her.

"General." Ava bowed her head. "This will have to be just for your ears, and then you can choose what you share with your lieutenants."

Raun-Tu bristled. "Avasu, you do not tell the general—"

The general lifted a hand and he snapped his mouth shut. "This concerns some things we spoke of earlier?" Her gaze flitted from Luc, to Massi and Dak, then came to rest on her again.

She nodded.

General Ru turned to her lieutenants, face impassive, and both of them reluctantly left the tent.

She would be hearing from Raun-Tu about this tomorrow, Ava thought, with a sinking sensation in her stomach.

"So, Avasu. What is so secret?" The general looked even more energized than she had before.

Ava reached into her cloak and pulled out the two scrolls. "Messages from the Speaker of the Grimwalt court to the Queen of Kassia."

"Is that so?" General Ru approached, looking at them critically. "They do look like they are sealed with the Grimwaldian crest."

"Oh. I haven't had a chance to really look at them." Ava bent closer. "He did use the official seal." For some reason, this sparked her anger and fear more than anything else she'd heard about the speaker of the Grimwalt court.

He was using official channels. Did that mean he had official backing, or was he simply abusing his position?

"And how did you know about these, and where to find them?" Massi stepped closer to have a look herself.

"The caravan is from Grimwalt. One of the traders in the caravan is a long acquaintance of my grandmother's housekeeper. He told me what he knew."

There were a few quick intakes of breath.

"He told you who the spies were?"

"He told her." Luc picked up one of the scrolls. "We were able to sneak into the spy's cart and find the messages, but we need to return them before they're missed."

"Better for them to not know they've been seen," General Ru agreed with a nod. "Then they will stick to their plans."

"Ava had the idea we could see what their plans are, and if possible, make some subtle changes to the text." Luc turned the scroll in his hands, looking for a way to open it.

"Who is the spy?" Dak stood back, a little apart from the rest of them.

"The wine merchant."

Dak jerked up his head to look at her. "I heard word from one of my captains that we weren't to touch the wine."

"One of the traders who tasted what he bought fell ill quickly, and if the wine merchant is a Kassian spy, he may be trying to delay us with poisoned drink." Luc handed the other scroll to the general, and then carefully lifted the seal on the one in his hands.

General Ru did the same, using delicate movements to remove it without breaking it.

They both read for long minutes, and the rest of the tent began to shift impatiently.

Luc gave a grunt of surprise and the general set her scroll down on the table.

"What?" Massi couldn't contain herself.

"Things are not well in Grimwalt." The general sent Ava a sympathetic look. "It seems the Speaker is offering an alliance with Kassia, in exchange for personal wealth for himself."

"Does he have the confidence of the court?" After everything that had happened, if Grimwalt allied itself to Kassia, it would be a massive betrayal. Ava couldn't believe so many of her parents' allies would forget what had happened to them at Kassia's hand.

"He says he can get it, if the Kassian Queen makes it worthwhile for him." The general glanced at Ava sidelong. "He says that he has a way."

Ava stared at her, frowning. The general was trying to convey something to Ava, but she didn't know—

It hit her.

She drew in a breath, and Luc glanced at her.

She managed to give a tiny shake of her head.

That was why the Speaker had tried to have her abducted from her grandmother's estate, and then had chased her for days afterward.

She had actually offered up this very explanation to Velda, her grandmother's housekeeper, when Velda had wondered why representatives of the Grimwaldian court were trying to kidnap her.

She had said perhaps it was for the same reason the Queen's Herald had taken her, but she hadn't wondered what would be behind it or even thought seriously about it.

She'd been too relieved to have escaped, and too excited about leaving to find Luc.

The Speaker wanted to use her to bend the court to his will. To force her to help him conspire with the very people who had killed her parents and imprisoned her for years.

She didn't have words.

The general was watching her face, and what she saw there had her giving a nod of approval.

The general knew she was a spell caster.

She would have to, to understand how the Speaker intended to change the minds of the Grimwaldian Court.

She had said before that she had met Ava's grandmother, now Ava realized she had been trying to say she knew what her grandmother could do. And that Ava could likely do the same.

Thread by thread, she was loosening the knot of secrets around her, and she was worried that in the end, she would be left completely exposed.

"What do you think he intends to do to get the court to support him?" Dak asked.

"Does it matter?" Luc gestured to the scroll he'd read. "What it says in this message is that he has embedded two spies in the Venyatux column, and he can let the queen know the Venyatux plans well in advance of their approach to Fernwell, as a gesture of goodwill."

The general snatched up the scroll and read it with eyes that were more alive than Ava had ever seen them. "I will discover who."

"The queen will not be that impressed. Although I'm sure she won't turn information down, we know there are still spies among the Rising Wave. Given so many of us came from the Chosen camps, and others from what's left of the Cervantes, it would be easy for them to slip some traitors in. Luc was captured because they turned one of our own Chosen brothers." Massi shrugged.

"Ava, you have an artistic hand. Can you alter the amount the Speaker is asking for? Either inflate it to an outrageous amount or make it much less?"

"The queen will be insulted by the one, and the Speaker will be insulted by the other." General Ru gave an evil chuckle.

Ava studied it. "He's asking for ten thousand gri?" She looked up, eyes wide.

Dak gave a snort at the amount.

"I could make it a hundred thousand." There was just enough space for an extra zero.

The general laughed out loud. "Yes. That is good."

Luc found a quill for her, and Ava used a sheet of paper to get used to it and check the ink was similar to the ink used on the scroll. When she was happy it was close, she carefully added the zero, and just in case, she thought of the Speaker; greedy, grasping and corrupt.

It wasn't an embroidered working, but it was worth a chance.

She left the scroll to dry and turned her attention to the second one.

"There is room for another sentence here." She pointed out the large gap between two paragraphs. "It's the place he's talking about his spies. Perhaps I could say the information from the spies would only be forthcoming if the Speaker sees some coin first?"

"Make the queen truly dislike him." Luc nodded. He held the scroll open for her and Ava carefully wrote out the sentence. It was harder, this time. She kept checking the way the Speaker formed his letters, taking excruciating care to match them.

"It looks the same." Dak peered over her shoulder.

She stepped back to look at it critically. It wasn't perfect, but hopefully the small differences wouldn't be noticed.

"We need to get these back." She had a low-level dread in the pit of her stomach over leaving the working in Karl's possession. If he gave it to someone, or they took it from him, what havoc would it cause? And would they begin to work out they had been enspelled?

"Your knowing one of the traders was one of those rare things, a serendipitous meeting." The general carefully rolled up one of the scrolls. "I need a candle."

Massi rummaged through a box, found one and lit it.

The general held the bottom of the seal over it for a few moments and then pressed it back into place.

"You're good at that," Luc commented.

The general smiled. "How do you think I got ahead in the military?"

She laughed at the surprise on everyone's faces. "I was a spy for a short time."

Luc handed the other scroll to her, and she did the same again.

"Tell your lieutenants what you think is best without revealing that Ava is Grimwaldian, if you can." Luc slid the scrolls into a bag and slung it across his chest. "Ava and I will return these."

"And we will need to talk about ambushes. Because we won't be moving toward Fernwell undetected. We already knew that, but these messages just confirm it. Everything we do is reported back. We will have to face them and we know they will want to fight us away from Fernwell." General Ru walked toward the tent flaps. "Let's speak tomorrow while the column moves. We cannot afford any more delay."

"Agreed." Luc waited until she was gone, then turned to Massi and Dak. "What's the news on Revek?"

"He's much better. Awake and even sitting on his own."

"I'll speak to him after Ava and I have returned the scrolls. We need to know what he told Haslia, and what she told him."

Dak nodded.

Massi hunched her shoulders and turned away.

"Massi." Luc waited until she'd turned back to face him. "You don't have to be there."

"I will be." She glared at him. "Someone has to be on his side."

"Let's first find out if he was on ours." Luc turned away, walking out the tent.

"You need to check yourself," Dak murmured, and Massi turned her hot, angry stare on him.

"Run along, Luc's waiting for you." Massi flicked her fingers dismissively at Ava.

Ava couldn't help the laugh that burst out of her throat. "Listen to Dak," she said.

She turned, and as she walked out, she heard the low, hissed conversation between Massi and Dak behind her.

She longed for the camaraderie of the Venyatux column, where the only thorn in her side was Nabi.

And the Speaker's spies.

She sighed. She would have to do something serious about them now. It was no longer a game of hide and seek.

CHAPTER 24

"It went well?" Dak asked.

Luc nodded as they stepped into the healer's new tent. He'd stood in the dark outside the spy's cart and listened as Ava gently coaxed the wine merchant into helping her put the scrolls back, convinced him she had brought him medicine that would ensure he felt completely well by the time he woke, and had taken back her spelled scrap of fabric.

It was disturbing. She had had Karl completely in her thrall.

And yet, she seemed uncertain about the efficacy of her workings. Hesitant to trust them.

"Did what go well?" Revek struggled to sit up as they came in.

"It doesn't matter." Luc wasn't going to say anything to him until he knew where Revek stood. "How are you?"

"Well. I could probably already be in my own tent, but Dorea insisted I stay under her eye one more night."

"That's good." Dak moved closer to him, pulling up a wooden stool and sitting beside his bed.

"What happened?" Revek looked between them. "Massi's been in here, all tight-lipped and upset, and no one says anything. Was it something I did that caused the other tent to burn down?"

"No." Massi stepped in at last. "It was nothing to do with you."

Luc had known she was standing just outside, listening. He worried about her. He didn't believe it was simply that she didn't like Ava coming among them.

That wasn't the Massi he knew. Open, warm, and positive.

She had helped him, Dak and Revek through the dark times of the Chosen camps with her laughter and her ability to always look on the bright side of things.

"I wouldn't say nothing," Luc said.

Revek stilled, looked between them. "What would you say, then?"

"Your lover, Haslia, tried to kill you, Rev. And if it wasn't for Ava, you'd be dead." Luc sat on the ground, as there were no more seats.

"Haslia wouldn't do that."

"She did. She spread some oil on your cheek." Luc used his thumb, just as Haslia had, drawing it across his cheekbone. "You suddenly got very sick. We'd all seen her rub her thumb across your face, but thought nothing of it. When we got you to the fire, so Ava could stitch you up with better light, the oil glistened and we realized she smeared it on you. As soon as Dorea wiped it away, you started improving."

Revek listened in silence, and then turned to Massi.

She shrugged.

Luc watched the byplay. "You don't trust my word now, Rev?"

He hunched his shoulders. "What about the fire?"

"Someone tried to kill you again when the oil didn't work. This time, with fire."

"Spell work?" Revek asked.

"That seems likely, but it might have been oil and a match." Luc hoped it was oil and a match. If the person who started the fire wasn't Haslia, they had a dangerous spell caster among them, who was not on their side.

"And Ava was in the thick of it again." Massi's voice held a nasty edge.

"If you mean she caught on fire instead of Revek, I suppose you're right." Luc slowly rose to his feet.

"Is she hurt?" Revek frowned. "You never told me that, Mas—"

"Her cloak was burned, but no, I got her out in time." Luc crossed his arms. He would deal with Massi after this. He could only sort out one betrayal at a time.

"Why did Haslia want you dead?" Dak spoke up, and the tension in Luc's gut eased a bit. He had one ally, at least.

"I don't know." Revek lifted his hands. "We only shared pillows a few times, I swear. We were in the same camp sector, and ate together most nights, but it wasn't serious. She told that story about you being enspelled a few times, Luc, and I should have challenged her on that, but other than that . . ." He looked around at them, eyes pleading.

"She thinks you know something that will harm her in some way, or harm the Kassian cause." Luc put it bluntly. "There's no way she would have risked trying to kill you right in front of me unless that's true."

"I don't know what. I'll think, Luc. I swear I'll go through everything we ever said or did together."

"Do that. It could be important." Luc turned to Massi. "A word?"

She followed him out into the now chill night air.

"Let's walk." He kept going, and after a moment, she caught up with him, saying nothing, hands in her pockets.

They reached the edge of the column and he kept going, out onto the open plain.

It was getting late now, and he wanted to be back in his tent, in bed with Ava.

He stopped and waited, looking up to the gleam of stars above. The night sky was so thick with them, it looked like a white plume of smoke across the darkness.

"I know what you think. I can hear myself, and I know what I think about it, so I have a good idea what you think." Massi hugged herself.

"Then why?"

"I look at her and I feel enraged. Truly enraged. I want to smack her, grind her down. It's illogical. Frightening, even."

Luc turned to stare at her in astonishment.

"I would say I was enspelled, except I know that sounds like an excuse." She sounded so miserable. "I would understand a little jealousy on my part. Revek and Dak have felt it, too. But they seem to have gotten over it."

"Has anyone given you something?" He asked it because he knew now how easy it would be to subvert someone's will.

"Given me something?" She frowned up at him.

"Anything that you've been given since Ava arrived."

She slowly loosened her arms and let them drop to her side. "You're saying in case I *have* been enspelled?"

"I have never known you to be like this, Massi. You don't behave like this. I'm saying, is it possible?"

She seemed astonished. "I found a cup outside my tent one morning. It had my name carved into it."

"And you've kept it?"

"I thought it was from an admirer." She hugged herself again. "Yes, I kept it. I drink out of it every day."

"Get rid of it." Luc put out an arm and held her shoulder. "Throw it in a fire."

"I'll do that right now." She seemed shaken.

"Don't touch it with your bare hands. Wear gloves, Mas."

"I will." She blew out a breath. "Could it be that simple?"

"Simple?" He gave a bitter laugh. "We have a spell caster among us with ill-intent. There's nothing simple about it."

"You think they also tried to burn Revek?"

"It might have been Haslia who left you the cup. She was invested in stoking suspicions against Ava, and having you openly hating her would have helped that story along. The fire could have been her, or someone else. I hope it was her, because at least she's gone."

"The cup might not be spelled." Massi's voice was small.

"This isn't you, Massi. You had a warm word of welcome for everyone. You were the most relentlessly cheerful person I know, even in the camps. If it isn't the cup, it's something else."

"Thank you."

He realized she was crying, and that it was the second time she'd cried since Ava had joined the column. Someone was truly trying to rip his life to shreds. Poison everything important to him.

This time, though, he pulled her into his arms instead of walking out.

"We'll sort this out. Come. I'll go with you to find the cup."

Because he remembered how Ava had to jerk the fabric out of Karl's grasp just an hour ago. The wine merchant hadn't wanted to let go of the source of his ensnarement.

He draped an arm over Massi's shoulder and they walked back together.

CHAPTER 25

Ava hesitated near the general's tent.

She could hear a low, serious conversation coming from within, and from the way the two guards at the entrance were leaning slightly inward, they were listening in.

That was dangerous.

Especially with the confirmation that there were two Grimwaldians spying for the Speaker within the column.

She had thought there were two people chasing her. Now she knew for sure.

She wanted to talk to the general, and she didn't want to wait. She knew her fear of revealing anything about herself would gnaw at her if she left it.

Best get this done.

Suddenly, Raun-Tu, and then the other three lieutenants, stepped from the tent, talking quietly among themselves.

Ava kept to the shadows, out of the light thrown by the lanterns set on poles outside the general's tent, and waited for them to go their own way before she approached.

"I've come to report to the general." She knew Catja, one of the guards.

Catja nodded, but put up a hand to tell her to wait, and disappeared inside. She appeared almost immediately. "Go in."

"Thanks." They shared a smile, and Ava felt the warm glow she often did in the Venyatu column. She had found camaraderie here. Something she never thought she would have.

"Your mission was successful?" The general had shed her jacket, and pulled her hair out of its high tail, so it fell in loose, black and gray waves around her shoulders.

Ava nodded. "We were able to return the scrolls with the wine merchant none the wiser."

"Good." The general tilted her head. "But that is not why you are here."

"No." She clasped her hands in front of her. "I only just understood tonight that you knew my grandmother."

"I told you before I'd met her."

"Yes." Ava looked up. "But am I correct that you . . ." She could not bring her tongue to move, or her throat to issue the words.

"That I knew she could work magic?" The general's voice was whisper soft. "Yes."

Ava breathed out. Breathed in. "That's what I thought."

"She made me something. I commissioned it." The general stepped behind the curtain that separated her sleeping quarters from the rest of the tent and Ava heard the creak of a wooden chest lid being opened.

General Ru stepped back with a jacket in her hands.

It was dark green silk, heavy brocade by the look of it. And along the bottom edge, in a thick border, and up the center and collar, was the work of her grandmother's hand.

Black silk.

That's what her grandmother had always used for her working. And her mother. Everyone except her.

Ava took the jacket the general had extended to her, and brushed her fingers over the fine work.

"It no longer works. But for two years after I got it . . ." General Ru shook her head in wonder. "Two years. I thought it would last me a few months at most and even then it would have been worth it, but for two years I knew when someone was planning to stab me in the back. Mostly figuratively, but once, literally."

"It's good to see something by her hand," Ava said. She handed it back. "I am here to offer to do the same. I have two suggestions. I can work something into this tent to make it impossible for anything said here to be heard by someone outside. I can also work on something to find the two Grimwaldian spies."

The general stood, one hip cocked, and lifted her brows. "That is a generous offer."

Ava lifted her shoulders. "It is likely my fault the Grimwaldians are here. I think they followed me out of Grimwalt. And you are my general, and your cause is my own. I want what is planned and arranged in here to remain only among those who should hear it."

"I accept."

Ava had brought some black thread with her. Unlike her mother and grandmother, she didn't need it for her workings to be effective, but she didn't have to reveal all her secrets to the general.

She walked to the tent entrance, and saw there were a row of toggles down the middle so the tent could be closed.

She chose the middle one, and began embroidering a design around it.

When she stepped back to look at it, she hoped it looked like it had always been there.

Then she turned and walked to the opposite side of the tent.

She had a feeling the working on the front flap was all that was needed, but she didn't know for sure, and it was worth doing it properly.

She crouched down and worked the same cloud design low to the ground, where it would be difficult to see.

"That's it?" The general's eyes were wide when she rose and slid the thread back into her pocket.

"I think so. Perhaps you can find some way to test it, without letting anyone know what I've done."

The general nodded. She had obviously gone back into her sleeping quarters while Ava had been working on the tent because she had put away the jacket and now had a scarf in her hands. It was of a soft, black fabric.

"I want you to use this item for your other working, so it is difficult to see the black thread," the general said. "If they are Grimwaldian, they may know your family's abilities. In fact, I think it's why they followed you."

Ava nodded. "Who do you want this to be for? Do you want me to wear it and find them?"

"No. The Grimwaldians are going to avoid you. Make it for me." The general handed it to her, and then pulled a small bag of coins from her trouser pocket. "You will need to replace the black silk thread."

Ava started to protest, and the general held up a hand. "Before you object, listen. I am going to ask you to change the working. Don't make it specifically to catch the Grimwaldians. Work something that tells me everyone who means my column ill."

There was a gleam in her eyes that told Ava she was looking forward to finding whoever those people were.

She took the money. She needed it, and she could see the general thought it was a fair bargain. "It'll take me a little time, but you'll have it tomorrow."

She walked out the tent, nodded to Catja, and made her way to Luc's tent.

When she returned and found him still gone, she considered going looking for him. The thought of sparring with Massi again was too wearying. Instead, she took out the knitting from her pack and found the closest campfire.

Her other job was to mingle, to forge the two columns into a team.

She had been doing precious little of that.

It was too dark to work on the black scarf with black thread anyway, and she enjoyed the sound of the needles clicking, the way the wool twisted in satisfying patterns, and the soothing mental mathematics as she counted stitch combinations.

"I always wondered how they did that." The soldier sitting with her shuffled closer. He shook his head in wonderment. "Who would have thought?"

"I just learned it myself." Ava held it up for him to see a little better.

The few others talking quietly and drinking something hot also shifted closer.

When she asked what patterns and motifs the Cervantes used, one of the woman shook her head.

"I was taken when I was twelve and put into a Chosen camp, so I don't know as much as I should." She sounded more subdued than she had before, and Ava didn't like to think her question had caused pain.

"After this battle, will you be able to find your family again?"

"I found them already. The Commander gave us all time to reunite before we joined the Rising Wave. My grandmother had passed while I was interned." She fingered the jacket she wore, as if it reminded her of her grandmother. "Perhaps my parents know, but they're protecting my brother and sister while we fight."

"Kali will know." The soldier's companion slid an arm around her shoulder in comfort. "She's one of the traders. She sells clothes with Cervantes patterns on them, but I think she's running low on her stock, and she doesn't make them herself."

"I'll find her tomorrow and ask." Ava knitted a few more rows, and tried to keep her mind from thinking of the tragedy of what had happened to the Cervantes. She didn't want to imbue anything like that into her work.

This was to protect Luc. To keep him safe.

She focused on strength and agility, on heightened senses and an impenetrable barrier.

"Are you up for another sparring session?" The question was from the soldier who had first admired her cable knitting. There was a hint of humor in his voice.

"Who with?" She flashed him a grin, pleased the conversation had turned to less serious things. "You?"

The others immediately began teasing him.

"Are you going to take on the Commander's lady?" One of them hooted. "Brave man!"

Ava laughed. "It doesn't matter who's lady I am." She put her knitting aside. "What happens in the ring, stays in the ring."

"Until the Commander comes in and carries you off." The woman who'd spoken about her grandmother said, a smug smile on her face.

"Ah. I can't help it if he's overcome by the sight of me fighting." She was glad she'd had more than a month of teasing with the Venyatux. She knew how this worked now. And she loved it.

The young soldier whooped at her response. "I've heard his sword is enspelled. Magical."

Ava had the sense he wasn't talking about Luc's actual sword.

"Yes. Can you confirm that for us?" The woman leaned closer to Ava and winked.

Oh!

Ava started to giggle. "I don't think I should . . ." She couldn't get the words out, she was laughing too hard, and the soldiers around her roared in appreciation.

"I think that's enough speculation about my sword." Luc's arms were suddenly around her, lifting her from her seat.

The soldiers were silent for a beat, and then burst out laughing again as Luc carried her the short distance to the tent.

He lifted his hand to make a gesture Ava couldn't see, and the laughter intensified.

"It's good to hear everyone laugh." Luc murmured into her ear, his lips brushing her skin. "It's good to hear you laugh."

"There hasn't been enough of that, in our lives, or theirs."

He set her on her feet once they were behind the canvas curtain that created his private space.

"Wait." She held up a hand as he reached for the buttons on her jacket.

She pulled the thread from her pocket and walked to the canvas.

"What are you doing?"

"Making sure no one can hear anything that happens behind this curtain."

His low chuckle brushed air across the back of her neck as he slid his arms around her from behind and then he rested his chin on the top of her head as she worked.

"Best I give you something to scream about, then." He kissed the side of her temple. "To test it."

CHAPTER 26

"You look rested." General Ru sent Luc a laughing glance as they rode together.

Massi and Dak were on his right, and Kurvin and Fervanti were on the general's left, ready to discuss the most likely Kassian points of attack.

"I got a quiet night," Luc said, with a straight face.

General Ru's quick look made him wonder if she somehow knew something about Ava's working a sound dampening spell into his tent.

He would have to ask Ava if there was a chance of that.

"Good." She gestured with her hand. "So what do we have?"

Kurvin leaned forward. "Dak and I looked at frontal attacks, and we think our approach to the Bartolo River is the most likely place for that. The map marks it as open plain, so it would be difficult for them to hide the size force they'd need to take us on in an ambush."

"However, an ambush would be much easier once we're all across the river, because we'd have to go through thick forest. They'd be wise to wait until we had all just gotten across, and then attack when we have no place to retreat except back into the water." Massi seemed calm, almost serene this morning.

Luc had thrown her cup into the fire for her last night. They had stood together and eventually Luc had had to tug it from her grasp.

He thought he saw a brief flare of green flame as it burned, but he couldn't say if that was his imagination or not.

"So the Bartolo River is the place?" The pace of the column meant it was easy to hold this talk on the move. He unrolled a map and leaned across so the general could look at it as well.

"I agree it's very likely, but they'll know we'll know that." General Ru studied the topography. "What's the most unlikely place?"

A lively conversation began, and Luc was pleased to see the way the lieutenants interacted with each other.

There was respect on both sides.

A call from the Venyatux side silenced everyone, though, and Luc saw it was Ava's friend, Deni, warning them of someone's approach.

The Skäddar rode up. He had a scarf around his neck that matched the markings on his face, and something about the style made him think that Ava had done it.

"Kikir." Fervanti nodded in warm greeting.

Luc had forgotten about the Skäddar. He knew the man had traveled with the Venyatu column in order to speak with him, but so much had happened in the time since he'd scooped Ava up after finding her sparring with him, he hadn't given the man a thought.

Obviously, the Skäddar warrior had been using his time to make friends amongst the Venyatu.

"If you are discussing the Kassian attack that is to come, I would like to be included in the discussion."

"I thought you wanted to return home as soon as possible." The general turned on her horse.

"I was waiting to speak with the Commander." Kikir nodded toward Luc. "But now I think it would make sense for me to continue on with you for a little while longer. I think I've learned a lot that would be useful to the Skäddar Collective."

Luc glanced over at General Ru, happy to allow her to make the decision.

"We accept." The general inclined her head. "We are talking about places where the Kassian army may try to intercept us on the way to Fernwell. What are your thoughts?"

Kikir held out his hand for the map, and Luc passed it to him.

They had to trust potential allies. It was how he'd got both the Venyatux and the Funabi to join the Rising Wave. His decision to trust others was also how the Kassian had managed to capture him, but even that had led to him meeting Ava.

So, on balance, it had always worked out for him.

And if the Skäddar wanted to be part of the Rising Wave, he would be pleased to let them in.

They could rise up and crash over Fernwell together.

"Shouldn't you be up there, plotting?" Kali waved a wrinkled hand at Luc, the general, and their lieutenants up ahead, heads close together.

Ava noticed Kikir had been invited to join in, and hoped it was a sign the Skäddar were going to become part of the Rising Wave.

"No. I'm not senior enough." She lifted her knitting and made sure her yarn was secure. You only had to drop a ball of yarn once from horseback to make sure you never did it again. She had forgotten her knitting at the fireside last night, but when she woke in the morning, it had been neatly set just inside the outer part of Luc's tent.

She had worked on the general's scarf early this morning, before the tents were packed up, behind the shielding walls of canvas. She didn't think it wise for her to be seen sewing with black thread anywhere in either column.

They were traveling slowly enough to make it possible to knit, though.

She and Kali had spent a happy time chatting about Cervantes embroidery motifs and knitting styles, and as people had overheard their conversations, they had joined in, talking about things specific to their region, or things their grandparents had done.

The heart's song motif was something she was shown more than any other.

"A heart's song is an outpouring of truth to your heart's choice," Kali explained. "And it can be in actual words, but it can also be shaped into a piece of jewelry or a garment, or even in a song, sung around the fire."

The Funabi and Venyatu passing by also couldn't help getting involved, talking about their own patterns and styles, as well as their versions of a heart song.

Her head was full of ideas by the time it came for lunch.

They were eating on the move today, trying to make up for the delays of the day before.

The trader caravan had been gone by the time the columns had started their lumbering movement and she wished them fair travels and a soft wind at their backs.

The leaders up ahead broke away from each other, the general and her lieutenants peeling left toward the Venyatu column, Luc, Massi and Dak wheeling their horses right.

Kikir followed the Venyatux, and Ava realized the Skäddar warrior had embedded himself well into the column. He barely raised a brow now, despite the markings on his face and his shorter, sturdier mount.

Kali had drifted off to get lunch, and Ava reached into her saddlebag to pull out the pie the cooks had handed out this morning at breakfast, made from yesterday's leftovers.

"Wait." Luc had doubled back, coming from behind her, and his hand clamped down on hers. "Will you follow me?"

She nodded, and he led them out of the Rising Wave and into the strip of neutral space between the two columns.

He slowed until they were in the middle section, where the carts and large wagons lumbered, protected from attack by the front soldiers and the rear guard. Then he leaned over and kissed her, holding her face in his hands and exploring her mouth.

When at last he leaned back, his eyes were crinkled in the corners. "I didn't want a large audience for that, but I have been thinking about it all day."

Ava looked around, and gave a laugh. "I'm afraid you misjudged the interest in us from the cart drivers."

He followed her gaze, to the waving drivers.

Whistles came from behind them, and when Ava looked back, the rear guard from both sides gave cheeky waves.

"Ah, well." Luc leaned forward and kissed her lightly again. "I tried." He unhooked a small basket from his saddle. "The cooks gave me this." He held out a small wild strawberry, and touched it to her lips.

She took a bite, and closed her eyes. She hadn't had anything like this since the days before she'd been abducted by the Queen's Herald. Sweet and tart at once.

Another berry touched her lips and she opened her eyes as she bit down.

"I learned today about a heart's song."

He froze as she spoke.

"You must know you are my heart's choice, Luc." He opened his mouth to speak and she put her hand over his lips. "Wait. I want you to hear my heart's song. I want you to understand you never have to fear me. I have only ever worked magic for your benefit. And if there is ever any reason for us to part ways—I hope there is not, but to put your mind at rest—I swear now on the memory of my grandmother and mother, I will never harm you."

Her fingers were still pressed against his lips and he took hold of them and kissed them, one by one.

"That is the heart song of a very strong heart's choice." His eyes danced. "I don't think I've ever heard the like." Then he grew serious. "I promised I would always come for you. That was my own heart song, but I will add, I will never fear you. I love you in all your strength and power."

She leaned forward, and touched her forehead to his shoulder, too embarrassed by the tears in her eyes to let him see them. When she had herself under control again, she pulled back, and found she had squashed her pie.

He laughed at her soft swearing, and then fed her the broken bits.

"Heyla." Massi's call caught Ava by surprise, and she felt herself tense.

Luc's friend was smiling when she pulled up beside them. "You are doing a good job of lifting the column's spirits."

There was no sarcastic edge to the words.

"Why were they low?" She addressed the question to Luc.

"They weren't low, but the daily grind of packing up and moving every day, with weeks of more of the same in sight, wears everyone down." Luc seemed relaxed with Massi again.

Ava looked between them.

"Massi found a cup in front of her tent the day after you arrived with the Venyatux," Luc said into the silence. "It had her name carved into it. She's been using it every day since then."

Ava turned to look at him.

"We threw it in the fire last night."

"Who gave it to you?" Ava asked.

"I don't know." Massi looked away. "It seems weak to say that was the excuse for my behavior. I take responsibility for my actions."

"No." Ava reached out and gripped her forearm. "We must find out who made it."

Massi's horse shifted uneasily. "Luc also thinks this is serious."

"It is," Ava agreed. "We have a spell caster with evil intent."

"As apposed to one with good intent?" Massi asked.

Ava drew herself up. Before she could speak, Luc leaned closer.

"Still listening to Haslia, Massi? Or Revek?"

Massi shook her head. "I spent the night thinking of spell castings, of people doing things they wouldn't do of their own free will, and I remembered Derek, and the way he sobbed when we caught up with him after you were captured by the Kassian."

"You think he was enspelled?" Luc sat back in his saddle, clearly horrified. "That whoever this is has been with us for that long?"

Massi nodded. "But I also remembered how he kept saying they had cut you to the bone, that he could see down to the bone on your arm."

Ava looked down at Luc's left forearm.

It felt like a very long time ago she had stitched it, but it was only two months.

Massi reached out and touched Luc. "There should at least be a scar." She ran a finger over his smooth skin. Look over at Ava with brows raised.

"There will be a scar on Revek's shoulder and on Frederik's cheek." Ava kept her voice soft.

She hoped.

She had tried her best to make sure some evidence of their injury remained.

"That's good. Probably for them as well as you." Massi still held her gaze.

"What happened to Derek?" Luc asked. "I've meant to ask you that a few times."

At last Massi looked away. "He killed himself. We were planning to execute him, but he somehow got a knife and did it himself."

"Somehow?" Luc's disbelief was audible.

"Yes." Massi shrugged. "Very convenient."

"This a private party?" Dak called.

Ava had caught a glimpse of someone approaching from behind her, and her heart sped a little faster. She did not want this conversation shared with anyone else.

She hadn't exactly admitted her spell casting to Massi, but it appeared the lieutenant had put the pieces together.

It made her feel like every eye, from both columns, was on her.

"Not anymore." There was a wry tone to Luc's response.

Dak grinned, unrepentant. "I was looking at the map again—"

Ava held up a hand. "Should I go?"

"Luc trusts you. That's good enough for me," Dak said. He pulled out a map. "I think the general is right to get us to consider other places of attack, and I wonder what you think about here."

Luc bent closer, and Ava did, too.

"You think they might hide in those hills?" Luc tapped at the place.

"They could get a lot of units in there, and we wouldn't see them until they rushed out." Dak sounded grim.

"We'll send a team there to keep watch," Luc said.

"That's three groups we'll need if we're also going to scout the other two places. How many are we going to include in each team?" Massi frowned as she nudged her mount closer to look at the map as well.

"Is the meeting here, now?"

Ava had watched Fervanti approach.

She clasped a fist to her chest in a salute to the Whispering Grasses and bowed to the lieutenant.

"Avasu. Should you be included in this?"

Ava lifted her shoulders. "Probably not."

"Then off with you." Her words weren't rude, though. They were laced with humor. "If you have time off, go enjoy yourself."

"I was trying to." She mumbled it, but Luc heard and shot her a delighted grin and Massi laughed.

"It's my fault. I interrupted them while they were trying to have a little time alone."

There were too many horses milling about for her to get close to Luc again, but he caught her eye and tapped his heart with two fingers and then brushed his hand downward just as she did the same.

Dak made a sound in the back of his throat. "Behold, and tremble. The mighty and feared Commander of the Rising Wave." He gave an exaggerated gesture in Luc's direction.

Luc's response was to throw back his head and laugh. He wheeled his horse around, blew Ava a kiss, and then raced toward the head of the column, managing to lean over and smack Dak in the back of the head as he passed him.

Dak had been teasing him, but Ava thought of the hyper-aggressions and chest thumping that went on in the Kassian fortress where she'd been held for two years. Luc was stronger than any of them.

As she watched them ride toward the head of the column, she thought about the problem of the Kassian attack points Dak had pointed to on the map, and the scouts who would be sent to watch for any sign of Kassian movement.

She could help.

She would just need to find the best way to do it. And the least obvious.

CHAPTER 27

Luc found Ava after the columns had ground to a halt for the evening, in the back of the store master's cart.

He had received a request earlier for permission to allow her access to the stores, and he had given it, even though Rustef, the store master's clerk, had seemed disapproving when he had waved him away with an 'anything Ava wants'.

She was sitting beside two lit lamps, head bent over her work, humming.

Pearl, the store master, watched her from her seat on a wooden bench, chewing on a piece of dried meat. Rustef was nowhere to be seen.

Luc reached up to grab the side of the cart and haul himself inside, but Pearl caught his eye and shook her head. She moved toward him quietly, and dropped down to the ground beside him.

"Wait until she's finished." Her voice was hushed.

Luc stared at her, because Pearl usually had no time for anything except buying more stock and bulk bargains.

She must have realized how out of character it was, because she shrugged. "I'm not one to coddle, but that girl is a master at her craft. And while maybe I think it's a waste of her time to spend so much effort on items that'll just get bloody and torn, it's her time to waste, isn't it?"

"What is she doing?"

It was Pearl's turn to stare at him. "Didn't Rustef come to you and ask if she had permission? He was certainly grumpy enough when he came back."

"He asked if she could have full access to the stores. I told him yes."

Pearl's face went smooth and blank, and Luc wondered if Rustef would be looking for a new job come tomorrow.

"That wasn't what was being asked. She asked whether I would let her work some designs into the padding the scouts wear when they go out on patrol."

"He asked for a lot more than that, hoping I'd say no." Luc was happy for Pearl to do as she wanted with him.

"She asked politely. Didn't assume I'd say yes, even though I know she's your lady." Pearl turned back to look at her, and Luc did the same.

The lamp light illuminated her cheekbones and the curve of her brows. Her hair was growing out, but it was still short from when it had been chopped off by her captors.

She was caught in her own world, unaware of anything around her as her needle flashed in and out.

"This is what she's already done." Pearl leaned into the cart and took out one of the vests. It was constructed to be sleeveless, with ties on the sides to secure it in place. It was made from a layer of silk, a thick layer of felted wool and then another layer of silk. It didn't stop an arrow or a sword, but it helped the wearer survive longer, even if just to get to a healer in time.

Luc held it in both hands, and had to angle the fabric toward the lamp light to see.

Ava had used thread that was a similar color to the raw silk, a pale yellow, and down one side of the vest she had embroidered a soldier holding up a shield to a field of arrows flying toward her. On the other side was a soldier blocking a sword blow with a sword of his own. Along the edges, he recognized patterns from the wall hangings from his village hall before the Kassian had raided them and taken him away.

Cervantes heritage.

Pearl traced the edge with a finger. "She spent the morning talking to Kali and others about our ways, and then she came and incorporated them into the protective vests."

Now Luc knew why his taciturn stores master was letting his lover have everything she needed. Pearl had joined the Rising Wave, left her people, because she wanted to personally have helped bring down the Kassian for what they had done to the Cervantes. The stealing of an entire generation, the loss that meant to the traditions and history of their people.

And Ava was trying to work a little of that back into their lives. As well as work some magic into it, too.

The humming stopped, and Ava looked up at him, then rubbed her eyes and yawned. "Time for dinner?"

"Yes."

"I've done four, Pearl. Thank you for letting me play."

"It's been a pleasure watching you work." Pearl watched as Luc lifted Ava down to the ground and gave an approving nod when he slid his arm around her shoulder. "You're welcome any time."

Luc gave her a wave and then steered Ava away. She was a little unsteady on her feet and rubbed the back of her neck.

"What were you doing that's drained you so much?" He had never thought of the toll working magic must take.

She leaned in close. "Protection against weapons. Maybe more."

"Maybe?"

She shrugged. "Sometimes the working does more than I thought it would. It takes on a wider interpretation of my original intent."

"Like?" He thought of his own improved reflexes and the way arrows bent out of his way.

"Like I worked a protection into my old cloak to warn me of people who meant me harm, but then I began to know what everyone thought of me, like or dislike. The working grew in scope."

"Like a handkerchief that was given to protect me, as a broad measure, but ended up making me able to anticipate the moves of three assassins almost before they struck."

She was silent, and he stopped, reached out to turn her to face him.

She worried her lip a little. "That might be from . . ." She looked up at him.

"From . . .?"

"From how I sewed strength, agility and health into you when I stitched up your wounds."

He studied her face. "That was two months ago, Ava. That surely couldn't still be in place, although, thank you for that. It has saved my life a few times."

"I think maybe my workings last more than a few months." She lifted her shoulders. "I'm not sure. But the general says something my grandmother made her lasted two years."

"You are at least as strong as your grandmother?" He asked the question softly, and she hesitated. Shrugged.

"I didn't realize the general knows your secret."

She turned, sliding her arm around him and tugged him forward. "She's known all along, but I only discovered that she knew last night. I offered to make something for her."

"I'm sure she was thrilled to accept."

She stopped, bringing them to a halt a little way from the campfire near his tent, out of earshot. "I said I'd create a working to help her find the two Grimwaldian spies in the Venyatux column. I'm the reason they're there, so I felt it was right to help find them. The general is going to wear what I'm making herself and hunt them down. Do you want something similar for the spies in the Rising Wave?"

He did. He really did.

He nodded.

"I'll work it into your shirt when I get a chance." She hesitated. "The general thinks I can only work magic into my embroidery if I use black silk thread. That's all my mother and grandmother used. But I don't need it to be black silk to work." She touched her hair. "I used strands of my hair once, that's why they cut it off. I can use anything I find. It works with canvas, with any cloth, and even with skin." She touched his arm, where once she had sewn up his injury, before he knew and loved her. "But that is a secret between only you and me."

She was building on her heart's song, he realized. On the oath she swore that he need not fear her. Because she wasn't hiding her skills from him. But still she stood, eyes down, hands clasped.

"There is something else." Her knuckles were white. "Something I haven't shared with you."

"And if it upsets you so much to tell me, then leave it for now." He drew her close, kissed her forehead. "I don't need all your secrets at once."

She looked up at him, gave a slow nod.

He didn't like that something weighed on her as much as this secret seemed to, but his words had soothed her, and when someone called to her, as they stepped into the light thrown by the fire, she called a laughing reply.

He would accept some secrets for a lightness in her step.

"I HAVE ANOTHER REQUEST." AVA HANDED THE BLACK SCARF TO THE general.

General Ru took it, studying Ava's work by the lamplight, and then lifted her jacket and shirt and wound the scarf around her waist.

"You aren't going to wear it around your neck?"

"No. If they suspect you have your grandmother's abilities, anything black will surely worry them. I decided last night it would be better to hide it completely."

"It will work even better close to your skin," Ava conceded. "So that's an added benefit."

The general inclined her head. "Good. So what is this request?"

"I overheard some of the plans being made to send scouting parties to check where you think the Kassian may attack. I would like to be in one of them." She knew Luc would be unhappy about this, but the scouts left tomorrow. The one way to find out what the enemy was going to do was to listen to them, and no one could get closer, unobserved, than she could.

It would be too dangerous, too revealing, to sew an invisibility cloak for someone else. It would take too much explaining, and reveal too much about herself.

She had woven a fine problem that had caught her in its web. But she wouldn't change anything. Her secrets were hers, and she would protect them. Protect herself.

"Why?" The general sat down on one of the cushions she kept in her meeting space, and Ava sank down opposite her.

"Because I would be useful."

The general stared at her for a long moment and gave a slow nod. "You would reveal yourself to the other scouts? Tell them what you can do?"

"Not if I can help it, no. But if it means the difference between the success or failure of the Rising Wave, I would expose myself in a heartbeat."

General Ru tapped her lips. "I agree that you would be a secret weapon. An extra chance at success. I was going to send Deni. I'll let him know you will be joining him."

"Thank you." She rose up. At least Deni was a good friend. It would be easier to tell him the truth, if it came to that, than someone she didn't know as well.

"Avasu."

She turned back. "Yes?"

"You tell your lover about this, and tell him tonight. I don't want to have to deal with his anger tomorrow morning."

"I intend to." As she walked out, she thought she saw the general give a rueful shake of her head.

She had always planned to tell Luc tonight. And she was glad that she had spelled their little bedroom to keep in all sound, because she feared it would get noisy. And not in the good way it had been last night.

CHAPTER 28

The feeling that someone meant her harm started the moment Ava stepped out of the general's tent.

She paused, and Catja, who was back on guard duty, looked over at her.

"What is it?"

"I feel eyes on me. Unfriendly eyes."

Catja nodded. "Sufro and I have been saying exactly that for the last half hour."

Ava glanced at her, surprised. "Have you worked out what direction it's coming from?"

The guard shook her head.

After another careful look around, Ava began to walk back to the Rising Wave.

Was the growing feeling of danger from the protective workings hidden in her cuffs and collar, or was it more visceral, like Catja and Sufro were experiencing?

In the past, when she had worn her old cloak, she had sensed this often, but it had felt like it came from a distance, someone watching her through the tents but who was too far away to harm her physically.

She had only had a closer brush with whoever it was who stalked her a few times, and they had moved away quickly each time.

Except for when they hunted her at night.

She had been roused from sleep many times over the weeks she'd traveled with the Venyatux, but they always moved away quickly and she had never wanted to chance poking her head out and revealing herself to see who they were.

Now, the feeling of imminent danger grew with every step, the embroidery touching the skin of her wrists and neck suddenly hot and chafing.

She gave in to the warnings suddenly, instinct causing her to crouch down and turn, just as a stick passed over her head with a whistle.

She let out a warning call, because this was an enemy in their midsts. The ululation seemed to bounce around her. Carila had taught her it was the carrying cry used in the high mountains to warn of Skäddar raids and mountain lion attacks.

"That won't help you." The stick was swung again, but Ava was already back on her feet, dancing out of the way.

"The Speaker's messenger," she said. She had thought it must be him who followed her through Grimwalt, but she hadn't caught sight of his face once in all the weeks she'd been with the Venyatu. She couldn't see his face now either in the darkness, but it was his voice.

She remembered it well as he'd tried to drag her from her grandmother's hall.

"You should have just come when you were told." He grunted with effort as he swung the stick again.

She wondered why he was using a stick when he had a sword hanging from his belt. But he was herding her with his attacks, she realized. Trying to maneuver her somewhere that suited him better.

"Your orders are to bring me back alive." She spun, trying to edge back toward the original spot where he'd attacked her. Trying to keep from going in the direction he wanted her to go. "Why did you shoot at me, then? Your arrows nearly got me twice."

"I was aiming for your shoulder." He struck out in frustration when she forced him full circle, back to where they started. She could see his face at last, and held back a gasp when it didn't match his voice at all. This was not the man she remembered.

She drew in a deep breath and ululated again, wondering why no one had come out to help her, or at least see what was going on.

"They can't hear you." She could hear the smile in his voice.

"What the fuck are you doing, Vane? You're supposed to be sending her my way." The voice came out of the darkness behind her attacker.

She remembered this voice, too. The second abductor who had appeared out of nowhere to help drag her away. He loomed out of the darkness, and to her relief, his face was as she remembered it.

"You try getting her to go the direction you want, then." Vane turned and hissed the words over his shoulder.

The moment his attention was off her, Ava jumped off the path into a small patch of ground surrounded by tents. There was a faint pop in her ears and she drew in a deep breath, and gave the warning cry again.

She could hear people stirring immediately.

Vane appeared suddenly beside her, and she realized he was shouting, although she couldn't hear a single sound.

She hoped her own silence working in Luc and the general's tents was as good as this and she wondered how they had done it.

Lights began to flare as people scrambled out into the night, and she ululated again as she finally had a chance to pull her knife from her boot sheath.

Vane's arm was raised to strike her again, and there was nowhere for her to go but toward him, but his companion must have called to him because he looked over his shoulder. The blooming lanterns all around them illuminated the two men fully for the first time.

The second abductor was winding up what looked like a length of black rope and suddenly she could hear them shouting to each other.

She tilted her head. The rope was spelled.

She wondered if she could do that.

The idea appealed to her greatly.

And she wouldn't need black for the rope, although she didn't know if they chose the color to make it all but invisible in the darkness or because the spell caster had to work in black.

Even as he turned to run, Vane swung his stick at her head.

She dived forward, avoiding the strike and tackling him around the waist as he tried to follow his friend.

His shout brought his companion running back, and Vane struck out at her with an elbow to her face.

She managed to turn her head in time but it loosened her hold on him, and then he was gone.

"What's happening?" Catja was suddenly beside her, and then the general, in some flowing garments she took to be their leader's silk pyjamas.

"The unfriendly eyes." She pointed in the direction they had run and then flopped back down.

"Are you hurt?" General Ru crouched beside her as Catja called to a few others and ran in the direction she had pointed.

Ava shook her head. "No. But I feel . . ." Suddenly, it was as if a weight had lifted off her, and the general crouched over her with her knife extended, a thin piece of rope hanging from it.

"It was over your shoulder," the general said. She brought the knife closer and looked at the short rope with interest.

"They also used rope to create an area of silence, so no one could hear us."

"Is that so?"

Ava sat up and looked carefully at the rope. Like the one they'd use for silence, this one was also black, although much finer.

"This could come in useful." The general seemed pleased. "Did you recognize them?"

"I recognized their voices but only one of their faces." She frowned. She was sure she wasn't mistaken.

"They would have had to have a way to change their faces if they wanted to keep you from finding them. Especially being around you every day."

The general spoke so casually of changing appearances, but Ava hadn't heard that was possible. "How would they do that?"

"I've heard of one person who could do that. But that was many years ago."

"Where is that spell caster from?"

"Grimwalt." The general smiled. "As so many of you are."

"Being in Grimwalt is what keeps us safe." Ava had heard that saying many times in her childhood. Now she wondered if it had ever been true, or whether it was only the rise of the new Speaker that meant spell casters had to be wary in what was once their safe haven.

And it had never been true for her mother. She needed to remember that.

"I've heard that said." The general rose up and offered Ava a hand up, keeping the rope balanced on her knife and away from both of them.

"They meant to use this on me to keep me weak so they could carry me away." Ava reached out to touch it, felt the bite on her fingers as the magic tried to grab her, and pulled her hand away, shaking it as if burned.

"They were fools if they thought they could get even half a mile away before your lover chased them down." The general turned, and as she did, Luc loomed suddenly out of the darkness, moving with that silent, deadly focus she had seen more than once.

The general went still, and Ava was impressed she hadn't flinched as he appeared.

She was right, though.

Vane and his friend would not have lasted ten minutes.

"Ava." He pulled her toward him, and she lifted a hand to his face.

"I'm fine."

"Who?" He looked around with a grim expression, and then his gaze snagged on the rope still dangling from the general's knife.

"Enspelled," the general said and Luc bent closer.

"What did it do?"

"Made me weak." Ava put her hands in her pockets, unwilling to touch it again. "They were trying to abduct me, not kill me."

"Who is they?" he asked again.

"The Grimwaldian spies." She heard the sound of Catja and the others calling up ahead.

"They'd have had everything ready to go," Ava said. "They were planning to grab me and run. They'll be long gone. And using magic to hide themselves, if what I saw in the attack is any indication."

"Why now?" The general asked.

"My guess is they learned we'd found the missives from the Speaker of Grimwalt, and that we knew they were in the column." Ava lifted her shoulders. "They probably had some magical means of finding that out. I don't think anyone is a traitor."

"Hmm." The general eyed the rope. "What you say is likely."

"I don't want them getting away and running back to tell the Speaker his plans have been spoiled." Luc was suddenly gone, and Ava peered into the darkness to try and see his silhouette.

"There is something almost otherworldly about the way he moves." The general's voice was soft.

"I have always thought so, too," Ava agreed, and then found the general looking at her with interest.

She turned and walked away.

"Don't forget to mention your assignment for tomorrow," the general called after her, and Ava winced as she waved in acknowledgment.

It was going to be a lot harder to convince Luc to let her go now than it had been before this attack.

CHAPTER 29

This time, Luc found Ava in his bed.

He was not at all unhappy about that.

Except she was fast asleep, holding a piece of cotton in her hand. She'd been embroidering it, and even in sleep her fingers were gripping the needle.

"Ava." He whispered her name and she stirred, then opened her eyes with a snap.

"Did you get them?" Her voice came out husky and something within him stirred.

"We shot one in the back, and he's dead. The other one got away." The spy hadn't ridden in the direction of Grimwalt though. That didn't mean he wasn't going to double back, but Luc wondered if he hadn't decided he would have better luck and a warmer welcome on the heels of the missives to the queen at Fernwell than to his scheming master in Grimwalt. Especially as he wasn't bringing a captured Ava back with him.

And Luc found he wasn't unhappy about that outcome. Especially not with the subtle changes to the letters that Ava had made.

The Grimwaldian was in for a cooler reception than he thought.

He looked Ava over, but she seemed unharmed by her clash with the two men.

"What were you doing?" He noticed two other strips of cloth beside the bed.

"This is for the Venyatux who will be part of the scout party. I can't ask to embroider their vests without letting the general know I don't need to use black thread, so I'm going to give these to them privately. Tell them it's for good luck, like I did for Deni yesterday."

"They'll be lucky to have your work protecting them on their scouting trip."

She sighed, and set her work aside. Then pulled him down beside her.

He felt a shift in the mood, and turned his head to look at her. Her expression was the most serious he had ever seen.

"Luc, I have to go with the scouts. I have to *be* a scout."

Everything in him said no. He forced himself to swallow the word and listen. But he didn't like it. At all.

"This is the most important thing we have to contend with before we get to Fernwell. We won't *get* to Fernwell if we don't stop or anticipate an attack along the route."

He gave a slow nod.

"And if I'm with the scouts, and we find a possible attack point, I can sneak unseen into the enemy camp and listen to their plans."

That was true. But the dangers . . . "The scouts are breaking up into three groups. You only have a one in three chance of being in the right place."

"My suggestion is I be allowed to move between the groups. In fact, I should go to all three places. I can set some . . . traps."

"Traps?"

She lifted her eyes, and he saw her hesitation, as if she wasn't sure how he would react.

"I could leave . . . things for people to pick up. Or for dogs to sniff out—"

"The dogs." He felt as if someone had hit him in the head. "When we were running from the Kassian, you turned the dogs away from us. And got them to ignore us the second time they came after us."

She nodded.

"What happened to them?" The memory suddenly came back to him, of him standing in the woods, back against a tree, hearing the pack of dogs coming after him and then they simply ran past, not even looking his way. They disappeared into the forest and he never saw them again.

"I had them meet me at the edge of the forest. I took them with me to Grimwalt. They're safe and happy."

"You had them meet you . . ." She didn't seem to realize how powerful she was. But she was right that he needed to put aside his need to shield her from a fight she was only too happy to jump into and use her like any good leader would.

But as she so eloquently stated, this was the most important issue they had to contend with until they got to Fernwell. Important enough he should be part of it, too.

If they were taken by surprise before they could get to Fernwell, their chances of taking the city were almost nothing.

"We'll need to get some sleep, then. We leave early tomorrow."

She blinked at him in surprise, studying him calmly. "You are coming with us."

"I am coming with you," he agreed.

"Because?"

"Because as you say, this is important. Important enough that one of the two column leaders should go. Also, I don't want you away from me. I think I've made that clear since you left me near the Grimwalt border two months ago."

She sighed and sank back into the pillows. "I hope you never have cause to regret it."

"And why would I do that?" He lowered himself down, a hand on either side of her head.

She was silent.

"Answer me this." He balanced on his elbows and pushed the hair back from her forehead. "Is this secret you find so hard to tell me something you've done, some confession you have to make for your own actions, or is it something you have no control over?"

She went still. "It's something I have no control over."

"Then tell me when you are ready, lover. But never believe I'll regret you being by my side."

She lifted up and placed her lips against his, and he sank down into her embrace.

He realized he truly didn't care what it was she found so hard to tell him, except that it obviously weighed on her.

As she rolled him under her and straddled him, eyes slumberous and heavy, he groaned.

They had to be up early, but there was surely time for this.

THEY HAD RIDDEN HARD, LEAVING THE COLUMNS FAR BEHIND THEM, and reached the first spot Dak had chosen as a possible ambush site in the early afternoon.

Ava was lagging at the back.

She was a lot better in the saddle than she had been two months ago when she escaped, but the Cervantes, the Venyatux, and the Funabi were all accomplished riders. More accomplished than she was, anyway.

As she rounded the bend, with only Catja in sight, Ava thought she glimpsed the hindquarters of a horse, just disappearing around the side of one of the small hills Dak had flagged as a good hiding spot for the Kassian army.

She considered giving a whoop to alert Catja, but instead gritted her teeth and urged her horse into a gallop.

Catja heard the hoofbeats and slowed, then turned in her saddle.

Ava fisted her left hand, lifted it to her right shoulder and gave a tap. The sign for danger.

Catja's eyes widened and she slowed even more, until Ava was abreast of her.

"There's someone in the hills to the right." Ava spoke softly. "Don't look that way. It's best right now we pretend I didn't see whoever it was."

"Agreed." Catja pretended to stretch out her back, lifting her hands over her head and twisting left and then right.

"I don't hear anything. And I don't know how many are there. I only saw one horse." Ava reached for a water pouch and drank.

"What should we do?" Catja patted her horse's neck. "Maybe if we keep walking, the Commander will stop and wait for us, or come back and see what's wrong."

"If they have chosen this spot as a place to ambush the Rising Wave, we need them to continue to believe we have no idea of their plan. We don't want them to find somewhere else." Ava reached back into her saddle bag and took out some flat bread. They had stopped for a quick meal two hours before, and it wasn't time for another break, but Catja took the bread and chewed with gusto, talking of inconsequential things.

It took less than ten minutes for Luc to come thundering back.

Deni rode behind him.

Luc was quick. So very, very quick.

Something in the way she and Catja were talking together told him everything she needed him to know.

He turned his head to say something to Deni, but the direction the wind was blowing made it impossible to hear.

She saw Deni freeze, but just for a moment, and then relax in his saddle.

"My horse has given up for the day," Ava called out when they got within earshot.

"Varik's has done the same, just up ahead. We thought you might be having the same problem." When Luc turned his horse back around, he put himself between Ava and the hills. "What did you see?" He leaned close to her.

"Someone on horseback ducking behind the hill just over my right shoulder."

Luc looked grim. "We shouldn't have let you get so far behind."

"I'm just not as at home in a saddle as the rest of you." She flashed him a smile. "And it had the benefit of making them think we'd all gone past, and they made a mistake."

"It won't happen again." He turned as Deni reached them. "We're going to walk slowly to join the others, as if Ava's horse is unable to go faster than a walk, and then we're going to find a place that's out of sight of anyone on this side of the hills, and set up camp for the night."

"What about those of us who're going to the river?" Deni asked.

They had all traveled together, but they had planned to split up a little way ahead, with one group staying in this area, the others heading for the massive Bartolo River to check the Kassian ambush spots there, one on each side of it.

Catja passed a piece of flatbread to Deni and he broke some off, then threw the last bit to Luc.

"The group that was going to stay here obviously can't do that anymore." Luc rose up in his saddle and waved, and Ava realized he could see far enough ahead to hail the others. "Not with the Kassian right here. They won't use this as their ambush spot if they know we've already identified it."

They rode the rest of the way in silence.

One of the Rising Wave scouts, Oscar, had noticed an outcrop around the back of one of the hills, which had a waterfall nearby, and they urged their mounts up the gentle slope until they found a place flat enough for the tents.

"They can't see us, but that means we can't see them, either," Deni said. "I don't like them behind us."

"Neither do I, but we have to let them think we're just stopping for the night on our way somewhere else."

"Are we going to try find out how many of them there are?" Varik, one of the Funabi faction of the Rising Wave, swung off his horse and began untying his tent.

"Ava and I will go later, when it's dark." Luc took the tent he'd brought for both of them, and set it up in quick, economical movements.

"You and Ava?" Hector, another Cervantes soldier, didn't hide his surprise.

"Ava's worked as a spy for General Ru." Deni's defense of her was edged in annoyance. "She's proven her abilities."

"A spy?" One of the women from the Funabi army, Talura, tilted her head. "I hadn't heard that."

"That's how she and the Commander met." Catja dropped to the ground herself. "They were imprisoned together."

"I've heard the tale." Oscar suddenly grinned. "Aren't you one of the Venyatu's sparring champions?"

Ava nodded, then flicked a smiling, sidelong look at her lover. "When Luc isn't whisking me away from the fights."

"I've lost some money because of that." Deni shook his head, and started setting up his tent.

Oscar chuckled, and gave him a commiserating thump on his shoulder as he walked past.

No one said anything more, but Ava thought the mood shifted a little, became less edgy.

Because they were stopping so much earlier than they'd planned, there was still plenty of light, and Ava settled down to embroider her cloak.

She had given the thin scarves she'd worked to Deni and Catja this morning, as a gift of good luck, she'd called it, and both had seemed delighted, exclaiming over the Venyatu designs.

The two of them made up the Venyatu faction, Hector and Oscar were Cervantes and Varik and Talura were Funabi. A nice even representation of the columns.

Ava and Luc had skewed that dynamic, and she understood they needed to readjust.

At least everyone had some protection.

The stores master, Pearl, had given out the vests to the four scouts from the Rising Wave and Ava was glad to see them wearing them.

She pulled out her small sewing pouch and threaded her needle.

She had managed to fit her knitting into her saddle bag, but her first priority was to work on her cloak. She felt naked without all the protections she'd once had.

"Why are you stitching on the inside where no one can see?" Catja sat beside her and started setting up the campfire.

"I'm practicing new stitches." Ava looked up from her work, hoping the lie sounded natural. "I don't have the right colors, either, and all the traders say they won't have what I'm looking for until they get to a big town. So I'm playing around where no one will see it."

Catja peered closer. "Your practice stitches look better than anything I've ever seen for sale."

Ava lifted her shoulders. "Thank you. I want it to be colorful, though. Oranges, blues, greens. Flowers, birds, leaves. The dark gray of the cloak will be a good background for it. So I'll play around until I can buy the thread I need."

The others had been listening in to their conversation, and Ava hoped they accepted her excuse. She didn't look at Luc, who was putting up a tent for them to share.

He would know she was lying, and it made her uncomfortable, but not enough to change her story.

She was stitching the part of her cloak that centered down her spine. Even if the wind blew the sides back and exposed the lining beneath, no one would see a single stitch.

She liked that idea. Liked it a lot.

"What are you humming?" Varik sat on her other side and began to help Catja stack logs.

"Nothing specific. It's a habit I've got into when I sew." Ava hunched her shoulders.

She could feel too many eyes on her now. Not in an unfriendly way, but she didn't like being the center of attention when she was doing a working.

"Why don't you sing for us, Varik?" Luc found space beside Ava and slung an arm around her shoulders. "I've heard from your captain you're considered one of the best."

The others began to tease the Funabi about his voice, and eventually he was persuaded to sing.

The fire was going, and Hector and Oscar began setting up the small pots they'd brought along, getting dinner on the go.

Ava leaned closer and gave a quick kiss to Luc's neck.

He'd seen her discomfort and distracted the others for her. She felt as if her heart could not be contained in her body as she relaxed against him, sewing in quick, sure movements as the last of the evening light washed over her.

She was working protection into her cloak, but her feelings for Luc kept creeping in, and she had to try and concentrate on deflecting arrows, and swords, and blows with fists.

Eventually dinner was ready and she set her cloak aside, eating and laughing with the others.

In a way it was good they could pretend they didn't know the Kassian were skulking about. They could enjoy themselves with a warm fire and hot stew, while the Kassian would have to stay quiet in the dark.

The fire burned lower, and Catja started yawning.

"When are you going on your little excursion?" Oscar asked, voice soft.

"Now. Make sure two of you are always on watch. If we get into trouble we can't get out of, we'll call."

Ava went to her saddle bag and got out the two scarves she'd woken before dawn this morning to embroider for herself and Luc, and slid them into her pocket.

"Ready?" Luc strapped his sword to his back and lifted the hood of his dark cloak.

She nodded and they slipped quietly down the hillside.

As soon as the darkness swallowed them, Ava handed Luc one of the scarves and pulled on the other one, winding it over her head and tying it at her throat.

Once it was on him, he disappeared completely, and she stopped for a moment, amazed at how well it worked.

"Ava?" he stopped himself, turning slowly to find her, and she reached out a hand to touch the air where she thought he was, her hand encountering his warm, hard body.

"It works really well." She smiled and found his hand and took it in hers.

"Don't let go or we'll lose each other." He squeezed her hand and she squeezed back.

Time to find out what the Kassian were up to.

CHAPTER 30

The Kassian said nothing.

Luc was reluctantly impressed.

He hadn't found the Kassian forces to be that impressive as a whole.

When they had first taken the older Chosen from the camps and tried to integrate them into the main Kassian military, it had been a disaster.

Luc had seen to that.

He smiled to himself at the memory.

The low-level insults he'd had his fellow Chosen murmur to the Kassian while they trained, needling them until they snapped, working out what made them furious the fastest.

There were fights every couple of hours, bad blood on both sides, until things got so bad it was decided the Chosen would form their own units. Be separate from the main Kassian army.

Luc had had a hard time pretending to be angry when he'd been told by the major in charge of his division that they realized the Chosen weren't civilized enough to work with the normal Kassian forces.

He'd lived under the eye of a rotating list of generals watching him as he was given the job of training his own people, and he'd had to be harsh to some of the younger ones who'd gotten a little too cocky and obvious about how happy they were to be back together.

He'd had his fellow Chosen all pretend to be a little less than they were. Not so much as to make the Kassian suspicious, but enough to look only slightly more impressive than the regular Kassian soldiers. Enough to make some of them wonder why the Cervantes children had been considered such a military prize in the first place.

He hoped that impression was still in the minds of the generals even after the Chosen had turned on them on the battlefield and wiped out the army the Queen's Herald had sent to crush the Venyatu.

Better to be underestimated.

And in the end, he'd done what he'd set out to do.

Made the Kassian rue the day they'd invaded Cervantes and stolen away their children.

He would make the queen herself regret it, personally, when they reached Fernwell.

But however ordinary the soldiers he'd originally trained with after the camps had been, these scouts were hardened. Professional.

He and Ava had found a tree to mark where they'd meet back up, and then they had drifted apart. Ava to search the saddle bags on the horses, him to walk through the camp and find out how many there were, and what they had to say.

There were five horses tied to a tree, and Luc counted three scouts sleeping, one sitting watch.

The scout on guard shifted uneasily as Luc walked past him, looking over his shoulder and then shaking his head before turning back to watch the trees in front of him.

The horses nickered and the guard stood up and walked over, more alert than he had been.

Luc started moving toward the horses as well, hand up on the hilt of his sword, but the guard walked around the horses, patted one, and then went back to sit down.

"What's wrong?" One of the men sleeping by the fire sat up.

"Nothing." The guard rubbed at his eyes.

"Boris back yet?"

Luc went still, and then saw a shadow separate itself from the darkness and move toward the low fire.

"I thought we weren't doing a fire?"

"They're on the other side of the hill, B. Fuck's sake. It's freezing." The man who had woken flopped back down. "Were you able to get close enough to hear them?"

"No." Boris went down on his haunches by the fire and rubbed his hands over the flames. "They picked a good spot. I could see their silhouettes around the fire, but I wasn't close enough to hear what they were saying. They're obviously on their way somewhere. One of their horses caught a stone or something and they stopped early, that's all."

"We're just lucky they didn't see us." The guard turned to join in the conversation.

"Can you imagine?" The man lying by the fire spoke quietly, and for a moment, absolute silence descended.

Luc knew all too well what their punishment would have been if they had let themselves be seen by the Rising Wave and ruined the ambush plans. He'd been in the Kassian military long enough. And in the Chosen camps before that. The Kassian didn't have any mercy to spare. Even for their own.

These scouts would lie about it even being a possibility to save their skins.

"If we're going to keep mapping the area for the Herald after they're gone tomorrow, some of us will need to get some sleep." The man yawned as he spoke.

"And we'll need to be cautious on our way back, because I doubt this lot is going one way. They'll be coming back. They're probably going to look at the river for good spots for their army to cross and then they'll return with the information." Boris lowered himself down.

Luc stood for a bit longer, while Boris got comfortable, and then the guard woke someone else to take their turn.

He slipped away as the new guard yawned and rubbed his eyes, trying to wake up.

When he got to the tree, he pulled off the scarf, and Ava did the same.

"Boris walked right past me. I could have reached out and touched him." She took his hand, her voice soft.

"They said they're mapping the area for the Herald, and the only reason they'd do that is so the generals can know how many soldiers they can hide among the hills." Luc admired the planning and the idea. Someone in the Kassian military was using their brains.

He was also very glad Ava had caught a glimpse of them.

If they'd left a team here, without realizing the Kassian were here already, who knew how it would have ended.

When they reached the camp, Oscar rose up from the shadows, and Deni turned from his place by the fire.

"That didn't take long."

They were all awake, Luc saw with satisfaction. Everyone came quietly from a hiding place.

"They sent a spy out here," Deni said.

"We crossed paths with him on the way back." Luc kept his voice low and sat beside Deni. "We'll have to assume they're always there."

Ava knelt close to him and put her hands out to warm them. He liked watching the way the light touched her face.

Oscar crowded in beside her, and the others drifted closer.

"They do plan to attack us here." Luc pulled his gaze off Ava, unable to hide his satisfaction. "They're mapping the area."

"So what do we do?" Talura's voice was barely a whisper.

"They think we're scouting ahead for places to cross the river, which isn't a bad guess. So that's what we're going to let them keep thinking." And when they came back, they'd have to make enough noise to warn the Kassian to keep out of sight.

They worked out a guard roster, and as he crawled into the tent behind Ava, and then wrapped her in his arms to sleep, Luc could almost taste the battle to come.

Between him and General Ru, they'd have to come up with a plan to turn the ambush against the Kassian.

It would be almost as satisfying as turning against them on the battlefield two years ago.

He would make sure the name they'd given him was something they'd live to regret, too.

CHAPTER 31

The Kassian scouts were still in the hills.

As they rode back, two days later, Ava sensed them.

They had to be close, hidden somewhere she couldn't see, because her new cloak was not as sensitive as her old one.

She needed time to work in the same number of protections, and she had a feeling some of the old cloak's strength had developed over time.

When they'd left the hills a few days before, someone had followed them all the way to the river and back. Luc had sensed it, too, and had warned everyone to assume that's what the Kassian would do.

The uneasiness had been a consistent tingle at the back of her neck. In her old cloak, she'd have been able to pinpoint where the spy was.

Now the hills were behind them, though, and they had nothing but open plain between themselves and the columns. The feeling of being watched had eased a few hours ago and she felt light now that the weight of the stare had lifted off her.

"What were you doing this morning?" Catja had been riding beside her for a while and Ava turned to look at her in surprise.

"With the strips of fabric," Catja clarified.

Ava hadn't realized anyone had seen her. Luc had kept the others distracted for her, but obviously not Catja.

"Marking locations," she said. This was one of the things that had taken time from working on her own cloak, or knitting Luc's tunic. But it was worth it.

"Isn't that dangerous?" Catja asked. "The Kassian might see them."

Ava hoped they did. Hoped they touched them.

She had thought a lot about them being drawn to look at them.

She really hoped they would be as attracted to those strips as the wine merchant had been to the fabric she had worked to influence him.

She shrugged. "It doesn't matter if they do. They mean nothing. Luc thought it would help with the idea that we were going over to scout crossing points. It won't matter if they find them or not, not if we're going to surprise them in the hills. And if they do find them, it'll make them think they were right about our reason for the trip."

"Oh." The Venyatux soldier gave a sudden laugh. "That's actually clever."

Suddenly, Luc gave a yip up ahead, then turned his horse in an arc, coming up beside her. "The columns are ahead."

Catja gave a ululation of joy and let her horse go, and as if they suddenly all knew home, and oats, and friends were ahead, the horses broke into a gallop.

The wind whipped her short hair and blew back her cloak, and Ava couldn't help but join in Catja's ululation.

She looked across at Luc and laughed, and he laughed back.

The tie at the end of Catja's long braid came loose, and her hair blew out like the unfurling of a banner as they thundered across the dry, cold ground.

They were a dusty, travel-worn group, and yet they moved well together, the accomplished riders at the front, back and sides which left Ava in the middle.

Ever since she'd been left behind in the hills, Luc had made sure she was always in the heart of the group, and no one had complained or tried to make her feel bad about it.

Like with Kikir, the Skäddar warrior, and his sudden friendliness toward her, she wondered if wearing protection she had created for them made them accept her more.

It disturbed her a little, but there was nothing she could do about it. She wanted them protected, and she hadn't done anything deliberate to make them like her.

Or maybe it had nothing to do with the workings. Maybe she was just likeable.

She laughed at the thought, and then a cry went up ahead of them and suddenly the scouts were around them, whooping their welcome.

It felt good to be back.

Especially after the cat and mouse games of the last three days.

The general was riding at the front of the column with Raun-Tu and Fervanti, and they slowed as they reached her.

Everyone but Luc, Deni and herself kept going, trotting into the slow moving column. Catja gave her a sympathetic smile and then disappeared with a wave, and Ava heard her call hello to a friend.

It was nearly time for the army to stop for the night, but this couldn't wait.

Dak and Massi arrived while they settled into the slower pace of the Rising Wave, and Ava thought their greetings to her were warmer than they'd been before.

See, she told herself. Likeable.

"So, let's have it." General Ru leaned back in her saddle.

"They're planning an ambush from the hills." Luc sent her a wide grin.

"Is that so? You saw them?"

"Even managed to sneak up on their camp and listen for a while."

The general lifted her brows at that, slid her gaze to Ava and gave a nod. "Hear anything interesting?"

"They thought we were surveying the crossing points for the river, so we let them think that. They were there to map the area for the Herald."

"We'll have to work on ways to surprise them." Massi rubbed her hands together and laughed in a way so similar to the way Luc had done when they'd worked out what the Kassian were up to, Ava blinked.

"I'm sure you'll come up with something good," she said, "but the Bartolo River is going to be difficult to cross afterward. It's really wide and deep." Ava knew they needed to concentrate on the ambush from the hills first, but she honestly could see no way the carts and wagons of the column would get across. In fact, the whole idea of it was laughable.

"Pontoons," Dak told her.

She frowned at him.

"Big, flat, wooden platforms which will float the carts over."

"And the yakkuna?"

"The yakkuna are excellent swimmers. They'll probably enjoy it." General Ru shaded her eyes against the last of the evening light.

"You were right that they could wait until we were about to go across and attack us at the crossing point. We'd be incapable of retreat." Deni pulled out the map and showed the general. "Hard to sneak up on us, though."

"Varik said they could wait until half of us were across, half still on the other side," Ava said. "They could hide in the forest, and then some could cross further down, out of sight, and come at us from behind and in front."

"I didn't think of that." Dak sounded intrigued. "An attack party on both sides?"

Luc nodded. "It could work, if they have enough people. There would be nowhere for us to go but into the river."

"We'd hardly be running away, though." Raun-Tu sounded insulted.

"No, but it's always good strategy to have a place to retreat to," General Ru said. "And they'd leave us none if they come at us from both sides."

"We need to consider moving the crossing point to the town of Bartolo, lower down the river." Luc tilted his head to Ava. "As Ava pointed out when we got there, the forest on the other side is a lot thicker than is shown on the map. The carts and wagons might not be able to get through. We need a road."

"If we defeat them in the hills first, we could take the town afterward." The general sat a little straighter in her saddle. "That's a definite possibility."

"And there's a bridge over the river in Bartolo," Deni put in.

The strategy talk continued on as the column slowed to a stop and began to set up for the night.

Ava had listened to it for the last three days, so she slipped away, rubbed down her horse and then went to find the bathing tent. When they'd set up camp by the river, they'd jumped in it and washed, but the water had been cold and the current strong. Ava had stayed in the shallows, shivering, even as she was grateful to be able to immerse herself in water.

Her two years in a cell, using a shallow bowl to wash in, meant even a cold river was a luxury to her.

The bathing tent in the Venyatu column was more wonderful still. The water was hot, and the soap smelled of lemon and rosemary.

As she sank down into the hard leather tub full of hot water she remembered the way Luc's arms had come around her from behind while she washed in the freezing water, enveloping her in sudden heat.

He'd chuckled in her ear. "I can hear your teeth chattering."

She'd felt his smooth, taut skin against her own, and the hard, poking evidence of his arousal at her back.

The memory had her rushing through her bath, pulling on a clean change of clothes, and heading for Luc's tent. He wasn't there, though, and she guessed they'd moved the strategy session to the general's quarters.

She stood for a moment, pack in hand, considering her options. Eventually she set her things beside his bed, on the side she favored, took out her knitting, and went to find a campfire to sit at.

She found one where a man was working on some leather boots, another was whittling a stick, and a few women sat companionably darning rips in their clothing. Oscar was there, too, sharpening the knife he wore on his belt.

He patted the spot beside him and she settled down to a warm welcome from the others. She let the conversation and the crackle of the fire soothe her, along with the click of her needles.

She was invisible here. Or unremarkable.

She was grateful for some space to concentrate on the tunic for

Luc. She wove impenetrability into every stitch she knit, every twist of the work. Nothing would get through this.

And it was almost done. Just a few more rows and she'd only have to sew the pieces together.

"Ava. There you are."

She looked up in surprise as Frederik stopped in front of her and then sat beside her.

"Look." He pointed to his face.

The stitches she'd put there had been taken out, most likely by Dorea, and the wound was just a thin white line on his warm brown skin.

She leaned closer for a better look. Her relief that there was an actual scar made her feel a little giddy. "That looks good."

"It's barely noticeable. Dorea says she's never seen the like. Never seen anyone heal so fast." He rubbed it. "I can't even feel it's there, so thank you. But the reason I came looking for you is that Revek asked me to find you and bring you to him."

Ava went still. "Is he all right?"

"He's fine. He had to do something for the Commander, and didn't know where you were so I said I'd find you and take you to him."

Ava packed away her knitting reluctantly, and stood. "Where is he?"

"The armoury tent. It's not far."

"Would you like me to come with you?" Oscar had been silent through the conversation with Frederik, and the young soldier seemed to start at his words, as if he hadn't noticed the warrior's presence.

"No need, Oscar, but thank you." Ava couldn't feel anything off about Frederik. Her new cloak may not be as sensitive as her old one, but there wasn't even the smallest of warnings.

Revek might be a different story, but she would deal with that when she had to.

She walked with Frederik, listening to him recount the training session he'd had that day, and laughing at his enthusiasm.

"Here we are." He waved toward a large, open tent which had a hot fire burning in front of it, and a man and a woman dressed in leather aprons working with hammer and tong.

She supposed their work day could only start when the column stopped and they could build a fire hot enough to repair damaged weapons and create items the stores manager needed.

Revek sat on a stool at the back of the tent, surrounded by crates, a wooden board with parchment clipped to it in his hand.

"I've got guard duty, so I'm off. Thanks again." Frederik tapped his cheek and then turned and walked away.

Revek had seen them arrive, and he watched her as she skirted the weapons smiths and approached him.

"You ever heard of someone who healed so fast?" he asked her, tilting his head in Frederik's direction. "The boy barely looks like he got scratched by a tree branch."

She didn't answer.

"Me, on the other hand." Revek pulled the neck of his tunic to the side, exposing the wound high on his left shoulder. "Why, I might have actually been hit by an arrow. Two months ago."

Ava came closer to look at it.

It did seem less healed than Frederik's, but not by much. It would end up looking very similar.

She thought of the resistance she'd felt to her healing while she'd stitched him, and realized the spell in the oil on Revek's face had interfered with her own working.

Maybe that was for the best.

"You wanted to talk to me?"

Revek pulled his tunic up again. He was holding the piece of board in both hands, and she saw his knuckles were white.

"I haven't felt sick since Haslia left. I didn't realise I felt sick until I didn't anymore, if you understand what I mean. I had gotten used to feeling ill, maybe." He looked up from whatever was written on the parchment. "I want to know if Haslia was enspelling me."

"Why do you think I'd know?" She shouldn't ask questions she didn't want the answers to, but it came out of her mouth anyway.

He simply stared at her for a beat. "What would she have done to me?"

Ava sighed. "I really don't know. But it could have been something she gave you to eat or drink, or even the crockery you used to eat or drink out of. Massi and Luc think someone, probably Haslia, gave her an enspelled cup to drink out of."

"She told me that, but the cup and plate I'm using I've had for years. It could have been in the tea we often shared in the morning."

"Does it matter?" Ava rose up from her crouch. "You're feeling normal again, so it was obviously something she was doing daily to you."

"Yes, it matters." His voice rose, and heads turned in their direction. "It matters." He lowered his voice, but there was no doubting his feelings. "I never want to be vulnerable like that again. I endured years of manipulation and mind games in the Chosen camps and I thought I was finally free. Now I know there's no such thing as completely safe."

"No. There is no such thing." She was sorry for it, but it was the truth.

"What I want to know is, are you doing the same to Luc? Are you playing the same games Haslia played with me?" At last Revek rose up from his stool, more than head and shoulders taller than her.

"If you want to know if I'm manipulating Luc, the answer is no." Ava took a step back. Her cloak's warning was kicking in, a faint bell ringing in her head.

Revek's mood had shifted.

More than her cloak, she could see it on his face.

He was considering hurting her, maybe killing her, just in case she was lying.

Despite her having healed him.

Maybe she didn't have to worry that she was affecting the way people responded to her. Revek certainly wasn't going out of his way to be friendly.

It almost made her cheerful.

"Have you figured out why Haslia wanted you dead?" She threw out the question more as a distraction than anything else, but he dropped what seemed to be the inventory checklist he'd been holding and flexed his hands.

"No. That's for Luc to ask me, not you. Most of the last few months are more a blur than not, when I think back on them now, and

I can't quite see clearly. But when I finally do," he glared at her, "I will go to Luc, not you."

"There a problem?" Oscar's voice came from behind her, and she looked over her shoulder to find him and Deni standing just inside the tent.

When she turned back, she saw Revek's posture had relaxed.

"No problem. Just thanking Ava for the patch-up job she gave me on my arrow wound."

Deni grunted in response and Ava turned toward him and Oscar, holding out both elbows.

"You finally going to spar with me, Oscar?" she asked as the two men linked arms with her and walked away. "Or are you too embarrassed to bet against yourself?"

"What was that about?" Deni asked her as soon as they were out of the glow thrown by the fire.

"He was enspelled by Haslia." She shrugged. "And Haslia did her best to convince him I had somehow enspelled Luc. He's trying to come to terms with the fact that he wasn't himself for a long time, and he's worried I'm doing the same to his friend."

"He's volatile," Oscar said. "Always was. Luc's the only reason Revek's still alive. And I think the Commander still remembers the person he was before the camps twisted him up, not the man he is now."

"You were in the camps with them both?" Deni asked.

Oscar nodded but didn't say any more, and Ava gave his arm an extra squeeze.

"What made you two come looking for me?"

"I wondered why Revek couldn't come find you himself," Oscar said. "Seemed strange to me. Deni and I decided we might as well take a stroll."

"It would have been fine, but thank you." She had managed to diffuse Revek's anger, but Ava was grateful to them anyway.

"So what are you planning, Avasu?" Deni asked.

She tilted her head to look up at him.

"Don't bat your eyelids innocently at me, I know you better than most, and I've watched you every time we talk about strategy, about the Kassian ambush, and you're planning something."

"Maybe," she admitted. "I'm still thinking through all the moving parts."

"If you think it'll work, we're in," Oscar said.

They walked her back to Luc's quarters, and then went to sit beside the campfire nearby.

Watching over her.

She ducked through the flaps and stood for a moment, fighting with the thought that she'd changed them, despite the evidence from Revek that she hadn't done so with him.

Or maybe they were just protective, and liked her. Wanted to keep her safe.

Or maybe it was complex, and she would learn over time what effect her workings had on those who wore her creations.

"That was a heavy sigh."

Luc stepped out from behind the curtain to their private space and she lifted a shoulder as she walked toward him, and slid her arms around his waist.

"You finally sick of strategizing?" she asked.

He chuckled. "The general is a believer in considering all the options, and I can't disagree."

"Did you sense that they were in the hills when we passed by around midday?" She hadn't had a chance to ask him until now.

He nodded. "They were watching us."

"So even if they left to go back to wherever the Kassian forces are based just after we passed through, how long do we have until the army arrives to hide there?"

"Not long." Luc drew her behind the curtain and she stepped away to remove her cloak and jacket. "Since you and Deni had that confrontation with the scouts, they haven't watched the columns as closely, but they'll know how fast we're moving and the Kassian generals will need to mobilize their own soldiers."

"How long will it take us to reach there, going at this pace?"

"We'll leave the slow moving parts of the column behind the day after tomorrow," Luc said. "We'll need to travel fast and light to get into place."

"The Kassian scouts watching us will report that."

He nodded. "We're going to pretend to try to take Bartolo. That'll make sense to them after our excursion to the river. But we'll split up, and only a small force will go to the town." He sat down and began to pull off his boots. "The rest of us will—"

"I should go to the hills before that. While you're drawing attention to Bartolo."

He let the first boot drop to the ground, and looked up at her.

She shrugged. "I can seed the area with some surprises. It will make things safer. Make the win more certain."

"And then? Because I can hear there's something else in there." He pulled off his second boot.

"And then I should go to Bartolo and convince the town of the positives of embracing the Rising Wave."

He sighed. Stood up to pull off his pants.

She watched his hands as he unbuckled his belt.

"I thought about us, about how we were in the river the other night when I was bathing earlier this evening, and hurried back here." She folded her jacket and set it on her pack. "But you weren't here."

"Are you trying to distract me?" He pulled the shirt she'd embroidered for him over his head and tossed it aside.

"I'm telling you the truth, but I was also trying to wipe that pained expression off your face," she admitted.

"Come here."

She discarded the last of her clothing and was pulled in close, skin against skin, although unlike at the river, this time they had all the privacy they needed.

"You smell delicious." He inhaled and kissed the side of her neck. "I knew I couldn't do without you the night we were on the run from the Kassian. The horse became lame and we had to leave it and run and when I helped you down from the saddle, I was overcome by the need to breathe in your scent and hold you close, even though they were right behind us."

"Really?" She remembered the moment, but she hadn't realized he had wanted to hold her. "I knew I couldn't do without you when you stepped out from behind the trees to draw the Kassian soldiers away from me. You sacrificed yourself to keep me safe."

"I always will," he said, and nipped at her ear. "Which sits uncomfortably with your proposal to race toward two places the Kassian control or are planning to infiltrate."

"I know." She feathered kisses along his jaw. "And yet, you know it's the right thing to do."

"I can't go with you this time. I have to lead the columns."

"Oscar and Deni can come with me. They've already offered."

He mulled it over. "You might have to reveal some of your secrets to them."

"I know, but I said before that I'd share my secrets if it means the Rising Wave has a better chance of winning, and I meant it. Deni is my friend, and Oscar is a good man; they came looking for me tonight while I was talking to Revek—"

"What happened." He went still, his hands running down her bare back and gripping her hips.

"Revek's worried I'm doing to you what Haslia did to him. I don't think he would have hurt me, but . . ."

"But?"

"But he was considering it. And Oscar and Deni made sure the feeling passed."

"I don't want you alone with him." Luc sounded grim.

"I won't make the same mistake again. I don't think he'll seek me out anymore. He asked his questions. I answered them."

Luc sighed. "I don't know what to do about him. It hurts to see someone I love as a brother so twisted up and angry."

"Give him something less annoying to do than stocktaking." She gave a wry smile.

"Is that what Massi has him doing? I left it to her." Luc sounded surprised.

"So what will it be?" Ava slid her hands up to his shoulders and pressed close again. "I'll have to leave as soon as I've had a chance to embroider a few things and finish your tunic."

"My tunic?"

She nodded. "That's what I've been knitting. It'll either be useless, or even more powerful than my embroidery, I can't decide which. But if it does work, it'll be the best protective armor you've ever worn."

He held her gaze. "You should wear it, not me."

She shook her head. "I made it specifically for you. I don't think it'll work for me. But anyway, I'm planning to sneak around at night, invisible. You're the one leading an army."

He studied her, lifting a hand to trace down her temple and then cup her face. "Promise me you are not neglecting your own protection."

She held his gaze. "I've been working on my cloak." Not as much as she should, she knew, but there were only so many hours in the day.

"I want you back as soon as possible."

She scoffed. "No, I was thinking of relaxing at an inn in Bartolo for a few days while you were fighting the Kassian forces."

His lips twitched. "I want you to always take the most cautious approach. I'll talk to Oscar and Deni myself about it."

"I'll be careful. I promise." She poked his chest with her finger. "And you do the same."

He nodded.

She left her finger in place, and traced down between his pectorals. "So we're not fighting? Everything is resolved?"

"Not quite everything." His gaze was locked onto her finger, and she had to swallow a squeal as he suddenly lifted her up.

"Well, let's get to it." She grinned at him. "We wouldn't want to leave anything unfinished."

CHAPTER 32

"So what was that?" Oscar spoke as soon as they had the hills behind them.

Ava didn't answer straight away. She'd been agonizing over what to say to them since they'd left the column at midday yesterday, after she'd had time to work on the traps she planned to set.

"That was spellwork," Deni said, and it was the lack of censor in his voice that gave her the ability to heave out a big breath.

"I can spell my embroidery." She sent a quick look at Oscar. "Your vest is spelled to protect you against arrows and swords, and to help you react to attack, that's all."

"My . . . vest?" He looked down at himself, and then rubbed the embroidery with a finger.

"You didn't know about the vest." She wanted to roll her eyes at herself. Why would they have even noticed? She'd specifically used the same color so it would be difficult to see.

"I knew," Deni said and she glanced over at him. "I suspected since that day when we surprised those scouts and one of them shot an arrow directly at me. There was no way he could have missed, and yet, he did." He fingered the scarf around his neck.

"And you're all right with it?"

"All right? I wrapped this scarf around my waist at training yesterday morning, and no one was able to connect a single blow."

"The Commander." Oscar suddenly turned in his saddle. "He's untouchable in training, as well."

Ava shrugged. "Some of that is me. Some of that is him."

"And what did you just leave in the hills?" Deni asked.

"I left useful things. Handkerchiefs. Scarves."

"What will happen to the soldiers who find them?" Oscar sounded less astonished, more interested, for the first time.

"They'll become resentful of their superiors, or even more resentful than they already are, and they'll find the courage to disrupt the Kassian army's plans in small ways that might not be noticed until it's too late."

"You'll create saboteurs from handkerchiefs and scarves?" Oscar's eyes went wide.

"I hope so. It is worth taking the chance, you would agree?"

"Most definitely. If it works as well as my scarf does, as well as that thin scrap of fabric you handed me the other day did, this will be a big help to the columns." Deni shielded his gaze to look ahead. "And what are we going to do in Bartolo?"

"We're going to encourage the people of Bartolo to feel sympathetic to the Rising Wave. And to hinder the Kassian army where they can."

"Except we're going to have to get through the Rising Wave to do it, aren't we?" Oscar frowned. "They'll already have left for the city this morning. If we come along from the same direction, we'll be pegged as spies straight away."

"That's why we're crossing the river and coming from the other direction," Ava said. She had proposed this to Luc herself, but she wasn't at all sure about crossing the river. It loomed large in her mind as an impenetrable barrier.

That feeling hadn't changed by the time they reached the river bank late that afternoon, nor as Oscar and Deni helped her across the swiftly flowing water.

She stood, shivering and miserable, on the other side as the two men made a fire, and only started to relax when the flames began to thaw her out.

Tomorrow they'd make their way through the forest onto the road into Bartolo, and start their campaign.

"How far do you think the Rising Wave would have got toward Bartolo?" she asked.

"Depends how fast they were moving, but maybe halfway there is my guess." Oscar stared down the river toward the town.

"They'll be splitting up tonight, doubling back to go around the back of the hills." Deni sounded a little wistful.

"Do you wish you were with them?" Ava asked.

He shook his head, his teeth gleaming white in the firelight. "I'm happy to sow seeds of discontent. It's what the Kassian did in Venyatu for a long time before they tried to annex us."

"And you, Oscar?"

Oscar leaned back, tipped his head back to look at the stars. "Ever since I was forced into a Chosen camp, I've dreamed of taking them on. I got to fight them hand to hand on the battlefield the day the Commander turned us against them, and it felt good, but this." He turned to look at her, and there was deep satisfaction in his eyes. "This is better. I want to subvert them. I want them to be confused about what's happening."

"Well then, let me get started." Ava had been feeling too cold and stiff to sew before now, but Oscar had inspired her.

She pulled out her sewing while the two soldiers kept watch.

THEY ENTERED A CHAOTIC BARTOLO A FEW HOURS BEHIND A LARGE part of the Kassian army.

It was easy to walk over the wide bridge and slip among the townspeople. The streets were crowded as everyone came out to gawk at the units marching through.

They'd plaited Deni's hair down his back and tucked it under his shirt, then looped his scarf around his neck to hide the Venyatux style of his hair. Ava kept glancing over at him, he looked so different without his high ponytail.

The three of them stayed together as a loose unit, wandering as if alone but always in sight of each other, eavesdropping on the gossiping citizenry.

"So, only some of them are staying in town, the rest are going out to meet the Rising Wave on the plains, is what I heard." Deni handed Ava a pie from a nearby cart and she bit into it suspiciously.

"Oh, it's actually nice. Apricot and spicy lamb."

He grinned, and handed one to Oscar as he joined them.

"I heard the same as you, a small contingent staying here in case any of the Rising Wave manage to get through the main army, the rest headed for open warfare on the plain." Ava didn't believe it, though.

"I also heard some of them were going north up the river to patrol it and stop the Rising Wave crossing anywhere along the way."

Ava smiled at the thought.

Deni gave her a look. "What's the smile?"

"I might have left some surprises for the ones on river patrol when we were there last week."

"Surprises?" Oscar asked around a mouthful of pie.

"Nasty ones."

Deni snorted and then leaned back against a wall. "So what's the plan?"

"The original plan was to turn public sentiment away from the Kassian to the Rising Wave, but with the army here, I'll have to be careful with that. It might be dangerous for the people I spell." She didn't want innocent people punished.

She could be subtle about it, though. She would have to think about how to do it.

"Let's find out what's happening, first. We need people who are in a position to know. Not gossip but actual facts."

"Like an official?"

She nodded at Oscar, then saw he was looking in the direction of a large building across the square with ornate doors. A woman stood in front of them, dressed in what looked like a ceremonial robe.

That did look official.

Ava began walking toward her.

"What's our job?" Deni kept pace with her.

"Watch the crowd for me. Look out for anyone who looks too interested in me."

They'd melted away by the time she was nearing the steps up to the door, and Ava saw the official was agitated, clasping and unclasping her hands.

It seemed likely that she was waiting for someone, and Ava needed her undivided attention, so she walked past, wandering through the pedestrians and continually looping back.

Finally a bell chimed the hour and the woman seemed to steel herself. She walked down the steps to the right and turned sharply into the narrow space between the town hall and the building beside it.

Ava followed her.

The woman had come to a stop a little way down from the entrance to the alleyway, and Ava made a snap decision when the woman looked at her with wild eyes.

She kept walking, giving the woman a friendly nod as she passed.

She casually drew out her scarf and looped it around her neck, then stopped and turned. She wanted to walk back, get closer to the woman, but every scrape of her boot on the stone flagging seemed to echo in the narrow space. Then she lost the opportunity completely, because the woman was finally joined by someone new; a woman in a dark cloak, her face obscured.

They didn't appear happy to see each other.

The newcomer looked down the length of the alley and gestured, and the woman in the official robe followed the direction of her hand and shrugged.

Maybe she'd seen Ava come in and was asking where she'd gone.

Then she pulled back her hood and stared directly at Ava for a long moment.

Ava tried to draw in breath without making any noise, but it sounded too loud to her ears.

Haslia.

Haslia was here in Bartolo.

Doing strange deals in alleyways.

When Ava forced herself to get over the shock, Haslia seemed to have relaxed. Her expression as she spoke to the official was sneering. The conversation was so quiet, Ava couldn't hear a word of it.

Haslia finally became impatient, gesturing with her hand.

Reluctantly, the official lifted both hands behind her neck and Ava realized she was unclasping a necklace.

She held the necklace out and Haslia drew something wrapped in cloth from her pocket and threaded it onto the chain without touching it.

With a shudder, the official put the necklace back on. As soon as she did, Haslia turned and walked back the way she'd come, into the square.

Ava watched her go, wondering if Deni or Oscar would see her and what they would do about it if they did.

She should probably go after her, but her sense was what had just happened to the official still standing in the alleyway was important. She pulled the scarf off her neck and walked toward the woman.

She was staring down at the necklace with loathing.

"Here." Ava held out a thin rectangular piece of fabric. "This'll help."

The woman reached out and took it so easily, Ava focused on the necklace. It was strung with a collection of six charms.

"Why don't you take that necklace off?" Ava suggested, and the woman heaved a sigh of relief.

"That's a good idea." She reached back, unclasped it, and instead of placing it down on the ground, she dropped it.

One ornament came loose and rolled away, and Ava put out a foot and trapped it under her boot. No way was she letting that be picked up by a curious child.

"Is that better?"

"I can't thank you enough." The woman shuddered. "The dread. It weighed on me. Every week they give me one, and I go home and vomit."

"What is it for?" Ava asked.

"For?" The woman seemed suddenly blank eyed.

"It doesn't matter. Take a deep breath, you don't have to worry about that anymore."

"I can't tell you what a relief that is." The woman traced a finger over the fabric in her hand. "They make me come out here to get it, because my staff are so worried about me."

"Do you know what the Kassian army's plans are?" Ava felt more than a twinge of guilt at manipulating this woman, who had obviously been manipulated enough.

She didn't think anyone had ever been in dread or afraid of her workings, and she wondered if whoever had created the ornament under her boot had deliberately added dread and fear to it for some kind of sick pleasure.

She felt a frisson of fear at the thought of who would do something like that if they didn't need to.

"The soldiers can't be gone soon enough." The woman's gaze cut to the alleyway entrance to the square.

"Will they be gone soon?"

"They don't tell me much." The woman looked down at the fabric in her hand and then leaned closer. "Just what they need to tell me for my cooperation. I've been told to say they're going to fight the Rising Wave on the plains, and they're just leaving a small garrison here, but I know they're lying."

"They are liars," Ava agreed.

"Yes." The woman nodded, face serious. "They're planning to hide a lot more soldiers under the town, in the cisterns."

The information was like a jolt to Ava's system. "Why?"

The woman shrugged. "To fool the Rising Wave?" She brushed a sudden tear from her cheek. "They're going to use this town as a battleground, and they're making me keep quiet about it." Her gaze strayed to Ava's boot and the charm beneath it.

"Are you the mayor?"

"I am. I am not a good mayor." The woman brushed another tear away.

"You are a good mayor," Ava assured her. "And the Rising Wave will not hurt your town if they can help it."

"They won't?"

"No. You can trust them to be as careful as possible. Is there a way to trap the Kassian units in the cisterns when they hide down there?"

The mayor nodded. "There are only two entrances. That's the only reason I was told about their plan. They needed the keys."

"Can you tell me where the entrances are to the cisterns?"

"Yes, of course." She gave Ava clear, concise directions and then stepped back, as if unburdened.

"You'll find the Rising Wave is a better ally than the Kassian. Thank you for your help." Ava reached out and covered the mayor's hand with her own. The mayor's fingers had the embroidered fabric in a death grip.

"Thank *you*." The mayor's eyes strayed back to Ava's boot. "I'm more grateful than you can know."

Ava tugged the fabric out of her hold, keeping it hidden in her fist. "It was a pleasure to meet you."

The mayor blinked at her and then looked down at her empty hand. Flexed her fingers. "Nice to meet you, too. I was . . . meeting someone—"

"They couldn't come," Ava said.

"Oh." The mayor laughed, the sound light. "I was dreading it, to be honest. I have so much to do."

She walked down the alley and disappeared, and Ava carefully lifted her boot and crouched down.

"You all right? We saw Haslia."

She looked up to find Oscar and Deni moving toward her. She nodded and took a piece of fabric out of her pocket.

"What was that?"

"That woman who just left has been spelled for the last five weeks at least and is finally free of it." She picked the necklace up, careful not to lose any of the charms.

"That's what kept her spelled?" Oscar went on his haunches beside her.

"Yes. One charm for every week." She captured the charm that had rolled off in the same wrapping, and then began to roll it up.

"What do we do with it?" Oscar eyed it with alarm.

Ava didn't know. "We can't let anyone touch it. Maybe melt it down?"

For now, she tied it securely and placed it in a side pocket of her pack.

"So, apparently the Kassian are going to pretend to keep a small force here, but there'll be a larger force hidden below in the cisterns."

Deni gave a half-laugh in astonishment. "The cisterns?"

Ava lifted her hands. "How many troops would they have to have?"

The Rising Wave seemed massive to her. Did the Kassian have so many more soldiers they could afford to keep a large cohort in reserve in case the Rising Wave made it through to Bartolo?

"Not enough to keep another small army hidden, I would have thought." Oscar turned his head to look toward the square.

They all started moving back that way until they stood together amid the bustle.

"You go do whatever you do, Avasu. Oscar and I will keep watch." Deni patted her shoulder.

They could both sense the urgency she was feeling herself, Ava saw. Something was happening, the Kassian had some plan that she couldn't discern, and she needed to find out what.

She nodded and made her way through the crowds, stopping at the stalls and buying a few small items with the money Luc had given her for this reconnaissance mission.

If the trader was alone, after she had handed over the money, she offered them a small square of fabric and talked a little about the Rising Wave, and how to help the columns if the battlefield came to Bartolo.

The traders interacted with the most people, so she'd decided they were the most efficient recipients of her workings.

She didn't have much persuading to do. There was already a feeling of ill-will toward the Kassian forces, even though Bartolo was a Kassian town.

They were behaving more like they were in an occupied territory than a friendly local city.

She kept the Kassian soldiers in view as she walked around, making sure to avoid getting too close to them.

They were boisterous and loud, and making her mission a lot easier.

When she was out of small squares, she walked away from the tables and Deni and Oscar drifted out of the crowd to stand beside her. "Let's go find an inn for the night, and make it one that's hosting Kassian soldiers."

"You get anything?" Oscar asked.

She shook her head. "Just the same gossip. We need to find someone who actually knows what the plans are, and that means a Kassian officer."

And they had better be quick about it. Ava didn't know what the Kassian were plotting, but she knew the Rising Wave was at stake.

CHAPTER 33

"So why is your hair so short?" The Kassian officer leering at her from his booth in the inn's dining area had to shout to be heard over the noise of his fellow soldiers.

"I had lice and had to shave it off a few months ago," Ava said.

He laughed uproariously. "Do you want to come up to my room?" He did something with his eyebrows that Ava thought was supposed to be suggestive, but he was too drunk to pull it off.

"Certainly. Let's go." She hopped down from the stool she was sitting on, and Oscar reached out to grab her by the shoulder.

"We'll be just outside the door."

She nodded, keeping her eyes on her target.

Oscar released her and she didn't look back at either him or Deni as she helped the officer up the stairs.

She had never tried a working on someone who was drunk, and she didn't know if it would help her or turn out to be a waste of time.

The problem was, all the officers below were drunk. She had to work with what she had.

"Hold this a minute, and I'll open the door," she said, taking his key from him and giving him a piece of embroidery.

She turned the key, stepping into the room warily. There didn't seem to be enough rooms at this particular inn for everyone getting drunk downstairs to have their own room, but she had obviously found someone with enough rank to warrant some privacy.

"Come in," she invited, and he clutched the fabric to his chest and stumbled after her.

"Would you like some water?" She found the pitcher on a table near the bed, and poured it into a glass.

He drank it down as if he were a child following orders.

"Why don't you sit?"

He didn't look for a chair, he simply folded his legs and landed on the floor.

It made her feel slightly queasy how easily she could manipulate him.

"You look like Princess Ava Valestri." He tried to waggle his eyebrows again. "Can I call you that while I fuck you?"

Ava went still. "How do you know what the princess looks like? Most people don't even know she exists."

"A drawing sent out by the Queen's Herald after she went missing. Only the senior officers know. We were told to look out for her." He held out his glass and she poured more water into it. "I think the Queen's Herald is in trouble about it." He snickered.

"That picture is wrong, you know. It doesn't look anything like the princess."

"Oh." He nodded sagely. "But can I still call you that when we—"

"That's not going to happen." Ava shuddered. "So tell me all the clever things the Kassian army are planning against the Rising Wave." She lowered herself into the chair by the fire.

"Got ourselves some flares." He grinned at her. "We're going to wait for the Rising Wave to pass the hills, where we've set up flare cannons, and when they come past, wooooooo, boom." He traced the air to show the trajectory of a flare and then threw his hands in the air for the boom. "And then," he leaned toward her and lowered his voice, "when they run for Bartolo, because its the only place for a quick river crossing, we'll come out from under the city and—" He made a sound at the back of his throat and ran a finger under his chin.

"How many flares?" she asked, trying to sound impressed.

"Ten canons, three flares each." He leaned back on his hands, as if expecting praise.

"That is amazing," she said. "Can you tell me what flares are, again?"

He chuckled indulgently. "Magical fire. Got them from Zilvana. Burns and burns. Spreads like water." He tapped his cheek, and she thought he meant to tap his nose but missed. "Got to be careful. Very dangerous to launch."

"Very dangerous." Ava thought through her options. "Where are they now? Are they in Bartolo?"

"No, silly." He shook his head. "Already gone two days ago. Probably already setting them in place. The Rising Wave could be coming past any day."

She, Oscar and Deni must have just missed them.

"Are you going to the hills?"

"No." He looked sad about it. "Would love to see it, but I'm stuck here to mop up the survivors."

Rage spiked in her chest, and she took a calming breath. "You know what you should do?"

He looked up at her and shook his head.

"You shouldn't take that kind of disrespect. A competent officer like you, stuck in Bartolo? You should pack your things and simply go home."

"I should. You're right, I should."

"Go tonight, if you can. Don't tell anyone. Why should you give them notice when they disrespect you like that? And when you get home? You throw that piece of fabric in the first fire you see and be done with it."

She left him packing his things, flinging them into a canvas bag with a sort of delighted outrage.

She hoped his disappearance caused all kinds of logistical trouble.

"He touch you?" Oscar asked as she stepped into the hallway, and she frowned at him in incomprehension.

"What?"

"Did he try—" Deni shut his mouth. "You were the more dangerous of the two, weren't you?"

She shook her head, dismissing the whole line of questioning. "Have you heard of flares?" She came to a stop at the top of the stairs. The noise coming from below told her they wouldn't be able to have a conversation down there.

"Flares?" Oscar shook his head, but Deni went pale.

"I've heard of them. Some kind of magical fire."

Ava nodded. "They aren't going to hide troops in the hills. They're setting up cannons on the hilltops and they're going to shoot flares at the columns. They'll only need a small force for that. It's how they have enough troops to hide an army in the cisterns to deal with whoever escapes the flares and tries to use the Bartolo bridge to cross the river."

"The fuckers." Deni's voice was hushed.

"We're leaving now?" Oscar asked.

She nodded. "You two go back the way we came in, get the horses where we left them and cross the river. Go find the columns before they try to surround the hills."

"And you?" Deni did not sound happy.

"I'm going out the other way. I'll get a horse or find a lift, but the Rising Wave has already split up. We need to warn both groups."

"Why don't I go out the other gate and you go with Oscar?" Deni asked uneasily.

"Because I can make it so that no one knows I was even there," she told him bluntly, and after a short staring match, he lowered his gaze and nodded.

The door opened behind them, and the officer came out, a pack slung over his shoulder.

"You should go out the back way," Ava told him. "There's too many people in the front."

"Good idea." He was still slurring his words and he walked past them and down the stairs, unsteady on his feet.

"Where's he going?" Oscar's voice was hushed.

"I persuaded him to desert. That should make things a little more difficult in Bartolo for the Kassian, as apparently he was in charge of the units going to hide in the cisterns."

"You are scary, Ava. As scary as the Commander." Oscar didn't sound scared, though. He sounded admiring.

"Guess we were made for each other, then." She grinned at him even as she thought about how the officer had recognized her from a picture circulated by her cousin. "Now let's take my own advice and leave out the back door."

CHAPTER 34

She walked into camp and looked around.

She'd left the horse she'd stolen to graze a little way back, and had wound her scarf over her head, mouth and neck, more to ward off the cold than to increase the effectiveness of the invisibility spell.

It looked as if Massi and Raun-Tu were in charge here.

General Ru and Luc would be with the main army.

She had passed two Kassian scout parties on her way here. She had thought, when she'd run into the second one, that she'd have to abandon her horse, because she hadn't thought it became invisible along with her, but she had been proved wrong.

They had walked past her, not quite within touching distance but close enough.

She'd kept her hand on her horse's neck and counted herself lucky.

She couldn't hide the sound of the hoofs on the hard ground, though, which is why she had left it behind to infiltrate the camp.

She just wanted to make sure everything was as it should be.

Massi and Raun-Tu were sitting together outside a small tent, arguing softly while most of the camp slept.

There were guards set all around, but there didn't seem to be a sense that they were on high alert.

Ava sat down on the other side of the fire.

"We can only pretend to be unaware of the scouts for so long," Massi was saying. "At some point they're going to get suspicious and realize we aren't as undisciplined as we look."

"And when they realize that, that's when we attack," Raun-Tu countered.

"Attack who?" Massi threw up her hands. "Two scout groups of four each?"

Ava stood up, walked away into the darkness, took off her scarf and walked back.

"It's me." She tilted her head at Raun-Tu's drawn bow, and wondered how he would react to it missing her completely.

Massi swore and Ava sent her a quick grin.

"How did you get through the guards?" Raun-Tu lowered his bow and sounded like he would like to go knock some heads together.

"Quietly and carefully." She shrugged. "I'm a well-trained spy for the general, remember?"

That little story kept coming in very handy.

Massi hissed out a breath. "What are you doing here?"

"That was always the plan, remember, to do some reconnaissance in Bartolo and then come straight back."

"To Luc, not us."

"Oscar and Deni have gone to warn Luc, I've come to warn you, then I'll be on my way to Luc, don't worry."

"Warn us?" Raun-Tu finally sat back down.

She walked over to sit between them and lowered her voice as she told them of the nasty surprise waiting below the city and in the hills.

"Shit." Massi leaned back. "I've never heard of these flares. Have you?"

Raun-Tu nodded. "Never seen one. I didn't know if they were a myth or real."

"I can't tell you what to do." Well, she could, and make them do it, too, but Ava recognized that would be crossing a line. "But I suggest you sneak into the city, lock the cistern exits and trap the army units hiding there, and take the small force above ground. The mayor is inclined to trust us over the Kassian, and most of the townspeople are supportive, as well."

"Take the city now?" Raun-Tu glanced over at Massi.

"That would be a feat to sing about." Massi rubbed her hands together. "You sure about the cistern exits?"

"I got it from the mayor herself."

"You sure she wasn't lying?" Raun-Tu leaned forward on his forearms.

"She's very angry with the Kassian for setting up her city to be a battleground. She wasn't lying." Ava paused. "Keep the damage in the city to a minimum and you'll be welcomed."

"Avasu, the general never once told me about you in all the years she was using you as her spy, but I have to say, your information is invaluable." Raun-Tu clasped a hand to her shoulder and squeezed.

"Yes." Massi's smile was wry. "We're lucky to have you among our number."

She sometimes forgot who knew the spy story was a lie, and just remembered Massi was one of that small number. She lifted her shoulders and twisted her lips. "Use the information well." She stood.

"You're going now?"

"I'll ride a little further, sleep for a few hours, then keep going."

"Be careful."

She nodded, then remembered something else.

"We saw Haslia in Bartolo. She was spelling the mayor, and I stopped her. So watch what you accept from strangers and keep your eyes peeled."

"You let her get away?" Massi hissed.

"It would have drawn too much attention to try and find her after she disappeared into the crowds, and I think you'll agree the information we got instead will be a lot more helpful to the Rising Wave than having Haslia as our prisoner."

Massi had stood while she explained, and she slowly lowered herself back down. "You're right. We'll watch out for her. I'll look under every rock in the city for her."

Ava nodded, then walked back into the darkness, donning her scarf again to avoid having to explain herself to anyone as she was leaving.

She'd gone the fast way out of Bartolo, and she actually might get to Luc before Oscar and Deni.

She didn't have a moment to lose.

LUC WOKE SUDDENLY.

He still slept with the handkerchief Ava had given him on his pillow—it had saved him from more than one assassination attempt—and he crushed it in his fist as he sat up.

Ava.

He dressed quickly, pulling on the shirt she had embroidered for him and stepping out into the misty predawn.

The first light of the sun lit the eastern sky pink and orange, and gave the mist a strange, golden glow.

He recognized this feeling. He'd given in to its call many times after he and Ava had parted, walking out of camp to stare in the direction of Grimwalt.

This time, though, he headed south, weaving through the close-pitched tents.

They had left the carts and wagons on the plain, protected by a small cohort of guards, and even so, he felt pleased with how many they were.

More than he had ever dreamed.

He had taken the scarf Ava had given him and gone for a wander last night in the hills, but although he'd heard a few calls in the distance, he didn't see any evidence of a hiding army.

The calls were probably scouts, patrolling the hills for signs of the Rising Wave approach.

They would be looking in the wrong direction.

The Rising Wave had swung north west, and was now crouched on the far side from where they were expected.

He reached the edge of the camp and kept going, into the thicker mist lower down in the shallow valley.

The sound of a horse blowing through its nostrils had him going still.

One moment it was simply swirls of white, and then suddenly Ava was there, looking at him from astride her mount.

He felt a sense of absolute lightness as she slid from her saddle and leaped into his arms.

He kissed her, arms tight around her as he held her off the ground.

She gasped as she pulled back, holding his face between her hands. "“Are Oscar and Deni here yet?”

“No.” He carefully looked her over.

She seemed tired but uninjured.

“I beat them here, then.” She gave a wan smile.

Someone shouted behind them, and Luc turned, his body shielding hers, to find Sybyl and Rafe looming out of the mist.

“Did you know she was coming?” Rafe asked, astonished, and Luc shook his head, but didn’t elaborate.

Sybyl walked up to them and reached for her horse’s reins. “I don’t recognize this one,” she said, patting the horse’s neck.

“I stole it.” Ava leaned on Luc’s shoulder, and he could hear the exhaustion in her voice.

“Come get something to eat and drink, and you can tell us about it.” He put his arm around her and walked her to his tent. She stood, looking a little lost, and he drew her over to the table, sat her down and went back outside to fetch her some hot tea.

He could see the dark bruises beneath her eyes.

“Avasu.” The general peered into the tent, and Luc gestured her in.

Ava looked up at them both over the rim of her cup. “The Kassian have bought thirty flares. They’re planning to launch them from these hilltops at the Rising Wave.”

“Evil.” The general’s hiss was full of fury and disgust. “That is pure evil. It is good we are going to break their power, Commander, because this is proof they do not deserve to have any.”

“I’ve never heard of flares.” Luc tried to think of any reference to them in his time in the camps and later in the Kassian forces, but he couldn’t.

“They make them in Zilvana. No one knows who supplies the magic but they are rare and difficult to obtain. Some countries, like Grimwalt, Venyatu, and Jatan have signed laws to ban them from ever being used." General Ru was almost panting with rage. "This will damage the Kassian reputation more than they realize."

"How do they work?"

"They'll shoot the flares, and when they hit the ground, I'm told the contents spread like water, as far as they can go, and they burn everything in their path. It takes a long time for the fire to burn itself out, and nothing is left behind."

"Then we stop them from firing them at all." Luc would not see the land he was reclaiming burned to nothing. That was not going to happen. "This explains why I couldn't find any sign of the Kassian in the hills last night."

The General nodded. "It didn't make sense that we were that far ahead of them. But if they're setting up flare cannons, they hardly need many people. You said thirty flares?"

Ava nodded. "I was told ten cannons, three flares each."

"Ten will cover a large area. That's what they were doing here with their mapping. They were working out which hills would give them the best coverage." General Ru had started to pace.

"At least we're not where they expect us." Luc was sure of that.

"That's true. You're sure of your information, Avasu?"

"Completely sure. The flare cannons left nearly four days ago from Bartolo, so they're most likely already here. The Kassian troops have split up, a few with the flare cannons, some to line the Bartolo River to make sure the Rising Wave can't easily cross, and the main force hiding under Bartolo, in the cisterns."

"Hiding under the city?" The general stopped pacing and turned to Ava.

"They've left a small force above ground, as a decoy, to pretend that's the only protection Bartolo has. They're hoping the Rising Wave soldiers who survive the flares will make a dash for Bartolo to cross at the bridge, and when they enter the city, the troops below will spill out and end things."

"We need to tell Raun-Tu—"

"I already did." Ava drained the last of her tea from her cup. "I went out the east gate to warn Massi and Raun-Tu. They're going into the city to deal with the Kassian troops. Oscar and Deni left through the west gate." She set her cup down and entwined her fingers. "I hope they were able to avoid the troops setting up guard along the river."

"That might be why they've been delayed. They're avoiding the Kassian. But what do you mean, Massi and Raun-Tu are going to deal with the Kassian troops in Bartolo?" Luc crouched down beside her.

"There are only two ways in and out of those underground cisterns. I told Massi and Raun-Tu where to find them, and they're going to block them off and trap the Kassian under the city." She made a pillow with her hands and lay her head down on them.

Luc looked over at General Ru, and saw the same astonishment on her face that must be on his.

"You learned all this in just a few days?" General Ru asked.

Ava said nothing, and Luc bent closer. She was asleep.

He lifted her up from the chair, and she forced her eyes open, looked at him blankly and then went back to sleep.

He set her in their bed and returned. The general had a look on her face . . . covetous, Luc thought.

She wanted Ava for her own.

And who could blame her?

"Would we have won this without her?" General Ru asked softly.

"We haven't won yet," Luc warned.

"I'm aware, Commander." General Ru put her hands on her hips. "But we have a lot better chance now."

CHAPTER 35

"Bait."

"What's that?" Dak looked up from the table they were all leaning over at Heival's words.

"We offer them bait."

"And if they decide to burn the bait with magical fire?" The general shook her head. "No one should die like that."

"Agreed." Luc was not seeing anyone burned. Or anything.

But it did give him an idea.

"This needs to be a stealth operation, not open battle." He looked over at the general and she nodded in agreement.

"Take each cannon unit out with a small group of well-trained warriors. Preferably at the same time."

"Do you want to form five teams, and so will I?" Luc didn't think the Venyatux would sit this one out. Not with the incandescent rage still burning in General Ru's eyes at the thought of the flares.

"Yes. Tell me what you've got in mind." General Ru glanced across at the curtain shielding a sleeping Ava from the lieutenants and officers in his tent, but Luc had no intention of involving Ava in this.

She had done enough.

"I would like to be in one of those teams." Kikir, the Skäddar warrior, had said nothing about the flares, but now Luc saw something in his eyes that told him the man simply hid his rage well.

The sound of shouting filtered through from outside, and everyone turned as Rafe stuck his head in.

"Oscar and Deni are back. And they have some news."

Luc gestured for them to come with his hand, and the two men walked in, a little wide-eyed.

"Encountered some trouble?" Luc asked.

Dak handed them each a cup of water, and neither answered until they had swallowed it down.

"We came over the river, but there were patrols all along the banks, and someone saw us and gave chase." Deni looked around for a seat, found a box and sank down on it.

"We didn't want to lead them back to where we knew you were headed, so we swung wide, toward the north east, in what we thought was a big loop that would put us out of their way." Oscar rubbed his face with a filthy hand.

"But?" General Ru asked.

"But instead we found a whole new army coming from the north west. Not fresh, like the ones we saw in Bartolo. Hardened, tired. Like they'd just been fighting. They'll probably reach what's left of our wagon train by midday tomorrow."

"The whole of the Kassian army was fighting the Jatan, but my latest information is they pulled more than half their force away a few months ago. Probably to rest and reequip to fight us. But they had to have left some forces to hold the border with Jatan. You think they've pulled those units?" Luc leaned over the map again.

"I think they've decided we're too dangerous. That they have to overwhelm us." General Ru tapped the map with a finger. "Or maybe the Jatan drove them back and they decided to cut their losses there. My guess is they've sent the contingent that was on the Jatan border to herd us toward the hills and the flares. The north east is where they thought the columns would be. They're coming up behind our old position."

"But the carts and wagons are still in the old position," Heival said. "They'll find something there, but it won't be the Rising Wave."

There was silence.

"Let's say Massi and Raun-Tu deal with the Kassian army in Bartolo." Luc bent over the map. "We've got Kassian troops waiting along the river and cannons in the hills, and now a whole new army coming from behind."

"We deal with the army behind, and the cannons, and then we take the river." General Ru crossed her arms over her chest.

"I agree." Luc stared down at the map. At their options. "We have to deal with the cannons now, but we can't leave the Jatan border contingent to take our carts and wagons. It's not just that's our supplies, they're more or less unprotected."

"Wait. How did you know about the troops in Bartolo?" Oscar had found a seat as well, and he looked up with red-rimmed eyes.

"Ava got here at dawn."

Both men slumped in relief.

"We hoped she'd beat us. We were driven so far off course, we were worried about the delay in letting you know about the cannons." Oscar rose to his feet, staggered a little.

"Now we know about the extra forces, so you did well." Dak clapped Oscar on the shoulder. "Go get a bath and some sleep."

The men left together and there was a moment of silence in the tent.

"This is bad." Fervanti said. "Kurvin is alone out there with just twenty soldiers, guarding the carts and wagons. While they won't be able to herd us toward the cannons like they planned, they can still wipe out all our supplies."

"Our plans have to change." Luc lifted his gaze to Ava, who was now standing quietly at the entrance to their sleeping space.

She must have been woken by the sound of Oscar and Deni's voices.

General Ru turned, following his line of sight, and nodded. "What do you suggest?"

"Everyone who's fresh, which is most of the camp, leaves with you, General. If you ride hard, you can come up behind the Jatan contingent of the Kassian army tonight. Deal with them."

"And you?" General Ru didn't show whether she would accept his strategy or not.

"Ava and I, and Oscar and Deni, and the few others left who were on night duty last night and are still asleep, will deal with the cannons when the sun sets."

Kikir looked up from the map. "I will help in the hills, Commander, if you'll have me. It's more what I'm used to than the plains."

Luc thought about it. He had no intention of using anyone but Ava, Oscar and Deni, and the sudden gleam in General Ru's eye told him she knew that.

"I would like you with me." The general turned to the Skäddar. "The hills where the cannons are situated are nothing like the mountains you know. But you've got a good rapport with all the teams, and you could assist Fervanti, Heival and Dak. We can split the two columns into four, and you could lead one."

Kikir looked between them, and while he may have suspected he was being steered in another direction for a mysterious reason, commanding half a column was not something he had expected to be offered. "General, you have me at your service."

"Good." General Ru gave a decisive nod. "Get everyone ready. We leave in half an hour."

The lieutenants sprinted from the tent.

"Good luck, Commander." General Ru thumped her chest in the Venyatux salute. "A lot weighs on your shoulders."

"No more than yours." Luc touched two fingers to his left cheek.

The general stepped up and slung an arm around him, pulled him into an embrace.

She was only slightly taller than Ava, he realized with surprise, as he returned the hug.

"We will win." General Ru's face was the most animated he'd ever seen it. "And we will remember this day."

She was suddenly gone, and it was just Ava and him in the tent.

"Are you up for taking the cannons?" Luc asked.

She stared at him through sleepy eyes. "Let me get my needle."

"I WANT TO GO HOME."

Ava crouched down to watch as the Kassian soldier stood up and looked around him.

"Not you, too." The woman who answered him sounded annoyed. "We all want to go home, Maynard."

"No. I mean right now." Maynard crouched beside his pack and threw a few things inside it, then stood.

"What're you talking about?" The third member of the four-person cannon unit stood as well.

"I don't think I could have been clearer, Vaten. I am leaving to go home. Now." Maynard strapped the pack on his back.

"What is going on here? How many people do we need to lose before someone comes out and says this place is cursed?" The woman sounded nervous. "It's not just the flares. People have been acting strangely since we got here."

"Can you hear yourself, Finley?" Maynard's tone was one of disgust. "I'm going to join the others who saw the light and left yesterday. This is bullshit."

"Enough. We're all just following orders." Vaten put a hand on Maynard's shoulder.

Maynard shrugged him off. "You got anything to say, Hamer?"

The fourth person stirred from where they'd been lying on the grass. "No."

"Good." Maynard put his hand in his pocket, and Ava knew that's where he'd slid the handkerchief he'd picked up when he went to relieve himself. His hand bunched into a fist, and she guessed he was holding it tight.

He sounded relieved. Like he'd been unburdened.

"Hopefully, I won't see any of you again." He started walking, and Vaten got in his way.

"Don't do this. We can't operate the cannon without you."

"You don't say?" Maynard gave a low laugh. "Sorry about that." He stepped around Vaten and kept walking.

The low fire they were sitting around illuminated Vaten just enough for Ava to see his mouth twist in rage.

He bent down, picked up a stick that was stacked beside the fire and swung it at Maynard's head.

The soldier went down without a sound.

Finley and Hamer scrambled to their feet and stared.

"He was deserting." Vaten threw the stick down. "Like Carter and Fal and Gador. Fuck." He looked around. "What is going on?"

"What's going on now is we're really stuck if we need to use this fucking cannon, because it needs four people to operate it." Finley kicked out at the stick Vaten had dropped. "What were you thinking?"

"I was thinking he was going to leave, whatever we said or did, just like the others." Vaten's voice rose, and then he rubbed his face. "I'll go down to the base camp, get one of the scouts to take his place. Watch him." Vaten picked up a belt and scabbard and buckled it low on his hips before he walked away.

The small items Ava had left in the hills before they'd gone on to Bartolo had certainly wreaked havoc here, by the sounds of things.

They were stretched thin and jumpy.

She waited, still crouched low.

This is where she let Luc, Oscar and Deni do their thing.

She was just as capable as they were of attacking the remaining soldiers, but unlike Oscar and Deni, she hadn't slept for more than an hour this morning.

She had spent the day embroidering, and she was exhausted, so now she waited, crouched low in the darkness, her scarf around her neck.

She was a killer, though, just as much as them.

Maybe warrior was a better word.

She hoped she wasn't just finding nicer, more palatable versions of the truth.

It was probably the exhaustion talking.

None of them had gone looking to be death bringers.

Kassia had forced this uprising, and they had upped the stakes with these flares.

The fact that Kassia remained without allies and with so many nations ranged against them, told the story of their missteps, greed and cruelty.

No one wanted to help them, unless, like the Speaker of Grimwalt, there was a personal benefit.

And her aunt, the queen, was behind each badly-made decision. Along with her cousin.

It pained Ava that she was related to them, although she wouldn't have endured what she had if there'd been no relationship between them.

She wanted revenge against them specifically, especially after what they'd done to her mother, but they were shielded behind the walls of Fernwell, and there would be a lot of blood that wasn't theirs on her hands before this was finished.

Luc stepped in front of her, searching for her in the darkness, and she pulled the scarf away.

"Site's cleared," he said and held out a hand to her.

There was a thin line of blood spray across his cheek.

She realized she hadn't even heard the fighting. She'd gone into a doze while she waited.

She closed her fingers around his and rose up, hooked a hand around his arm, and glanced at what they were calling a cannon nest.

Everyone was dead.

Oscar crouched beside the cannon, opening the wooden box beside it.

She walked over to Maynard's body and pulled the handkerchief from his pocket. No sense leaving any evidence behind.

"They all there?" Luc asked.

Oscar turned and nodded. "All three accounted for."

This was the ninth nest they'd cleared. They had one more to go.

The sound of footsteps had them all turning, but it was Deni.

"There is a base camp," he said. "I'm amazed we didn't stumble across it by accident before now."

"How many in it?" Luc moved toward the cannon.

"Just four that I could see. Probably off-duty scouts. This one," he toed Vaten, who they'd dragged back up the hill after killing, "said he'd get a scout to stand in for his deserting friend, so it's possible there are others patrolling the valley."

"That makes sense. They wouldn't want anyone to stumble across this by accident. They aren't expecting us but anyone could be wandering around." Oscar took out the hammer they'd brought with them, and Luc carefully tipped the small cannon over.

They systematically smashed the levers and then pulled it apart.

A shout went up, coming from a hill they had cleared earlier, and they all rose to their feet.

"Looks like one of the scouts stopped in to say hello and got a surprise," Deni said.

"We need to get to the last hill. Now."

Luc ran and they fell in line behind him. The others were faster than she was and Ava had just lost sight of them when she remembered the flares.

She stopped. Damn! There was no good choice here.

She needed to help the others, but hiding the flares was her job, and it was vital no one could find them.

She turned and ran back.

Oscar had already moved the wooden crate to the side, but not under bushes as they had done at the other sites.

She tried to lift it, but it was too heavy and she was too afraid of knocking the glass canisters together or dropping the box.

She turned in a circle, looking for inspiration, and ran at the closest tree, jumping up to grab a leafy branch, and ripping it off the main trunk.

It wasn't much, but it just needed to obscure.

She didn't know if it was even necessary. It was possible her working would hide the crate even if it were out on the plains in full sunlight, but she wasn't prepared to take that chance.

They were planning to come back and find a way to destroy all the flares, but right now they just needed to hide them and keep them out of Kassian hands.

She tied the long strip of fabric she'd embroidered with invisibility to the box and arranged the branch on top, then ran back toward the trail. She felt lightheaded by the time she reached the bottom and stood, head bent over her knees, to get herself together.

"You sure you saw someone come this way?"

"Yes."

Ava slowly raised her head, grateful beyond words she'd decided to put her scarf back on.

Her cloak hadn't warned her of the small group's approach, but then, they couldn't mean her harm if they didn't know she existed.

Her old cloak would have alerted her, though.

She knew it.

And there was nothing she could do about it, so she focused on what she could do.

Five soldiers moved in single file up the narrow path to the hilltop, and Ava stepped out of the way to let them pass.

They had their weapons drawn, and they were dressed in the brown and gray of scouting parties, not the more formal uniform of the Kassian soldiers.

This must be the four scouts Deni had checked out earlier, and the fifth soldier who'd sent up the cry of alarm.

Ava followed behind the last in line, and then kicked the back of his knee.

He went down, hands splayed out to stop himself, and she threw a piece of fabric in front of him.

"You all right, Rogers?" The scout in front of him turned to look.

"Just tripped." Rogers stood, holding the small square in his hand.

"It's not good, is it, Rogers? Guarding flare cannons?" Ava asked from behind him.

He stopped, turned to look, and frowned.

"I'm here, you just can't see me. You have to be sick to your stomach at the thought of it. Of burning all those people." She had found most of the soldiers at the cannon nests had needed almost no persuasion to leave their posts. Maybe it was the havoc she had already sown by leaving her little surprises behind, or maybe they truly did have a conscience.

She had started working a compulsion to leave the hills into the fabric she had left for them to find, and ended up not having to talk to them at all after the third nest.

"Like how I feel about it would make any difference." Rogers scoffed. "At least I don't have to fire the things."

"You could stop it. You *should* stop it."

"How?" He started to scramble up a steep section of path, and Ava realized she was in danger of falling behind.

"Run home." She could get him to kill some of the others, but she didn't want to do that. It was easier to just make them run away.

"Now?"

"Now. And when you get home, you should throw that square of fabric in the fire." It was her last one, as it happened.

She stepped aside as he turned and went back down the hill.

One down.

She stepped off the path as the scout in front of Rogers turned and saw him leaving.

"Hey, where're you going?"

"Home." Rogers waved without turning and disappeared into the darkness.

"What . . . ?" The soldier moved down the path to follow after him, and Ava stepped behind him and slit his throat.

It was the first actual person she'd killed with her own hands.

She felt sick, and she was already not well from the exertion. She bent over and retched, her skin clammy.

She had no time for this.

She straightened and started up the path again, then heard the sound of someone gasp in surprise up ahead and then the death rattle as they were stabbed in the chest.

Luc.

Working his way back through the scouts to her.

"I'm all right, I went back for the flares," she said into the darkness.

"Ava." He sounded at his wit's end.

"Sorry, I didn't want to leave them." She pulled her scarf away, and felt invisible arms go around her.

"There were two others, but I sent one home and killed one," she whispered in his ear.

His hold tightened at the word 'kill' and then he let her go.

"Let's go help Oscar and Deni." She couldn't see him, but she knew from his tone he had turned back to look at her. "Stay behind me this time."

She didn't answer, except to pull her scarf back on.

He wanted to go faster, she could tell, but there was no way she could push herself any more.

She stepped around each of the bodies of the three scouts he'd killed, and then stopped.

"Go ahead. There's no one left to hurt me back here. I'll catch you up." Oscar and Deni needed him more than she did right now. "Go."

He made a sound of frustration and then he went, she could hear him running along the path.

This would be the first nest they would clear without help from her, and she pushed herself a little faster.

When she reached the top, she slowed to a stop and tried not to make a single sound.

Three Kassian soldiers lay dead and a fourth held a glass flare canister in his hand.

"It's over," Luc said to him. "We've taken all the cannons. You are the only one left."

"Then I'm dead, whether I let this go or not. I'm the officer in charge of this whole operation, so there is no way this will go well for me. At least this death will be a lot quicker than if my general gets hold of me. That's if you don't torture me for information and then kill me, first." The officer lifted his arm. "I don't know what went wrong with this operation, but people were deserting or obstructing the mission from the moment we got here."

Ava pulled off her scarf. "Stop."

He stopped, hand still raised. Stared at her in the low firelight. "Where did you come from? Wait, are you . . .?" He leaned closer.

"I hear it's a good likeness." She remembered how quickly the officer in Bartolo had recognized her.

"It is." He stared.

"So, I'll make you a deal. Put down the flare and you can take me with you. You'll be rewarded, not killed."

"Ava, what are you doing?" Luc turned to look at her.

"What will it be? An agonizing death for everyone, or you going back with the prize the Herald has been searching for for months?" She lifted her hands as she ignored Luc.

"I won't get far with you, not with these three after me." The officer lowered his hand, though. "Although . . ."

He shuffled around Luc, holding the flare out. "Move, or we'll see what happens if I splash some on you."

Luc moved slowly out of the way.

"Ava, what's going on?"

"When I was in Bartolo, one of the Kassian officers recognized me. Apparently the Queen's Herald sent a drawing of me to the senior officers with instructions to be on the lookout."

He said nothing, and she looked over at him.

His face was impossible to read.

"Better to be in enemy hands than for all of us to be dead, and the hills burning."

He couldn't argue with that. Although, she saw with a surprise that punched the air from her lungs, he looked like he wanted to.

"If you follow me down, I'll douse her in the stuff." The officer waggled the bottle, then thought better of it and held it still.

Ava started to slide her hand into her pocket, but he gave a shout.

"Don't move. Keep your hands up."

He reached her and put the flare into her hands, then pulled her up against his chest. "You spill it, we both die. You try to attack me," his gaze went to Luc, "she spills it on herself."

He fumbled with something on his belt, and came up with the thin restraints Ava had seen carried by every Kassian soldier at the fort where she'd been held.

He looped them around her wrists and pulled her back against him.

They moved in an awkward shuffle down the path, and when they reached the first body, Ava's cloak let her know the man holding onto her had become even more dangerous.

"I would think long and hard before you take the flare from me and toss it down on the path." She spoke quietly.

"And why's that?" He didn't deny he was considering it.

"Because I've heard it reacts like water, and water flows downhill."

He hesitated and then tightened his grip so he was hurting her. "These are my people lying dead here."

"And you were planning to burn my people to death. Including the ground beneath their feet." She waited for a response, and when none was forthcoming, she shrugged.

He loosened his hold a little and kept pulling her back. The path was uneven, and he kept stumbling. "Keep a good hold on that flare."

Her heart lurched as they slid down a little way, and she tightened her grip on the glass canister.

Luc would be following them, scarf on, she knew. And Oscar and Deni wouldn't be far behind.

She wished she'd had time to work more protection into her cloak. She had added a working for flare fire this afternoon, to hers and to Luc, Oscar and Deni's clothing, but she hadn't really known what the flare light was when she'd done it, and she didn't know if her magic would stand against the magic in the canister.

She wouldn't want to take that chance. And neither would Luc. She'd warned him that she didn't know whether the magic in the flares could override hers. And to assume it could.

She would definitely be protected against a sword strike or an arrow, but she had a feeling that with her new cloak, there were big gaps in her protective shield.

They finally reached the bottom of the slope, and a horse nickered to the left.

"Captain Rangar?"

She felt a chill that her cloak had not warned her of the group of soldiers who were waiting quietly in the darkness. It might be because they meant her no specific harm, but she had become too complacent, too used to the sensitive, fine-tuned warnings of her old cloak.

"Who's there?" The officer swung her around so he could see both the path and down the valley.

"I'm Captain Farr. What's going on?" The officer was no more than a dark shadow on a horse.

Ava thought there might be another five soldiers behind him.

"What unit?" Rangar asked.

"I'm with the Jatan Border Force. I've orders to requisition some of your flares."

"You were going to herd the Rising Wave within shooting distance of my cannons. Why do you need my flares?"

"Because the Rising Wave ambushed us, and there's barely any of us left. We're not going to be herding them anywhere. But if you give us the flares, we could fire them into their columns and deal with them. Take them by surprise." He sounded viciously pleased with the idea. Then he leaned forward. "Who's that with you?"

Rangar hesitated. "A Rising Wave prisoner. She and her friends have taken out the cannons, but you're welcome to the flares. Take as many as you like." Rangar began to edge around the small group.

"Is that a flare in her hand?" Farr leaned forward for a closer look.

"It's my insurance. There are twenty-nine left for you."

"Don't let them get the flares," Ava said into the darkness. "That has to be your main priority."

She wanted to crow at the knowledge that General Ru had won her battle. It was good news, despite her current situation.

"Who's she talking to?" Farr brought his horse closer, and Ava could tell Rangar didn't like it at all.

"Her friends. Who I hope haven't followed us down the hill."

"You're not going to douse me in flare." Ava turned her head to look at Rangar. "I'm your ticket out of this mess." She looked up the slope again. "Better to stop them getting the flares at all than have to get them back later."

She felt vindicated in her decision to go back and hide the last lot of flares, now. There were only two available to take.

"How many 'friends' are there?" Farr asked, his gaze going up the hill.

"At least three."

"Four people took your whole position of ten cannons?" Farr sounded shocked.

"I said 'at least'. I'm assuming there are more of them." Rangar was getting twitchy. He wanted to get away clean from here with Ava, and have the ability to spin the story any way he liked.

Farr was ruining that for him.

"Tie up the woman and then show us where to find the flares." Farr slid off the horse at last, and moved closer to them.

"The only flares left are up this hill." Ava didn't want the soldiers splitting up. It would be harder for Luc, Oscar and Deni to hunt them down that way.

"What?" Rangar tightened his grip.

"As we cleared each position, we took the flares. There are only two left above."

"And the one in your hands," Farr said.

"And the one in my hands." Ava smiled.

"I don't believe you. You haven't had time." Rangar gave her a little shake. "They're difficult to transport."

"Just imagine," Ava said. "The Rising Wave heading for Fernwell with at least twenty seven flares, all courtesy of the Kassian military itself."

She couldn't see Rangar's face, but the look on Farr's told her he was thinking of the many ways he could be killed by his generals.

"No." Rangar shook his head. "It took nearly fifty soldiers all day to get them into place. You couldn't have taken them."

She shrugged. Said nothing. She wished she could get her hand into her pocket. But she would surely get the chance soon.

"Head up that hill there. There should be three at the top." Rangar pointed to the ninth cannon nest.

"If she's right, then her friends might already be taking the two that are left, which would leave us with just one." Farr waved a hand at the soldiers behind him and they slid off their horses and started up the slope.

"She wants your people to go up there, she's manipulated you into doing it, so her fellow Rising Wave friends can kill them."

"Five against three. I'm sure my unit will be fine."

Ava saw the five soldiers disappear up the path. They wouldn't be coming back down.

"You don't think they will, do you?" Farr must have seen something on her face.

She shrugged. "Who can say?"

He was much closer to them now, and she felt Rangar's tension in the way he held himself behind her. He didn't want Farr to recognize her.

If he'd just come from the Jatan border, he might not have seen the drawing.

Rangar wanted her for himself. She was his ticket out of the disaster that had just hit him.

Not that she was planning to oblige.

She looked down at the flare canister in her hands.

She thought it would feel warm, but it was cool to the touch, and the contents were a pale, luminous blue.

If the general's reaction to the news of it hadn't been enough to warn her, though, Rangar's palpable fear would have done it.

It was hard to work out what to do when she was holding so much potential for destruction in her hands.

And then, suddenly it wasn't in her hands.

Farr had snatched it from her.

"I think she was telling the truth about the other flares, and I need as many of these as I can get if I'm to go back without losing my rank." Farr slid the canister into a pocket in his saddle bag.

"You have no right." Rangar lifted a knife to Ava's throat. "That was mine."

"It belongs to the Kassian army, and I have orders to bring it out to the plains."

The knife pricked at Ava's skin and now that she was no longer holding the flare, she moved her tied hands to her pocket.

"Don't move." The knife dug deeper, and she stopped.

Rangar sounded desperate enough to cut her. And it hurt. Her protection was definitely not what it had been.

Ava looked up the path and wondered where Luc and the others were.

A sudden scream from above had Farr jerking his gaze in the direction of the hill.

"One of yours?" Rangar asked. He lifted the knife from Ava's throat and tightened his hold on her neck.

Ava gasped and began to claw at his arm. He was choking her.

"What—?" Farr turned back to face them, and as he did, Rangar threw the knife that he'd been using on Ava. It cut Farr's question short as it entered his throat, and just before she lost all her air and the world went black, Ava saw the bloom of blood.

CHAPTER 36

Luc didn't question the sudden urgency he felt to get back to Ava. He had killed two of the soldiers who had come up the hill looking for flares, and he was confident Oscar and Deni could deal with the other three.

This need to get to her, though, was more than just general worry that she was being held by two men who were his enemies.

It felt like a warning from the protections she had sewn into his shirt and tunic. As if her safety was part of his own protection.

He didn't disagree.

He would . . . not do well if anything happened to her.

He raced back down the path, trying to hold on to the fact that Rangar seemed to need Ava.

The Queen's Herald would do anything to keep Ava under his control, and the fact that he was actively looking for her was a bad sign.

Desperate men did desperate things.

Rangar obviously thought his problems would disappear if he produced her.

He was probably right.

And she had made the choice to bargain herself for their lives and safety, betting on the same calculation.

He heard muttering up ahead, like Rangar talking to himself, and he crept the last stretch of path to hide the sound of his steps.

He reared back at the change in scene from only a few minutes ago.

Farr was dead, lying in an expanding pool of blood from his throat.

Ava was slung over Farr's mount and Rangar was looping her bound hands through the shortened stirrup on one side.

"The only way," Rangar was saying. "Just have to chance it." When he turned, he had the flare canister in his hand, the lid off.

He tilted the canister and swung his arm, and a thin spray of luminous blue liquid flew through the air.

Some of it hit Luc in the chest, and there seemed to be a thunderclap, a lightning strike of cold, white light, that threw him backward.

He landed hard and scrambled to his feet to find a thin line of fire blocking his way to Ava.

It was spreading so fast, running like water just as the general had said.

But he wasn't burning, he suddenly realized. The flare had hit him, thrown him back, but he wasn't even scorched.

Ava had sewn protection against flare fire into his shirt.

She hadn't been confident about it, but once again, she proved she had no reason to doubt herself.

He pulled off his shirt and began to beat the flames so he could get to her.

Suddenly Oscar and Deni were on either side of him, the protective vests Ava had made them for tonight off, helping him beat the fire.

It took them almost half an hour to douse it completely, and by the time they did, Rangar was long gone.

"He's got Ava?" Oscar looked at the charred body they'd found once the flames were out.

"That's Farr," Luc said. "Rangar stabbed him in the throat and then threw some of the flare liquid up the hill."

"Why?" Deni stared at the blackened corpse in horror.

"Because he knew he wouldn't get far with Ava if we were after him, and he didn't want Farr going back with tales of how his whole mission was rendered useless." Luc started jogging toward where they had hidden their horses, and Oscar and Deni followed.

"Where's he taking her?" Oscar asked.

"The river, to wherever they've set up their headquarters." Luc wanted to catch them long before they reached the riverbanks.

"The Queen's Herald is looking for her?" Deni asked as they swung into their saddles.

Luc gestured to Deni's vest, which he'd put back on, and then to his own shirt. Neither of them were even singed. "If you were a greedy, power-hungry ruler, wouldn't you do whatever you could to have her?"

THEY FOUND THE FLARE CANISTER TWO HOURS LATER.

Dawn had yet to break, although it wasn't far off, but the luminous blue was easy to see in the darkness.

"Why did he leave it?" Oscar wondered.

"Maybe it was slowing him down," Luc said. "He was worried about it spilling or dropping." He picked it up and wrapped it in his shirt, then put it in his saddlebag.

It worried him, though. That Rangar would give up such a powerful weapon.

He'd sent Deni back to the general, to give her an update on the situation, and it was just him and Oscar chasing Rangar across the plains.

The smell of fire shortly after they found the flare canister worried him enough that they followed it to its source.

It was nothing more than a scout camp, the coals in the fire pit still glowing.

"He must have stumbled across the scout camp." Luc circled the small area. "He didn't want to be seen with the flare canister on him. He must have worked out a story that doesn't suit him having one."

"So he just left it on the plain? Out in the open where anyone could have found it?" Oscar sounded grim.

"He doesn't care about anything except saving his own ass." Luc caught sight of the churned up earth of many hooves, and felt his heart sink. "And having Ava to present to the Queen's Herald is the ultimate ass-saver."

At least that meant she was would be kept safe. For now.

But Rangar would have spun his story to the scouts and it looked like they had been persuaded to escort him on his journey.

"Let's go." Luc leaned down to see which path they'd taken, and he and Deni galloped in the direction of the river as the sun rose behind them and turned the plains pink and orange.

They found the base camp easily enough.

The smoke led them right to it.

They had burned the pontoons they'd used to get their equipment over the river, and they'd burned their supply wagons and their massive wooden slings.

"Why?" Oscar's horse danced nervously around the smoke-hazed camp.

"Rangar's told them we've decimated the Jatan border units and taken the hills and the flares. They may have decided it was too dangerous to trust we hadn't taken Bartolo, or maybe they'd heard we had, and that lent veracity to his story."

"They've taken Ava, and they've destroyed everything that would slow them down." Oscar slid off his horse and led her to the river bank to let her drink.

Luc looked over the river, but there was no obvious route that he could see. They'd split up, breaking into groups to make themselves a more difficult target, and Ava could be in any one of those units.

Finding her would be impossible.

Except he knew where they would be taking her, and he had long been planning to go there himself.

"Where is she, do you think?" Oscar came to stand beside him.

"Not sure where she is now, but I know where she'll be by tonight, or tomorrow morning."

"Fernwell?"

He nodded. "Fernwell."

"So what do we do?" Oscar eyed the river as if expecting Luc to say they needed to cross and give chase.

"We go down to Bartolo, make sure we have actually taken it, and wait for the general. She won't be far behind."

And then they would march on Fernwell, and get his lover back.

CHAPTER 37

There was a delay in her getting brought to the palace.

Ava gathered it was because Rangar wasn't initially believed.

She didn't blame whoever had dismissed his story as farfetched, because it was—a mixture of half-truths and outright lies that somehow pointed most of the blame at the murdered Captain Farr.

She clung to the idea it was lies layered on lies, because he had also told her that he had burned Luc and the others with flare fire, and she refused to believe it.

Refused.

Someone eventually believed him, though. And now they were scrambling.

She could hear the panic in the voices of those around him.

They were in trouble, and she wondered how Herron had heard she was here.

The Queen's Herald would not react well to the idea that his prize possession had been under his nose for two days and he hadn't known it.

"You're sure it's the princess?" Whoever was in charge sounded like he didn't want to produce her, only to find she wasn't the one all the fuss was about, but didn't want to refuse to bring her to the palace, either.

He walked to the cell and stared at her.

She stared back.

"All right, she looks very like the drawing." There was relief in his voice. "Although she looks like she's been mistreated. What did you do to her?"

It was what they hadn't done that was the problem. They hadn't given her access to her needle and thread, or the squares of fabric in her cloak pocket.

She had been tied over a horse for the first part of her journey, then in metal cuffs since the river, her hands tied above her head in the little cart they had transported her in.

When they'd entered Fernwell, Rangar had been directed to one of the military barracks, and they had taken her cloak away when they'd thrown her into the cell.

Standard practice, it seemed, not an indication that they knew her secrets.

At least she could take some comfort in that.

"I've been trying to get the palace to grant me an audience for the last two days so I can hand her over to the Queen's Herald. I haven't had time to coddle her." Rangar's voice was indignant.

"Well, you've got the audience now. I suggest you do something to make her look like you haven't been abusing her for the last week."

The sound of shouting and horses filtered through into her cell, all the way at the back of the barracks, and Ava forced herself to keep relaxed and still.

Her cousin had arrived himself.

She should have guessed he would be too impatient to wait for her to be brought to him.

The captain of the guard realized it, too. He looked panicked.

"Where is she?" The Queen's Herald's impatience could be heard in every syllable.

"My lord." Rangar had stepped out into the passage. "I am the one who found her. She is here."

He was shoved aside and there was Herron. Looking a little more dissipated, a little more seedy than when she'd last seen him.

She hoped the scar on his side still gave him trouble.

"Ava."

"Herron." She leaned back against the wall and took him in.

"How long has she been here?" Herron turned to the captain of the guard accusingly.

"Two days. Captain Rangar apparently approached your steward three times about her, and was told not to waste your time."

Ava had wondered who would be sacrificed for the greater good of the captain of the guard's career.

"My steward?" Herron's rage was icy cold.

He'd probably told the poor man he wasn't to be disturbed, Ava thought.

"I recognized her immediately, Herald." Rangar had stepped back into the room. "And I did everything I could to make sure I got here with her."

Herron flicked his gaze over Rangar, sizing him up.

He would know a liar when he saw one, being such a prolific liar himself.

"You did your duty, captain. Well done." He gestured to the cell door and the captain of the guard unlocked it.

"Did she have anything on her?" Herron suddenly remembered she had teeth, and leaned against the door to keep it closed.

"Just a gray cloak and a knife," Rangar said. "I think they took them from her when they put her in the cell."

"Where are they?" Herron looked around, and there was some low, fierce whispers as the captain of the guard stepped out.

"They appear to have gone missing." The captain of the guard was sweating when he came back.

Someone had stolen them, perhaps, or it was some kind of perk of the job to be given the prisoner's belongings.

There was a handkerchief in her cloak pocket, which she'd taken off the dead soldier at the ninth cannon nest, along with her scarf. She knew the scarf would only work for her, but she wondered about the handkerchief. Hopefully, whoever held it would feel nothing more than the desire to head home.

"Missing?" Herron gave a smile. "Who was in charge when she was brought in? And why didn't they recognize her?"

She recognized that smile. He wanted to make someone pay for not bringing her to him sooner, and his steward wasn't in front of him right now. He followed the captain of the guard out, and she closed her eyes until the screaming stopped.

When she opened them again, Rangar was standing by the door to her cell, eyes wide, expression stricken.

"You might have bitten off more than you can chew, captain," she told him.

In his face she saw his dreams of fame and promotion wither and die. Now he would be glad just to get out from under her cousin's notice unscathed.

"It appears your cloak and knife have been sold at the market." Herron returned, wiping bloody hands on a cloth.

She shrugged. "I guessed as much."

He studied her face, looking for evidence of her being upset about it, and when he couldn't find it, he turned away.

"Bring her out to my carriage. I'm taking her to the palace."

He strode out, and the captain of the guard opened the door and held it for her.

She stood carefully, and felt herself sliding to the side. The captain caught her before she went down.

"You're going to owe me your life before this night is through," he hissed at Rangar. "Is she injured?"

"No!" Rangar sounded sick.

"If you're lying and I'm in any way implicated later, you will suffer all the consequences I can arrange." The captain of the guard lifted her into his arms and walked out into a room Ava only had a brief impression of before.

It appeared to be an armory with a few tables for note taking and inventory, and armor and weapons lining the walls.

The body of the warden lay in one corner.

A soldier stood, staring at the blood.

"Keys," the captain of the guard snapped at him, and he jolted, then looked at the warden's body in horror.

"The Herald is waiting."

The soldier moved as if struck by lightning, finding the keys on the body and holding them out with shaking hands.

Ava was bundled into the coach with hands still bound, though, and the captain handed her cousin the key.

As soon as the coach rumbled away, Herron crossed his arms over his chest.

"What's wrong with you?" He asked the question politely.

"No food for two days," she said.

He gave a grunt. "Unfortunately, the queen knows you're here." He flicked his gaze over her, top to bottom, and grimaced. "We'll have to clean you up."

"How did she discover my presence?" Ava had an inkling, and it both filled her with joy and worried her.

"Apparently you are going by Ava Yngstra of Grimwalt now, which upset our aunt slightly, but the Commander of the Rising Wave, the Turncoat King himself, asked after you personally. It appears they have captured all thirty flares we purchased at great expense and they have surrounded the city. If we don't produce you, what we had planned to rain down on them, they will rain down on us." Herron's lips were a thin line. "I think I'm quoting almost word for word."

The Commander of the Rising Wave could not have been burned with flare fire, then. Unless General Ru was pretending he was still alive.

But, no. Rangar was a liar. And she would not believe he had killed Luc and her other friends. She simply would not.

"So, the queen was taken by surprise about the flares?" Ava looked Herron directly in the eyes. "You in trouble, cousin?"

He struck out at her.

A backhanded arc from left to right.

The collar and cuffs of her shirt warmed slightly and she dropped to the side, flat on the seat, and at the same time, the coach seemed to lurch, as if it had gone over a stone.

He hit the wall near the window instead of her, and she rose up slowly as he sucked on his bruised fingers.

"Probably better this way. She might not take well to any marks on you. She wants to see you as soon as possible." He leaned back in his seat. "We'll have to clean you up a bit first."

That might mean having to remove her shirt, and she didn't want to be stripped of her only remaining protection.

"Why not take me straight away? Show her you can follow orders."

He shot her a nasty smile. "I'd love to drag you into the throne room looking like a half-dead peasant, but our aunt might take it into her head that I had something to do with it. And I am, as you've surmised, in enough trouble already."

She said nothing more as the coach rumbled over the flagstones. She hadn't been to Fernwell in more than twelve years, and she tried to see out between the gaps as the blinds swung with the rocking motion of the coach.

She caught glimpses of house-lined streets and trees.

The briny smell of the ocean was everywhere, even in the cell she'd been held in, and if you listened carefully, no matter where you were, you could hear the crash and retreat of the waves on the city walls.

The coach slowed as it turned, and then the going was a lot smoother for a short distance.

It came to a stop and the door opened instantly.

A man looked in. He was familiar, Ava realized, and had probably been here the last time she was in Fernwell with her parents.

"The princess's hands are bound." The man looked from Ava to Herron with distaste.

"I must have forgotten to unlock them, Balrick." Herron lifted up the key as if taunting the man. "Would you like to keep her restrained until she's inside?"

"If Her Highness discovers that her niece was brought into the palace in restraints, I assure you, she will not be happy." Balrick stared Herron down. "And she will discover it. I'll make sure of that."

There was no love lost between these two. Ava wondered if Balrick had an escape plan for when her cousin became king, because he would need one.

She rubbed at her wrists as the metal shackles fell to her lap, and then stepped out of the coach.

The palace rose up above her, the peach marble catching the light in a way that was meant to delight.

It had always captivated her.

Just beyond the wall she could hear the sea, and she remembered the time she was last here with her mother and father. Her father had been sick with anger and outrage. He had learned about the Chosen camps, although they been going for nearly a year already by the time he'd gotten word, and he had come to beg his half-sister, the queen, to close them down and release the children.

Her aunt had refused, and they never came back to Fernwell again.

"Do you remember me?" Balrick asked.

She hadn't remembered his name, but Ava did remember his face. She nodded.

"Good. Come with me."

She followed him, not looking back at her cousin, but he caught up to them, clamped a hand on her shoulder.

Balrick turned, his eyes narrowed.

"I'm warning you now, Balrick. Do not let her have anything. Not a thing."

"She will have the clothing appropriate for an audience with the queen." Balrick's nostrils flared, and his lips thinned.

"Nothing else. Not a piece of paper, not even a length of thread."

So he hadn't told her aunt what she could do. Ava had always wondered. And he was trying to keep it that way.

Of course, he still thought she had to use black silk thread, or her own hair, which was also dark, for her embroidery to be dangerous, but he couldn't be so specific without looking like he was hiding something.

Ava laughed, looked at her cousin sidelong. "Not even a needle and thread to darn my socks?"

"Nothing." He took a step closer. "I'm warning you, Balrick, be careful or you will regret it." For the first time, he looked a little unhinged, a little out of control.

She had seen him that way before, up at the fortress, and she guessed it was his true self, covered over by a loose grasp of manners and some veneer of civility.

But it was so easily cracked.

She was led up to a suite of rooms more suited to a guest than a prisoner, but she didn't doubt her aunt would change her status in the blink of an eye, if she wanted to.

A bath had already been drawn for her, and she undressed behind a screen and sank into it, taking her shirt with her to wash it as well as keep it safe.

She wouldn't put it past Balrick to burn everything she had on.

She wasn't given long. A woman in the gray and white uniform she remembered from her last visit came in to hurry her up, and took the wet shirt from Ava's hand with a shake of her head.

"I'll hang it to dry. It looks well enough, I suppose."

"It's my favorite shirt, I don't want to lose it."

The woman sniffed, but she seemed willing to do as Ava asked, and that was as much as she could hope for.

The clothing set out for her on the bed was a dress, silk embroidered with flowers, birds and leaves.

Ava smiled, tracing the design with a finger, looking carefully at the stitching. She had told Catja she was going to do something like this for her cloak. At the time, she'd been lying, making excuses for why she wasn't embroidering the outside of her cloak, but this was beautiful enough she might consider it.

She wondered what would happen if she wore the spell workings of another spell caster like herself. She felt no danger from the dress, though, although she was in nothing but a towel. She had no way to tell whether it was dangerous or not.

"What are you doing?" The woman who'd taken her shirt away came back, wringing her hands. "Don't look at it, put it on."

Ava had no choice, so she stepped into it and the woman tugged on the lacing at the back to make it fit snugly.

"Where did you get such a beautiful dress so quickly?" Ava asked, smoothing the skirt with her hand.

"It was left behind by one of the queen's guests a few years ago. I thought it was too beautiful to throw away, and that turned out to be a good decision." The woman shrugged. "Do the slippers fit?"

Ava slid them on. "Slightly too big, but good enough."

The woman gave a nod of relief. "You're due immediately in the throne room." She led the way out, and the two guards who'd followed her and Balrick up, fell in behind her as she was led down the stairs.

Balrick was waiting for her outside the door to the throne room, and he gave the woman a nod.

"In the time you had, this is good work, Lucinde."

She curtsied and then hurried away, happy to be shot of the whole thing.

Ava didn't blame her.

The sound of footsteps ringing on the marble floor made Balrick stop as he reached for the door handle.

Herron was wearing an ornate jacket, and Ava recognized her mother's stitchwork in the black silk design that was sewn into the two front panels.

He was wearing protection. Protection he had obtained by chaining her mother to a wall and threatening Ava's life if she didn't work it for him. And to make matters worse, he'd forced her mother to unpick her own cloak's protection for the black silk thread.

In that moment, she didn't think she could hate him more.

And yet . . . her mother had worked that design knowing Ava was at Herron's mercy. There might be a few surprises worked in for Ava to use, even though it had to have been around a year ago since the item was sewn.

"You watch your tongue in there, Ava." Herron's hand clamped down on her shoulder and he squeezed hard enough for her to try to get out from under him.

"Or?" She wrenched herself away. She despised this man, and she would not even pretend to obey him.

He said nothing in response, and Ava was aware not only Balrick but the guards as well were listening to every word.

Herron's eyes told her she would be very sorry if she told her aunt what he'd been doing to her for the last few years.

She was going to be sorry no matter what, so she'd make his life as difficult as possible.

She turned her back on him, and Balrick looked at her with a flash of approval before he opened the door.

The throne room was just as Ava remembered it. It didn't seem to be altered at all in the twelve years since she'd been here.

It was a simple room in some ways. There wasn't a lot of furniture or wall hangings.

The focus of attention was the throne and the queen herself, and the gloss and beauty of the veined peach marble that clad the walls and floor.

A long carpet ran from the door to the throne.

It tended to focus the eyes on the dark wooden chair on which the queen sat, carved with images of the sea. The back of the chair resembled a rising wave, and Ava wondered if Luc had known that when he'd named his rebel army.

She'd forgotten about it until now, but it surely couldn't be coincidence.

"Ava!" The queen stood as they entered, and Ava walked the long carpet train, hands demurely together, head bowed, until she reached the bottom of the dais.

"Aunt Freida."

"You don't go by Valestri anymore." It was a strange opening statement, and Ava wondered if her aunt was still smarting from the final words she'd had with Ava's father.

"My father took my mother's name after you refused to disband the Chosen camps," Ava said. "I've used Yngstra for the last twelve years."

"Was it that long ago?" the queen mused. "It feels like yesterday. How is my brother?"

Ava blinked, looked up at her to see if she was being cruel, or if she really didn't know.

"Herron had him murdered two years ago." She stated it as calmly as she could.

It was the queen's turn to blink. "Herron?"

Herron had followed her down the length of the room, but off to the side, where guards lined the walls.

"She is—"

"Did you have my father killed?" Ava snapped, her voice cold as she cut through his bluster.

"Yes."

He looked surprised to have answered her, and Ava hid her elation by looking at her feet.

Her mother *had* worked some extra details into the jacket. Like the ability for her daughter to be obeyed, if she should ever be in the same room as Herron while he was wearing it.

"How?" the queen leaned forward on her throne, and Herron looked as if he were weighing up the benefits of coming clean.

"I paid bandits to ambush him and his wife."

"Why?"

"He was coming to rescue me. Herron had abducted me by then and was holding me in your northern fortress." Ava linked her fingers together. "You held me for two years, didn't you, Herron?"

"Yes." His answer this time was slightly weary.

"Explain." The queen stood, and Ava saw her mouth was in a tight line.

She looked ill.

She had looked ill twelve years ago, and Ava had wondered a few times while she was held in the fortress whether she had possibly died.

"I thought we should have her under our control. She is your niece, after all, and would be considered a prize to some." Herron held his hands palms up.

"You just forgot to tell me about it. Like the flares?" The queen slowly sat back down. "You ruin my reputation with our allies and neighbors, and I don't even know what has been done in my name."

"You aren't in the best of health, I'm trying to shield you from the nastier side of running a country."

Frieda laughed at that. It was not a happy sound. "Herron. I'm afraid you will force me to execute you one of these days."

Herron tried to smile, but Ava guessed it was close to what he feared himself.

"And you? How are you known to the Commander of the Rising

Wave?" The queen's ire turned on Ava as suddenly as it had turned on Herron.

"I joined his army. I have traveled with the Rising Wave for some time."

"And why would you do such a terrible thing against your own aunt?"

Ava stared at her, held up a hand and ticked the reasons off with her fingers. "I was abducted and lost two years of my life. My parents were murdered. I wanted revenge." Ava held her aunt's gaze, steady and serious.

The queen leaned back. "That, I understand." She turned to Herron. "Again, your actions have consequences that affect me far more than they affect you."

He said nothing.

Ava assumed they had already had a shouting match about the flares, which it was clear her aunt hadn't authorized.

"Flares, Herron? Paid for with my money. In the hands of the army that has now besieged my city. Could you think of a scenario that is worse than this?"

"The generals let this happen. They were supposed to take the Rising Wave by surprise, and they did not. I thought we had competent military leaders." Herron began to pace.

"Surely making sure they are competent is your job," the queen said. She sounded tired. "I should be killing you, but instead, I have to kill Ava for her betrayal, even though I understand her motivations completely. How do you always survive when your betters do not? I cannot understand it."

There was silence. Herron had stopped pacing and stood looking at the floor, as if hoping the queen's attention would move off him.

"When do you plan to kill me?" Ava asked.

"Tomorrow, when the Commander of the Rising Wave comes to fetch you." The queen leaned back as if exhausted. "I've told him I concede to his demand to have you back, but I insisted he come in person to talk terms."

"And you're planning to kill him, too?" Ava asked.

"I have no choice. I cannot surrender, I will be turning over Kassia to the Rising Wave, if I do."

"Yes," Ava said. "That does tend to be how surrendering works."

The queen gave her a ghost of a smile. "You think I'm foolish, or deluded, but I'm clear eyed. It may be there are competent leaders in the Rising Wave who can take the Commander's place, and then, we are done. Or killing him might be enough to throw them into disarray and buy us some time to save ourselves."

"How will you kill him?" she asked. She would need all the information she could get to stop this from happening.

"An arrow from the wall." The queen shrugged. "The coward's way. I can claim it was a rogue soldier, deny all responsibility."

"I am sorry that it is going to end like this." Ava turned away from her, and started walking back toward the doors.

"I am sorry, too," the queen said. "I wish I could see another way."

There was another way, but it would mean putting someone other than herself first, and Ava knew her aunt was incapable of that.

Herron was suddenly beside her, roughly grasping her arm. "You leave the queen's presence when the queen tells you that you can leave." He gave her a shake.

"What's she going to do?" Ava asked, lifting mocking eyes up at him. "Have me killed?"

The queen laughed from her perch on the throne. "I really am sorry I'm forced to kill you, Ava. And Herron, I'll remember you are responsible for this situation. I won't forget. Take your hands off her and don't touch her again."

"What do you want done with her." Herron let go but he was still standing too close.

"Balrick knows what to do. It's none of your concern."

Ava started walking again and Herron started after her, getting to the door in time to open it.

"You should wear your best clothes tomorrow to see me murdered," Ava told him as she stepped out into the airy atrium. "You'll want to make a good impression given how angry the queen is at you. Something beautiful and ornate." She gestured to his jacket. "You'll never have a jacket like that again when I am gone. I'm the last of my line."

Herron stared at her for a moment, then turned on his heel and stalked off.

When she had conceived of embroidering the shirt she had made for him, she had never envisaged being in Fernwell to see it work.

But now, Luc and her lives depended on his wearing it.

At least her mother's magic in his jacket meant he would most likely wear the shirt tomorrow, if he had it.

The final gift from her mother, from the grave.

CHAPTER 38

Lucinde didn't ask her how she'd slept, or engage in any chitchat with her at all when she arrived the next morning with breakfast.

Ava respected that.

There was nothing either of them could do about her situation, no matter what anyone thought of it.

She had tried to get access to a needle, but needles were sharp, and Balrick must have thought she planned to use it as some kind of weapon.

She had, but not in the way he thought.

Ava ate the fruit and pastry and looked for the shirt that Lucinde had taken yesterday. The only thing for her to wear was the silk dress with the embroidered flowers and birds on it.

When Lucinde came back in, she clicked her tongue at the fact that Ava hadn't gotten dressed yet.

"I'm looking for my shirt and trousers."

"Oh." She shook her head. "The queen doesn't want that. She wants you to look like her niece. Like a princess."

Ava did not try to hide her disappointment, but she pulled on the dress. What Lucinde meant was her aunt was going to use her to strike fear into her court's hearts. It didn't matter how high you ranked, you could still be executed.

It would be harder to make that stick if Ava was in a plain shirt and pants.

"Do you know when the Commander of the Rising Wave is due to arrive?" she asked.

Lucinde shook her head. "Not my business." She led Ava out the room again, and once again two guards followed behind.

As they reached the ground floor of the high atrium, one of the guards tripped on the last step, and fell with a shout.

His companion bent to help him. Lucinde turned as well.

"I'm telling you, I felt a foot. It had to have been you." The fallen guard glared up at his partner.

"I'm here." The whisper in her ear was so welcome, so wonderful, Ava had to look down and clench both hands to stop herself looking for Luc. Reaching for him.

"They plan to kill you when you come for me." She breathed out the words in quick gasps. "With an arrow."

The guard was getting to his feet, and his friend was teasing him.

"Wear the tunic as well as your cloak."

"I already am." His lips touched her neck. "So when they called you princess at the fortress when we met, they weren't taunting you, they were addressing you by your title." There was a laugh in his voice.

He didn't care, she realized. He truly didn't care.

She felt lightheaded with relief.

Lucinde had turned and was looking at her. "Did you say something, Princess?"

"Just muttering to myself," Ava said. "Does my aunt intend to execute me in public or just in front of the court?"

She felt Luc go still behind her.

He was shocked at that, although he had obviously suspected her aunt intended to assassinate him.

Lucinde shook her head. "I don't know."

"Public's what I heard," one of the guards said. "When the Turncoat King comes to get you."

The guards were standing to attention again, so close to her. Lucinde stood beside them.

They were all looking at her, and she felt a flare of panic that they would somehow be able to sense Luc's presence.

Ava could feel the heat of Luc's body behind her, and she moved her hand back, hidden by the skirt of her dress, and touched his thigh.

His hand came around her fingers and squeezed.

"Well, I hope my cousin is there in all his feathered finery to see his plans come to fruition."

Luc touched her shoulder to let her know he understood what she had just told him, and then she couldn't feel him anymore.

He was gone.

She felt suddenly bereft.

She knew she would see him all too soon in whatever pageantry her aunt had arranged for both their murders, but she couldn't help the tear that escaped and ran down her cheek.

"Ah. And here I was thinking you were unnatural in your calm." Lucinde was watching at her with a sympathetic gaze. "You're a credit to your father, girlie, and I'm sorry to be leading you to your death."

Ava was sorry, too, but she was planning not to be the one who died today.

Princess Ava Valestri.

His lover was a dark one.

Luc slipped through the palace and out into the gardens that covered the clifftop.

The marble walls that lined them plunged into the sea, slippery and impossible to climb.

It didn't matter. He had managed to get Oscar and Deni into the city with him by twisting the invisibility scarf around all of them.

Dak and and number of others had been unhappy about missing out, but Luc had told them Oscar and Deni had worked with Ava before and would be the best two to help. It was true, but it was also to keep the pool of people who knew her secrets to a minimum. And now he would have to reveal one more.

They had discovered the gardens after they'd snuck into the city, and had designated a meeting place. They had agreed a time to meet back here, and he was overdue.

As soon as he was among the trees, he removed his scarf, walked down the twisting path beside a small pond, and then gave a whistle.

He was answered by a whistle in return, and Oscar and Deni stepped through a curtain of vines and leaves.

"We were getting worried," Deni whispered.

"I found Ava." He held up a hand when their faces changed. "Only briefly. I couldn't get her out, she was too well guarded, but I need to warn you about something now, so that you're prepared."

They both frowned, almost in unison, as if they couldn't think of anything they didn't already know.

"Ava is known here as Princess Ava Valestri."

There was dead silence.

"It seems the queen is her aunt."

Oscar gave an audible intake of breath.

"And the queen plans to execute her for treason when I come to fetch her, and kill me at the same time by arrow strike."

"She's a princess?" Oscar shook his head. "If a few days from now you came and told me she's the Goddess Beris herself, I think I'd believe you."

Deni gave a sudden, low chuckle at that. "I knew there was something about her from the moment I met her. She told me one day the story about her would change, but I didn't suspect this."

"So she gave herself up to stop the Kassian officer burning us and the hills with flare fire, knowing if she ended up here she would be in serious danger?" Oscar made it a question, but they already knew the answer.

"And the queen is really going to kill her own niece?" Deni asked.

"Yes." Luc checked his weapons, tugged on the hem of his tunic. "As far as I understand things, I'll be taken to the queen in the main square, where she'll try to have me killed, and then she'll execute Ava.

It would be good if I had someone close to me on the ground and someone on the walls."

They both nodded.

He touched two fingers to his left cheek. "You know my signal. Wait for it."

He stepped back out of the greenery and ducked between the trees to loop his scarf over his neck again.

He had half an hour before he was due at the gates to speak with the queen, and he wanted to hear what the citizens of Fernwell had to say about the siege, their leaders, and the Rising Wave.

He wandered the city, looking for places to hide, places to run, places to hunker down, all the while keeping an ear out for what the people were saying.

Deni would be looking for high ground—perches that would give him a good angle into the main square.

Oscar would be blending in, finding a place that would give him a good view of the proceedings from the ground.

One thing that pleased him a lot was the lack of soldiers. There were palace guards, but not many, and only one unit guarding the gate.

The Queen's Herald had thrown everything he had at the Rising Wave, and he had nothing left for Fernwell.

That suited Luc.

He found himself close to the square where he was meant to meet the queen and decided it wasn't a bad idea to get the lay of the land but before he could turn down the main street toward it, a woman caught his eye. She was standing surrounded by a small group of people dressed in bright silks and brocade and they seemed to be giving her money.

"Go away now," she said to them in a bored voice, and they left without a word.

Haslia.

Ava had told him she'd seen her in Bartolo, and that Massi would look for her there, but Massi hadn't found her.

She probably ran for Fernwell the moment she heard the Rising Wave was about to crash on Bartolo.

And now she'd trapped herself.

Luc smiled slowly and walked over to her.

Her head rose, and her gaze swung left to right, looking for something.

"Looking for me?" Luc asked her from behind, and touched his knife to her neck.

"The Commander himself, all dressed up in Princess Ava's workings." Haslia tried to sound bored, but Luc could hear the jump of nerves in her voice.

"That's right. So tell me, Haslia, who were you working for?"

"Were? How do you know I'm not still working for them?"

"Because you're using your gifts to swindle money from the wealthy on the street, which tells me you're not being sponsored by anyone. So tell me. Might as well."

"Do you remember General Daikin?"

"There have been so many generals," Luc said. "No, I don't."

"He's the one who I helped to ambush you using poor little Derek nearly three months ago now." Haslia drew something from her pocket and held it up, but Luc felt no compunction to take it from her and with a sigh of disappointment, she put it back.

"So it was you behind that betrayal. I thought so after you tried to kill Revek. Was it you who managed to get Derek the knife and tell him to kill himself, too?"

"Well, you do know a lot." Haslia relaxed.

"Was the general working under the instruction of the Queen's Herald?"

Haslia chuckled. "No. He'd seen how Herron abused his poor cousin, locking her away, forcing her mother with terrible threats and then letting her die so carelessly. Daikin knew if the Queen's Herald ever found out about me, he would take me away. And the general didn't like that idea. He'd stumbled upon me a few years ago, taken me prisoner, and we'd eventually negotiated a deal. I would help him, he would give me a long leash."

"So what was his plan?" Luc wondered what the general had been trying to do.

"Firstly, he was simply trying to get ahead. Capturing you was a coup for him, he was sure to get promoted with proof he had captured the Turncoat King. But then, it all went wrong. You and Ava escaped, and then she humiliated him. I don't think he's quite recovered from it."

"Humiliated him by escaping?" Luc frowned.

"No, the way she forced them to stay in their tents and not follow after you when you got away from them the second time."

Luc thought back to that. "I was badly injured, I don't know what she did."

Haslia trilled out a laugh. "She hasn't shared the delicious details with you? I can't believe it. She managed a working that made them too scared to come out of their tents. They were only able to crawl out when they were so dehydrated they had to find water to stay alive." Haslia snorted. "I gather it was over a day. And they took a while to recover." She sounded so gleeful, Luc guessed she was quite happy with what had happened to her former captor.

"I never knew that."

"Well, the general did not like that. Not one bit." Haslia tilted her head to glance at him sidelong. "So he got me to keep up my spy routine, sending information to the scouts that went to main headquarters, but he also wanted me to make life hard for you and Ava. Make people hate her, or suspicious of her. Make your friends try to kill her or make you choose between her and them." She shrugged. "It was harder to do than I thought, and when it started to fall apart, I had to run."

"Why did you try to kill Revek?" Luc asked.

"Spoke too freely. It got lonely being a spy in the Rising Wave." She shrugged. "It's possible he'll never remember, but no use taking a chance."

"But you're not working for Daikin anymore."

Haslia shrugged. "I thought I was at the time. I made it to Bartolo and went to the person the general told me to find if we ever got that far. He's a spell caster, too."

Something in her voice told Luc she had not liked discovering she wasn't the general's only acquisition.

"He was weak, though. His workings only have a very short life, and he ordered me to go do his dirty work for him when I got there, like I was his servant." She gritted her teeth. "I was his better."

"The mayor of Bartolo," Luc said. "This spell caster was the one enspelling her with the charms?"

Haslia truly was shocked now. He felt her go still.

"Ava saw you. She reversed it."

"I thought I caught a glimpse of her in the alley . . ." She shook her head. "That's how the Rising Wave took Bartolo so easily." She sounded resigned. Then she lifted a shoulder. "After I did that . . . errand . . . for the general's Bartolo spell caster, I had a good, hard look at my prospects. And didn't like what I saw. I decided it was time to go my own way."

Above them, a big bell rang the hour, and Luc realized he was supposed to be meeting the guards at the gate.

He had promised Ava he would always come for her, and he always would. Dealing with Haslia would have to wait for another day.

"I'm going to let you go, Haslia. I don't want to, but I've got more pressing things to do. I suggest you find a way to not be in Fernwell any more when this is over."

"I was planning on taking a nice journey on a ship, as it happens." Haslia jingled the coins in her coin bag. "I have heard the general is probably dead, killed with the Jatan Border Forces. The money he promised me certainly wasn't waiting for me. But just in case he did survive, I'd prefer not to be here should he return."

"Good. If I see your face again, you're dead." Luc stepped back and Haslia walked away from him, her step unhurried and slightly jaunty.

He made his way to the main city gate and leaned against it, listening to the guards as they stood nervously waiting for his knock.

"I heard he's never been beaten in a fight."

"That might be gossip."

"Or it might be true. He *has* assembled an army and surrounded us. And has the ability to raze us." The guard looked above the gate nervously.

"There's someone approaching," one of the guards above called, and while they all turned to look up, Luc slid off his scarf, put it in his pocket, and straightened.

"I think the queen is waiting for me." He spoke normally, but the guards spun around as if he'd shouted.

"The Turncoat—" The guard cut himself off.

"Himself." Luc smiled.

"How did you get in?" One of the guards gulped as he spoke.

"Most walls aren't as impenetrable as we think," Luc said. "The queen?"

For a long moment, no one spoke.

Luc crossed his arms over his chest and waited.

The guards looked at each other and eventually one stepped away from the gate and swept his arm toward the palace.

"This way." There was a tremble in his voice.

They were afraid of him, and Luc was glad of it.

They had killed his mother. They had killed her without having the courage of their convictions, just as they planned to kill him today.

They'd pointed the finger of blame at some zealous officer off the leash of command when his mother had been run through on the Cervantes plains all those years ago, but she'd been targeted because she'd come to Fernwell to speak to the queen about ending the Chosen camps.

She was making too much noise and they wanted to silence her.

They planned to do the same to him today.

This time, they would regret it.

CHAPTER 39

Something was wrong.

Luc approached the square, following behind the guard, but he had expected announcements, or at least someone addressing the crowd, but it was quiet.

A group of people in front of him broke apart, and he caught sight of a slight woman in gold brocade on a platform, trying not to pace, and trying not to show any emotion.

What was leaking from her was rage and impatience.

She had chosen an interesting setting for this confrontation.

The square was lined with beautiful, three story houses, with old, established trees in their small front gardens.

Men and women in finery stood on balconies looking down, although the people standing around the platform wore more modest clothing.

The queen wanted all her subjects to witness this.

That the only person who stood on the platform with her was a general of the Kassian army was interesting, too.

Luc had heard the queen had become more and more paranoid about her advisers, relying on them less and less.

She stood all but alone in this piece of theater.

The guard leading him stopped at the wooden steps up to the platform and whispered to one of the two uniformed palace guards, and one went to murmur quietly to the queen.

She looked at him with dislike and a hint of panic.

The general turned to face him, as did the second set of palace guards at the other end of the platform.

"Weapons." The palace guard held out a hand, and Luc unbuckled his sword from his back and the knife at his belt.

He was patted down, and his boots checked, and then the guard stood back with a grunt.

"The Turncoat King." The queen turned as Luc climbed up to the platform, her voice strident.

The crowd suddenly hushed as they realized he had arrived.

He smiled at the pettiness of her words. It gave him permission for his own. "Child Stealer," he said to her.

She flinched back visibly, her composure gone.

The crowd began to murmur again, but there was a tone to it, an undercurrent.

Something rose in the queen's eyes, a complex mix of fear and hate, and she flicked her hand out at her side.

An arrow slammed into his back.

It hurt, a little, but no more than a training hit.

Luc turned and stared down at the broken shaft lying behind him.

Ava had said his knitted tunic would either be the best protection he had ever had or a failure.

Except nothing of hers had ever failed, that he could see.

Another arrow flew toward him, this time aimed at his head, but he heard the whistle as it flew and leaned back slightly. It sped past his nose and narrowly missed the queen herself.

Her scream was panicked and high-pitched, and the crowd was suddenly shouting and screaming as well.

"Want to try again?" He shouted the words as he turned toward the source of the arrows, opened his arms wide and presented himself as a target.

The crowd quietened down, he could feel every eye on him.

Another arrow shot toward him, hit his stomach and snapped like kindling.

A scream sounded, audible in the stillness of the square, and then a body fell to the ground from the wall of the palace.

Deni had obviously found the queen's assassin.

"Where is Ava?" He turned to the queen.

"She'll be here soon. There is some delay." The queen clasped and unclasped her hands. Her eyes looked jaundiced, and her clothes looked like they were too big for her, as if she had lost weight since they were fitted. "But it doesn't matter. Not to you, because you will be dead. Kill him." She took a few steps back and looked over at her general.

He had already unsheathed his sword when the first arrow flew and he swung it. Luc didn't even try to move. He felt the blade go through the wool of his cloak and then vibrate as it connected with his side as if it had hit stone.

The general swore, swapped his sword into his other hand and shook his sword hand out.

"What is it?" There was fear in the queen's voice.

"He's wearing a steel plate under there. That's why the arrows broke."

"I don't see a steel plate around his throat." The queen's voice was high.

"No." The general moved again, looked over at the palace guards. "A little help?"

The guards had climbed the steps when the queen had ordered Luc killed, and had hesitated there, waiting for orders.

Before they could move, Luc leaped from the platform, scooped up his sword from where it had been left leaning against the steps, and drew it as he ran back up them.

Oscar was suddenly beside him, sword drawn as well, and they struck together.

Luc ran his blade underneath the palace guard's arm, and kicked him off the platform into the crowd.

It was a large group of people, and it might occur to some of them to assist the queen. He had created worry and doubt he could be taken though, and that would hold most of them for a while. He would still need to move fast.

He left the second guard to Oscar and engaged with the general.

Luc recognized him. He'd visited the Chosen camps to observe the children's progress many times.

He was wearing thick armor, far thicker than the palace guards.

Luc blocked his first blow, then spun low and cut the backs of the general's legs, spun back as he straightened and then slashed the general's throat with his knife.

He didn't wait to watch the general fall. He ran straight at the other two palace guards.

One was standing in front of the queen, the other behind.

He shouted a battle cry as he leaped high, sword above his head, and with a cry of fear, the guard in front jumped to the side and rolled off the platform.

The guard left behind the queen stared at his partner in horror, and while he hesitated, Luc spun again and slashed at his arm.

He dropped his sword with a scream and grabbed hold of the wound, scuttling backward down the stairs.

Luc brought his bloody blade up to the queen's throat. "Where is Ava?"

"I don't know." The queen's words were clear over the hush that fell over the crowd when his sword touched her throat.

"You are lying."

He heard a murmur wash through the crowd. Saw the look in her eyes that told him she would delay for as long as she had to until someone came up to help her.

He stepped behind her, pulled her up against him and let his sword blade rest across her whole throat.

"They aren't coming to help you. They don't think I can be defeated. Both your assassin and your general have proved that. Now, tell me where Ava is, or I'll do what I've wanted to do since the day my mother was murdered in your name."

"Herron has her." She cleared her throat. "He said he had taken her to his house."

"Then let's go to his house."

Ava stared down at the jacket on the table before her. She was still amazed at the way her cousin had been able to intercept her and divert the guards to his private residence, which lay between the main square and the palace.

Change was in the wind, obviously, and the guards were calculating that the queen wouldn't last too much longer.

Better obey their new master now.

They had hedged their bets, though, because she'd seen them pay a messenger to run and inform the queen of the situation.

"Don't threaten me with death," she said, looking up at Herron, who was wearing a robe over his trousers, not the shirt she had hoped to see. Her plans had centered around it, but she acknowledged the foolishness of that. She had laid her hopes on things she couldn't control. She would have to work with what she had. "The queen wants to kill me in public, remember? As a lesson to others."

He grabbed his hair in both hands and stared at her. "Why are you so difficult?"

She gave a bitter laugh and lifted her hands. "Why *won't* I cooperate with the man who murdered my father and chained up my mother and starved her to death? I wonder."

"Your mother's death was an accident. The stores manager for the inventory in the dungeons was watching her and making sure she had food while I was away, but then he died, and . . ."

Ava leaned her elbows on the table, her bound hands in front of her, and shook her head. That pathetic excuse did not deserve a reply.

She had to squeeze her eyes shut for a moment, to calm her rage.

He hadn't given her a needle yet, for the magic he wanted her to work into his jacket—the same jacket he had forced her mother to work on, too—and she wondered if it was worth lying to get her hands on one. At least he would have to untie her hands for her to sew, and that alone would be worth it.

"All right." She slumped lower. "Give me a needle and I'll—"

She stopped talking at the knock on his front door.

He turned toward it eagerly. Full of anticipation.

He left the small room they were in, off the main reception area, without a word, and she heard the sound of boots ringing on marble—one of the palace guards coming to check on the door from the kitchen where they were waiting.

The guard and Herron spoke quietly to each other, and the door was opened.

She heard Herron's voice rise in pleasure and excitement, and she thought she might recognize the other voice as well, although she couldn't remember where she'd heard it.

The palace guard loomed in the doorway, taking in the garment on the table in front of her with curious eyes.

"He wants me to embroider his jacket before I die," she said to the guard. Then she rolled her eyes, communicating how strange that was.

The guard shifted, suddenly a little unsure of what he was doing straying from the plan he had been given.

"I'm sure my aunt is annoyed at the delay, but I don't mind it," Ava told him. "The longer Herron wants me to sit and sew his jacket, the longer I have to live."

"I'll take over now." Herron's voice made the guard flinch, and he turned, and sidled out of the doorway.

Herron stepped into the room, and Ava stared at him.

"Look at your face!" He laughed. "It is the most sought-after garment in the city."

He stretched out an arm and admired the feathers that danced up the sleeve.

"It is beautiful." Ava didn't mind if she said so herself.

"And not a black stitch in the whole piece." Herron winked at her. "I wouldn't buy it until that had been checked."

"Very wise. I think we need to go to the queen now."

He frowned down at the jacket on the table, but then nodded. "Yes. This was worth a try, but you aren't going to sew a working for me, are you?"

"I'm afraid not."

He shrugged, philosophical, and took the jacket off the table, shrugged into it. "Come then."

"Do we need the guards?" Ava asked, lifting her bound hands. "You can handle me, surely?"

"I can, but—" He looked through the door, and she saw both guards had returned.

She had spooked them, before she'd realized the knock at the door had been her Grimwaldian trader, delivering her revenge.

"We're leaving?" one of the guards asked, relieved.

"Yes." Herron walked from the room, and she rose to her feet and followed him out the house, a guard on either side of her.

They walked along a main street, almost completely empty of people.

"Everyone is at the square," the one guard said, and Ava heard the nerves in his voice.

He was just realizing the impact of this delay.

"We'll make an entrance." Herron sounded pleased. He kept stretching out his arms to admire the shirt cuffs sticking out from the jacket sleeves, or smoothing his fingers over the design.

"Incoming crowd," a guard warned.

Ava looked up ahead, and couldn't work out what she was seeing. It looked like . . .

Luc. With his blade at her aunt's throat as he dragged her down the street.

She could see Oscar walking backwards behind Luc, covering his back as hundreds of people followed behind. She guessed Deni must be somewhere around, too.

"I understand why no one is attacking him on the ground, because he could easily kill the queen, but why isn't someone climbing a wall and shooting him in the back?" One of the guards wondered quietly to the other.

"I think the queen had already arranged for him to be assassinated in that way." Herron frowned. "I'm not sure why it hasn't happened yet."

"A stray arrow, or a poor shot, and the queen would be hit," the other guard said. "I wouldn't take the chance."

"I don't like him holding the blade to her throat," Herron said. He sounded annoyed.

Ava wondered if it was because *he* would prefer to be the one holding the blade to her throat.

The shirt would bring out his hidden self. All his truths. Truths he would be desperate to share.

She had gambled that that version of himself would be far worse than his public face. Would in fact inspire her aunt to finally rid herself of him.

It looked as if the opposite was also true.

They were close enough now for Ava to see the fury and fear in her aunt's eyes at her situation. And the calm and strength in Luc's.

He actually did seem to have been shot a few times from the walls as he'd made his way down the street. Two arrows had caught on his cloak, and were hanging like snapped twigs. As she watched, another arrow flew at him, hit him in the back and fell off him.

"They *are* trying to shoot him in the back," the guard to her left whispered. "And they're just bouncing off."

"You all right, princess?" Luc asked, and she raised her eyebrows at the title.

"I'm all right, Commander." He was close enough now she could see he had been fighting. There was blood on his cloak and his hands. "You?"

He shot her a grin at that. "All good." He tipped his head at Herron. "That's the Queen's Herald?"

"Yes."

How were they going to get out of this situation?

The street behind Luc was heaving with people. They could be overrun at any moment, except the queen would surely die.

Someone lunged from the crowd with a sword, but Oscar moved, almost fast enough to seem a blur, and the man retreated, screaming in agony.

"Anyone else?" Oscar called into the crowd.

Most likely, if more of the military were here, they would be in serious trouble, but Ava hadn't seen many soldiers, not even in the barracks where she'd been held in the heart of the city.

They were either prisoners in Bartolo or they'd died on the plains under General Ru's sword.

The sound of voices behind her made her turn, and she saw people beginning to spill from side streets to surround them, as if the ones at the back of the group following Luc had spread out and down toward the palace for a better view.

Everyone wanted a front row seat.

"Why aren't you doing something, Herron?" Her aunt's voice shook with anger. "Deal with this!"

"I wouldn't help you even if it meant my personal fortunes doubled," Herron told her, and there was a sudden hush in the crowd.

"Why would you say something like that to our aunt?" Ava asked.

"Because she won't die!" Herron's scream cut off every sound. He stopped, staring in horror at his own revelation. He looked down at his jacket, at the black embroidery on it, and then at Ava. He ripped the jacket off, kicking it away from him in panic. "That bitch did something to it. She worked something in."

"Who's she?" Ava asked. "Don't be so cryptic, not everyone knows what you're talking about."

"Your mother." Herron shouted the words. "She did something to it, made it so I would have to answer you."

"It seems you're still answering her," the queen said. "So it can't be the jacket. Now do something to get me free."

Herron shook his head as if dealing with an irritating fly. "I've waited patiently for my turn on the throne, but whatever makes you look like you're about to fall down dead isn't killing you fast enough." He stopped talking, looked at Ava in shock. "How are you still making me talk?"

"Making you tell the truth, you mean?" Ava shrugged. "Maybe you just need to get it off your chest?"

"Maybe." Herron gave a slow nod. He lunged suddenly, grabbing the queen in a hug, and Luc lifted his sword from her throat when Herron tugged her out of his hold.

For a moment, Herron and the queen stood in each other's arms, and then Herron stepped back, raising his arms at his sides. He held a long knife in his right hand, and it dripped blood.

The queen's hands went to her chest, and she looked down. "I'm protected." She looked around wildly. "I'm protected. My chemise is spelled to protect me."

"Those protections don't last forever," Herron told her. "How long have you had it?"

"Nearly thirty years. It made me sick, but it protected me. I survived two assassination attempts thanks to it."

"Thirty years is a long time." Herron shrugged. "I should have known you had some protection."

The queen fell to the ground and Ava crouched beside her.

"If it doesn't work anymore, how was it still making me sick?" the queen whispered.

The golden brocade gown had slid off the queen's shoulder, and Ava saw the black silk edging on the bodice of the chemise.

Suddenly, as if getting a second wind, the queen batted at Ava to get her to shuffle back and then struggled up on an elbow. "What are you waiting for?" She pointed at the palace guards. "Kill him." She moved her finger to Herron.

The guards hesitated.

"Kill. Him."

They moved together, one striking Herron's neck, the other his torso.

He went down with a cry and lay beside the queen, blinking slowly and then he closed his eyes.

The queen started to laugh, and then coughed, blood spraying from her lips. "The queen is dead," she said, her voice a weak croak. "Long live the queen."

Ava rose to her feet, frowning at the words.

"Going to kill her, too, warlord?" Her aunt turned her head to Luc. Laughed again and then fell silent.

The palace guards who had killed Herron stood, anchorless and confused.

"What should we do?" The one who Luc had tripped this morning asked.

"Take off my restraints." Ava held out her hands, and the man couldn't move fast enough to get them off.

"And them?" The other guard asked, pointing to Luc and Oscar.

"They are on my side."

"Then who is against us?" The guard lowered his sword.

"Are any of you against me?" Ava asked the crowd.

There were murmurs. It sounded like plenty were against her, but none brave enough to step forward.

"I was just getting used to you being a princess." Luc turned in a circle as he spoke, looking for threats. "Now you're a queen."

"Funny." She turned as well, watching the roofs and walls for shooters, but if they were there, they weren't shooting.

Perhaps because their paymasters were both lying dead at Ava's feet.

"What should we do now?" The guard asked her.

"Now, you should go open the city gates."

CHAPTER 40

"I've put the clothes you came in on the bed for you." Lucinde called.

"Thank you." Ava rinsed off her arms in the bath. She listened for Lucinde's footsteps to leave the room, and for the door to swing shut before she stood.

She didn't have time to linger in the hot water, although she really would have loved to.

She wiped herself down with the linen cloth Lucinde had set out for her, and wrapped it under her armpits.

She stopped short when she stepped out from behind the screen and found a man standing beside her window.

"The messenger from the Grimwalt Court." She should have remembered he was somewhere in the city. She knew this was his likely destination when he'd run from the Rising Wave.

Too much going on, she acknowledged to herself. Too many balls in the air.

He moved over and sat on her bed, checking over her clothes. He looked like himself this time. So whatever working he'd used to hide his face had either faded or he'd stopped using it.

"No black silk, that I can see," he said and tossed them to her. "Put them on."

She moved back to step behind the screen.

"No." He held a throwing knife in his hand. "I'm very accurate. You put them on where I can see you."

She slid the pants up under the linen wrap, and then shrugged the shirt over her head and tugged the wrap down.

It fluttered to the floor.

"How long have you been in Fernwell?" she asked him.

"Long enough to know I was lied to by my boss." He gave a grimace. "The welcome here was not at all the warm one I was told to expect."

"So, why are you still doing his bidding?" Ava asked.

"There's still something in it for me, as long as I have you with me."

"How are you going to get the Queen of Kassia out of the city?" The Rising Wave was everywhere. He had to know it would be difficult to get far.

"This." He held up a necklace. "The last of its kind, I'm told, since the Grimwaldian who made it died. Changes your appearance. They won't think I'm leaving with the queen, because you will not look like the queen."

She knew the necklace worked. She'd seen it with her own eyes.

"The Speaker never told me about your connection to Kassia. I had no idea." He shook his head in disappointment. "But we won't worry about him, because you'll be making me some things on our way there that will put me in charge, not him."

These people who kept thinking she could be coerced into doing their bidding.

"No."

"That's not the answer I'm looking for."

"Throw your knife at me, then, because I'm not interested in being dragged to Grimwalt by a deluded criminal. I have no idea what these things are you're talking about, and I don't care, either way."

He stared at her. Threw the knife.

Not to kill her, she noticed, as he aimed for high on her right shoulder. It somehow missed.

"That should have hit you." He rose from the corner of her bed. "There is no way I could have missed."

Ava shrugged. "But you did."

He threw a second one, and Ava saw he had five sheaths along his belt.

He aimed at the same spot, and it went astray again.

He stared at her in horror. "You've got some protection. Something I missed."

Ava looked around for a weapon. Her own knife was gone, and she hadn't had a chance to look for something in the armory.

The two knives he'd thrown at her would do, she decided, and turned to see where they'd landed.

"You know exactly what I'm talking about," he said, suddenly. "You're wearing something magic-worked. You were just feigning ignorance."

As Ava bent to pick up the first knife, he threw a third, and she felt the handle skim along her back and clatter to the floor.

"Maybe hands around your throat will work." The words were guttural.

She had misjudged his rage and frustration.

He slammed her up against the wall, and began choking her, but where he was touching her shirt she smelled burning and then he threw himself back with a scream, batting at his chest.

The door flew open, and Luc suddenly filled the doorway.

The messenger calmed suddenly, lifting his shirt.

Ava could see red welts across his stomach.

"I've tried and tried, and I can never get her," he said to Luc. "I really hate her and I'm glad her friends in Grimwalt are in prison. I hope they die there."

He moved slowly to the window, a throwing knife in his hand.

"I'll find a way to get you," he said to her. "Don't think I won't." He climbed out, clutching at the sill. "You can't be wrapped in protection all the time."

A knife suddenly lodged in his eye, and he fell back with a scream.

Ava looked across at Luc, who was lowering his hand from the knife throw.

"He might have known which friends and where they're are being held," she said.

He shook his head. "Or he might have come back while you were in your bath and killed you."

"Maybe."

The palace guards burst into the room, and Luc waved at the window.

By the time Dak and Deni had spoken to them about how he got in, and the body had been removed, the sun had set.

As soon as they were alone, they walked toward each other, and Luc bent down to kiss her.

"I'm sorry I didn't tell you I was related to the queen."

"I should have guessed." He nuzzled her neck just under her ear. "They called you princess enough times in the fortress. And I remember now how they didn't care what happened to me when they were hunting us after we escaped. But you had to be brought home no matter what the cost."

"That was more to do with my other secret than the princess thing."

He chuckled. "Maybe. Anyway, you aren't a princess any more." He kissed her again. "Queen."

She sighed. "We'll have to work on putting together a system like the Grimwalt court, or the Skäddar Collective. Even the Venyatu principalities are more representative than Kassia has been."

"We can do that, but you'll need to be in charge for a while until it's all settled. You'll leave Kassia open to invaders, otherwise."

She leaned back and smiled at him. "I think it's already been invaded, hasn't it?"

"True." He lifted her onto the bed, and settled over her. "But I'm a reasonable warlord. We can come to some accommodation."

"Is that so?" She bit the cord on the side of his neck, and he made a sound that lit a fire in her. "Well then, accommodate me."

ABOUT THE AUTHOR

Michelle Diener is an award winning author of historical fiction, science fiction and fantasy.

Michelle was born in London and currently lives in Australia with her husband and children.

You can contact Michelle through her website or sign up to receive notification when she has a new book out on her New Release Notification page.

Connect with Michelle
www.michellediener.com

Sign up to Michelle Diener's New Release Notification list on her website to find out when to expect the second book in the Rising Wave series, THE THREADBARE QUEEN—coming late 2021.

ACKNOWLEDGMENTS

A huge thank you to Edie and Jo, who always help make my stories the best they can be. Also a huge thank you to Book Coverology for the amazing cover. Thanks also to Diane on my reader team for her eagle eyes.

Made in the USA
Middletown, DE
17 July 2021

44316112R00184